David Mathew creates a world that's familiar but seen through a deviant lens. There are shades of Clive Barker and JG Ballard in these stories – fiction that's all the more unsettling for having its roots in the everyday – but Mathew has his own voice and vision for the twenty-first century.

Julie Travis, Author of
We Are All Falling Towards the Centre of the Earth

Characters' messy lives intersect with danger in this nervy, gritty, warped collection from David Mathew. These tales feature aphrodisiac bombs, illegal tritium deals, giant hedgehogs, dream angels, and the impending anxiety of parenthood. The urban sprawl and rural dystopia reflect the sordid emotional and inner world of the characters who are fighting, sometimes for their lives, sometimes to be understood, or sometimes for just a pint. *Panic Soup* is best served with shots, in a noisy neighbourhood pub where all the patrons are insane.

Stephen Scott Whitaker, National Book Critics Circle,
Managing Editor of *The Broadkill Review*

If you love stories with bite, brutality, wit and wonder, you will love *Panic Soup*. As the title suggests, there is dread here, warmth, trepidation, a multitude of flavours. Drink deep.

Paul Meloy, Author of *Adornments of the Storm*

David Mathew has an eye for nudging characters from the everyday to the disturbing.

CC Adams, Author of *But Worse Will Come*

Panic Soup

First Montag Press E-Book and Paperback Original Edition August 2019

Montag Press
ISBN: 978-1-940233-63-5
Cover art © 2019 Daniele Serra
Design © 2019 Rick Febré
Author photo © 2019 Jacqueline Mathew

Montag Press Team:
Project Editor – Charlie Franco
Managing Director – Charlie Franco

A Montag Press Book
www.montagpress.com
Montag Press
777 Morton St. Unit B
San Francisco CA 94129

Montag Press, the burning book with the hatchet cover, the skewed word mark and the portrayal of the long-suffering fireman mascot are trademarks of Montag Press.

Printed & Digitally Originated in the United States of America
10 9 8 7 6 5 4 3 2 1

By the Same Author

Fiction

Paranoid Landscapes
O My Days
Creature Feature (with M.F. Korn)
Ventriloquists
Sick Dice
The Parry and the Lunge
Dreadnought Flex
Panic Soup
Nostalgia's Boat

Academic

Fragile Learning: The Influence of Anxiety
The Care Factory
Psychic River: Storms and Safe Harbours in Lifelong Learning

David Mathew

Panic Soup

MONTAG

Contents

For Charlie Franco

A Difficult Angle

CERTAIN THAT HE'D BE DISCOVERED and called back, Stuey walked away from the vendor with his Marlboro Lights in one hand and his change in the other. He re-entered the building. Phil and Becky were still on their stools. Stuey wondered if they'd said a single word to each other in his absence.

'Hey,' said Stuey, attempting to lighten the mood, 'you'll never guess what just happened to me. I gave the guy a ten and he gave me change for a twenty. Look!' He displayed the notes and coins with pride.

'Are you sure?' asked Becky, ever the optimist.

'Of course I'm sure. It all looks the same but I'm not stupid.'

'I didn't say you were stupid, dear.'

Brightening up, Phil added: 'Well, it looks like it's your round then, mate.'

'Okay.' Stuey looked at the back of the bargirl's head, willing her to turn around and notice him.

'What can I get you?' she asked as she approached.

'I'll have another Bud Light. Phil?'

'Bud Light.'

'Becky?'

'A Manhattan, please,' she answered. 'When in Rome…'

It was the hotel bar of the Ramada New Yorker on Eighth Avenue, on a Tuesday afternoon, the room full of accents that sparked off one another, an inquisitive path of smoke making its way towards the restrooms.

'Last one, though,' said Stuey. 'We can't spend all day in here.'

'Why not?' asked Phil. 'I'm not going out in *that*.'

The blizzard was two feet and counting, of immaculate snow, drilling crosswinds and dangerous conditions underfoot.

'Yesterday was cold enough for me.'

'Don't be a wimp.'

The bargirl delivered two glasses of beer.

'Your prerogative, mate – you wanna catch hypothermia, that's *your* lookout. Me, I'm staying in where it's nice and warm. I've seen the views from the Empire State Building already. I'm happy,' Phil said.

Saying anything more, Stuey knew, would goad his half-brother, and the atmosphere had been sharp enough since the holiday had begun. What good would another argument do? After two weeks they were tired of each other. Louisiana had been fine; it was only as they'd travelled north, and the temperature had dropped, that their moods had worsened.

'Becky?' said Stuey. 'What do *you* wanna do?'

'Go shopping.'

Stuey wasn't afraid of his own company, not even in a foreign city. By the time he returned to the south coast of England he wanted to have a few more stories to tell than those he'd heard in the place where they were staying. Determined to see the East River, to eat in Chinatown, to watch the skaters in Central Park, he resolved to finish his beer and trek out into the wastes, no matter the chill. He was already dressed – multi-layered, with his hat and gloves on the next stool along –for the expedition.

Stuey stood up at the same time Becky did. 'I'm going to the bathroom,' Becky said.

'I'll see you later then,' said Stuey, intending to be gone by the time she returned. 'Can I pay, please?' he said to the bargirl.

Phil checked that Becky had moved out of earshot, then

he said, thumb over his shoulder: 'Half an hour with her and I'd be a new man.' He nodded to the woman by the till in case his point wasn't clear.

'You're married,' said Stuey.

'Only just,' Phil countered, as if the recency of the vows made them somehow less valid, like a tile-paste that had not quite set rigid. Indeed, Phil and Becky had only taken the plunge four days earlier. A thin Elvis Presley had held the book and invited the sanctifying kiss in a Las Vegas chapel last Friday. Instead of rings the couple had each purchased modest and easy-to-hide tattoos: two small green birds, conures to be exact, on their left shoulders.

Stuey handed the bargirl a twenty and a lingering smile.

'I'll bet she'd do anything you wanted,' Phil opined further.

'Enough,' said Stuey, close to being embarrassed. 'Thanks.' This was to the bargirl, now handing him his change. His scalp bristled. She'd said fifteen-fifty and he'd given her a twenty. Now here she was passing over the change he'd expected, plus a twenty-dollar bill and a ten.

Change from fifty bucks. Scarcely able to believe his luck, Stuey dug in his jeans for a five and slipped what he'd been handed into his shirt pocket. The five he left on the bar was a tip, anchored down by the sheriff's-badge ashtray.

He wished he'd had such good fortune while in Vegas. Though no gambler, he'd plugged more than a few dollars into machines and pulled handles. Wheels had clunked: fruit salads of strawberries and pears had come up. He'd won a few times: 75 cents here, a buck and half there. Nothing like this.

Taking it as a good sign, Stuey wrapped himself up warm and left the building. The snow fell vertically and at a slant, making perfect right angled triangles of precipitation. He climbed into the yellow cab and said, 'Little Italy, please.

Somewhere touristy.'

Not thinking about what he was doing, he handed the driver his new twenty and said, 'Keep the change,' cherishing his generosity. In the mirror the driver's brown eyes were a delicacy of suspicion and joy.

'Thank you, man,' said driver 8J22.

Late in the afternoon Stuey dined on ravioli in a low-morale joint near a bright souvenir store and a check-cashing office. He was nervous at the thought of paying. What if his luck shifted the other way? What if he handed the waitress a twenty and she read it as a one-dollar bill? He was obviously from overseas; he could surely claim dimwit immunity, seeing that all the bills looked the same to him. So why not go the whole hog? Leave a one-dollar bill on the table and say 'The rest is your tip, darling'? See what happened. In the end, he decided to stick to his tried and tested formula. The bill was for $14.49. Stuey readied his twenty.

Outside, he had no choice but to sit down; his legs were as weak as wet cardboard. He sat on a cushion of snow on a bench by the souvenir store, risking all by counting the money in the open air, instead of stuffing it blindly into his pockets.

He'd been given change from a hundred-dollar bill.

It was like a dream that he kept expecting to be dragged from. The next transaction would surely be the acid test, he figured, if his math was correct.

Warily observed by the souvenir store guy, Stuey perused the array of sub-quality hats on offer, two for ten. He didn't need a hat; he was already wearing one. But he knew that this was make or break when it came to theories: the fourth go.

'How much is one?' he asked, fingering a baseball cap.

'Siss dollar.'

'Okay, I'll take it.' Deliberately – very deliberately – he

handed the man a one-dollar bill. And thought: *I'm rich, or I could be rich, if I can take this home with me.* Stuey wasn't referring to the headwear.

'Can't break it,' said the vendor. 'You gore anyfing smaller?'

'Sorry.' Stuey walked away with his tail in the air, smoking a celebratory cigarette and singing to himself: 'Start spreadin' the news…'

He got back to the hotel at six-fifteen. A line of people was waiting to check in: wet coats, luggage. A lot of British passports were on display. Grimly Stuey remembered his own check-in, two nights before; the waiting had been horrendous, conducted as it had been on an empty stomach and with several NO SMOKING signs on display. For the duration of his time in the line, while Phil and Becky had sat in the very bar in which Stuey now found them again, he had believed that the hotel had sold his room on, just because they'd arrived late at JFK.

5

'A nice afternoon?' Stuey asked Becky. Phil had gone off for a pee.

'Not bad. We went upstairs, watched a movie…' Becky giggled. 'I was just down to my bra and knickers – you know how I like to be nude in bed when I watch a film…'

'Yes, I remember.'

'…when the maid knocked to clean the room. Phil was in the bath. God knows what she must have thought when I answered,' said Becky.

Stuey laughed. 'Heaven forbid she might have thought a married couple was about to have sex.'

'Chance'd be a fine thing.'

'You're newlyweds!' said Stuey.

Becky was quiet for second or two. 'A nag doesn't become a thoroughbred just because you put a rosette on its mane.

Think about it.'

Stuey thought about it. 'That's a ridiculous comparison,' he told her. 'Anyway, you've been drinking all afternoon; you might think twice about telling me this in the morning. Let's change the subject before he gets back.'

Becky shrugged. 'Some men are good at carpentry; some aren't. Some men are good in bed; some aren't. That's all there is to it.'

'I don't want to know.'

'*You* were.'

'Thank you. But my carpentry days are over. Did you go shopping?'

'Nah. What did you do?'

Stuey gave her a précis of the afternoon's events, but chose to expunge any reference to money, even though by his rough calculations he was a hundred bucks up on that morning. If he talked about what was happening it would stop, that was one thing he was sure of.

Phil sat down. 'Dinner? Us?' he suggested.

'Yeah,' said Stuey. 'If you're not too afraid to brave those big, bad winds.'

'I didn't say I was *afraid*…'

'Okay, then. I'll get this.' And Stuey reached for his wad of new notes.

'You're all right,' said Phil. 'You weren't even here; we don't expect you to pay.' Phil pulled a twenty from his wallet; they'd paid round by round so the money would be sufficient. For different reasons entirely, Stuey kept a hawkish eye on the proceedings.

A five, a couple of ones. The correct change was given.

Together they left the bar. In the hotel lobby, the line had inched forwards, but seemed to have carried on reproducing

6

at the back, the queue as long as ever. A Japanese family with nine cases, all of them identical hard shells, on a trolley, trundled in front of the three of them, heading for the elevator. The current idea was to get changed, or at least to don more clothes, and to walk to the nearest place that looked good.

Rounding the back of the queue, Stuey looked at the last party in line. Like at least half of the congregation, the two adults carried British passports in readiness for their check-in. The tiny child at their feet, two years old, possibly three, was tired, probably jetlagged, but was doggedly playing with his dinosaurs. The woman's upper lip was perky and fragile with cracking plum lipstick. She looked familiar to Stuey.

Halfway up the building, still ascending, he remembered why.

'Did you see that couple on the end?' Stuey asked the oc-
cupants of the lift, not all of whom he had met before. 'I *know* her. I went to school with her.'

'Who?' Becky asked. For the first time tonight she sounded drunk.

'The woman at the back of the queue. Her name's Claire Drury.'

'Bully for her,' said Phil. 'She's got to sleep somewhere.'

And Becky said, 'We've all got a double, you know.'

Stuey nodded.

'Twenty minutes?' Phil suggested, outside their two rooms.

'Just bang on my door when you're ready,' said Stuey. His room had not been made up while he had been out; an announcement had gone round that the hotel was understaffed because of the freak weather. Still, he reflected, Becky had said that the maid had knocked on *their* door, one room along. He turned on the television; the news was dominated by the blizzard. A man in Queens had been killed when his car had slid like a hockey puck into a gritting truck; a dog had whined long enough for its elderly owner, who had slipped on steps in Harlem, for a neighbour to call the services. She'd survived.

Phil's twenty minutes could easily stretch to an hour, so Stuey knew that he had time enough for a quick bath to warm himself up. The pipes performed an industrial symphony as the water made its way up the side of the building and into the tub, freezing cold at first. In his wait Stuey found himself sitting on his bed, with the travel guide open on his lap, thinking about Claire Drury.

When the knock came at the door, Stuey was convinced that Claire had remembered and found him. His face had even constructed a smile.

'Hi. My hairdryer's knackered,' said Becky. 'Can I use yours, please?'

'Sure.' Stuey stepped aside. Becky entered. She was wearing only the first of the many layers that the New York winter would demand of her; water dripped onto her shoulders, down her neck.

The hotel hairdryer was near the TV. As Stuey closed the bathroom door and began to disrobe, he could hear it fire up – it sounded like a jet engine, sucking in sparrows. He could hear Becky sing: 'I'm gonna BE a part of it...'

He slid into the now hot water.

A few minutes later, the hairdryer's mumbles ceased and Stuey figured that he'd spent enough time soaking. Stepping out, he wrapped himself up.

Steaming as he entered the bedroom, Stuey gasped.

'What are you still doing here?' he asked.

'Waiting for my hair to dry,' said Becky.

'Does Phil know you're here?'

'Of course. What do you think I did – tell him I was going

out for peanuts? Roasted chestnuts? I just told the truth: our hairdryer's on the blink. Come closer.'

'I can't, Becks,' I said. 'That's my brother in there.'

'Your *half*-brother,' said Becky. 'And it didn't stop you before.'

'Well, you're married now.' Stuey knew it to be a ludicrous line of defence. 'There's no way I could do it…'

'Do what?' Becky cocked her head.

Stuey opened his towelly toga; Becky looked on. Not tilting her head up by one inch, Becky said, 'Help me, Stuey. Help me out of this marriage. I've made a mistake.'

Stuey covered himself up again. 'Too early to tell,' he said.

'I've settled for second best.'

Stuey began to dry himself off. He didn't see any point in being modest.

9

'I want someone to think about me the way *you* think about that girl in the lobby, the one from school,' Becky said. 'Or thought. Whatever's the case.'

'Think,' admitted Stuey. 'I was fifteen, I had a crush.'

Becky stood up. 'I'm hungry. Let's go out.'

Despite the time that they had spent getting ready for dinner, when they descended to the lobby, the check-in queue was still long. Stuey looked about for Claire Drury. There she was, next in line for individualised attention, looking bored.

'I'll meet you outside,' Stuey said. 'Hold the cab. I'll pay.'

'I thought we were walking,' said Phil.

Stuey considered tipping the nearby porter to go over and have a word. But say what? Instead Stuey walked around the line of people and leaned against the far end of the check-in desk, where there was no one serving and where you could hire a key for a safe deposit box. He wanted to hear them as they were served.

'Hi,' said Claire's companion. 'We have a reservation. Carter.'

Claire Carter, thought Stuey. It didn't suit her. He tried to look at Claire, but the angle was a difficult one: she was on the far side of her husband. The little boy was now on his feet, still playing with his dinosaurs. The tyrannosaurus had learned how to fly. Is it really her? Stuey wondered.

'Room 2822,' said the guy behind the desk.

'Come on, Josh,' said Claire to her son. They walked away from the desk and Stuey got a good look at his old crush. It was her; it had to be.

Stuey, Phil and Becky dined locally: a Greek place called Mitzi's. Stuey was in no mood for retsina and sipped on his Sprite with little enthusiasm. Hoping that neither of his friends would want a dessert, Stuey finished his vine leaves, dabbed his lips with a paper napkin, and reached inside his jacket for his wallet. 'On me,' he said, laying down a fifty.

It came as no surprise when the waitress brought him back nearly two hundred dollars in twenties and tens. 'Have a good evening,' she implored them.

Along with a brace of other people, they stopped outside The New Yorker's revolving gold door and snacked on cigarettes for five minutes. Once inside, Phil announced that he was going for a nightcap in the bar. Becky and Stuey rode the elevator to floor 26. They were alone in the car.

'Do you know what my new year's resolution was?' asked Becky. 'This was going to be my year of not letting chances pass me by. My year of not having any regrets.'

Stuey knew that he had to say something, and he presumed that she was referring to her marriage. 'Don't worry,' he offered, 'it's just first-month jitters. You'll be fine.'

The doors opened. 'I had the chance to say no, to run away. I couldn't even get *that* right, could I?' Becky laughed.

They had reached Stuey's door. 'Can I come in?' she asked. 'Let's watch a movie or something. Get one of the rude ones.'

'Not if you're going to undress and get into my bed, I'm not.'

'No. We'll watch it like normal people. If you prefer.'

'Okay. But just for a bit.'

Becky waved away the suggestion. 'Oh, you know what *his* nightcaps mean,' she said. 'He'll be down there for another two hours, drinking beer and watching the ice hockey. Like he's ever shown a *scintilla* of interest in ice hockey before. Maybe he'll flirt with that barmaid. She is his type.'

Stuey closed the door. He felt uncomfortable. *Why didn't I tell her I was sleepy?* he thought. He wanted to call 2822. 'Something strange is happening,' he said. 'With money.'

It felt good to explain.

'Could you run a bath, please?' said Becky.

'You're not taking a bath!'

'I just want to hear running water.'

When Stuey came back into the bedroom, Becky was down to her bra. She smiled. 'Don't worry, Stuey: your luck seems to be sky-high at the moment. He'll never know.'

'We'll have to be quick,' said Stuey, 'just in case.'

'Spoken like a true romantic. Come on.'

Stuey began to disrobe. Worried that the headboard would make a noise, he led Becky by the hand into the bathroom. To the sounds of crashing hot water, the steam filling up the room, she firmed up her grip on the side of the tub and bent her legs slightly, her head up.

After she'd left, Stuey thought about some of the things she'd said. Eschewing the option of pornography, he neverthe-

11

less remained naked – with the heaters on full blast – and he picked up the telephone receiver.

2822, he dialled. What if Claire's husband answered? What if *her son* did? True, the little boy was probably in bed, but what with jetlag, who could tell?

Just hang up, thought Stuey. *Your luck is sky-high at the moment.*

'Hello,' said Claire.

'Hi.'

'Where *are* you?' she asked. 'Still in the bar?'

'In my room,' said Stuey. 'This isn't your husband. Is your boy asleep?'

'Who is this?'

'Stuey. I knew you in school. Do you remember me?'

'Vaguely. What do you want?'

Stuey sighed – and plunged. 'I can help you out of your marriage,' he said.

'What? Who says I want help out of my marriage?' Claire asked.

'You didn't look very happy in the lobby.'

'Are you *watching* me?'

Stuey plunged again. 'Come to my room. Please.'

'*No*,' said Claire.

Despondently and with anger, Stuey reached for the remote. *Angelina's Mouth* was five minutes in; he was asleep a quarter of an hour before his erection decided to give up the ghost as well.

Bright and early the next morning, Stuey descended to the lobby and bought *The New York Times*. His dollar earned him a hundred and seven bucks in change, handed over by a woman in a flower-print smock. He found a chair in the coffee shop that had a decent view of the elevators; he ordered a coffee and piled in sugar, much more than usual. Then he pretended to read.

The Carter family emerged at a little before eight. They were not dressed for the outside, where snow still fell heavy and thick. Silently they made their way past Stuey's table, en route for the Tick Tock Diner. Stuey stood up. About to follow them, he suddenly had a better idea. Quickly he made his way back to the elevators and ascended to the twenty-eighth floor.

A maid's trolley was in the hallway. Stuey made sure that the young woman saw him insert his keycard and try the door handle a couple of times. Then he took a step towards her. 'Excuse me,' he said, 'this doesn't seem to be working. Could you let me in, please?'

The room was larger than his own. There were two queen-sized beds, the covers in knots and tangles. While the little boy, Josh, had evidently slept on only one side of his bed, the other bed was more of a shipwreck. Stuey leaned on it – his knees sank deep – and sniffed both pillows to learn what side Claire had slept on. The far side smelt of shampoo; it was also lightly thatched with a few strands of her dark hair. He picked up her nightdress and held it to his face, inhaling.

I wonder if she told her husband about my call, thought Stuey. And it was at this instant that he heard a keycard in the slot. His thoughts were atomised.

Two strides took him into Claire's bathroom. He climbed into the bath as the front door opened. Someone had forgotten something; that was the only explanation for so swift a return. 'Bloody dinosaurs,' he heard Claire mutter. Behind the shower curtain Stuey smiled. But not for long. The dinosaurs that the boy had been playing with were with him, in the tub. Stuey had neither the time nor the confidence to reach past the curtain and plant the toys in the sink. He gasped as Claire pulled back the curtain…

Claire gasped louder.

'What the hell are you doing in my room?' she demanded when her breath had returned.

'Do you recognise me?' asked Stuey, stepping out of the bath.

'That's hardly the point. Get out.'

'I've come to help you.' Stuey held up her nightdress.

'You're sick. I'm calling the cops.'

'No, don't. Please. I don't mean any harm.' Stuey was confused. Why *was* he here? 'I thought you might have been expecting me.'

Claire copied his frown. 'After your phone call, nothing would have surprised me. That's what I believed anyway. Drop the nightdress on your way out.'

At the door, Stuey turned. 'Can I keep it? Something to remember you by.'

'You never knew me. And I'm a different person now anyway. It was fifteen years ago, Stuey,' said Claire. 'Okay, then. Keep it. But don't bother me again.'

His heart had slowed down by the time he reached his room. He fell backwards onto his bed. Then there was a knock at his door.

'You bastard.'

'And good morning to you, Phil,' said Stuey. 'What's wrong?'

'You did it, didn't you? Couldn't keep your hands off her. Don't deny it. I come up from the bar and she's asleep with come on her thighs.' Phil used both hands to push Stuey backwards. 'And I'm thinking: it can't be Stuey. *Stuey* wouldn't do it…'

'I haven't done anything,' Stuey lied.

'You're a mangy little dog. Why the hell are we on holiday together?' Phil asked.

Stuey closed his eyes. He could take a cab to JFK. He would probably make a few hundred dollars on that. Then he could try to get on the next flight home, for a quarter, a dime, a nickel…

When Phil had left, Stuey packed his bag. As he stepped out of the elevator on the ground floor, Claire and her family were waiting to step in. Very briefly panic fought for control of her features, but she held it at bay. They passed one another silently. He joined the queue for checking in and checking out.

'Checking out,' he told the receptionist. She charged him five dollars for *Angelina's Mouth* and confirmed that he hadn't made any phone calls. He handed her a red penny. She rewarded his audacity with a grenade-sized brace of fifties, and counted them carefully in front of his eyes. A thousand dollars. Pretty soon people would be paying him just to breathe. The thought raised a quivering smile.

'Where to?' asked the cabbie. The windshield wipers massaged the snowflakes from the screen. Horns hooted. Stuey thought of ducks.

'Somewhere south. Somewhere warm,' said Stuey.

'You wanna be more specific?'

'How much to drive me to Las Vegas?' Stuey replied. He wanted to see if good luck was transferable. How long would it take to bleed a casino dry?

What do you mean, good *luck?* he asked himself sourly.

'The airport. JFK.'

15

Trite

'SOUL WINDOWS, MATE,' said Piper, lighting a cigarette. 'It was the *soul windows* done it.' Greedily, and with a liquid sigh, he inhaled, and exhaled.

Though yearning for clarity, Ray left a respectful pause. 'The what?' he asked quietly as he averted his attention to the Union Jack ashtray – whiskery with coals and dead smuts.

'The windows to the soul,' Piper elaborated, enjoying the beat. 'The *eyes*.' He flicked ash; spores of it missed the cross-beams of the flag and swam idly in the table's beer-rings.

'I'm lost,' admitted Ray. 'His eyes were shifty, were they?'

Piper nodded. 'Well yeah, but that's not what I mean. So'd yours be if you knew the bloke in front of you 'ad a grenade in his jacket pocket. No. What I *mean* is, his eyes – Ray – Raymond – you listening?'

'Yeah…'

'What I mean is,' said Piper, 'his eyes were the wrong fucking *colour*, you daft slag. *That* was the clue.'

'I didn't notice.' Nor did Ray have any idea what Piper was talking about.

'Obviously. What did Leonardo tell us? What was our brief?'

Defensively, Ray answered, 'To pick up the trite.'

'Right. Who from?'

'The geezer – from the geezer in the navy blue whistle.'

Piper waved Ray on; his movements elicited a loop-the-loop of fagsmoke. 'His chief characteristics being?' Piper asked.

'A crew cut…'

'Yeah?'

'A skull ring on his thumb…'

'*Yeah…*'

'Oh. Oh Christ…' And Ray recalled the initial meeting: the warehouse, the back room, the dirty light and the unbelievable heat; Ray had looked up at the overhead fan, cutting the blue smoke into identical packages, and a fat spider had ridden a blade, round and round. 'And blue eyes,' Ray concluded. That was what Leonardo had said. 'Eyes like the Indian Ocean.'

'Right. So what colour were matey's?' asked Piper.

'I didn't notice,' Ray repeated. 'I'm sorry, boss.'

As he had yet to make his point, Piper ignored the apology. 'Let me tell you summing, Ray: that's *just* the sort of inattention to detail that's gonna get you pulverized under some cunt's boot one of these days.' Piper paused. 'I mean, honestly, Ray. You really want me to send you out on your own? You think you're *ready?*'

'Sorry, boss.'

'He had green eyes, Ray. Not blue…'

Busying herself in the kitchen, Fee knew that something had gone wrong. She was nervous. With a trembling hand she used a hob to light a cigarette while leafing through the possibilities in her mind. Either Ray had been hurt or someone else had: surely there was no other reason for Ray arriving home sober. Fee stirred the casserole and wondered if she should offer Ray a consoling can of lager.

It took her the length of her smoke to make up her mind. He'd prefer to take the initiative, she thought – and feeling his approach through the flat Fee turned and offered him a smile. He was in the doorway.

'That's disgusting, that is,' Ray opined. 'Smoking while

you're cooking.'

'Sorry.' Fee stirred the food again, cigarette on her lips. She hated his unpredictability when he hadn't had a drink; it was as though he was still working. And he was probably spoiling for an argument; he had certainly never complained of her smoking while cooking before. Indeed, he'd once wondered aloud what a cigarette stew would come out like. 'How was your day?'

'Why'd you ask?'

Fee's temper had lost her boyfriends in the past, but she knew, now that she'd entered her twenties, that she wouldn't be changing her demeanour anytime soon. She said: 'I always ask, Ray.' She abandoned the long wooden spoon in the casserole. 'And you know what? It'd be nice if I could add something like: *you know that*. But you *don't* know that, do you, Ray? Because you never listen to half of what I'm saying.'

Ray lingered on the threshold. 'Not you an' all,' he complained.

Four steps took him to the bathroom door, which he closed with an unwarranted force. The lock was snapped into place and Fee heard the toilet seat make contact with the cistern. Had he gone in there to examine a wound? Nothing so romantic, it seemed: the sound of Ray farting in C-Minor rose above the noises of the food cooking, and Fee sighed.

She heard him leave the room. He entered their bedroom and said, 'Jesus, Fee. Couldn't you tidy up a bit?' he called through the wall.

Ray stepped back into the kitchen, with a pair of her knickers, as wrangled as a dishcloth, on an extended forefinger. 'These have been on the floor since *Sunday*!'

'What you doing,' asked Fee, 'keeping an inventory? You forgotten which one of us schleps from house to house, cutting hair all day? Why don't *you* clear up for a change?'

DAVID MATHEW

'I'm going out,' Ray decided.

Piper raised the weights. *Too much*, he almost caught himself thinking (while noticing the silent shriek that his face had become in the floor-to-ceiling mirror); quickly he reassessed the situation. *I can do it*, he told himself.

'That enough?' asked Ollie, the young black man who worked at the HeartLines Club, giving guidance to the pullers and the pushers, the groaners and the sighers, when it was needed (about once a day) and who at all other times maintained an air of seigniorial agitation as he viewed and compared the backsides of the women training.

'It'll do.' Piper reached for the bottle of water and the towel. Ollie, similarly, lifted his own canister to his lips – to toast his client's achievements.

Piper stood up. The shower was the best bit, and as he stood beneath the water, clearing his nose between thumb and middle finger and micturating into the gel foam and shampoo slick, Piper relished an instance of peace. Not that his day was over – far from it, though it was pushing nine at night – but just for the moment he was able to forget the pressures that lined up to confront the busy entrepreneur in this day and age.

'Night, Ollie,' Piper said a quarter of an hour later.

'Night, Mr Piper. Drive safe.'

Fucking chill on it, thought Piper as the doors slid closed behind him. November: bonfire perfume in the air; Piper's breath danced whitely in front of his face. He paused to ignite a compensational smoke; cracked open a can of fizz as he forced himself to become accustomed to the evening wind. He wasn't alone. Some kids were dicking about, doing kids' things, near the bicycle railings, with their tracksuits, their bags of wet clothes, and their damp and spiky hair. *Just had a game*, Piper

19

deduced. He had heard their roars.

From ten metres away he shot a laser beam at the Bentley. The lights blinked twice, indicating that the burglar alarm had been disarmed. Equally reassuring was the fact that the car had been untouched. On emerging from a building, the fact that his beloved motor had suffered no abuse never failed to produce a warm glow in Piper's belly: it helped him to build faith in his fellow man. Piper had even heard of the sort of scum that stole people's number plates in order to fasten them to getaway cars and vehicles used in ramraiding, the better to frame an innocent victim on the CCTV. Unforgivable. Piper's homage to his musical god, Tom Jones, had so far remained unscathed. The plate read YYY DELILAH, and this rarely failed to make him feel proud either. Piper unlocked the driver's side and tossed his sports bag onto the passenger seat. He was just about to climb in.

'Taking a risk, intcha?' someone asked.

Piper turned.

'You must think you're cock of the walk or summing.'

The man was five-six, five-seven – the same as Piper. He was dressed for winter: a big dark coat, a scarf across his face, a blue baseball cap dipped low. Earrings caught the car park lights.

'Me?' said Piper. But the spanner in the other man's right hand had already answered this question.

'Who else? Give it back.'

The man took a step towards Piper.

'And we can avoid all this nonsense,' he went on in his real voice. Piper had no way of knowing that in fact he had met this man before.

'I don't 'ave it,' Piper told him, not panicking. 'Leonardo's got it.'

'No he ain't. Do you want me to start? Show I mean business.'

'The deal went rotten; what can I say? You sent the wrong man. You stitched us up.'

'I didn't send no one, mate. I'm just the collector. Nice car.'

'You touch it...' Piper warned, his voice hardening.

'How long you been in there. Hour?'

'About that.'

'Long enough for me to fuck your brakes up, agreed?'

'I suppose so,' Piper conceded.

'Listen. I don't want this and you don't want this. Just give me the fucking tritium and we're all laughing. It's not yours!'

'It's not yours either! We had a deal.'

'Which soured. You give our boy a thump and take the gear anyway! What sort of cunt trick's that?'

It's business, thought Piper, recalling how he'd leaned across the table to jab the visitor in the eyes – the eyes that failed to be ocean blue. He had said, 'His arms, Ray!' and Ray had stood up swiftly, upending a chair, in order to secure the impostor. Ray had wrapped himself around the other man, restraining him to his own chair, as Piper had slapped him on the nose.

Who you working for? Piper had demanded.

Shakey.

No you not. He was sending a cunt called Billy, with blue eyes. Who are you? Last chance... or this fucking grenade's going off in your face...

'Come on,' said the man in the car park. 'Time to pay the piper.'

'Is that supposed to be funny?'

The bescarfed man took a swing with the spanner. Catching Piper unawares, the blow connected with Piper's left temple – a hollow clang.

'You don't do it,' Sam the Fridge was opining. 'You just don't.'

Ray returned from the bar at The Speckled Frog. Exhibiting great talent for a future in the waiting business, he was carrying four pint glasses in his banana-bunch hands. *Not this still*, he thought. He'd hoped that the conversation might have moved on following the important phone call that he'd just made and during his stay at the three-deep bar.

Nobby and John were discussing football: the international game that had been played a week earlier. They had reached no consensus on whether the ref had been blind or simply corrupt. And here was Sam the Fridge, on and on, in the same line – like a parrot. 'You just don't *do it*. Not to your mum,' he was saying.

'Here you go, lads,' said Ray.

'I don't *care* what she done,' said Sam. 'It's not on. It's not cricket.'

Ray sat down and started on his fifth of the evening.

John asked him: 'So how did it go today, Ray?'

'Don't ask. Nightmare,' Ray replied.

'It's the lowest of the low…'

Ray was not supposed to tell the boys anything about his work with Piper: it was one of the latter's rules, laid down from the off. But Ray spilled every bean there was to spill.

'They turned us over.'

'Not to your old *mum*,' said Sam the Fridge.

'Someone found out we were buying the tritium,' Ray continued. 'We don't know all the ins and outs yet, but they sent a ringer. Took out the bloke we were supposed to be meeting and got someone off the subs' bench. Same hairdo, nicked his ring…' Ray shook his head. 'But they couldn't change the colour of the cunt's eyes, could they? So Piper smelt a rat. Things got perky, mate, I can tell you that.'

'Damage?' asked Nobby.

Ray sniffed. 'We busted his nose for him,' he lied. 'Shoed him around a bit.' Or rather, Piper had done so – the latter; Ray had been the restraining order. 'So we took the stuff and legged it.'

'Even if she *does* give you a bit of lip,' said Sam. 'Not your *old girl.*'

'What *is* tritium anyway?' John enquired.

Again, Ray sniffed; he could do this one now. 'It's basically a lot more stable than plutonium,' he said. 'And it's more expensive – hence the hassle. You can carry it round in water, it's light, and it don't react like plutonium, nuking every cunt for half a mile in diameter. And everyone wants some…'

'You just don't get your mum in a *headlock*,' said Sam.

'So where is it now?' John wanted to know.

'Piper put it in his sports bag and dumped the case.'

'It ain't right. It's wrong.'

Ray turned. 'Sam?' he said. 'You don't shut up I'm gonna put *you* in a fucking headlock. Do you understand me? Had enough for one day.'

'Drink your drink,' said Sam, frowning. 'There's nothing to see here.'

Fee turned off the quiz show. She was ready to pacify Ray and to attempt to reach the heart of the matter. It was with a light but fluttering heart that Fee entered the square of hallway in response to the bell that had rattled a few seconds earlier. Ray always rang when he knew that he'd behaved intolerably; it was the equivalent of the writhing white hanky. And besides, he knew that she would have put the chain on and rolled the deadbolt.

23

She opened the door.

'Where is he?' asked a man that Fee had never seen before. 'I said, *where is he?*'

'Where am I?' Piper wanted to know. His vision was ambiguous at best, but he recognized the aromas: the room, the aftershave.

'It's me. Ollie. Don't worry, you're safe. He gave you some juice but he's gone.'

Piper was lying on his back, on a changing room bench: in the pluvial air he could smell the evening's b.o. and deodorant. Ollie knelt beside him, explaining the few moments after consciousness had escaped.

'A coupla kids came and got me,' he was saying. 'I thought it was a trick to get me away from the till. But they said you was being attacked, and when I got out there he was driving away. I didn't get the plate.'

'My car?' Piper wondered aloud.

Ollie smiled understandingly. 'It's secure. He didn't even take your wallet, man. He only wanted your sports bag…'

'Oh shit,' said Piper, sitting up quickly.

'Come on, man. So he gets your sweaty knickers: big deal.'

A wave of nausea lurched within Piper's head.

'Lie down, Mr Piper. You're not ready. Just rest.'

Leonardo would go spare. Only two hours earlier, Piper had informed Leonardo – not altogether truthfully – that things had gone according to plan. Although it was a fact that Piper intended to return Leonardo's money when he handed over the trite (perhaps there would even be a small reward), it was equally the case that Piper knew how much Leonardo detested unforeseen complications.

What's going on? Leonardo had wanted to know.

24

Nothing; it's all in hand.

I've heard otherwise, mate, Leonardo had continued. *I've had Shakey on the phone. Wanting to know where Billy with the blue eyes has got to...*

And Piper had sighed. *It's all in hand,* he had repeated in the tone of voice suggestive of playful indulgence with another's silliness. *I'll explain everything when I get to yours. Say ten tonight?*

Ten's good.

A squeaky version of 'The Green, Green Grass of Home' piped up. Remaining prostrate, Piper reached for the mobile in his inside pocket.

'It's Fee,' said the voice on the other end. 'Is he with you?'

'Whoss matter?' asked Piper, responding to the tears in the question.

'Is he? Please, Piper...'

'No. Whoss matter?'

'This guy was here looking for him,' Fee continued. 'He shit me up summing chronic. What you *done*?'

'Your boy's all right,' said Piper, astonished by the swiftness of the work and the location. It was like they had radar. 'He's useful.'

'I don't *want* him fighting, Piper! This guy was *mean*.'

Join the real world, Piper thought about saying. *You and your scissors and your curlers – what do you know about the lives of real men?*

'What you tell him?'

'What could I? We had a row; he stormed out. I said he must be in the pub, but I don't even know what pub you go to. Not thighed tell him.'

'I'll protect him,' said Piper. 'Sweetheart, I promise.' *Protect him,* thought the man. *I can't even protect a sports bag*

He took out his cigarettes.

Ollie winced and said, 'No, man. No smoking.'

'Time, ladies and gentlemen, please,' called Dave the barman.

Ladies? thought Ray. *What ladies?* Surely he couldn't be referring to that gaggle of hounds by the fruity. He stood up. 'I'm off.'

When last orders had been announced, Nobby had taken the precaution of ordering in another three pints for everyone, but Ray had abstained. *Big day tomorrow,* he'd confided. More of this trite nonsense, no doubt.

He left The Speckled Frog. High above, a firework expanded like an accordion; the air had the tang of burning guys about it. Loops of sound emerged from a car alarm, nearby; a motorbike snarled, restrained by the red eye of a traffic light. Ray ducked into his Ford Amoeba.

Almost immediately his mobile trilled. Deliberately, so as not to be bothered by Fee, Ray had left the phone in the glove compartment. Now he answered it, after checking the number of the one who was making the call.

'Where are you?' Ray asked.

'Two cars behind,' the voice answered. 'Car park of the Angel Hotel.'

The call that Ray had made in The Speckled Frog had gone like this:

'Leonardo? Name's Ray. Been a slight change of arrangement.'

'With reference to what?' asked the man on the other end – cautious and astute.

'With reference to the trite, mate.'

'The what?'

'The tritium,' Ray elaborated. 'It's me you'll be dealing

with from now on. And I got what you need. You got my money?'

There was a pause. And then Leonardo said, 'Where's Piper?'

Ready for this, Ray replied, 'Piper's off the job. He fucked you, mate. But I got it back, and if you want me to get the negotiation money from him then that can be sorted. But for now, I have the trite and I'm sure you got my cash.'

'I have your cash,' said Leonardo.

This left only one more matter to attend to.

'Where's he at?' Ray asked the man with the scarf around his face.

'Boot.'

Ray smiled. He felt more important than ever. 'You're kidding,' he said. 'How'd you get him to keep quiet?'

'I showed him my spanner. Asked him nicely.'

It really *was* a buyer's market. You could get any damned thing you wanted, for a price. It used to require three thousand pounds to whack an opponent out; nowadays there were refugees willing to do it for a ton. What did it matter?

Or there were guys like this – whose name, as far as Ray was concerned or could care less about, was Barry: guys who were willing to abduct someone, and steal his ring, and pretend to be him *and then get slapped about* on his behalf – all for two hundred pounds. It was a miracle.

'Open it up,' Ray said.

The boot of the other man's car sprung open.

'Peek-a-boo,' Ray greeted the man within – the man with the eyes so blue that they had been compared to summer skies, to oceans deep.

It was beautiful. Ray would be paid a grand, of which

he'd only need to relinquish two hundred. All for a bit of false modesty and feigned stupidity. 'You listening, mate?'

Billy in the boot, his mouth stuffed full of a golf ball that had been Sellotaped secure, nodded briskly. He had the score.

'I'm gonna expect some repercussions over this,' Ray said, 'but I won't expect them tonight, you got it? Because I was never here and I never touched you. My missus has even been threatened tonight...' Ray turned towards the man in the scarf, who smiled briefly. 'I'm innocent, mate,' he finished.

Again, Billy nodded his head.

'Now. I'm going to phone a man named Shakey – your boss. You're gonna tell him we've treated you well. And then we're gonna ask for a few quid for your safe release, mate. Okay? So tell me: how much you think those lovely blue eyes are actually worth, eh? Gimme a price.'

Ray began tearing sticky tape from Billy's face. As he did so, Barry removed the only disguise he'd adopted: the clip-on earrings. Then he pulled off Billy's thumbring – the skull – and Ray thought about keeping it as a souvenir.

Billy's eyes were bright. His lips said nothing.

City Went A-Courtin'

THERE WAS TIME for one more murder before she went home.

On the trolley beside her chair were five DVDs. Such was her lot in life that these she had to bodybag and classify – before the end of the week. Belinda Coffey had used the line before, but she used it now, internally: *The dead have deadlines too.* She shuffled the array like a cardsharp. And although she was tired she thought she could at least begin the next offering before the end of the day; before the lure of the swollen tube station at Aldgate East. What else was she going to do to fill ten minutes?

Belinda selected a Vietnamese film called *Heavy Duty*.   29

The first murder was a pool-cue job.

At exactly the same time as the murderer – with his face the colour of clay and his eyes warmly wet – arrived home, Belinda's own door opened. It was Becky. They didn't much like each other, but they often walked to the station side by side. On some days it would be the only person that Belinda had spoken to in the preceding eight hours of work.

'Ready?'

'Sure,' she answered. The killer's eyes could now be rested.

In the street – with the delis belching pastrami and odd lingoes, and the Jewish foodstores smiling out kosher salt-breaths – she turned to Becky and said: 'Is it me? Or does it feel like a storm?'

'A storm?' said Becky, not missing an opportunity to pounce upon her colleague's weakness of mind. 'Just look at the sky! Electric blue!'

Belinda frowned. 'I didn't mention the sky,' she said.

But what then?

The pulse, she thought. The pulse that was aggravating her ribcage. Something like nervousness, lovesickness and belly rot, all in one... *Am I coming down with something?* she wondered. Everything seemed so *bright*.

He hadn't eaten for such a long time that the slice of discarded pizza – left drooping over a pile of rubbish in a bin and resembling a leaf on a drain – made him feel drunk as he wolfed it down. Feast completed, he sat near the supermarket and licked his paws clean, like a cat.

His name was George Feathers.

At five minutes to six he stood up again. Although his clothes – mainly dark, mainly heavy – had clearly seen better days, George made a quick show of straightening his jacket and adjusting his belt buckle. Then he strolled through the heat and the swarms of bee-lining crowds to the jaws of the tube.

However, the station was temporarily taking nil by mouth. On the pavement, a scrum of thwarted commuters swore and awaited further developments. The old newscaller, in his sentry-box straitjacket, glanced around, perplexed by his lack of sales during such developments.

George looked skywards slightly and to his left. 'What's up?' he asked.

The woman looked down at the questioner, but without disapproval: they were all in this together. Besides, George had made a few pounds in Brick Lane Market the day before, unloading and loading vans, and he'd spent the money, not on food, but on a packet of cheap razor blades, some toothpaste, deodorant, and a new clothes brush to replace the near spineless hedgehog that had previously lived in the inside pocket of his black jacket. Having long since learned to shave by touch

30

alone, and without a mirror, last night he had locked himself into a cubicle in the Pizza Express gents, near Liverpool Street, and shaved in the toilet bowl. He had spruced himself up. Then George had spent the early hours in a doorway behind a curry house.

The woman said, 'Bomb scare.'

'Again?' George enquired. The last time he'd visited this part of East London, a bomb scare had closed down Waltham-stow. George's work had been delayed by an hour.

The woman nodded. She turned to the woman who was on the other side and shared a few words with her. George plucked at the air with his brow; it had gone into involuntary but eminent spasm, and he was pleased that the convulsion, which would not last long, was not being witnessed.

George's mind had fangs and he allowed the animal free reign as he stood in the sun, in the melee. He breathed the ozone. The print from the newsvendor's wares met his nose, but it was a thin strain, diluted by the pong of bodies around him. The animal rose, its outcry silent. George felt the warm-ing of his own blood; not to mention the slick of perspiration that now fell towards his butt-line through the fabric of his shirt.

The animal was twice as tall as George stood. Unseen by the vast majority, it resembled a huge inverted teardrop. Its apex was the point by which it was attached to George's scalp, follicled-in like a hair-weave. The torso rippled, as wide as a sail on a catamaran. All but featureless too, apart from what would be the head, its lower body was amoebic, unfinished. There was no neck. The head began as an extension of the teardrop, on which three gashes were intended to represent the eyes and the nose, or possibly the eye and the noses. George had never been able to tell. The only thing that was clear was

31

the maw: octagonal, it boasted six fangs of light-show smoke.

George felt the burden of that pizza in his belly. He burped. But this was London, and no one turned. Everyone wanted to get home.

Amazing, thought George, *that the patterns have scarcely changed.* At the unheard bell, here they were, the working masses of the capital, running home for a meal, for the news and the evening soaps. In their heads a gong banged and they slipped into a morning rhythm: muesli and tea; getting the children ready; defrosting the windscreen of the car. And then, ten hours later, this *pandemonium.*

It wasn't natural.

The beast bent swiftly at the waist. It now resembled, if only to George alone, a buxom pillow bent in two. And down the fangs descended...

The teeth punctured into Belinda's skull.

Nicky Reef mended eyes for a living. He spent most of the week in a darkened room, with a patient present – sometimes a patient and the patient's mother or father. He gave advice on the subject of contact lens payment plans; he slotted circles of glass into the monstrous apparatus that he'd fixed to the patient's head. To age his boyish good looks he had grown a beard; what no one had told him was that the resulting scruff of peach-fuzz made him seem younger than ever. Notwithstanding his tender years, however, he made a point of ensuring professionalism: after all, he was still on probation at the practice. Every day he arrived thirty minutes before his first appointment. He made reassuring noises and ensured that his breath was minty before each examination. He wore suits that he alternated by the week. And these days he rarely even touched the bottle of Coward's Whiskey that was kept in the bottom drawer of the filing cabinet; but he liked to know that it was there.

Pulling it free of the drawer's hanging files, Nicky adopted a hunchbacked rugby player's attitude; then he scuttled over to the door. He leaned against it. If it were to open suddenly, he would at least have a second in which to slip the bottle into his inside pocket. He unscrewed the cap and swigged. Then he left the building.

No sooner had he reached the throng at Aldgate East than he realised that this was as far as he would be permitted to go. The entrance was closed.

Nicky was standing half a metre to George's left. He heard George ask 'What's up?' and he also heard Belinda's response. What were Nicky's choices? A walk to Liverpool Street station? But that was so close that it might also be shut, for the good of the general public. And the Central Line was no particular help anyway: he needed to get to Goldhawk Road, to the house he shared with two dieticians and a diabetic stonemason. The best bet was surely a walk to Aldgate and the Circle Line south, and then a bus.

Suddenly dizzy, Nicky felt as though his upper brainpan had been recently mopped. Scents and sights played with his senses. To his right, just beyond the slight body of George Feathers, the woman named Belinda was also feeling the worst. Bending slightly at the waist, she gripped her knees. Her discomfiture was loud – a subject of concern to the woman who stood beside her...

A few minutes later the gate opened.

Throughout the thirty-five minute wait in the tunnel, while the authorities had decided if Aldgate East was a safe port, the passengers on the train travelling west from Barking had moved through distinct shifts in mood. The train had eased to a halt. Following a throat-clearance of static, the P.A. had announced:

'This is Geoff, your driver. I'm afraid we're going to be banked here for a short while. I've just been told there's a security alert at Aldgate East. There's nothing I can do about it, ladies and gentlemen.' Only on the last word did Geoff let his guard down and allow his true voice to crawl through: *jellmin*.

London, born and bred, thought a man named Dan, who clutched the leather case that encased his expensive cello.

Grim resignation was the first wave that swept through the carriages. Resignation gave way to frustration, to anger; the patterns were identical from one carriage to the next. Dan tried to keep things in perspective. Geoff was doing his best to keep temperatures down: his three-minute updates could be heard by one and all.

Then, a new mood entirely...

Dan Waremond had once been on a bad plane flight. Not bad in the sense that most voyagers would have defined the word – as the result of a few bumps and curtsies in the sky – but *really bad*. The aircraft should never have taken off, given the evidence that had been available: that of ball lightning, gales and whirlwinds sucking skywards. For three hours, Dan and his co-travellers had been of the opinion that there was nothing to do but hope; but at one point, so dreadful had the journey become, that he'd considered the ultimate in death defiance. He had almost, but not quite, said to the woman who had then been his wife: 'Let's go into the toilets. This might be our last chance.' And then, a second later, he had almost curled his body around so that he could slip his hand up between skin and blouse.

It hadn't happened. But opposite Dan, now, two young

adults were clearly thinking along similar lines. Dan could almost read their minds: if this was the end – if the explosion
was about to saw the faces from their skins – then what did they
have to lose? Certainly, the canoodling that had been part of
Dan's journey so far on the Hammersmith and City line from
Stepney Green had stepped up a gear.

They were feasting on the heat. Gorging on the panic.
An awareness of doom had brought with it an exhibitionistic
streak. The two lovers were in their early twenties, with the fad-
ing beechwood-skin colours of a recent foreign holiday. The
man had thrust his right hand up the woman's denim skirt. But
playing her own part, the woman now tore her paramour's
shirt, as efficiently as if she were slitting open an envelope.

Throughout the thirty-five minute wait in the tunnel, a   35
man named Bob Dooley asked: *Am I really awake? Am I here?*

He'd asked himself this more and more in the last few
weeks. Although he'd been too frightened to confirm his suspicions, he was certain that others among the track crew had
experienced similar sensations.

Then again, maybe he had relapsed; maybe he was still ill.

The nervous breakdown he'd suffered was three years old.
It was, he sometimes joked with his second wife, Jessica, whom
he'd met while in therapy, their third anniversary together: he
and his madness. But behind his joviality was fear. The exit in-
terview from the police force had taken place in an atmosphere
of sincerity, committed support and deep, rich understanding.
Police work wasn't for everyone, he'd been told, but Dooley
could have been found a desk job. No; Dooley had made up his
mind to leave. Unwilling to give up working outdoors, he had
taken a drop in salary and begun work on the railways.

He and his colleagues spent part of every day living like

moles. Armed sometimes with nothing more than torches, they patrolled the lines, clearing up trainkill and checking out points and electrical connections. Since arriving on shift today, Dooley had suffered from what he took to be hay fever: his symptoms had consisted of a clamp to his sinuses that no amount of Sudafed and sweet tea had been able to shift. However, things had developed for the worse. In the last hour Bob Dooley had started to sweat. The overalls and waterproofs (unneeded in the current climate) had conspired to turn his legs into waterfalls, his groin into marshland. Worse still, that groin had another treachery to bestow upon its owner. Eight times since clocking on, Dooley had looked up from a routine task to find that beneath his clothing his manhood was saluting, waiting, and sniffing around. Nor could he attribute his sudden longing to a lack of feeling shown him in the bedroom; last night alone he and Jessica had found their favourite places in the gloom, and had gone to sleep happy, fulfilled and feeling that they'd earned their rest. When Dooley had been aware of his erections, he had summoned up Jessica's face, her back, in an attempt to convince himself that he'd been lusting after her all along.

It wasn't so. And Dooley knew it.

He was seeing things, worst of all. How many times so far had he witnessed uneven tubes of something transparent, sliding along the tunnel walls and ceiling? How many times had he seen these shapes as they stroked along the sides of a moving train, barely shunned by the velocity? And every time that he saw a shape – an elongated bubble – he would feel the stirring, the unwanted pressure at his midriff.

Dooley was now beside the stopped train. Its progress had been postponed for nearly twenty minutes, and keeping close to the blackened bricks, Dooley took a heated walk along its

36

dirty length. He breathed heavily. He thought: *It's like being a peeping tom...* Inside the carriages the lights were still on, and Dooley could raise his head and see some of the sexual activity within. What he saw set shivers plucking at his moisturized spine.

They don't see me, he thought. *They don't care.*

A sound startled Dooley: scratching and nail-on-concrete squeaks. He hooked in a desperate breath. He shone the torch in the direction that he believed the noise to have come from. To Dooley's right, near a rampart in the tunnel, on a bed of broken paving slabs, were two fat rats, throbbing like organs. The fatter of the two rats, perched on the less obese, resumed its frenzied thrusting.

Dooley watched the act in the spotlight. A certain guilt and shame prevailed, but more than that, a certain sadness; sniffing loudly, almost as an attempt to dissuade the animals from their congress, Dooley knew that the sweat on his neck signalled longing. He was fixed on the spectacle. He hoisted free what had swollen in his pants. He leaned his head backwards and gripped hard. Returned his gaze. The male rat was fit to burst, or so it seemed; and so was Dooley.

The air was rocky with currents.

Had Dooley not been so absorbed, he might well have heard the booted approach of another member of the team. But he heard this:

'Jesus.'

And he turned, his panhandle in a trusted grip. His face seemed to shrink in the torchlight. Not that he would have admitted it, but his face was smiling.

'What the hell do you think you're *doing*, Bob?'

'Paddy?' said Dooley. Pissed Paddy was Dooley's Team Leader.

37

'What you *doing*?'

Dooley turned. Presenting his interlocutor with a full-frontal view of what his genes had seen fit to bequeath him, Dooley said, 'Don't you feel it?'

The other man was clearly unsure. 'Feel what?' Pissed Paddy replied.

'Take the light out of my face,' said Dooley.

'And put it where, Bob?' Sarcastic and caustic.

A semblance of rationality had returned. Face reddening, Dooley added: 'I was just taking a squirt.' The way he spread his arms threw beams of light into the carriage; they splashed up to the ceiling, where long, hollow teardrops were waiting for the next stage of events.

'No you weren't. There are *people* on that train…'

'I know. They feel the same way…'

'As what?'

Dooley took a step towards his team leader. 'As you and me.'

'Stay away.'

Another step. 'I've been burning for months,' said Dooley.

'I'm serious, Bob. Stay right away from me. I don't wanna know.'

'Yes you do.'

By now no more than two metres separated the two men, but Paddy was standing his ground. Having taken a huge sniff, he now spat on the stones, the flint, the wood. And in the face of such defiance, a cliché was all that Bob could muster.

'It's bigger than both of us,' he said

He reached out. He touched his superior's identical leggings, saying:

'See? You're a *liar*, Pissed Paddy. You're a liar.'

The place where a man named Dan had recently visited – the offices of Withing and McGraw, independent song publishers – was one of the first places in London, near Bromley-by-Bow, to feel the quake of the expulsion.

The tunnels were full of need-to-do.

The beasts and the force rumbled skywards.

Released from the silent embarrassment that he'd felt for the duration of the threat, the newspaper seller started up again on his précis of the day's world events.

'Prince Harry,' he called, as if anyone cared. 'Love scandal.'

No one listened. *It's like the start of the Marathon*, thought Nicky, whose own father had once described the experience in a brief flight away from the alcoholism that had killed him. Nicky Senior had been quite an athlete in his time, before the realisation that those skills had themselves run away, and before the slow slide away from life that had been lubricated by Coward's Whiskey and Diet Coke.

More or less booting each other out of the way – there was no community spirit – the crowd blazed its trail to the ticket barriers. No less violent in his intentions than the next man, Nicky was nevertheless aware that the woman who had experienced difficulties above ground was but one punter behind him as he rode the escalator into the capital's bowels.

Like a telegram, the train arrived on time.

When Belinda and Becky boarded, a step or two behind Nicky, and two in front of George, they were presented with a scene straight out of European cinema. The young couple had by now relinquished one of its two seats: the man was standing behind the woman, who was kneeling on the second chair. And although her face was mainly visible only in the reflection in the glass, anyone close by could pay witness to her gooey pleasure and her rolling eyeballs.

George smiled like the loon the woman had become.

Others were not so exhilarated.

'It's the sun,' Belinda heard from somewhere to her right. 'Brings out the horny in us all.' *Well, that may well be the case*, she thought; *but there are times and places to be acting like pigs in heat.*

I'd rather watch another murder, she continued.

'Mind the gap,' said Geoff, omnipotently.

The doors slid closed.

But there was no denying that Belinda herself was feeling the burn of too little, too late, at her core. George's beast had performed its trick.

George had been hard at work for the previous seven months.

He often began the week in the white room. He would wake on the narrow cot and move to the corner of the room, where he showered. His clothes would have been ironed and hung up during the night. He dressed, and felt in his pockets as a matter of instinct.

There was almost a second, if that, of consternated surprise at what he found in there. His eyes atavistic, he would pull free a handful of the small objects. They resembled two contact lenses stuck together.

Inside the casing was a drop of milky white fluid: thick. When George held a capsule up to the light, the liquid rolled about with the unhurried determination of mercury in a thermometer. Very briefly, before the darkness started to crawl into his line of vision – the darkness that George always felt to be inside the room, but which was really inside his head – he had cause to wonder if he should burst one of the capsules open. He was curious.

Then, before his very eyes – still blurry, often, but not myopic, and not, as far as he was aware, given to hallucination – the capsule or capsules would begin to disappear. The vanishing was such a neat magician's trick that George would query whether his hand had been full in the first place.

Sometimes he fought the disappearance: he was certain that it was a bad sign – an omen of looming insanity. When Dr Chidzoy came in, she would find George staring at his palms or rummaging in his pockets, bringing out great fistfuls of the chemical but seeing nothing at all but his own moistened skin.

'What have you got there, George?' she would ask.

'Nothing.'

'And what have you got in your pockets, George?'

'Nothing.'

'Good man. This week we'd like you to travel on the Piccadilly Line.'

'Okay.'

For the last seven months, George had taken the capsules down deep into the womb of London, and then released them. George would leave the white room, and the laboratories, and Docklands behind, travelling north on the DLR. Only at his given destination would his digits begin to assume a life of their own. Digging deep into his pockets, he would squeeze a capsule like a pimple, or leave a breadcrumb trail of them on the platform, for a tourist or a worker to stamp on or pierce with a high heel.

For the rest of the week George lived rough.

By the time the train reached Euston Square, the physical display had ended. The lovers sat back in their chairs, blissed out. However, there was plenty more love in the air. Looking left and right, Dan was able to see a few not-so-furtive kisses, including those between people he'd assumed to be strangers.

A few metres from him, Belinda seemed remote and alien. Rogue thoughts shook her imagination, like a bone in a wild dog's mouth. Standing directly behind Belinda was Nicky, buzzing with booze. It came as no great surprise when he felt the woman's hand on his erection. There was something in the rancorous air.

Dan saw George, although he did not, of course, know the name. Dan saw George as he pinched a bud of plastic between his thumb and forefinger. Clutching the cello's neck harder, Dan worried about the scent that was sure to follow – but which didn't. The poison was odourless. Dan found himself thinking of the man who was now being fondled: and he was shocked that he knew the man's name to be Nicky.

George was smiling. He had no idea that he'd just released the latest in a thousand-fold selection of aphrodisiac pellets; all he could see was the beast, writhing now like smoke along the roof of the carriage. His work, he believed, was being done; the people in the white room would be proud.

The train dogged on through the darkness.

Bella Chidzoy was also aboard. She had left her doctorate at the office, and was currently present in the form of a private detective. She wanted to know – and her managers wanted to know – if George was doing everything that he'd been programmed to do. After all, there was a lot of money riding on this project.

As soon as she'd followed George down into Aldgate East, she had been aware of the heat in the air – and not just in terms of the temperature. Over the last seven months, the product had been released at most of the stations in the city. Using her contact in London Underground (a stupid man, but obliging), Bella had discovered that trainkill of animals was up by a good thirty per cent on the same figure for the previous year. Encouraging. The drug was working its way through the country's private parts.

Rabbits, humping on the tracks, oblivious; now dead. Foxes decapitated in the act of violent procreation: also gathered to God. Rats squashed. The power was immense.

Bella found some of the actions disturbing. What she and the consortium had hoped for was *energy* – witless and furious energy. The aim had been to convert whatever *ennui* and apathy that embraced the miles of wriggling tunnels and chasms – into life. To see if it could work; to see if sadness could be warped...

Dogs had caught the scent. They howled at the ends of their owners' leashes.

Suspended in disbelief, dog owners around Euston Square were left bewildered by their animals' sudden roils in heat.

It all commenced suddenly, after such a long wait. Against the law of nature and despite the hour of the day, the light was becoming *brighter*. High above, the sky was in motion but it was not in flight. Whatever wind tugged at the clouds was not drawing them across the great blue canvas; it was more that the clouds circled, like crows, making rings of vapour against whose outer and inner surfaces the sun played its gold.

The clouds were *approaching*.

Even as Belinda turned to face a bemused young man named Nicky – and even as Becky, her colleague, asked her pointedly what she was doing – she knew that her actions were uncontrolled. They were the simple manifestations of the heat, the drug.

She dirtied her knees on the floor of the carriage. She wrenched what Nicky had hidden, from its harness…

The tide was in the air. It reached for the synapses; it reached for the settled tectonic plate of the Londoners' repression. It bit into faces and minds.

It flipped both man, woman and beast onto their backs.

Traffic was halted. Adults and children were coupling on zebra crossings. A policewoman bared her chest to the shop owner whose premises she had just saved from a violent burglary. A market trader fell in love with his own pumpkins.

Buildings groaned. The light became whiter. The air got hotter.

44

On! On! And the disease had spread quickly.

The invisible mist rose. Above ground, but still in the stations into which it had leaked, the fog caused all manner of sexual distraction. A guard had stripped to the waist, from the feet upwards, and was attempting to push his body into a ticket slot; an old woman, feeling as she hadn't in years, lay on the ground, waiting, legs in the air, while her small yapping dog on her bosom licked at the rouge on her cheek. Energetically a Chinese couple bounced in a photo-booth.

Outside, spontaneous acts of fertility were abroad.

Even vehicles seemed to have caught the bug as they mounted each other from behind, their drivers distracted. In the Chrome Café, near Paddington, a waitress named Giselda took a complicated order while a different punter knelt down to her rear with his face deep in her musky knickers.

Meanwhile the beasts had taken a grip on each carriage. Like overambitious parents, responding to the children's cries to go higher on the swings, faster on the roundabout, the beasts were starting to push just that little bit harder…

The smile was like a magnet.

Among the po-faced fornicators, and the even-more-so features of those crying 'This is the Devil's work' and variations on the same, a smile was bound to stand out like a pimple on a prick.

But George did not so much see it as *feel* it.

He turned to his left. He blinked and squinted. And then he said:

'Bella?'

Dr Chidzoy cocked her head. 'The very same,' she said.

George frowned. 'What are *you* doing here?' he asked.

'Just travelling home, George,' she answered.

George was fiddling in his coat pocket for the capsules that his fingers knew were present. Nervously he squeezed one.

(*What the hell has he got in there?* wondered Dan.)

For George the meeting was nothing less than apocalyptic: the violent concatenation of two distinct realities that should always be kept apart. Seeing Bella in this way, on his turf, during work-time, was no less distressing than it would have been if he had seen his own doppelganger.

Seven seats away, a middle-aged man in a rumpled suit dis-impaled himself from his new boyfriend's lap. Blinking owlishly he said to the compartment: 'Does anyone think we're moving too fast?' as he pulled up his grey trousers.

The compartment was thick with beasts. George closed his eyes, trying to shut them all out; trying to think. His past flashed through his head: staccato bursts of sights, sounds and aromas. The white room; the capsules…

Sensing this moment – that the drawbridge was down – George's hand emerged from his coat pocket; it was stuffed with the mind control substance.

'Why are we immune?' asked George, cutting to the chase.

'We've been protected.'

'From what?'

'From the power of suggestion,' Bella replied, still smiling and seemingly unbothered by her subject's revelation.

George shook his head. 'I've got to ask you why,' he told her. 'What point are you trying to prove?'

'Crush them all,' said Bella. 'Do it now.'

George dropped the capsules to the floor. In the next second or two, it was all he could do not to stamp upon them as if they were slugs.

'No,' he said. 'I won't.'

Shedding her cool façade, Bella made a move to execute her own command. While she attempted to crush the capsules, however, George took hold of her shoulders and pushed her back. Some people protested, but others had seen what was unravelling.

Stepping backwards from Belinda's mouth, Nicky moved over to where Bella struggled in George's arms. His depreciating, wet erection led the way. He joined George in wrestling Bella to the filthy floor. They held her in place as if a gust of wind would yank her up from her moorings.

At the same time, Dan stood. Leaning his cello against the seat, as if to save his place, he stepped into the vestibule and began picking up the capsules from where they'd been scattered. He might not have any idea of what they were, but he could sense their significance and taste their danger.

It was more than the rigorous, almost *violent*, nature of the sunlight that drew Bob Dooley from the tunnel and back into the open air. Whatever happened next, he knew that he had to get as far from Pissed Paddy's opened forehead as he could. For although Dooley had done his best to hide the body behind a rampart, he knew that it was simply a matter of time before his team leader's corpse was discovered.

What's wrong with the light? Dooley asked himself.

At the mouth of the tunnel he paused and looked down, as if to check himself for tell-tale signs of culpability. It wouldn't take a detective to deduce that he had been up to no good. Despite his best efforts, there was blood on his hands, his overalls – for all he knew, even on his face. A few more seconds elapsed before Dooley understood that he was *weeping*. Even as a policeman the sight of blood had distressed him; and this was a new occupation, and blood had no place on the railroad. Wiping his nose on his sleeve, he left the tunnel and moved into the descended cloud.

47

It was so luminescent as to be hard to look at directly. In its moving folds there was heat; memories, too, or so it seemed. Dooley thought back to the rag he'd just made of Paddy. *They'll catch me*, he thought, referring to the men and women of his previous industry. If the blood wasn't giveaway enough, there would be copious semen deposits on the other man's face, in his mouth, in his nostrils (he'd attempted even this incursion), and even on the man's skull, unless the latter had leaked free with the blood from the gash that Dooley had made for the purpose of sexual ingress. The thought had amused him at the time – that he'd found another interpretation, finally, of having one's head fucked with – but the joke had paled into insignificance in the vapour.

London as he'd known it was gone.

Although this was no dream, Dooley experienced the same sort of dream-helplessness that thwarted his slumber on a regular basis. All he could see was white and gold – flowers of it blooming and dissolving in the tide – and the occasional presence of one or more of the long thin beasts that he had doubted viewing before. The latter at least set his mind partly at rest. *I'm not going mad*, he thought with some relief as he struggled once more to free what was baking to perfection in his boxer shorts. *London is.*

The city is losing its marbles.

Deciding to go the whole hog, Dooley stripped. By this point he could barely see the metal lines between which he stood; the ground had disappeared. The mist was eating its way up his hairy legs, questing. His penis was as bloody as fresh beef, nosing in gulping motions for what its owner failed to detect. Here there was no smell; no smell at all.

Life and longing plucked at his scrotum.

48   'I'm ready,' he whispered, and waited not long at all.

In the driver's cabin, Geoff knew that he had no control. The observation was almost a blessing: it meant that he could ignore the radio warnings leaping into his head; ignore the dials, the blinding light looming ahead. Instead, with one further twist of his nipple-ring, he stumbled, half blind and fully naked, into the first carriage, where his people were preparing themselves for him.

'This all came from my head,' George either protested or attempted to convey, through guilt, to his witnesses. 'So I can parcel it all back again.'

'From *your* head?' Bella queried, her face as close to a humorous question mark as the human face can become. Then she gave in, and cackled like a fishwife. 'What on earth gave you that idea?'

'What on earth gave me *these* ideas?' George retorted. His

arms widened as though he were ushering on fresh attractions. 'You!'

Bella was still on the floor, her skirt around her thighs: the thighs that Dan, one of her kidnappers, was now examining with his eyes. He had to fight with his natural instincts not to put his hands there. 'You're *miles* off, George. These are all from *my* head,' Bella finished. Her eyes widened.

What had caused this latter surprise was Belinda. Dejected to have been left alone, on her knees, she had stood up and thought through any number of possible revenges. In the end, it was the last film she'd viewed that day – *Heavy Duty* – that had loaned her the inspiration. In lieu of a pool cue with which to do damage to the man who had deserted her – Nicky – she had a large unattended musical instrument in a leather case. Carrying this, she moved closer to where Nicky was holding down the madwoman's ankles.

The dead have their deadlines too, thought Belinda, apropos of nothing at all. And then continued: *The dead like to play games. What else are they expected to do all day?*

George shouted, 'NO!'

In spite of the confines, Belinda managed a decent parabola of swing, holding the cello by its neck. The body came down on the back of Nicky's head, to a howl of pain and the bonfire crackle of splitting wood.

The instrument offered one solitary discordant note.

Scalp leaking, Nicky fell forward – on top of Bella, who wriggled like a worm on a salted leaf. Her vocal protestations were loud and insistent. It was everything Dan could do to hold her still, but his resolve was waning. Bright light brimmed in his head, and he began to see snake- and eel-like creatures slithering along the ceiling and wrapping themselves around the handrails and the dangling hand-grippers. *God help me*, he thought as he viewed dispassionately his shattered cello, bent in its flimsy leather. Dan scooped a good hold of Bella's breasts, and was gratified when the buttons popped and he could touch the decorative contours of her brassiere.

Come back to me! thought George – a lover's cry from a man who had yet to become a lover. He wanted the animals back in his head. And some – those closest, perhaps – obeyed, like puppies, slipping back through his skin as dried-up perspiration. But there were thousands of the beasts abroad by now, and more by the second as they dallied with what had fallen from the sky. The carriage was bathed in more gold-white than ever, and George, through his panic, through the ravages of his guilt, knew that the command was hopeless.

Bella sank her teeth into Dan's neck. She drew blood.

Otherwise, white was the colour.

Up above, in what had become a swamp of blinding vapour, some of the people-turned-moles staggered around, stoned on lust, with their eyeballs melting down their cheeks. Not that this summer of love had had its currency spent so soon. Through the swirls and eddies, there were twos, threes and more's worth of writhing flesh and ambition. This was the manifestation of repression, and it didn't look at all as anyone had dared to imagine.

The train line was only so long.

When the vehicle hit the buffers at Hammersmith, proceeded by a pillow of gusting cloud and a small army of sprites that curled like commas, all above ground felt the pavement, the park, the car suddenly lurch. The earth moved.

And so, after a second of indecision, did the train.

It thumped and ravaged its way past the barriers, and squealed into the station, scoring supine couples in half beneath its spark-chattering metal wheels. The noise was on a par with the heat, with the city-wide contrast. The noise alone was a reminder that the summer of love was just beginning.

Delivery Night

(with Paul Meloy)

DELILAH FOUND HER MOTHER in the park. She was sitting on a bench, a smile on her face, patiently conversing with a bicycle that someone had chained to the fence around the bowling green. A few pigeons waited by her feet.

'Come on, Mum,' said Delilah, 'it's time to go home.'

What always amazed Delilah, whenever her mother went walkabout, was how far she'd get in so little time. Delilah would berate herself, but afterwards, in a more rational mood, would think: *What more can I possibly do?* She'd already accepted her mother into a home that could scarcely contain the two of them – not to mention the ugly cat that her mother had insisted on bringing, and not to mention a good deal of the creepy furniture that she claimed to be unable to part with. Delilah had even given up her own bed.

Patricia's efficiency when it came to travelling was alarming. The woman had no money – Delilah saw to that – so the bus was never an option, unless a string of drivers had taken pity on her over the months. So how had she made it as far as the park in the hour that Delilah had taken to collect her car from the tyre replacement centre?

'Who brought you here, Mum?' Delilah would ask, for the park was a favourite destination, on her runaway days.

'The angels,' her mother would reply.

And into the car they'd climb.

As they drew up outside the terrace, Delilah glanced across at her mother, who was strapped into the passenger seat, where she gazed ahead, her lips pressed together and moving constantly as if suppressing a mumbled monologue. Coming to a stop, Delilah felt a sudden and desperate urge well up in her to reach out to take one of her mother's small, trembling hands.

She gave it a squeeze, sighed and unbuckled the seat belt. She climbed out of the driver side and went around to open the door for her mother. Delilah helped her out and they both stood there for a moment in the sunshine. Delilah looked up at the little terrace house and tried not to think about what the future held. She'd read an article once about a woman who had tried to look after her dementing father at home. She had woken one morning and found him gone from his bed. The front door was open so she had flown from the house, in the pouring rain, to find him. She found him eventually, in a neighbour's back garden, happily drinking from the birdbath.

53

'What's in here, then? Pipes?' he had apparently remarked – and that comment had stuck in Delilah's mind ever since. It summed up all the banal, bewildered disorientation that organic loss of function represented.

'Come on, Mum,' Delilah said as she stepped up onto the curb.

As she looked down to guide her mother onto the path, Delilah saw that she was standing in a recently drawn hopscotch grid. It was sketched in bright yellow chalk and looked like the blueprint of a box you could try but never quite fold. Despite herself, she smiled. Nice to see the PlayStation hadn't kept some children indoors on a day as sunny as this.

Delilah heard her mother gasp. She looked up and was surprised to see a beaming smile on the old woman's face. She followed her mother's gaze and could see nothing that might have caused this fascination to shine in her mother's eyes.

'What is it, Mum?'

'The dustmen are here.'

At the end of the street a dustcart nosed into view, like a mammal searching for insects. It shuddered to a stop and groaned as its compressor yawned open. A group of men in green council boiler suits tramped behind it and lobbed their swag into the back and then turned and went off for more. Collecting nutrition for their insatiable Queen, the town tip. Apparently, a fully-grown dustman can carry eight times his own body weight in bins. Delilah shook the joke out of her head. One of the dustmen had stopped and was standing at the top of the street, staring back at them. Delilah had to shield her eyes against the midmorning sun just to see. He was a short black man wearing a non-regulation flat cap. Strangely, his overalls were dark blue, like the filthy fabric things the dustmen used to wear when Delilah was a child, when they still used to reverse the dustcarts round the back alleys and collect the rubbish in bins from your garden. These days, Delilah was surprised they didn't stand over you and watch you heave the garbage into the crusher yourself.

Delilah began to feel uneasy. The dustman continued to stare at them, even as his *compadres* traipsed back with another load. They seemed unmindful that he was just standing still. Then he was on his own again and the dustcart was sloping off across the intersection.

When he stopped, he waved at them.

Delilah's mother waved back.

'Do you know him, Mum?' Delilah asked. She also wondered what business they had collecting so late in the day.

'Just being friendly. Let's go inside; I'm getting cold.'

The sun strained overhead. Under its blanket Delilah recognized the sensation of being duped. Inside, Patricia accepted Delilah's offer of a cheese salad and a glass of port. Late lunch or early dinner – either way, the day was too young for alcohol, but what the hell: Delilah felt that she needed it. As she busied herself in the kitchen, Patricia became rooted in her favourite chair and watched her soap with a concentration as impenetrable as obsidian.

Unoriginal but potent thoughts formed inside her head. However unlikely it sounded, maybe the *dustmen* were the ones that gave her mother a lift to the park every time she vanished. It had never occurred to Delilah to note which day (or days) of the week the breakouts occurred, so was it possible that today being Thursday, a rubbish-collection day, she'd hitched a ride with a mangler?

At a little after four, on schedule, Patricia fell asleep, and Delilah juggled her options. Eschewing the tidying up of the kitchen, she made for the telephone and used the local directory to call the council authorities. Though initially baffled by the request, the representative operator was happy enough to assist – to provide the route that the dustbin lorries followed through the town. Delilah thanked her. She clutched the gonk attached to her keyring and wondered if she was doing the right thing. To do as she planned meant leaving her mother alone. What if she woke early? Even as she bit into the chilly wind with a gasp, Delilah imagined returning home to a burnt-out shell.

All the more reason to hurry, she told herself. With decreasing attention, Delilah traced the road. She was honked at several times—but it was only twenty-five minutes before she'd caught up. She overtook, parked, locked up; the alarm signal chirped.

'Excuse me,' she said to the nearest collector, looking around for the man who had waved to her mother. While explaining who she was – into an attentive but baffled façade –Delilah began to doubt the sense of what she was doing. The impulse was running dry. The moment was folding in on itself.

55

'She's the friendly old girl on Worthington Avenue,' said the dustman. 'What can I say?'

Delilah felt frustrated. 'And what about the little guy, dressed in blue?' she asked.

'Eh?'

'Blue overalls.'

The dustman shook his head. 'We wear green, darlin,' he replied.

'But *he* was wearing blue,' Delilah protested. 'The black guy – dressed in blue? Does *he* know my mother a bit better?'

'What black guy?'

Even silence could have an echo, Delilah realised in the following few seconds. Nothing was said, but the absence reverberated like a ball on a roulette wheel. *The black guy's nothing to do with them*, she told herself.

Who comes to get you, Mum?

The angels.

'I feel sick,' Delilah declared.

'Get away from the wagon,' she was told. 'Takes a while to get used to it.' By way of compensation, almost, he offered his loose-change smile.

Delilah was conscious enough to understand that he was proffering a kindness, and she smiled back. What was more, she believed him.

In the car she watched the dustmen work. The operation reminded her of the heave-ho machinations of a pirate ship. Desultorily she drove home.

They were dustmen. They weren't angels.

But the black man in blue overalls was not one of the dustbin crew.

Friday morning.

Delilah awoke to a scream. It was her own – although she spent a few breath-lagged seconds trying to convince herself that it had been her mother calling for help. A bad dream, then... Delilah rose and deplored her hips in the mirror, then donned her dressing-gown and went about her day. Between dressing and performing the first of the day's activities she checked on Mum, with a lump in her throat.

Gone were the days on which a check could be done from the threshold. Her feet be-slippered, Delilah would creep into her mother's room. It smelled of talc. Satisfied on hearing Patricia sniff, Delilah tiptoed out again and closed the door in time to protect her mother from the sudden phone's drilling.

'Hello?'

'Hi, it's Carly. You've got to come in.'

'Why? I can't, I haven't arranged anything.'

'You've got to, Del: the peanut people are going crazy.'

'What's up?'

Delilah's work was in web design. It was exactly as dull as it sounded, but she could work from home, keeping an eye on Patricia. Three months earlier, she had been commissioned to design a new website for a company called McManamon's— purveyors of party snacks.

'They're going spazzymodo, babe,' said Carly. 'Wrong tones, wrong specs. You've gotta come in.'

'I *can't*. It's my mother,' said Delilah. 'She's worse than ever.' Said out loud, it sounded cold, insensitive.

Maybe Carly picked up on the lack of feeling. 'Well, I'm sorry to hear that, but so are we – losing this account. An hour. That's all I ask, Del.'

Delilah was focussed. She pressed the flesh with the McManamon's Bar Snacks and Crisps rep, and coolly proved

57

that she had delivered what she'd been asked to deliver; that it was the peanut people's administrative error. When he left, the rep did so still riding high on his camel, but with his chin down hard on his chest. Delilah, meanwhile, took no sense of achievement from the encounter. More than anything else she resented the wasted time.

'Minor tweaking,' she said to Carly, on her way out. 'End of the week, okay. I'm going home.'

The bus's engine chatted to the other cars in the mid-morning traffic jam. It appeared that there was to be no sense of satisfaction about today. The red lights held their quarry for too long; the bus was overstuffed with aromatic passengers; and a child was seeing how loudly she could squeal.

It was a relief to disembark. A relief to speed-walk from the furniture showroom stop to her home. A relief to scratch the key into the lock, to open the door, to call 'Mum?'

Her mother had run away.

Bedtime came as the biggest relief of all: her mother's bedtime. Anything between half-seven and half-nine was customary, but on this day, no doubt bushed by two satisfactory breakouts, Patricia collapsed into a doze at a quarter past seven, with a quiz show blaring. Delilah woke her and led her to the room. 'Spit 'em out,' Delilah said, referring to her mother's dentures; her mother complied, and they clacked like castanets into her daughter's palm. Delilah dropped them into the water.

Patricia found peace.

Delilah knew that her own sleep would not come so easily, unassisted. She had a miserable glass of the last of the port, and then she shuffled clothes from the airing cupboard, in search of a small cube of resin. Back in the lounge she had a smoke.

It was the weekend.

Patricia was finishing her porridge when Delilah said, 'Do you remember what happened to you yesterday, Mum?'

The slop on the older woman's spoon, now suspended between the bowl and the mouth, was like cement. Cautiously Patricia said, 'No.'

'You ran away again. Twice.'

Her lined face smoothed with relief. 'Oh, that.'

'Why, what did you think I was talking about?'

'Nothing, Delly. Leave me alone.'

Delilah frowned. Kowtowing to irrationality she asked, and she asked slowly, 'Did the *angels* come to get you?'

Patricia smiled. 'Of course.'

The frown remained. 'In their big metal chariot.'

'What?'

'That they were driving around yesterday.'

'Who were?'

'The angels. You waved to one, Mum.'

'No I didn't,' Patricia protested.

'Outside, in the road. The little black man,' Delilah persisted.

Her mother was becoming cross. '*You* can't see 'em anyway!'

'Why not?' Delilah asked.

'Because *you're* not dying! You're not the one who needs to be prepared.'

Delilah paused. 'Do you get into the dustmen's lorry, Mum? Do they take you to the park?' She was wrestling with the significance of the man in blue.

'No.'

'So how do you get there so quickly?' said Delilah.

59

'The angels take me.'

'So do you get into the *angels'* lorry?'

'In a manner of speaking. What business is it of yours?'

'And why the park? What's there, Mum?'

Patricia smiled again. 'Because that's where I've been scheduled to haunt, when I go. That's where I'm going to live. After I die there.'

That night, Delilah slept badly. She dreamed that she had lost her mother. Delilah found herself running through the back streets in her dressing gown, calling Patricia's name, frantic with worry. Patricia had reached the park. Standing ankle deep in the fountain, her face in the bubbling marble dish, she peered up at Delilah and mouthed something through the frothing, collapsing water.

'They buried my Billy,' she said, although the name came out like *Blulululililly*. 'Somebody burnt his shoes.'

Delilah groaned and sat up among sheets that felt as thin and damp as over moistened Rizlas. She put her face in her hands and wept.

Perhaps her midnight catharsis eased her passage back into dreams of a more gentle variety. She found herself standing at her curtained bedroom window, cooled by a breeze drifting from between the heavy material. Behind and beneath her she could make out movement through the house. She wasn't alarmed; she remembered a recurring nightmare she'd had as a child. She would wake to sunlight – sunlight that was somehow *alive*, as if a bolt of it had crept back to shine in. In reality, it was night, the house was empty. Everywhere was silent and she knew that she was alone, lit by a cold night sun, and now the furniture in her parents' bedroom was coming alive.

'Creepy furniture,' Delilah said aloud.

In this dream she would make it to the stairwell and freeze because she had caught a glimpse of the sun-drenched room, mysteriously vacated by her parents, and she would begin to hear the sneaky whispered voices of the items of furniture plotting with each other. Standing there, nightmare-rooted, she'd hear the furtive sound of drawers sliding open and shut.

Then she heard another sound, from outside. She was unsure which chamber of dream she was now inhabiting, her breath shallow in her lungs; her face felt parched.

Flat slaps, she could hear those clearly − flat slaps and a skitter of pebbles. Delilah reached out and parted the curtains.

Outside it was night. Delilah gasped. The entire pavement, from one end of the street to the other, on both sides of the road, was hatched with clearly marked bright yellow hopscotch grids, lurid in the streetlight.

And there, outside her house, the little black dustman danced and pirouetted, plucking up a stone and lobbing it carefully into the required square. His overalls were a blue that looked black in the lack of light.

The dustman lifted a leg and hopped, slapped both feet down flat-footed in a brace of squares, hopped again, bent, re-trieved his stone, and looked up at Delilah's window. His smile resembled the death-gash on a slaughtered animal's neck.

Reality kicked her in the heart. Delilah let out a shriek and dropped the curtain. Breathing hard, feeling panic drench her system, Delilah span the floor and flew from the bedroom. Around her the comforting night sounds had been replaced with a sudden and frightful whispering. She turned at the top of the stairs and ran down them to the front door. Outside, she could still hear the sound of the dustman playing hopscotch. She reached out for the door handle and froze. Something moved in a shadow behind her. She looked up at the door handle above the letterbox, her eyes blurring with tears that felt more angry than disconsolate.

'Why don't you leave us alone!' she hollered.

Distantly she heard her own voice whining with terror and was aware that it had become a scream as her parent's chest of drawers slid menacingly into the stairwell above her and a small mouth opened in the keyhole before her and spoke to her in her mother's voice:

'And where the fuck do *you* think you're going?'

Delilah froze. Her clothes clung to her skin like a funeral shroud.

Where was Mum?

Pulling her consciousness clear of the black man who was hopscotching outside, like the separating of Siamese twins, Delilah felt queasy. Panic took hold of her legs, and she understood. The hopscotch, the black man – these were all bloody *decoys* to keep her distracted and quiet as she struggled for a stranglehold on the truth.

Hamfistedly she fought towards her mother's room.

Mum was gone.

Delilah swore so hard that her left lung throbbed. During the course of the next few minutes, she ransacked the available space in the terrace. She ran to the road, for a better view. No cars cruised, but the street was crammed with energies and forces; the air deliquescent with possibility.

Her mouth sluiced spittle as Delilah ran from her home. There she saw Patricia. The older woman was being spun and wrenched, as if in an undertow of powerful pulls: being lopsided, now inverted, now rotated like an engine component – sucked in through the vortex.

Delilah ran towards the *melange*. She felt dumb that she'd been so duped, but there was nothing now she could do about that. In order to rescue her mother she surged into the angels' show of energies. She could hear herself screaming 'Mum!' – even as the heat sheared her face from her skull with a liquid pop.

She understood a minute too late: what was good for one believer was disastrous for a non-believer. Patricia ricocheted past Delilah's field of vision, and her mother had a broad and genuine smile on her face.

Delilah, however, was being stripped of her skin. To the bone.

The air was red, electrically charged.

And just for sport, the angels burst her swollen heart.

In the seconds before this happened, Delilah screamed loudly, but she felt happy for her mother. Patricia was going somewhere else, somewhere without her. Her mother had had the right idea about dying. Delilah. Seeing her, Patricia was smiling like a two year-old. But then again, she had somewhere to go to; somewhere to haunt: the park. She'd been prepared.

The sky copied the expression.

Delilah knew the angels' might as they plucked the arms from her torso.

Heart of the Seahorse

ALTHOUGH I KNEW the temperamental Katherine as a friend of but recent acquaintance, her pleasured face gave away her tickled thoughts with ease. The previous Sunday, outside the church of St Nathaniel the Decisive, after another of my brother's interminable services, she had revealed her fascination with her nephew's versatile ears. Marvels, she had said. His ears, she had declared, are marvels and nothing but. She had grinned. However, her nephew was only one reason why Katherine was returning with haste to the capital.

The door clicked open to a sneeze of rain, and the tall man entered the waiting room. Her expression did not change.

'A beast of a night, is it not?' the man asked the room's reluctant inhabitants.

Consensus followed; no other opinion was plausible. The storm had laughed at the village for a day and a half, and tonight the coach to the capital was already two hours late. Dead-meat cold was the air. Snow would follow.

The tall man sat and brushed water from his clothes, using movements that were like the swatting of insects.

His actions burst a bubble.

Up to the point of this man's entrance, very little conversation had been shared between Katherine Wollington, with her portmanteau at her feet like a terrier, and my brother and I on the opposite bench.

'My name is Alexander Mondo,' said he. 'But perhaps you know me better by my stage name: Mondo the Magnificent. I am told by many to be the greatest magician who ever lived.'

The name meant nothing – I confess that I had always

regarded the practice of magic as entertainment overrated – but it was plain to sense that Edward and Katherine were of a different opinion. The room shimmered as it adjusted to the volume of their excitement.

'I do indeed know your name, sir,' said Edward warmly (Katherine was silent), 'but I fear I may represent a body opposed to your art.'

'You are a man of the cloth?'

'Yes.'

Mondo nodded. 'Sad business. But I believe, if I am not mistaken, that you still have your mind open to suggestion. Am I right?'

'You may well be correct, sir,' Edward replied, 'if you can assure me that suggestion is what we witness when you perform one of your spells.'

At this Mr Mondo looked puzzled. 'Why, sir, what else but suggestion could it be? Surely a man such as yourself cannot believe that what we mere *entertainers* ply is *necromancy*...or some such.'

'I wish not to believe such a thing.'

'And you long for proof to ease your mind?' said Mondo.

'Indeed.'

'And you, madam.' He had turned to face Katherine. 'May I ask after your views on the subject?'

'Sir, I have none,' was Katherine's response; and she held his eyes wide open with her gaze.

Mondo laughed. It was a small brittle ejaculation, more like a chirrup than the hearty roar I might have imagined from such a fellow. 'Surely, madam,' he pressed, 'you know your mind well enough to decide if what I do is the devil's work or simply some fancy? Then let me tell you, I have a conjuror's nimble fingers and a brain like a termitary. But nothing sinister

65

guides my hands, believe me.'

With which Mondo reached inside the waves of his heavy cape, still beaded from the rain, and retrieved a small deck of cards with dragons on the back. He wanted to prove his skill, though not to Edward, who was clearly a believer, however reluctantly, nor indeed to me, an abstainer as yet in the debate. 'Madam,' he addressed Katherine again, 'will you indulge me?'

When I made my next utterance, was I trying to protect Katherine? Or was I, perchance, somewhat *nervous* about Alexander Mondo, and what we were about to receive? After all, his prestidigitations were more elaborate than sleight-of-hand, perhaps. Vanishing frogs, snakes standing up on the very tips of their tails. What I offered was:

'Perhaps we should all introduce ourselves...' and I smiled '...if fate has decided that we will be spending such time together as this. My name, Mr Mondo, is Lucy Layton.' Gesturing to my brother I tried to read the expression in Mondo's eyes. 'And this is Edward – *mon frère.*'

Mondo also smiled. 'And you, madam, who might you be?' he asked a few seconds later.

'I might be Katherine. Katherine Wollington.'

'Delighted to meet you, Miss Wollington.' And he leaned to a more advantageous incline, the better to kiss her knuckles.

'Charmed, I'm sure,' she told him, her voice slightly quieter, softer, for once.

'The card trick, Mr Mondo,' said Edward, and for the second time since the man had arrived a moment snapped.

Suddenly Mondo the Magnificent was a different person; he was a tidal wave, a barrage of showmanship, and his voice had risen as Katherine's had fallen. When he snapped the cards, fire flickered behind the lantern's glass. 'A few items to amuse you,' he announced, fanning the deck. 'Miss Wollington,

66

would you be so kind as to choose a card? Any card.'

Katherine pinched a card between her thumb and forefinger. And as if it were a love-letter, she clutched it to her bosom.

Mondo's face was placid. 'I fear, Miss Wollington,' he said, 'that you have selected a card that scarcely befits your delicate composition.'

'I do not remember telling you, sir, that my composition was delicate.'

'The evidence is before my eyes. Miss Wollington, you have picked a masculine card – a club or a spade.'

'If you think you can disarm me with a lame little weapon like that, Mr Mondo, I must tell you that a different thought is heading your way.' Katherine sounded smug.

The pediment crumbled, and the façade toppled in on itself. Mondo was vexed, although he tried not to show it. 'Miss Wollington,' he declared, 'I am certain that you appreciate that every workman needs a tool. It just so happens that one of my tools is a line of questioning.'

'I am well aware of the fact, Mr Mondo. As I am well aware you appreciate that not all jobs require the *self-same* tool. Your strategy has not wrongfooted me, Mr Mondo, even if your *legerdemain* might have done so.'

Matters were spiralling out of control, and I felt the push from within me to intercede. Evidently, so did Edward; his voice was as round and clear as when he addressed the congregation. 'Miss Wollington,' he said, 'I am sure there is no need to affront our guest as he attempts to entertain us.'

The word *guest* was fired wide of the mark, and I fear that *attempts* would hardly have made Mr Mondo feel much better, but the reproof, I was certain, would find its target.

I was wrong.

'Affront?' Katherine repeated. 'Mr Mondo, for it is you I

must ask, have I *affronted* you with my words?'

'Not at all, Miss Wollington,' Mondo replied.

'For if I have…'

Mondo held up his hands. Could he, as I did, with ease, see the humour in Katherine's eyes? Did he acknowledge that even now, by playing to this so-called wounded soldier, he was being made to look a fool?

'Your card is the three of spades,' said Mondo. 'If you'd be so kind as to show your acquaintances…'

The shock on Katherine's face was but a snack, I am sure, to a conjuror such as Mr Mondo; but his eyes ate it greedily. Katherine flipped the card round for us to see. There were indeed three spades on its face, but Katherine, duped, as helpless as a butterfly on a pin, was beginning to protest.

68

'I don't see how you could have known that unless you had arranged the cards beforehand,' she said, returning Mondo's weapon to its arsenal.

'In that case, perhaps you would like to arrange the cards yourself and we can try again.' Mondo placed the deck in Katherine's hands, holding them closed, and said, 'Please shuffle.'

The following thirty seconds were akin to watching a horse stamping for its food – its movements increasingly clumsy. The shuffle started slowly, Katherine easing her chosen cards into the mouth of the pack, time and time again. But by and by she became increasingly confident, and clumsy.

She passed the cards to Mondo.

'I will do it slowly to show you that there is no trick involved,' he said.

'But Mr Mondo,' my brother replied, 'you told us, not five minutes ago, that your trade *was* built on a foundation of trickery!'

Just the sort of invitation that any good showman requires! 'But, sir, that was when we were *discussing* my art, not participating in it!' he dismissed. As he said this he fanned the cards. Without a word Katherine chose one and clasped it to her breast as before and Mondo continued, 'If I were to give my work anything less than the respect of *belief*, what possible use would it be?'

My brother always had an extremely noisy frown. Although I was not looking at his face, I was well aware that his brow had now crinkled. What would follow? Dreading as I was a return to the subject of necromancy, I was pleased when Mondo resumed his act.

'The four of clubs,' said he.

Katherine offered, this time, a good-natured protest. 'Mr Mondo,' she said, 'you will surely do me the courtesy of allowing me to look at my card before you guess it.'

'Guess? I assure you, Miss Wollington, there is no guesswork involved.'

One glance at its face, and then Katherine slapped it down into the palm of her other hand. It was of course the four of clubs. 'Quite impressive, sir,' she conceded. She sliced it back into the pack still fanned in his hands.

Mr Mondo shuffled the cards once more. 'Trust me, we could joust like this all evening, Miss Wollington, and you would never win.' At which he bent the cards nearly double; on their release, each card flew out from the family nest, describing an arc, and landed in the man's other palm. It was as if the cards, knowing of their purpose, had leapt of their own accord.

His confidence wrankled Katherine. 'Perhaps, in that case,' she said, 'you wouldn't mind playing a game of my own devising. May I?' She reached out for the deck.

The cards were passed across. With no greater expertise

than before, Katherine rearranged their order. 'This time,' she had decided, '*I* will spread the cards and Lucy? – would you mind? – Lucy will choose one.'

Mondo nodded: a graceful decline of his well-bescarfed neck. However, on seeing this almost longsuffering gesture, Katherine made her eyebrows pinch together. 'Mr Mondo,' she addressed him, 'surely you cannot presume to know a card that you have not manipulated into my grasp.'

'Miss Wollington,' was the reply, 'you misunderstand my art, I am pleased to say. I did no such thing in the first place.'

'Lucy?'

How I wanted, at this point, to assist my associate! The rainbow of dragon-faces had a zenith, and I tweezered the card away from the rest. I regarded it swiftly before plastering it to my bodice, like my friend before.

Mr Mondo put on a show of fixing his fingertips to his temples. He stared at the back of the card as though he were trying to control flames. The attention, I must say, did not make me feel comfortable. The oddest fabrication – that somehow Mr Mondo could see through my *clothing* – fluttered through my consciousness.

'Your card is the four of hearts.'

I gasped. While showing the card to Edward and to Katherine I rather fear that I sputtered out something like, 'But how... how did you...?'

Mr Mondo enjoyed my candid admiration. All thoughts of travelling had long since left my head, and the chill that had settled in my bones could be tolerated.

'The strangest of beasts, is it not?' Mondo asked before I could put in my request.

'What is, sir?' said Edward.

'*Magic.*'

70

'Would you show us a different trick, Mr Mondo?' said Katherine. By this point, of course, Katherine had long since caught the Mondo Fever as well, despite her early resistance to the virus.

'My pleasure. The cards, if I may?' Katherine handed the deck to its owner. This time he executed a yet-more elaborate shuffle than before: he separated the deck into two small piles, and with his wrists at inappropriate angles, he managed to *tear* the cards together – or so it seemed at first, by the sound.

'One more trick. Miss Katherine,' said Mondo, 'would you be so kind as to choose one card, take a look at the card, and then return it. Do not say a word to our assembled audience here.'

Katherine followed Mondo's instructions, after which the Magnificent laid the deck on the bench, beside his right hip. Again, he attached his fingertips to his temples, where they wandered slightly, as though Mr Mondo were blind, and his forehead were his prayer-sheet.

Evidently connecting himself to a higher power – or proving that his hands could not be engaged in any monkey business – Mr Mondo allowed his brain to collapse under a series of loud hums. He mumbled; he gurgled. Then, with a sharp theatrical gasp, far more exclamatory than my own feeble effort a few minutes earlier, Mondo said, 'Your hem!'

Katherine and Edward said, 'Excuse me, sir,' at the same time.

'The five of clubs! It is tucked into the hem of your skirt!'

'Mr Mondo, I must protest,' Edward started, but Mondo silenced him by closing his eyes and breathing deeply, as if he had been playing under water.

Katherine was visibly fascinated. 'Gentlemen? Would you turn away?' she asked, but as the two of them abided by her

71

wishes (with Edward scarcely thrilled at the recent turn of events) I kept my eyes on her. She turned up the hem of her skirt… and a card was indeed entwined in the stitching.

'Astonishing!' I remarked.

'Please name the card,' replied Mondo, which I did even though the actual card was not the height of the prestidigitation, as far as I was concerned. How on earth had he lodged a card *down there*?

Mr Mondo absorbed the concentrated praise in the waiting room with an air about him of the cat who had taken the cream. When questioned and quizzed by Katherine – indeed, by Edward and myself – Mr Mondo would only answer, 'It's magic.' Before long we ceased our interrogation, and let the man have his moment.

72

Or rather, Edward and I did. Because very evidently a bee still buzzed in Katherine's bonnet, and although neither Edward nor I had never seen her behave in this fashion, she was determined, even now, to upstage the trickster.

'Fine, I cannot match your magic, Mr Mondo,' she said, 'but I can show you something as equally incredible. A piece of history, no less.'

For a second Mr Mondo strummed his jawline, and then 'Do tell, Miss Wollington,' he said.

'Are you aware, sir, of the name of Leonardo Da Vinci?' Katherine asked, but asked with her eyes shining into mine.

I told her there and then that she absolutely must not, although I did not do so aloud. In horror, I watched as Katherine unfastened her portmanteau. One Sunday a few months earlier, Katherine had shown me what I was certain she was about to show my brother – and a rank stranger.

'He was born in the year of Our Lord 1452 and died in 1519,' said Katherine. The paper was pressed between two uneven pieces of thin wood. 'But he produced this plan,' Katherine continued, 'for a vehicle called The Seahorse.'

The paper was in good condition.

'What is it?' asked Edward. He was handed the flimsy article.

Katherine said, 'It is the original of Da Vinci's plans for a vehicle that travels underwater. He called it The Seahorse, as I say.'

'Good grief,' said Mondo. 'May I?'

As though he were handing over the Crown Jewels, Edward passed the parcel. Mondo could only shake his head.

'I have to ask, Katherine,' he said. 'How did such an item come into your possession?'

Katherine cocked her head. 'A long story, sir. And one from which my family line, I fear, does not emerge unscathed or unsullied.'

'Do tell,' said Edward.

I happened to know the story: Katherine had given me all of the salient details on that same occasion. Nor was I ignorant to the fact that Katherine, a spinster and only supported financially by occasional jobs in a laundry, was keeping the plan for a rainy day.

I also knew why Katherine was travelling to the capital. She had accepted a cleaning job in that expensive city in order to be nearer to her ailing sister – the mother to the nephew with the comically-advantageous ears.

'My family has served for generations,' said Katherine. 'A cousin of mine worked for a German aristocrat named Count Hugh Von Bargeld. He did not treat her well, sir. When he got her with child, he discarded her onto the street – but not before Eliza took her parting gifts. Some ornate spoons, some etchings, a silver goblet – and this Da Vinci, which had been accumulating wealth in the old man's study. When Eliza died, it came to me, and I confess that I knew not what to do with it.'

'It is gold,' said Mondo. 'Goodness gracious… words fail me, Kathy.' His frown was as loud as my brother's. Quickly he added: 'I must have this.' He spoke into her eyes with his own. 'What price are you asking?'

Katherine smiled. 'Are you expecting me to discard a family heirloom, sir?' she replied.

'*Someone else's* family heirloom.'

'Well, yes…' she conceded.

'You cannot,' I finally offered. 'Not now, not here, Katherine.'

Edward turned to face me. It was at this moment that I realised that silence as a natural state is bestowed with powerful benefits: when one does eventually unburden one's concerns, the telling is all the more potent for what has not come before.

'Lucy?' he either asked or demanded: at that moment it was hard to tell which. With holy men it often is.

Mondo ignored me. 'Kath, I'll give you fifty pounds for this,' he said.

'No, Katherine,' I interjected.

'*Lucy?*' said Katherine. The quizzical expression was love itself, I was certain; it made my heart soar, and sore: it was a grate of woodchips, awaiting the spark.

The door opened. Rain-soaked, as sleek as an eel, the waiting room porter popped his head over the threshold to apologise for the lateness of the coach. 'It won't be much longer, ladies and gentlemen,' the boy offered.

Such warm air as was present soon evaporated, and was briskly replaced. The chill of the night raced in to pinch our noses.

The door closed and I was aware of three pairs of eyes on

me. 'I've been saving.'

Mondo was losing patience. 'Sixty, Miss Wollington,' he said, but looked at me.

'What would you want The Seahorse for?' asked my brother.

What could I tell him? As proof of an independent thought? A life? As a chance to give someone the sort of freedom that I personally yearned for?

'I'll give you seventy,' I said. In truth, I think I even surprised myself. Where on earth would I obtain such a sum?

But it had to be me.

Edward was still staring. Again he repeated my name, and I almost told him to be quiet. It was only the fear of the belt – the buckle, the strap – that sealed my lips. There was no doubt that Edward could be kind, but kindness was a fraction of his emotional repertoire.

I faced him. My moment had arrived. 'Please, Edward,' I said.

Outside, a commotion. It was not the result of the storm, but rather of what had defied it: the coach had arrived.

'Please what, my sister?'

'The money, Edward,' I replied. 'Consider it an investment.'

'Seventy-five,' said Mondo the Magnificent.

'Please, Edward.' For the first time I was aware of tears in my eyes.

'Lucy?' said Katherine.

'Please,' I said once more, softly, intending to convey a host of emotions, the predominant one being that of desperation. I could not bear the thought of a stranger owning my loved one's keepsake.

I was jealous.

75

Of a sudden, Edward flailed. 'My dear sister,' he said, embarrassed, 'don't cry.'

Horse-hooves clipped closer.

'Darling?'

'I'm all right, Edward,' I responded with my face imprisoned in my fingers. Where was luck? Where was joy? And had it been Edward who had spoken anyway?

His arm an anchor on my shoulders, Edward led me through the rain to the coach. Katherine and Mondo followed. The night was grim; it was a trap.

Money changed hands. Eighty pounds.

Mondo resembled a man who had just had his home burned to the ground. He was seething. He was worth a fortune in bile...

76

I felt good. Having given Katherine a step aboard a new ship, I experienced a sense of proud delight – of exultation and *release*.

'Enjoy,' I told Katherine as the horses snorted, drank the air, and pulled us forward. My skin was as cold as wine-bottle glass in a cellar. I closed my eyes and smiled.

But now – do you wish to hear the truth of it all? Dear Reader, here it comes. Not once since that evening have I seen or heard of my *confidante*, my friend; no, not once. Nor has she adhered to her promise to write to me regularly. I have yet to receive a reply to a single letter that I have written.

Never again have I heard of Mondo the Magnificent. To nobody else whom I have asked is the famous showman's name familiar.

And I am frightened of viewing what it was that I bought at so high a price.

I don't want to know.

Nod Your Own Head

'I'M SICK OF IT,' he told her, even laying down the tea towel, like a gauntlet, for the fight that would ensue. 'Couldn't you have *asked* me before you accepted?'

'Well pardon *me*,' said Annie, stung by the suddenness of the display, 'I should've thought – what with you and your hectic social life! Blimey. How often do we get invited to places like that?'

'*We* weren't invited at all,' Seb replied. '*You* were. And I'm to be your mascot again for the evening, I suppose.'

'You're being ridiculous.'

'I'm being honest! I always feel out of place.' I'm a loner,   77
he fought shy of saying. 'I hate chit-chat, I *hate* small-talk – and to be honest, I hate most of your friends.'

Seb closed his eyes tight for a full second. When he unstuck them he was astonished to witness not anger but pain in his girlfriend's features. He hadn't seen pain there for quite some time – not since her sister, Lucy, had died.

'Sorry…'

'No *I'm* sorry, Seb. This has obviously been percolating for a while.'

'Annie…' Seb held up his hand, not fully aware that he'd gone too far but suspecting as much. He knew what it meant when emotion started to fray Annie's voice.

'But if you think that a relationship can survive on the dictates of *one* of the partners, you're wrong.'

Seb was twenty four. He therefore knew *precisely* the stupidest thing to say, and he chose this moment to say it.

'That's what I'm fighting against, dear,' he replied. And

closed his eyes again.

There was always plenty of blood after an argument, both figuratively and actually. They both had to deal with the figurative stuff – dragging the bodies from the field and shooing away the vultures. But Seb had another step to take. When he was upset, it wasn't alcohol – Annie's road to enlightenment – that he had recourse to; nor did he sweat out his angst in the gym. What Seb did was run a shower and take a razor from the cabinet.

He'd long since grown bored of tracing the veins along the undersides of his arms. These days Seb was interested in more artistic explorations of the form.

Pinching the razorblade between thumb and forefinger, Seb followed the grooves beneath his pectoral muscles. His teeth were chomped together as though he were posing for a cheesy photograph. And pleasure twinned with pain; the burn of leaking blood set the back of his head aflame. Feeling weak, Seb sat on the edge of the bathtub as lines of blood raced down for the finishing line of his heavy leather belt. As if in prayer he dipped his head. He felt both worthless and appeased. He listened to the shower.

'Okay,' said Annie, 'we won't go.'
'Yes we will.'
This was two hours later, but nothing on the subject had been said in the interim. To facilitate the making-up process Annie had put on her sexiest dress. It wouldn't work.

Seb was piecing together a jigsaw puzzle on the dining room table: his penchant for such amusements was one of the things that had first drawn Annie to him. He wasn't like any of the others.

'Christ, Seb, you could at least make an effort.'

'And do what?'

'Look at me maybe?'

Seb sighed. 'Right, I'm looking. I've *said* we'd go, what more do you want?'

Annie sat on the next chair along, a glass of white wine in her hand. Sydney Opera House was taking shape on the table's surface, and to change the subject Annie said, 'It's going well, isn't it?'

'The relationship or the jigsaw?'

'The jigsaw.'

'Yes, it's fine,' Seb replied. 'What about the relationship?'

'We've been better,' Annie admitted. 'Look, okay – we won't go. And I'm sorry I nodded my head for both of us and I'll try not to do it again.'

Seb smiled. He admired the honesty in that *try*: it was clear how different they were, but Annie was right – the bare minimum Seb could do was meet her halfway. He took her hand. If not for the fact that Annie had to be a *part* of everything that she could be a part of, he sometimes thought they would have an idyllic existence.

'Tell me *why* you hate going to functions so much,' Annie said.

'You *know* why!'

'But that was eighteen years ago, Seb!'

'Not in my head it wasn't.' Reclaiming his hand, Seb turned away from Annie and picked up a jigsaw piece; it was shaped like a star. 'I don't want to talk about it, all right.'

'Then how do you expect it to go away?' Annie asked, exasperated.

'I *don't*. It's the uniform I'm forced to wear, okay. Now change the subject: please. I'll go with you if you want to go and if you don't want to go, fine.'

'I want to share things,' said Annie – and there was a ru-minative quality to the words. 'Let's compromise. Leave the jigsaw alone and look at me, please. Tell me what you want from me.'

'I don't want anything. I'm happy,' said Seb.

'Are you really?'

'*Yes*. I just don't like going out. Is that a crime?'

'You're becoming a hermit.'

'There's no *becoming* about it, Annie. You were happy with the way I was, this time last year.'

Immediately Annie was on the back foot. 'I'm *still* happy,' she insisted.

Seb turned her own question back on her. 'Are you really?'

For nearly a minute she said nothing. 'Let me tell you what I want from you, Seb, or what I don't want. I don't want you to keep disappearing from me as soon as I suggest we mix with other members of the human race.'

Seb snorted. 'We're talking about your work friends, re-member. We're talking about Mr Big's Retirement Showdown.'

Annie sounded weary. 'All right, Seb, there's no need to make fun of people you've only met a few times.'

'Who looked down on me.'

'They did not look down on you! They aren't even thinking about you.' Surprising both of them, Annie kept reins on her temper. 'For crying out loud, Seb, I can't believe we're here again.'

Seb felt like a spoilt brat; unable to exhibit any magnanim-ity, even though he'd got his own way. The thin cuts he'd made under his chest stung badly.

Annie finished her glass of wine. Reflexively she stood up: Seb knew that she could not bear to have an empty glass in the evening, but he didn't know when this failure of tolerance had begun. He watched her backside, all the way to the door. As an afterthought she enquired, over her shoulder, if Seb wanted anything while she was in the kitchen.

'No, thanks.' Not unless Annie could serve out a bowl of peace and quiet. All he wanted now was an hour of solitude in order to work on the jigsaw and pick over his feeling of self-disgust. Couldn't Annie go and take a bath or something? She enjoyed listening to early Miles Davis in the bath, sipping on a glass of chardonnay.

He wanted to be left alone in the company of his incisions, and their collective burn.

Already half-cut, Annie took her drink into the bathroom and started to fill the tub. Having locked the door, she carried off her usual performance: she pretended to be a stripper as Miles' trumpet shimmied around the deep acoustics of the room. Steam folded around her pores; into the mirror she pouted at herself with longing. Her head felt spongy as it did on good strong wine.

Annie dried the corner of the tub: it had to be bone dry, despite the moisture in the air. From the cabinet she removed the box of sanitary towels, and dug beneath the three ever-present decoys for the balloon she'd hidden there two days earlier. She replaced the box and untied the balloon's pliant foreskin; very carefully Annie squeezed and shook the powder onto the corner of the bathtub. On her knees she licked inside the rubber for any stray grains – before lowering her head to the beautiful mound.

A second craving was exhorting Annie to bow, to pray; but some of the granules needed to be chopped. Joints clicking, she stood and took out one of Seb's razorblades, thinking: Thank

God for a man who had no time for anything so fancy or modern as a disposable! Again, she genuflected, and stayed down. The steam was all over her skin; her heart galloped. The razor had some blood between its awkward teeth; it looked wet, or moist, but Annie couldn't believe that this could be anything other than a drink- and steam-riddled illusion. As quietly as possible she cut, using a slow clapperboard motion rather than the more enthusiastic guillotine.

A pinhead of Seb's blood was transferred into the powder. When Annie took this part of Seb into her system, via her right nostril, she felt powerful and lovestruck. The argument had moved out of her head.

Tears moved into her eyes.

82   To cover the wounds Seb pulled on a t-shirt, and he climbed into bed, feeling like a humming wire. The day, including the fight, had exhausted him. But it was the wrong sort of tiredness to fall asleep to. Besides, he had one more errand to complete. For a few minutes he lay on Annie's side – to warm the sheets, thinking forward. With luck she'd be so drunk and toasty that she'd fall asleep immediately. At any rate, by the time she joined him – still wet, because she rarely dried herself properly – Seb would be pretending to have fallen asleep himself. And it only took minimal planning to ensure that she didn't see any area that he'd been slicing: not even the chest. Indeed it was amazing to Seb just how rarely he and Annie saw each other's bodies, fully naked, in good light.

Seb had been cutting himself for longer than he'd been seeing Annie, and strategy and deception came easily. Of course Annie knew he *used* to do it – but that was back in his teens, a plausible consequence of the defining moment, however brief it had been, of Seb's childhood. Which Seb could not bear not to play again, every once in a while: the grownups' party below, with Seb being kept awake by the carousing from the ground floor. The opening of the bedroom door; the entrance of Dad's business partner, Jake, enmisted and encouraged by drink; the cold, cracked hands, a rummaging, mirthless fondle. And the tears – such tears – as the door opened again, Mum checking on her son, and Jake saying, 'I heard him crying, he had a nightmare…'

'Thank you, Jake,' Seb could still hear her say, down through the column of years.

The failure of words: Seb's failure.

Thank you?

She'd had of course no inkling, but that expression of gratitude had polluted Seb's thinking, on and off, until the current day. Self-mutilation, for Seb, had become a habit; it made him feel better by making him feel worse. What happened when Seb was eight was not the reason that he bought razorblades…. But buying razorblades never failed to remind him of that part of it.

Seb moved over onto his side of the bed. Miles Davis was abruptly curtailed; the vinyl's needle pulled off and the music's neck snapped in two – and Annie padded in through. There was nothing tentative about her climb under the covers: so old was the bed that Seb was catapulted out of his position into the centre where it sagged.

There she kissed him. And Seb could always tell when Annie had ingested the cocaine that she believed he knew nothing about: her breath tasted different, metallic, he was certain, and a ravenous quality pervaded her ardour. The good news was, if he had to raise a smile, cocaine usually hotwired Annie so that she could gallop her way quickly on his hips to her synaptic destination.

Seb had never mentioned that he'd found out. Annie had a right to her secret. But *she* wanted in on *his* inner workings, on *his* thoughts: the emotional high tide earlier had confirmed as much. How was that fair?

'I've got something to tell you,' Seb whispered, '…something to share' – almost hoping that the pillow would swallow his words. That way, when Annie informed him that she hadn't heard, he would be obliged to lean up and say it clearly – declare it into the darkness and imagine the expression on his partner's face. But the pillowcase resented the responsibility: the words went around the room like a fat fly, butting its way from bulb to bulb.

Annie responded immediately. 'I know,' she said; 'you've started again, haven't you.'

84

'I never stopped.' Seb's voice crumbled like cake.

Tensing his muscles, Seb prepared himself to leave the bed. His eyes burned at the ceiling. He imagined indignity and shame to be *en route*… Surely Annie would retreat from him, even by a couple of inches; or she would force him to set up base camp in the lounge.

'Seb…'

She was whispering. Seb couldn't read her right. He whispered back, 'Yes…'

'Does it make you feel good?'

'…Yes.'

He heard her gulp; it was as loud as an old jalopy clunking into gear. She moved closer. 'Is it something we could share?'

Seb was stunned. 'What do you mean?' he asked.

It was sharp, what Annie had in her hand; what she pressed against the pucker of his navel. 'Is that what you want?' she asked.

'Yes.'

Annie increased the pressure. The darkness was too full for Seb to see the blood that had been drawn, but he knew that the skin had been punctured. The wound sang sharply in his ears; its tone shrill.

'Up or down?' Annie asked.

Seb was scared. She was drunk enough to do anything, he knew, and having found a way of making amends, was likely to overdo any action taken. Excitedly Seb sweated; fear and longing jostled, competed, barked at one another.

'*You* decide,' he whispered, taking Annie in his arm and kissing the top of her head.

Hell of a West

MARCHING TOWARDS THE WINDMILL, Annie noticed that there were no mountains in view, and there were no clumps of grass underfoot. *I'm walking on the flat face of the earth*, she thought, *and that windmill's the nose.*

As she got closer, the faint whine in the silence grew louder, and she could hear clanking – as though she had crept up on the windmill and had caught it talking to itself. The thought gave her the creeps.

Outside the door Annie called, 'Anybody home?'

No reply. Annie opened the door and called again. There was no reply, but any thoughts she might have had about the windmill being a long-abandoned structure were quickly squashed. A candle still burned in a night lamp on the table. Next to the light was a Bible with a few of the pages loose and dangling out like cows' tongues. With the candle burning someone must be here now, or had just been here recently and had stepped out upon her arrival – the candle was not that tall.

Against her better senses, knowing that she was in trespass, Annie stepped in, closed the door and looked around. A thin flight of wooden stairs led up and around. In the small room in front of her, a chair, and one chair only, accompanied the book, table and candle. There was nothing else.

Knowing it was ill advised, Annie hoped that the fella or fellas who lived here would take kindly to her intrusion, or at least let it pass. *He'll be as big as a bear,* she thought, *and as angry as a hornet in mud.*

With a rattle the door opened, and Annie and the wind-mill-keeper gasped. Under the door frame Annie saw the

86

smallest women she'd ever seen. She wasn't more than ninety pounds in weight; like a child, though she was dressed in a schoolmarm's fashion. In the candlelight it was impossible to judge her age. Her emotion, however, was simple. The woman was furious, and she was pointing a rifle at Annie.

'I saw your footprints in the dirt. I knew them to be fresh,' the woman said. 'What do you want here?'

Annie displayed her empty palms seeking forgiveness. 'I need somewhere to rest.'

The woman thought about this and those few seconds Annie decided to capitalise. 'I don't have a horse. I've walked here all the way from Tombstone.'

'What is it that you have done to bring you here all the way from such a place?' the woman asked, her eyes unwavering, lowering the weapon.

'I'll tell you – gladly. May I have a drink of water first?'

'First sit down,' the woman said. 'I'll fetch some from the well.' She placed the rifle by the door as she went out. 'I want to say that I am sorry about my unchristian welcome, but I can't be too careful.'

Minutes later she returned with a pail half-full of clear water that she poured in an old teacup that she pulled from the shadows. Annie drank deeply and gratefully from a chipped cup. She had three refills before she spoke any more words.

'I can also offer you some buffalo meat, it's hanging above, but that's it.'

'The water's filled me up for now,' Annie said. 'Maybe shortly, thank you.'

'It's strange for me to have company. Name's Bonnie.'

'I'm called Annie. I'm sorry; I should've waited outside. You live here alone?'

'Just me and my shadow,' Bonnie replied. 'And the Holy

Ghost, of course.' Smiling, she patted the tatty Bible. 'The Lord, he gives me the strength to endure.' Bonnie said standing on the floorboards with her back pressed against the door.

'So you hunt the buffalo for yourself?'

'Buffalo's too rare,' Bonnie said. 'But the Lord will provide. I have a well for water, and a Bible and a rifle. I know my place.'

The words almost caught in Annie's throat but she forced them out. 'Are you one to have committed a crime? Is that why you are here far from Tombstone?'

Bonnie stood up again and reached for the weapon.

'Mind your own business,' she whispered when the noise had died down.

I Shop At Night

(with Lawrence Dyer)

I WAS AT THE CHECKOUT when I saw the Quatilati looking at me.

Behind the row of tills, the plate glass windows revealed the supermarket car park bathed in March sunlight, attentive mothers with toddlers and hover-trolleys gliding by. I saw myself crashing through the glass in slowmo.

I brought my glance back to the Quatilati's eyes. What did he want? Why was he pursuing me here? The Agents ought to be protecting me. It probably was here to add another band to my arm, restrict what I could do even more. I already had two, like swimming pool rubber bands on my left arm, rows of numbers and symbols setting out clearly what I could and couldn't do. Even the Agents I worked for couldn't get them off my skin, they were that permanent.

With a heave I lobbed my old-fashioned wire basket of heavy sauce and pickle jars and my bags of fruit at his chest. He took the impact badly, just like a till assistant would, flailing his arms, face distorted, a jar of pickled walnuts rolling up one shoulder, ripe grapes bursting over his pimply chin. Then, before it could react, I was gone, racing down the row of checkout stands, people parting with my barks as they saw me coming, my mind on the knife that would hit me square between the shoulders at any moment. To avoid it, weaving as I ran, I dived down between the last row of self-service tills and a seasonal display of discount starts and tulips.

Nothing happened.

'Are you all right?' a grey-haired man in a corduroy suit

standing over me asked. I told him I was fine, just checking out the buy-one-get-one-free kitchen herb starts. Looking back I couldn't see the Quatilati anymore.

Since then I shop at night. There is no good reason not to – not if you're careful – despite what I'm told about Quatilatis sometimes venturing out after dark.

I doubt it myself, they are daylight lovers, they ought to be.

But nothing is more dangerous than routine, *they* tell me. So I visit different places for my supplies; but now it's always at night. The daylight scares me.

The first sign of recognition on a shopkeeper's face and I'm away. I complete the purchase – I don't want to stir suspicion – but I never go back there.

Even pleasantries makes me twitchy, and there are pleasantries are all around me, especially here in the Tourist district. They all want the business I bring.

I'm not being honest – I've returned a time or two, pretending I'm a Tourist. Then as far as they know I've gone back home, wherever that might be. All they know is I'm not from around these parts. My accent is different – even in the limited words I use.

I wish I *could* go home.

When I think of home I think of simplicity, in spite of the arguments. A fire in the grate. The smell of meat cooking in the kitchen. The strange walk Granddad struggled by with, after the second new hip. The cat we called Umbrella, shortened to Brolly (she loved the rain). I think of simplicity.

I think of the slow bus down the hill to the butcher's shop. Meat in greaseproof paper. Edible bodies. Divided and subdivided, meal after meal of it – lasting longer than commonsense suggested it could. Weeks of soups and broths from the bones, thought any weather outside. Crunchy texture to cartilage, to gristle. Warmth and sickness to the stomach. 'We're not made of money,' I was told again and again. Bleached vegetables, the consistency of trifle. The bones always bubbling in a cauldron of onion water for extra stock to be used the next day soon, so that the meal never ended: it merely passed from one onto the next meal, the next time some wages came in.

I don't eat meat now – none. I don't ever take any buses, I don't have to. I shop at night because it's not only daylight and Quatilati that I'm afraid of. It's the simplicity.

My town here sprawls for miles. There is always more construction – you can hear the noise anywhere you go – and as fast as things crumble into the river, it seems, new buildings are erected into a sky that has seen better days. Not that the town has that look – parched by war – that haunts other towns. But it definitely has that feel.

I have never reached its boundaries. I have tried. Although I don't take buses, I have studied their routes and attempted to follow them on foot, searching for a perimeter fence, a checkpoint. But each time I do my wrist bands will start to sting, telling me I'm close to going as far as I'm allowed to go, and I never reach what I assume must be the end of the town. I'll turn a corner or crest a rise, and in front of me, all I see – another nightmare of beige housing, the pimply lights of ad boards selling sparkling drinks or handbags, off into the distance, for as far as I can see.

On one occasion I asked. I was at a terminus.

I asked a stranger – possibly an Agent. She gave me a look like I was way out of bounds, like I was suggesting something criminal. She shuffled away from me, shooing her wheeled luggage in front of her like lazy children. I felt guilty for asking all day.

It was round about then that I made the decision: to stick to the night, that and hiding beside the kitchen herb starts.

I find that at night the air is full of fake lights, neon and humming, small and glittering with gusts of smoke from the restaurants and the drains. Everywhere I look there are animals, unwanted and roaming, feral and dangerous. I know how they feel. They have the same job as occupies me. Up above us, the sky is slimy with a meniscus of unshed rain. The pollution in this town – it is really no joke, or maybe that is exactly what it is.

I do worry about this town.

But not when I am at the fights. I like the fight nights.

I like losing my money that way. They give me too much for a job that is so large that I have never understood exactly how to do it. I do not understand my part in the overall proceedings – and I've tried to, believe me. I have made the same sort of enquiries that always seem to get me locked in the sights of some sort of eventual trouble from my superiors. I am told, 'you don't need to know.' I am told, 'it is a matter that needn't concern you.'

I have learned not to persevere with my questioning. No one enjoys being challenged in such a fashion, I am told. And it's no use complaining that my aim is not to challenge – it is to learn – because I am threatened with my wages being docked for insubordination.

I do not deny that the idea of having my wages docked is actually quite exciting considering what I make. There is nothing more dangerous than routine, they say. Surely this applies to the regularity of my pay day as well.

The best fights are in the southern districts, in the converted Warehouses. There is something about the proximity of the river that brings out a good cold fever in the crowds. You can lose yourself in the Warehouses, they are like warrens to me.

These nights I am careful not to let anything pass my lips while I'm at the fights. It has been close once or twice. A couple of times I have nearly failed to get home before the dawn started to leak in. The unfamiliarity frightened me. It didn't matter where I walked, I couldn't find a tram or a taxi. Or even anything I recognised from my time in the town. When that happened I was lucky to get home alive.

Yesterday I went out during daylight hours. I felt like the only woman there, but I have perfected my outfit of rough overalls, my cap pulled down over my face. So yesterday, when I saw that I was out of milk and bread, I decided to risk it. I went to a corner shop in a remote district where both wrist bands stung, a place I have never been to before. The wrist bands work automatically, they don't alert any Quatilati until they start to burn; so as long as I didn't go any further the Quatilati shouldn't know I was there. But once inside the shop, right at the back by a frozen food cabinet, that's when I saw her.

At first I couldn't think who she was, her familiarity was so obvious. I realised then that I had seen her a couple of times before, out of the corner of my eye, watching me. I knew she was no Quatilati though I had tried to avoid her the times before. Now I couldn't, I was practically face-to-face with her as she leaned over the cabinet, a packet of frozen coley held delicately between the thumb and forefinger of her right hand. Not surprisingly, our eyes met. She seemed lost for words too. She knew she was me, just as I knew I was her. She was the daylight version of me, the one me that shopped by day.

Just how far she was *actually* me I wasn't sure. She wasn't me in the sense that she had come back from the future, or in

93

the sense that she was my twin. She was just *me*, and for a moment I saw her seeing myself through her eyes, still wearing the overalls from the night before.

'Well,' she said. 'We meet at last.'

She said it as if it had all been planned. Or was it me being sarcastic with myself?

I don't know if I reacted correctly. Perhaps I should have been outraged or frightened. After all, it isn't every day you meet yourself. I remember saying quickly, 'Perhaps we should team up. It'd be safer from the Quatilati.'

Her eyebrows twitched upward. 'All right, maybe,' she said. 'There could be some advantages. But let's be clear about what we are talking about, I'm not going to shop at night.'

My smile, I am sure, was suitably bitter.

94   'I'm not known for my tendency to compromise either,' I told her.

Her smile was bitterer still.

'Oh yes you are. I hear you play by rules that you sometimes manage to convince yourself are your own but are really the Agents'. You're no freer than I am, don't you think otherwise. So you can lose the attitude.'

That shut me up for a second. I don't know what bothered me more: the possibility that there was a me who was bolshier than I was, or the possibility that I was the same as this me in the eyes of other people.

Nothing like confronting yourself to gauge your bitch rating.

'So what happens next?' I asked.

'You're going home, I would imagine.'

'I meant for you.'

'That's none of your business,' she told me. She dropped the frozen coley into her basket; as she sauntered away, the basket took a second to compute that she had gone, and then it was in pursuit of its mistress down the aisle – hovering after her like an abandoned pet.

Not wanting her to have the last word I called after her. To my surprise she stopped, the basket gently bumped into her rump. She turned around.

'Babe, I think that qualifies as irony,' I informed her. 'You're the reason I don't know half of what I don't know: because it's been told *to you*, not to me.'

'Do you expect me to break down and cry?' she asked.

'I expect *something*.'

'You've *got* something. You've got my indifference. So why don't you stop whining and crawl back to your hole?'

'*Our* hole.'

'No, *your* hole,' she spat back. Her brow tensed and puckered. 'Do you think we *live* together – share the space? How incestuous.' She almost laughed. Her voice could scarcely have sounded more disgusted with the very notion. I was even hurt at the sound of it.   95

'So you've seen it then,' I said. 'My hole, I mean.'

I think I was trying to trap her, but it didn't quite work out that way. For one thing, I hadn't expected her to admit it.

'Of course I've seen where you live. Who do you think gets you out of trouble after the sun comes up?'

'What trouble?'

'The *expensive* kind of trouble you seem to enjoy swilling around in. *Me*.'

'Well in that case, I owe me a bunch of flowers,' I replied sarcastically.

'You owe me a *florist's*.'

The basket floated higher, trying to get her attention. I read in a weekly that some of these baskets had been programmed to be neurotic – those were the very popular ones; and of course, that said a lot about the people who chose them when they entered a shop. Except in this case, of course, the choice said a lot about the other *me*. After all, it was *I* who had chosen the basket, even if it was a *different* I. *Me*, I preferred the old fashioned wire baskets – the ones without the programming. Supermarkets usually kept a few for older for their less adventurous customers.

'What's a florist's?' I asked the back of her shoulders.

She didn't answer me. Despite the less-than-flattering results of the conversation, I was left with one assured positive. I looked a lot better from behind than I had thought I did. It helped some to explain all the attention I get when I pass people, men in particular.

It took a second for me to make a decision.

Could I *really* let her out of my life? I didn't think I could – or should. Legging it after the other me meant that it was I who had to abandon my basket, for which I felt briefly guilty, but the basket was one with a chilled hippie character programmed in that didn't mind what I bought or thought, it was all cool and groovy.

Barging through the checkout queues I emerged red-faced into a day much too bright to be healthy. In the glare I saw her rear as she approached the bus stop, trailing her personal shopping trolley at shoulder height behind her. To have exited the shop so swiftly she must have paid extra for the Instawrap service. Evidently I have more money than sense during the daylight hours.

But I do not take buses. I'm not *that* reckless. I am afraid, I thought.

I didn't really have a choice though.

I tried to duck between the cars, to get across the road

to her before the arriving bus did, but the traffic warden – a blob of silver with outstretched arms and a maternal smile — 'saved' me from myself. By the time I had gone around via the pedestrian crossing, the bus was gone, and with it the other me.

Though somehow she had left her personal shopping trolley behind. Perhaps she wasn't as in control as she made herself out to be. Why she wanted to lose me, I had no idea; weren't we supposed to be working together? The shopping trolley was blancmange pink, with retro 50s-style silver wings; it was running up against the pole of the bus stop sign, backing off, rolling forward, backing off, like a disturbed person slowly head-butting a wall again and again. Its flexi-eye caught sight of me, and with an electronic sigh of satisfaction it nestled up against my leg. There was nothing to do but take it home with me. Perhaps my other self would come for it there – she already knew where I lived.

97

When I arrived home the door was open. The place had been ransacked. My stuff was thrown about on the floor, my neo-Victorian wardrobe dragged over, a long curved split grinning at me down one of its plexi-wood sides. I don't have a lot of stuff, but what I do have I don't like being messed with. She was going to pay for this.

That it was she who was to blame I had no doubts – until Utterson stepped out of the bathroom. He was one of the Agents I worked for – usually I did not know their names, but I knew his all right, the slimy bastard.

'What do you think you're doing?' I began, but he raised a hand to silence me.

'Not here,' he said with a simple finality. Being simplicity-intolerant, I wanted to strangle him.

A couple of minutes later, as we were whisked along at

speed through the underpasses by his driver, I could contain myself no longer.

'You had to wreck my place, didn't you!'

He gave me a long thin look, with one eyebrow pressed up. 'The Quatilati have her.'

With that everything fell into place. It hadn't been Utterson who had wrecked my place. And it wasn't the other me. It had been the Quatilati, when they had come to kidnapped her.

Back at HQ, Utterson was less than composed. He came out of his office into the cigarette-butt space called the waiting area, fingering his collar. 'I've gotten a message,' he said. 'She's come to see you in person. It is most irregular. She doesn't see operatives, but this time she's insisting.'

'She? Who is she?' I asked.

98   'My boss,' he said.

I didn't know he had a boss. I'd always assumed he *was* the boss, or one of them at least. Still wondering I followed him up two flights of stairs. I had never been in this part of the building before: but clearly it had no elevator. He led me down a long corridor: carpeted and much more luxurious than the stark metal-lined basement of the building that I was so used to seeing the inside of.

He stopped outside a heavily panelled wooden door. It looked like it was made of real wood. Utterson hesitated; again he fingered his collar.

'Look, there's no easy way to say this. She's different. The boss.' With a flick of his head he indicated at whoever was waiting for me behind the wooden door.

Then he got behind me and pushed me inside.

A animal smell burnt my nostrils and I felt my legs back me against a wall, my chest breathing hard. The adrenaline of the night time fights I frequented, my life as an operative, my fleeing the Quatilati – nothing could have prepared me for this.

Utterson's boss was large, stinking, and from what I could understand telling me to sit down. I wasn't able to take it all in at once. I didn't sit down but stayed where I was, my back pressed against the wall, my fingernails digging into the soft plaster boards.

I took a deep breath to assess the situation. Utterson's boss – so by default *my* boss – appeared to be a giant clothes-wearing hedgehog. An orange-brown tweed skirt and jacket, to be precise. One of her spines stuck through the tweed of the skirt and pricked the black leather of her office chair. She half-filled the small room and her animal presence was overwhelming.

'Do sit down!' she insisted again in a high-pitched and not very strong voice, waving with a hairy, clawed paw at the upright wooden chair in front of her desk.

I couldn't move, nor could I speak.

'Very well, as you wish, stay were you are,' she mumbled as she picked up a sheet of paper, perusing it for a moment or two. There was a flicker of movement along one of the translucent spines just above her eye and I saw a tiny insect run to the end of the spine then double back on itself. In response, the giant she-hedgehog scratched vigorously at her brow, sending a shower of tiny baby lice onto the papers on the desk before her. The minute insects raced back to reintegrate themselves, jumping from the desk back into her fur and spines. She didn't seem to notice, or care and continued to study the paper the she clutched in her paws.

'It appears you have been taken by the Quatilati Veris Ba,' she observed, as she looked at me over the top of her winged spectacles. 'Or rather, to be precise, your *other* you has.'

I turned my head to look for Utterson, but he was gone. It

is just like an Agent to slip away when you need him most.

'Most unusual case, yours,' the boss added, looking me up and down. I wondered if it was already too late to ask her name.

Dropping her gaze from me she reached for what I now saw was an enormous chunk of cheese on an ornate plate on one side of the desk. Holding it up to she took a delicate bite and I saw her long teeth exposed for a moment. She then rubbed her greasy paws together.

'Do you know how this has happened? Fragmentation. Usually it works on a mental level only, but in your case the fragmentation appears to be physical. One operative has split into two operatives. You have divided, my dear.'

She paused and studied me over the top of her glasses again, gauging my reaction to the news. Frankly I was still too reeling from the fact that she was a giant hedgehog to have much of a reaction to the news that I had split into two.

'What's more,' she went on, looking back at the paper, 'the Quatilati Veris Ba now possess the other you. You came to their attention and they were as intrigued as I am by what has happened. The fact that they have a you – or one of the 'yous', so to speak – poses a grave threat to us. More so than if they had just captured you in your entirety, that is.'

I managed to look curious about this and she saw my reaction.

'Because, my dear,' she explained in answer to my silent question, 'physical fragmentation – although known to be theoretically possible – has never been known to occur before. Of course, there've been *stories* of it. Worse still, their having *one* of the yous while we have the other one is going to give them a huge *advantage*. This will allow them to find a way to tap into our systems while you are still with us. So, you see, we really do have a big problem, my dear.'

With a hard swallow I found my voice. 'I'm going to find her, Ma'am.' I found that my words sounded composed and reassuring, not like those of someone who was unexpectedly speaking to a giant hedgehog.

'That's all well and good, but what do you have in mind to *do*, exactly?' She said as fixed with me a stare.

'I think I *will* sit down, if that's okay, Ma'am. Allow myself to think out loud. If it's not stating the obvious – I know me very well. I know myself. And if it was *me* who was abducted…'

'It *is* you who was abducted.'

'…then I'd be damn sure I left the other me enough clues to find me.

'And how will you go about searching for these so-called clues that the other you would have tossed out willy-nilly?'

By confronting the matters that I don't wish to confront, I wanted to say. *By travelling on a bus, perhaps; facing the simplicity I couldn't bear.*

I would shop by day.

'I don't know,' I admitted, 'not exactly. For starters, how do we know it was *me* that was captured?'

Her whiskers twitched. 'Curiously enough, they sent a severed finger as proof. Yours, we presume. And a note.'

'But I haven't lost a finger,' I protested.

'So you haven't. I saw that to be the case as soon as you entered,' the hedgehog replied. 'The note also said that they had you and that we were to await further orders.'

'Then there's this: I know myself to be simplicity-intolerant,' I said quickly. 'I'll find her in simplicity.'

'*Her?*'

'Myself, I mean. I'm going to live in my negative. I'll find her that way,' I continued. 'As soon as it's night I'll go to bed. I'll need to fight my instincts. I'll be able to find out how the other half, *my* other half, lives.'

Calm, I told myself. *Deep breaths*. All the alarm bells were going off in my head as I walked into the supermarket. Sun streamed through the plate glass, regular shoppers moved along the aisles, muzak trickling out of the speakers: everything appearing normal. With a brief sigh of regret I pulled my fingers from the little stack of wire baskets and selected a modern trolley.

A shiny green ball with silver side pouches floated up from the stand. 'Pleased to be of service. Thank you for selecting me.' Its voice was tinny and brittle. 'Where shall we begin? Do you need eggs today?'

Ignoring it, I set off down the cereals and biscuits aisle.

'Do you like chocolate creams? They're on special offer today,' the trolley went on in its metallic voice. What was wrong with it? Trolley's should sound sweet and seductive. 'Or perhaps some Cokey Flakes? Two for the price of one for you for the next hour only?'

Reminding myself to do everything differently from what I would have usually done, I headed for the meat counter. I needed to get a great big lump of meat, one that would last for weeks; one that would fill my flat with that old simmering meat smell from so long ago. As I headed towards the long low Perspex cabinets filled with wet, pink body parts I glanced at the other shoppers. They all seemed hypnotised by the machine-like melody that played from the speakers mounted in the ceilings, mesmerised by the gentle cooing suggestions and persuasions of their trolleys.

Whereas 'Beef is 10% reduced today, so buy some now!' my trolley shouted at me.

'Shut up!' I snapped and thumped the trolley hard on its

shiny green nose.

For a moment it sat there in the air, actually trembling, as if it felt for the blow.

'You shouldn't have done that. I've been waiting for you to come in here all day, dodging fat grannies and spotty teenagers who tried to choose me instead, and now you have gone and hit me? That hurt, y'know, and not just on my nose.'

I stared at the trolley.

'Don't look at me like that, you'll draw attention! Haven't I taught you anything?'

I continued to stare, unable to figure out what was happening.

'Now don't tell me you don't recognise me!'

'Don't *recognise* you? I recognise you're a shopping trolley!'

I was about to walk away in disgust when the trolley made a kind of snorting noise. 'Duh! Hey bimbo, don't you know me? It's me, airhead, your other self.'

I took a deep breath and looked the trolley right in the lens of its mechanical eye. 'So, you're telling me you've now become a shopping trolley?'

'Strewth! We *are* on top form today aren't we? Have I become a shopping trolley? No. Am I speaking to you from somewhere else *through* a shopping trolley? Yes. I suppose if I give you enough time you'd have gotten there in the end! But time is not a luxury that we have right now.'

The trolley moved closer to me, looked to one side as if to make sure no one was listening, then turned back to me with an air of confidentiality. 'I'm being held in a white room with no windows. What I do know is that it was a bloody great hedgehog, dressed in orange-brown tweed, the size of a small car that put me in here!'

103

An image of Utterson's boss eating cheese sped through my mind. Had she lied to me? She had said that members of the Quatilati Veris Ba had abducted my other self, but what if *she* was responsible, and what if she was a member and been telling me the truth?

I walked away from the trolley, in the direction of the tills. Noise crowded my brain, as intrusive as smoke; two wings of distant headache flapping against my temples. I didn't care about the public announcements for special offers or for a lost child. I didn't even care about what the trolley had to say.

'Where are you going?' it asked.

'To the edge of town,' I answered.

'I'm coming with you!' And I heard its soft hum come up behind me.

I turned. 'You're bloody well not! It's going to be stressful enough for me getting on public transport. I'll be damned if I'm going to wrestle *you* onto the bus or tram!'

The trolley made a tutting noise of disrespect.

'I can take you to me!'

'How? You just said you didn't know where you were.'

'I don't. But this trolley might.'

Turning my back on her once more, I told her that she was talking gibberish. 'I don't have time for this. I want my old life back, and something tells me that the only way I'm going to get that it is to solve this riddle as quickly as possible.'

A uniformed man the size of a grizzly stood, arms crossed, by the doors, the insignia of the supermarket on both his lapels. His skin was sunburnt and flaky. He looked straight at me.

'Allow me to point out your mistake, madam.'

'Me?' I said. 'What mistake?'

'Your mistake in thinking that you'll be leaving without paying for those items.'

'I haven't bought anything,' I told him.

'My point precisely, madam.'

'I haven't *chosen* anything, I mean.'

He uncrossed his arms and pointed past me.

'Is that your trolley?'

It was half-full of junk food, though I'd left it a few seconds ago empty. Had the other me managed to pull the stuff right off the shelves?

'I don't want any of it,' I said to the guard.

'Then I suppose you'd better put it back then, what do you say?'

'I say you're overstepping your line.'

'The authorities will beg to differ.'

I could feel myself getting flustered. I needed a fight. Not an argument with this bear, but an actual physical presence at a brawl. I missed all of it, worse than acutely.

'I seem to have forgotten my purse at home, there's nothing I can do for you.'

'No. You've forgotten your purse. Or you've *left* your purse at home. You can't forget something at home. Your grammar's half-baked,' the guard informed me.

'I've had enough of this…' I muttered.

'You tell him,' said the trolley.

'And *you* can shut up as well,' I told the other me.

'Are you telling me to shut up?' asked the guard. 'I regard that as confrontational. We have policies about customer-to-staff bullying. You could be barred from this store…'

'Oh, *bar* me then! I was talking to the trolley if you must know.'

'To the *trolley*, madam?'

'Yes. The trolley wants to follow me. I won't let it. Isn't that clear enough?'

'Not really, madam, no.'

'Well, it's all I've got time for. If you'd excuse me, I'd like to pass.'

With a look on his face of reluctant acquiescence, the guard stepped aside. 'You might ought to be thinking of some oily fish, madam,' he seemed to advise. 'It's good for your brain, *they* say.'

'I'm not buying *anything*,' I repeated, ignoring his slur to my intelligence.

As fast as I could I walked to the terminal building, my need to take a bus now like an addiction. I both wanted it and didn't want it. I feared it and adored it. I would need to take a bus if I was to reach the edge of town before the sun sunk away. There being no higher notch for my terror to reach, it made sense to do all the things that I was scared of while under the umbrella of one overarching terror. It was only a bus, I tried to say to myself.

Lined up against the walls were about a hundred ticket machines. Many of them were doing no business, and I chose one at random – the one nearest to where I had stopped in my tracks. The machine asked me where I wanted to go.

'To the outskirts,' I replied.

'Selection not recognised,' it's monitor flashed. 'Please state where would you like to go.'

'To the edge of town.'

The machine hummed. '…To H Town? Please confirm or make a different selection.'

'No. I want to go near the river.'

'To the river,' the machine agreed. 'Single journey or return?'

Let's show some confidence, I thought. 'A return.'

'A return ticket to The River Nightclub. Please insert…'

'No! I don't want to go to a *nightclub!*' I shouted.

'People are staring,' a voice seemed to say from behind me. Expecting to see the trolley again, I pirouetted and was ready to tell myself to *FUCK off* and leave me alone.

But it wasn't the trolley.

It was another, different giant hedgehog. Not Utterson's boss but one much larger. I stared, unable to respond. The animal was half the size of a bus, and it held under its right arm a small girlish figure who raised her head towards me. I could hardly see her, so amazed was I by the sheer size and scale of this hedgehog. This one was clearly a male: it was much more bristly, much more muscular than the other one.

Studying him, something collapsed in my mind. Before I knew what I was doing I was lunging halfway to the departure quays, my breath scorching hot and corrosive in my throat and lungs.

By accelerating slightly, and leaping at the last moment, I managed to get on board a bus as the doors flapped shut behind me. I didn't have a ticket but at least I was out of that terminal building, away from those who wanted to talk to me, too.

But I wasn't.

It didn't matter how impossible it was, but the hedgehog had beaten me to the bus and had boarded – without me seeing it do either thing. There it was! Taking up most of the rear of the vehicle, sitting on top of the rows of head rests, as snug as a bug in a rug.

And yet there were fifteen or so other passengers on the bus. Not one of them had turned to see this intruder in their midst; all of them were looking at *me*. They were oblivious to the great spiny animal in their midst; even now as I pointed toward the back, my hand shaking, not one so much as glanced at the vast creature. Then, as I stared at it aghast, the fabric of its velvet jacket began to strain; its left arm flexed away from its shoulder. There was a popping as stitching snapped, and a tearing as the arm detached itself entirely and moved out sideways on metal struts. Between the structure of the struts a padded seat with a headrest was revealed, like an old leather car seat.

'Get in!' the other me called from her position in the hedge-hog's right armpit.

Get in what?

'GET IN!' the hedgehog roared – and I was blasted by its rancid breath. Despite the fact that this vile gale tousled the hair-dos of the other passengers (and even lifted up a toupee), not one of the people shifted even an iota.

'Get in *now!*' the supermarket security guard shouted, coming around the right side of the great hedgehog – this even though logic stated clearly that there was nowhere near enough space inside the bus for such a manoeuvre. The rules of physical space had been abandoned, or so it seemed. And how had the guard got on the moving bus? Had he followed me here? He must have done just that. Had he been hiding behind the hedgehog all along?

Defiant I shook my head. 'No way.' But the guard was quick, much quicker than I would have given him credit for, at his size, and as I turned to run down the aisle of the bus, back toward the doors at the front, he caught and held me by one wrist. Then he twisted my arm.

Dragged to the ground, I was confronted by the bland façade of the bus machine that had wanted me to go to the River Nightclub. 'Get in,' it droned without emotion.

I didn't understand the command. Get in *what*, for Christ's sake?

The seat that had emerged from the hedgehog's left side?

Get into that?

Barely seconds after I'd got on the bus, or so it seemed, I could feel it decelerating. Perhaps as it stopped to pick up more passengers I could make a break for it.

'You don't have to be afraid of me,' the guard said.

I don't know if I couldn't speak or if I chose to stay silent. Either way, no words emerged: apart from anything else, most of my air had been knocked out of my body when I landed on the road. Not that the guard's ministrations were complete. Far from it. Having picked me up bodily he thrust me down hard into the padded leather seat that had emerged from the side of the great hedgehog.

I noticed some people stepping up onto the bus. It appeared that one could see me, I was certain of it now. It wasn't that they chose to ignore me and the hedgehog: *they couldn't see us.*

'You have to go where I put you,' the security guard explained.

My last glimpse of the outside world was of his smug face before I felt my seat shooting sideways again and I was engulfed in the dark, suffocating side of the hedgehog. Then there was a loud roaring, as I choked on the musky fumes and lost consciousness.

When I came to I was in a pure white room, no windows, no door. The furniture was white too, what little there was of it. I could breathe more easily now, but vestiges of the smell of the great hedgehog clung to my clothes and hair. And there was another smell as well.

'I think she's awake,' a voice said, and I recognised it as belonging to the other me.

I turned and sat up. Behind me, sitting at a steel table sat the other me and two large hedgehogs. I did not recognise either of them, but they were each about the size of Utterson's boss; both were evidently female from their clothes.

I could smell the aroma of cooking meat.

I didn't want to think about cooking meat at such a time.

Quickly I got to my feet and faced them. 'Are you the Quatilati Veris Ba?'

The other me smirked, her nostrils quivering.

'It's much more complicated than that, child,' one of the hedgehogs said. She had a kind face that emerged straight out of the neck of her puce cardigan.

'You're safe now,' the other hedgehog said. 'You're a long way from the city. Well beyond its boundaries. Nearly home, in fact.'

I didn't know whether to believe her or not.

'What's going on?' I asked the other me.

She replied: 'Have you never been here before?'

'No.'

'Good answer. Have *we* been here before?'

I was expected to say yes: her sentence construction told me as much.

'No,' I answered.

'Good answer. Have *they* been here before?'

The hedgehogs? I wondered. 'Who they? What they?' I asked.

'The ones in the boiling pot,' said the hedgehog on my left – the one who had spoken first.

More riddles? Surely, so late in the day of my story, I was entitled to the simple courtesy of an explanation.

I waited a few seconds before asking wearily, knowing it was a trap: 'What boiling pot?'

'The one you remember from an earlier time,' the second hedgehog replied. 'When meals went on for months. Literally. Just adding a bit to the bottom of the pot every night. It was never really *finished*, was it?'

Standing up made me feel marginally better. It was good to hear my knees crack.

'The town is where we grow cultures. It's our Petri dish.'

'We went in there to *watch evolution,*' the other me said, 'in real time!'

'I didn't see anything of the kind,' I protested.

The other me made a face. '*Who* didn't?'

'*We* didn't.'

'That's better. And you're wrong. We saw it grow from nothing: we *were there.* And then we got lost in there and forgot the nature of the experiment. It wasn't cheap to split us, by the way. But someone had to rescue you, cost or no cost.' The other me shrugged.

'Are you hungry, child?' the second hedgehog asked me.

I spent a few seconds walking from one wall to the other, my stomach rumbling like trucks on a distant road.

'What do I smell in the oven? Is it food?' I asked.

The other me took the question.

'That's not food in the oven. That's the town,' the other me said. 'That's the smell of progress. That's *science* being done, babe. That's our future.'

Shaking my head, I looked for a door. There *had* to be a door.

'Am I prisoner?' I asked, tired of questions.

The first hedgehog said, 'Whatever makes you think that, child?'

'Good. What time is it?'

'Bedtime, it's bedtime,' said the second hedgehog. 'We're

all tired.'

'Good,' I said. 'You mean it's night. It's dark outside this room, right?'

The other me said, 'Yes.'

'Are you coming with me?' I asked her. 'We have a lot of catching up to do.'

She stood up but I could tell she wasn't certain of what I was asking of her. Nor were the hedgehogs. But I was going to fight my way out of that white room, or die trying. Or at least that's the kind of bravado nonsense that we tell ourselves when the handsome stench of meat baking is in your throat and on your taste buds. I wanted food – I wanted meat – like a woman possessed.

There was only one place to go for meat and a night at the fights.

112

'Where did you have in mind?' the other me asked.

My answer was immediate, and much to her pleasure.

'We're going shopping, together,' I said.

The Pigeon

JONATHAN MOVED INTO Stephanie's house in the country. They were both in their early thirties, professional, and scared of commitment.

Three months in, and things were going smoothly. Every morning before the drive to the station, Jonathan went outside to feed Stephanie's rabbit in its hutch. It was always pleased to see him. Jonathan sat on the bench by one of the neglected flower beds, drinking his morning coffee and smoking his cigarette. From the bench he could see for miles across the farmer's wheat fields, all the way to the next village.

One Saturday, the farmer was shooting pigeons. Jonathan sat on the bench in his dressing gown. In the distance he saw the makeshift hideout, constructed of bales of hay, in the shape of an igloo. The previous Wednesday he and Stephanie had dined at The Swan, the village pub. Jonathan had eaten pigeon pie, and now regretted it. He soon lost count of the number of birds the farmer blasted out of the sky; when he stood up to go in, he found he had drunk only half his coffee, and it was now stone cold.

'Why does he have to kill them?' Jonathan asked Stephanie in the bedroom.

As she pulled on her tights she smiled at him. 'Oh, you city boy you. So they don't eat his vegetable crops and things.'

'But does he have to *shoot* them?'

'He probably thinks strangulation's not worth the effort.'

'Hardy-har.'

'Give me a hand making the bed, you silly fool. Then we'll go shopping. I've got an eye test at ten.'

When they returned in the afternoon, Stephanie started putting the shopping away, gratified to have learned that her recent headaches could be put down to an out-of-date prescription for her lenses. On his way through the lean-to to play darts in the garage, Jonathan stopped at the back door. He stared at the glass pane. There was a splodge and then a streak of red, as though someone had thrown a paint ball.

'That's blood,' Stephanie told him, unlocking the door. 'You know what's happened, don't you. He's shot one down but didn't kill it right then and it's crash-landed against our door, the poor thing.'

The bird was in the narrow passage between the side of the garage and the fence belonging to the neighbours. It had nestled up against the padlocked wooden gate that led out to the drive, having got as far from the field and the farmer as it could. A smear of red decorated its back and side, like punky plumage.

'What do we do?' asked Jonathan.

'It'll die,' Stephanie replied. 'We put it out of its misery, or we place it back in the field for the farmer's dog to find.'

'Great choice.'

Stephanie shrugged. 'I don't make the rules. But it can't stay there,' she said. 'It's scared to death. Get one of the dust sheets from the garage. I think if you throw something over their heads they fall asleep.'

Jonathan tried to throw the stained dust sheet at the pigeon. So weak was the throw, he couldn't have meant it: the dust sheet flapped to the concrete floor, half a metre short.

Nevertheless, it was enough to scare the creature. Feebly flapping its wings, it tried to *vamoose*, but had no strength left. Jonathan walked forward to pick up the sheet. Spine arched, bending low, he approached the pigeon as though it were dan-

114

gerous, its black eye regarding him seemingly with insouciance.

It started to panic. Jonathan tried again to cover it with the dust sheet, but as big as the sheet was and as small as the area was to cover, he missed again.

'Give it here,' Stephanie said. She strode forward and dropped the sheet on top of the bird. She picked it up gently by its sides; it didn't struggle.

'What now?' Jonathan asked.

'I can't kill it. I'll put it over the fence.'

That night in bed Jonathan said, 'We should make a complaint to the farmer.'

Stephanie had been thinking about the event as well: 'What, that the bird he shot over his own property fell into our garden?'

Not caring much for her tone, Jonathan complained, 'It freaked me out.'

'I noticed.'

'A Hemingway moment, and I failed. I couldn't do it.'

Stephanie turned to him and let the book she was reading drop to the duvet. 'But your skills lie in other directions, my darling.'

Jonathan dreamed that he was a pigeon, or at least a bird, flying high over fields of corn and soy. Swooping towards the farmer's hideout, he used his zoom-in eyesight to peek through a gap in the hay that a shotgun would poke through. He saw the farmer, and though it was dark in there, Jonathan clearly saw the man's furrowed forehead, his hedgerow eyebrows, and even the drinker's broken capillaries on his wide nose, and the crusty crenellations on his dried lips.

At that moment, the gun barrel appeared, sliding out through the hole in the hay bales. Jonathan flapped his arms powerfully to get away. Behind him, the explosion. And then the shock of pain and the blissful held breath of falling.

Gasping a denial, Jonathan woke.

'What's wrong?' Stephanie mumbled. 'You were thrashing about.'

'Sorry. Bad dream.' He breathed heavily. 'Do you want a drink?'

'Mmmm.' She was already slipping back into the rear of her head.

Jonathan got up. After closing the bedroom door behind him, he put on the landing light, took the alarm keys from the dish on the small table, and walked downstairs, avoiding the steps with the pressure points that would set off the security. In the downstairs toilet he deactivated the system and went into the kitchen.

Looking out the back window, he drank iced juice with a splash of vodka. Medicinal purposes, he said to himself: to get him back to sleep. The back garden and the field were an undulating alien landscape in the dead of night.

A soft pop: an unmistakable sound. Jonathan frowned. What on earth could the farmer be firing at so late at night? Maybe nothing. The farmer was a well-known drunk; he was always falling over and abusing the staff in The Swan. Perhaps he'd had a skin-full and was shooting for the sake of shooting.

Not bothering to reactivate the security system, Jonathan returned to bed. He kissed Stephanie's breast and lay on his back, staring up at the ceiling.

Feeling groggy and helpless, Jonathan showered, shaved and checked his hairline – a habit that took up more and more of his free time these days. From beyond the bathroom window came the sound of more gunfire.

Stephanie munched the toast and jam that Jonathan had brought her with her coffee. Jonathan picked his own drink off the tray. 'That farmer was at it early this morning,' he said. 'Shooting, I mean. Do pigeons even *fly* during the night?'

'I'll look in my pigeon-flight-plan book.'

A few minutes later Jonathan stood up to get dressed. Behind his back Stephanie groaned. He turned. 'What's wrong?'

'What happened to your backside?'

Twisting himself around, Jonathan looked in the full-length mirror. On his left buttock was a deep and red groove, about three centimetres long, and half that wide.

'Does it hurt?' Stephanie asked.

'No. Was it there yesterday?'

'Wouldn't I have mentioned it yesterday?' she answered. 'Lie on your front.' He did so. 'I can get my thumb in that.'

'Well don't. I'll go to the doctor tomorrow.'

When they went downstairs they had more coffee and heard another rally of gunshots. 'What is his *problem*?' Jonathan asked. His fingers froze on the handle of the *cafetiere* plunger. 'God, I've just remembered something,' he said to Stephanie. 'A dream I had. I was a pigeon and that mad sod shot me out the air. From behind.'

He waited until Stephanie said, 'Diddums.'

'And now I've got a weird thing on my arse. Like a pellet wound.'

They opted for a drive into town, for a swim and a sauna. On their way back, to counteract any good effects they'd had on their bodies, they stopped at The Swan, like usual. Jonathan drank three pints of a dubious brew called Harmful, each with a dropped shot in there. Stephanie opted for her too-stiff, off the menu, Bloody Marys. Knackered, they decided to leave the car in the car-park and return for it later on, when they'd sobered.

After they'd made love, Jonathan fell asleep on the sofa. Stephanie climbed off and pulled the spare duvet from the airing cupboard over him. She didn't want him catching cold as the sweat dried on his chest.

Feeling the fabric against his skin, Jonathan dreamed again of being a pigeon. Slipping further down the sofa, the duvet covered his head, like the dust sheet had covered the pigeon. Stephanie's hands were on his body, lifting him. There he flexed his wings.

Even under the dust sheet (and its strange aromas of unknown chemicals) he could feel the breeze as Stephanie moved him to the end of the garden.

She lowered him to the ground. The stalks around him whispered and rattled in the wind. Jonathan fluffed his feathers; numbness crawled over his body. He knew he would never fly again, and that the farmer's dogs would find him. Their method of putting him to sleep would be fiercer than a snap of the neck.

Jonathan heard barking. His heart beat quickly. He looked up at the sky with a flick of his head; the sky was changing shape. His perspective was changing. He blinked, his breaths coming raspily, as though he had a hole in his throat. Suddenly he felt colder, and he wrapped his arms around his body. The ground was prickly under his feet. His skin was the colour of milky-tea; his fingernails were grubby.

And he was naked in a farmer's field with no idea as to how he had got there.

Quickly Jonathan climbed back into Stephanie's garden. Halfway to the house (his hand cupping his genitals) he picked up the duvet that he must have discarded. How long he'd been out of the building he had no way of telling – he assumed it

118

had been hours and not days.

Inside he found Stephanie upstairs, reading. She looked up as he entered, wearing the duvet like a caftan.

'What's wrong?'

She had seen the hollow look in her lover's eyes.

He went to bed early. Feeling Stephanie's accusative stare on his back, he tried to sleep. She had tried to get Jonathan to look at the situation logically; in her opinion, the wound on his buttock might have gone septic, causing hallucinatory dream walks. Although Jonathan had pooh-poohed the idea, he couldn't deny *anything*.

He woke at three a.m. Repeating the same procedure as the previous morning, Jonathan went downstairs and drank juice. And listened to the gunshots from the field.

Phone the police, Jonathan told himself. But he'd already had a better idea. In the dark of the bedroom, with Stephanie murmuring in assent, Jonathan picked up some clothes from the floor. He was a sock short, but it was a reasonable harvest. Then he went out the back door into the garden. Stephanie's rabbit jumped up against the wire mesh of its hutch (didn't it *ever* sleep?) but Jonathan, for once, ignored it. At the back of the garden he climbed into the field. The farmer's hideout was at an angle, to the right.

Another shot rang out, amazingly loud. It made Jonathan's ears ring.

For the first time it occurred to Jonathan that the farmer might be incensed or drunk enough to start shooting at *him*. Daunted, but unable to think of anything else to do, Jonathan continued walking, his trouser legs rasping.

At the hideout Jonathan whispered, 'Excuse me.' The embarrassment was ludicrously timed, but he realised that at that moment he did not know the farmer's name. Jonathan peered past the gun barrel, into the darkness, wishing his vision was as clear as it had been when he was a bird.

Two eyelids opened in the darkness. Luminous red eyes were revealed.

With a roar the farmer leapt from within the blind towards Jonathan, and bounced against the side of the hay bales. Jonathan stepped backwards.

'I won't let you tell them that I am here,' came the strained, creaky-door voice.

This was a mistake. The farmer was smashed.

'I only came over to ask if you'd stop shooting for five minutes and let us all have a good night's sleep.' It sounded confident. Jonathan dealt with sales directors at the top companies every day of his working life; he knew he could handle this old soak. And the eyes? he asked himself. The eyes weren't real. The eyes looked the way they did because Jonathan was tired. Deal closed.

'They won't get me, do you understand?'

'Fine. Just stop shooting. Please.'

'I should put a pellet in your head right now,' the farmer replied.

A car will continue moving even after the foot has come off the accelerator, but will eventually lose momentum and stop. The same was true of Jonathan's fearlessness. He was running out of steam. He needed something to keep him going: a way of knowing that his words were having an effect.

By the time he reached the fence into Stephanie's garden he had his shoulder blades pinched together, anticipating a pellet between them. His nerves were raw; his eyes were sore; he was getting a headache.

But the farmer had ceased shooting.

Needing warmth during the night, Stephanie clung to him

snoozily as soon as he eased himself between the sheets. She murmured nonsense to him and he told her to go to sleep. His limbs shook. He saw his neighbour's red eyes in the darkness.

'You had a bad night,' Stephanie told him in the morning. He watched her applying make-up in the bathroom as he towelled himself down after a shower.

'You don't know the half of it. What's the farmer's name?'

'I have no idea.' Stephanie had a meeting with her employer today about her performance review. She always left for work before Jonathan. She wouldn't know he had no intention of going straight to the company doctor. In the kitchen he smoked a cigarette.

'I'm feeling awful,' he told the team secretary on the phone. 'I'm going back to bed.'

'Flu?'

'What flew?'

'Have you *got* the flu?'

'Or something like that.'

'Well, you wrap yourself up warm, my lamb, and sleep it out.' Mel was only twenty-two, but she had three children and a motherly air.

Jonathan went out into the garden for another cigarette. He'd already fed the rabbit, but it headbutted the wire mesh anyway demanding more food. At the back of the garden he smoked and looked at the farmer's hideout. How much of what he remembered from last night had happened?

It's his property, Jonathan thought as he climbed over the fence. And you're in your work clothes, suit and all, you silly arse. This last criticism was delivered in Stephanie's voice.

He had to see. Round the back of the hideout was the low entrance, supported by worn planks of timber. Inside it smelt of male proximity: beery farts, curiously collected, but nothing worse. There were tins of triple strength lager, crushed and mangled on the floor.

An average alcoholic, gun-wielding loony.

At lunchtime Jonathan walked to The Swan, determined to take on the challenge of Harmful Ale. He had two pints, depth shots and all, and read the papers that the barman always bought. Since he wasn't going to work, he had changed out of his suit. To Jonathan's surprise, the farmer from next door arrived and ordered lager. His courage buoyed by alcohol, Jonathan went over to him at the bar.

'Not shooting today then?' he asked.

'Don't look like it, I'm here ain't I?' the farmer replied.

'I've been thinking about what you said last night.'

The farmer shook his head. 'Didn't say nothing to you, nor anybody, last night.'

'Well, this morning then. It was early enough to be last night.'

'Nor then either.'

Jonathan nodded. 'You were drunk. I visited your hidey-hole. You said something about not letting me tell them where you are.' He forced a smile. 'What was *that* all about?'

The farmer frowned. 'Are you mad?'

'It happened, I swear.'

'Going out there to *him*. What got into you?' He was angry. 'To who?'

The farmer hastily swallowed the remains of his pint and left the pub, with Jonathan following and urging him to wait and slow down.

'I just want to understand what all the fuss is about,' he pleaded.

Ten metres from the pub, the farmer stopped on the pavement. 'Son, this is none of your business, so stay out of it. Your own good.'

Feeling he could confess to this man what he'd been too scared to say to Stephanie, Jonathan added, 'I've got a gash on my backside. I had a dream I was a bird, the bird. You shot me, and the next day I had this wound. If it's nothing to do with me, what's *this* all about?'

'We'd better go back to The Swan,' the farmer replied.

Jonathan ordered the drinks. Now that the farmer had decided to tell all, he was chatty; but his mood was still sombre.

'Look, son,' he said, 'I'm not going to pretend I know what he is because I don't. All I know is, he's taken over the village. If I thought it was safe for you, I'd show him to you. Just so's you know it weren't me you were talking to last night.'

Jonathan felt as though he'd got pepper in his nose.

'He had red eyes.'

'And that didn't strike you as odd?' The farmer laughed.

On the defensive, Jonathan replied, 'Well, yeah, it did, but I wasn't sure how much I was seeing and how much I was dreaming.'

The farmer nodded. 'They'll put that on the gravestone marker for this whole village. *They didn't know how much was a dream and how much was real.* Assuming of course there's any difference anymore; and I'm not so sure there is.'

'I want to know about who I talked to last night,' Jonathan said.

'He fell from the sky, I can tell you that much. Busted wings. Someone shot him.' The farmer sipped his lager. 'His flock, or swarm, or whatever − they left him. Now he hates anything that flies. Spends half his time drunk and shooting at things no one else can see. Not to mention sparrows, crows. Don't matter the gun hasn't got half the range he thinks it's got. I mean, he's

123

taken pops at crop-spraying helicopters. Jumbo jets. If a plane leaves a vapour trail he gets paranoid; he thinks it's a message in the sky to him.'

'He's insane, is that what you're telling me?' said Jonathan.

'Make no mistake about it.'

'And are we talking about an *angel*?'

The farmer shrugged. 'Alien. Angel. What's the difference? A couple of letters. An *I* or a *G*. Still *here*, innee? Still making our lives miserable.'

Good job I'm drunk, Jonathan was sober enough to note.

'But my wound?'

'He's got it into his head that we're all trying to warn his flock he's here. So they can pick him up. Take him up and away from where he is.'

124

Jonathan exhaled a gush of smoke. 'He really is mad.'

In a move of shocking suddenness, the farmer placed his tree-bark hand on top of Jonathan's on the table. There was terror in his eyes.

'No, son. That bit is *true*. We try to send up signal flares. We do it in our sleep, when we're most powerful. When we got nothing else on our minds. We fly out and try to flag the spaceship down like an 'itch-hiker. Problem is, he sees us flying in our dreams just as easily as he sees us as us here now. And he can still shoot us down. But the wounds that happen in dreams don't hurt in the real world. If this *is* the real world.' He was unfastening a couple of shirt buttons. On his chest was an ugly gash.

'It was me who fell into your garden, the one you threw a drop cloth on, or that's what I've come to think.'

Stephanie returned at six-thirty. She'd had a good day: her pay rise had been agreed – an additional two grand a year.

'Let's celebrate,' she said wagging a bottle of expensive Spanish merlot.

'I have something to tell you.'

Jonathan described his day. To make Stephanie feel better he shared a few glasses of her wine with her, but his heart was not in it. In the kitchen he made her a colossal vodka and orange, while he had just the orange. Jonathan wanted to keep his wits sharp. When she fell asleep on the sofa, he brewed himself coffee.

The air in the back garden was chilly. The visitor had only fired a few shots tonight; possibly Jonathan's words had had an effect. When he got close, the barrel pointed out.

'Look, I know what you're doing,' Jonathan said. 'And I want you to know, you don't need to. We're not going to tell your clan, or group.'

The farmer fired.

'Can you hear me? You leave us alone, and we'll leave you alone. You have my word.'

Another gunshot. Growing impatient, Jonathan leaned into the gap. 'You're not listening to me,' he said. He wasn't frightened by the red eyes, nor by the whiskery chops, or the melted appearance of the face. The jowls connected directly with the shoulders. 'You're safe here,' said Jonathan. 'But I need to see your wings.'

The visitor pushed Jonathan's head from the gap. The hand that did so was stubbly, four-fingered, with long curling black nails.

Jonathan's heart beat madly. Although the push had not been violent, he had lost his footing, and had fallen on top of some bean stalks planted nearby.

The gun was pointing at him.

Quickly Jonathan raised his hand in surrender. 'Okay, I'm

going,' as he scrambled to his feet. He ran back towards the house, hurdling the boundary fence.

'Stephanie!' he called. She was not in the house; nor was she anywhere on the premises. Jonathan checked the garage, where their cars were parked. The laundry room, the lean-to. He should not have left her sleeping, he realised. Who knew where her dreams might be taking her?

In despair, Jonathan heard a knock at the door. It was midnight. Unless the visitor was a very polite burglar, Jonathan reasoned that it had to be…

'Stephanie!'

Crying, she fell into his arms. 'I've been shot,' she said, 'but it doesn't hurt. I was flying, like you said. I saw it. He looks like the farmer, but *exaggerated*. Look at my leg.' There was a dry creek through the back of her thigh, about six centimetres long.

'I think we should move to the city,' they said, almost simultaneously.

Rivereyes

LIGHT CATCHING ON WATER always made him think of Celeste.

The memories could arrive at the most unfortunate of times. In a meeting at work, for instance, with the overheads dunking two pins of whiteness in a colleague's drink. Or on a drive somewhere late, with a red traffic signal striping through a puddle. On such occasions it was difficult to keep hold, to maintain control. He missed her.

Other times, he deliberately sought out her presence over the waters, such as now, by coming here to London Bridge, which was where they'd first met and where they'd first kissed and where he'd proposed to her with her tiny mittened fingers in his hands. Tonight the clouds had bitten the moon into the shape of an anvil; on the water, crescents of light, a million of them, stretched away into the distance. He could feel her close. His eyes blood-red from staring, he believed that if he breathed very slowly and denied the intrusion of the constant pulse of traffic, he could summon back the scent of her perfume.

Celeste on London Bridge, that was his goal.

'Look at the lights on the water,' she'd said to him, although they'd been strangers only five minutes earlier. A small woman now akin to a child, she'd hustled her way closer to his body, seeking warmth. 'This river has more stars than there are numbers.'

He had fallen in love with other people before hearing those words, of course, but never with such haste, such finality. His heart had been parked on London Bridge ever since that moment.

'Can I meet you here again?' he'd asked.

Celeste had ignored the question. 'Can you imagine what sights the river must have seen since the beginning?'

He had thought that he was being rejected. With a heaviness in his voice that matched that inside his ribcage he had murmured, 'Yes I can imagine.'

She had turned to him, a smile on her face. 'No you can't, no one can,' she'd said. 'Tomorrow night.'

As she was walking away he'd called, 'The same time?'

'We'll both know when to meet when we're ready.'

The memory warmed him: the air had been milder on that evening. The wind was playful and fresh tonight, and the river's eyes gazed back. His elbow stung with a psychosomatic injury: one night, as midnight had edged closer and the breath of the river had smelt sootier, with their bare arms around one another, in late-summer dress, they had watched the cautious approach of a wasp. It had a drugged look about it, and was crawling along the handrail.

'Scared to fly,' Celeste had remarked.

By this point he had long since learned to take her comments and savour them. 'Why?' he'd asked.

'Lost his aerial licence.'

He'd been disappointed in both of them, and he had watched the wasp as it inched nearer, transferring the blame onto its thorax.

'The last wasp of summer,' Celeste had said. 'Isn't it romantic?'

'Shall I put it out of its misery?' he'd replied.

'What makes you think he's in misery? Don't you dare.'

The wasp had stung him on the elbow. Celeste had thought this hilarious. As she watched him recoil, while he rubbed the blighted pimple, she'd told him that it had served him right for thinking bad thoughts. This was the first time that he had wanted to be apart from Celeste, and by admitting this to himself – by comprehending that he could feel rationally about her, that he was not cherishing her as if she were a doll – something snapped and he had appreciated the true, hidden nature of the love he felt.

'Will you marry me?' he'd asked with his elbow in his palm.

'Come here,' she'd said, and as usual he'd grinned at the way she'd needed time to answer the question. 'I'll kiss it better.'

'Kiss my *life* better,' he'd told her. 'Marry me.'

She'd actually set her lips to his beating wound. 'Tomorrow night,' she'd said, though not as an answer to his proposal.

I frightened her, he knew. A cloud or a bank of clouds now chewed up the moon and made many of the river's eyes close. He felt ashamed. He felt sick. He felt haunted.

London Bridge came alive with the traffic that he had ignored. London Bridge: where they'd met, where they'd shared an eager first kiss; where he'd made a decision about constructing a future with Celeste. And London Bridge: where she'd stamped on his dream, on his ego; and from where she'd attempted to hurl herself into the freezing sea of stars.

'Celeste,' he whispered.

Startling him badly, a voice to his left said, 'Was that her name?'

He turned. 'Excuse me?'

The other man, tall but with a slight stoop, with wire-brush sideburns and a pate only scratched with a few loose whips of greying hair, said clearly, 'The one who hurt you. Her name was Celeste?'

'It's none of your business, mate.' Turning away, he acknowledged the canny winks of the river's glowing eyes.

'Oh but it is,' the other man answered. 'If she hurt you, it's

129

very much so my business. She dumped you?'

'Among other things.' He was aware that his interlocutor was stepping closer. Every car behind him, across the strip of pavement, was making a sniffing noise as it passed.

'And you're thinking right now that your life couldn't get any worse, aren't you?'

He frowned. Determined not to pay this intruder the compliment of a sympathetic counsel, he continued to stare at the Thames.

'I *do* have something of the kind in mind, mate, yeah – thanks for asking.'

'You're wrong,' he was told. 'Things can always get worse. Haven't you *learned* that?'

He faced the other man. 'What's your game?' he said. 'What are you selling?'

130

'Selling? You amuse me. I'm *taking*.'

'Taking what?' His arms instinctively tightened against his body, to protect the wallet in his jacket pocket.

'Taking anything I desire. Have you ever heard of Sweet Tooth?'

By now a mild nervousness had changed its wings; the colours differed. He was frightened – and not of being pickpocketed either.

Acidic Slime-smells slid off the water. The clouds opened up like a flesh wound. Even the traffic seemed to gasp.

'No, I've never heard of Sweet Tooth,' he said. 'What is it?'

'Good. That means you haven't learned everything you need to know about fear. I'll be your teacher.'

'You'll do fuck, mate. I'm in a bad mood,' he bluffed. 'Piss off.'

'I love that. Dying-ember arrogance.'

'I'll call the police.'

'When? Tell me when. You're already fish-food, and believe me, there's nothing tastier than grief. You'll be quite in demand.'

'I'm warning you…' he said.

The proffered smile was carefree, was cheeky. The air seemed to gulp. 'You strolled into my plot,' was the response – the weird response.

Immediately uncertain of why he'd said it, he replied, 'But this is *my* story. It's nothing to do with you.' Nor was he certain that what he'd said was true.

'Your story is nothing without somebody else's intervention,' said Sweet Tooth. 'And she's gone. So now it's my turn. Say goodbye.'

And then their bodies met.

For the last time he thought of Celeste.   131

And then, as if in shame, the river closed its eyes.

Needles and Threes

THE SISTERS DROVE HOME in the car that they shared, with Beth at the wheel, occasionally squinting into the freckled light of dusk. 'How's your bruise?' she asked Kelly.

Although Kelly took a quick look at the grape-coloured patch in the crook of her left arm, she had already decided that the next subject of discussion would be that which they'd kept at anchor till now. 'She looked worse,' said Kelly, turning to judge Beth's profile for a reaction.

'I know.'

'One of us should have stayed with her.'

'We weren't allowed to.'

'Stayed closer then,' Kelly added.

Beth told her: 'Only tramps sleep in hospital waiting rooms, Kel.' That hair-thin inflection of sarcastic superiority – the one that they'd both secretly despised since girlhood – was in her voice. It wasn't the time to score points. 'Dr Lance made it perfectly clear: we're no help to anyone, loitering.'

Kelly pounced upon the last word. 'Loitering? Paying respect was more what I had in mind. Showing concern.'

'You've given three pints of blood in as many weeks, Kel,' said Beth. 'You've shown plenty of concern.'

In part, this seemed to mollify Kelly; the stranglehold logic took away some of her guilt's sourness.

While Beth garaged the car, Kelly opened up the house, having offered to make toast. She hushed the warning pips of their expensive burglar alarm with its numbered code. She entered the kitchen. Sensitive as ever to sudden illumination, the fish in their tank increased their varying velocities, their movements quarrelsome. By the time Beth joined her, Kelly had fed their four fish, sprinkling flakes on the surface with the dainty precision of a gourmet chef adding ingredients.

Kelly announced that she would take a bath. Naked at the basin, she fingertipped her eyes free of their lenses and flicked them at the bin, single-use as they were, the room filling with steam. Her left arm was slightly sore, a little bit heavy. Today's blood donation had been the worst yet, that zealous trainee ferreting his needle around in her bicep, gouging for a vein, like a hopeful but incompetent electrician wielding a screwdriver in a fuse box, probing for a spark. She sank into the water.

The door opened and Beth walked in. This was not unusual. 'Kelly,' she said, 'I think we've got a problem. 'We left the outside door open this afternoon. I say *we*. My fault: I thought I'd checked. But all of the *vegetables* have gone from the lean-to. The shed keys. Your polystyrene collection.'

133

Abruptly Kelly sat up, as tensed as a headache. 'Did he empty the shed?'

'I didn't look. Why steal our vegetables, for crying out loud?' Beth mused.

'Check the lawnmower.'

'Who'd want a *lawnmower*?'

'Me! Go and check!' Kelly barked, rising. Spectacles she always kept in the soap dish (a long-running bone of disagreement) and having stepped, racing with water, onto the checkerboard tiles, she hydroplaned over to fetch them.

The shed was empty. Gone were the shears, the trowels, the heavy gloves; and gone was the worm-menacing mower.

'The insurance, I suppose,' Beth was saying, 'will pick up the tab. God! Can't believe I was so stupid. But why take vegetables?'

'For a soup?' Kelly answered. 'You sound like Mum. We're

turning into her and she's not even dead yet.'

Years earlier there had been a game, a tease, as unfair as glass shards in ice-cream: a game with a young man named Nathan. They had shared him. They had taken turns going out with him. Disbelieving of their luck, Beth and Kelly had compared notes at the finalisation of a date: his words, his equally slippery tongue. Sooner or later, naturally – three weeks in – the talk had turned to sex. To the subject of who first, and what limits. Nathan simply couldn't tell them apart. Would he be able to do so in bed?

They had both yawned open to his valedictory will, one jealous of the other but neither able, unless circumstance compelled them to commit to a memory, to recall who was following whom. Their lives were blurred. They had troublingly vowed never again.

But it *was* happening again. Not sex, of course; the third party being gutted on this occasion was their mother. However, the feelings were similar.

Kelly said suddenly, 'I feel bloodless.'

'I wish,' said Beth, 'I could help. It's no fun, believe me.'

'I believe you.'

'I feel *healthy*. Feel good.'

Kelly nodded. Both rattling with secondary anger (the burglary would pass), they re-entered the house, glowing with knowledge. The evening had yet to deepen darker into a named colour; autumn would be closer than spring.

There was a chance.

Don't Drown the Man Who Taught You to Swim

(with D.F. Lewis)

'IT'S ABOUT SOMEONE who discovers the secrets of the universe as he's drowning.'

Nathaniel looked up. 'What is?'

'The story I'm writing,' said Paul with a pinched expression on his face. 'You could pay attention you know, Nat, it wouldn't hurt you.'

'Sorry. I just can't make these figures balance.'

'Then leave them unbalanced, like the rest of us,' Paul replied. He honestly believed that he was being witty. 'Do you want some squash?'

'Yes, please. And put some vodka in it while you're there.'

Paul couldn't resist a crack as he left the room. 'Yes, you're always better at eyeing up figures when you've had a few drinks, aren't you, dear.'

What had Nathaniel missed? He returned his attention to the towering totals on the sheets of paper before him. Talk about drowning by numbers! He'd have a word with a few of the team on Monday, that was for sure. Look at that! Bloody Katie: her expenses were always good for an extra few notches up the blood pressure pole, but putting *flowers* on her claims now, was she? No way.

'Here.' Paul laid down a glass, which dripped.

'For crying out loud, Paul, not on the papers!' Nathaniel transferred the glass onto a clothing catalogue, but when he wiped at the ring of moisture on the training cost breakdowns

135

for the Marketing Department, the numbers merged and ran like mascara.

'Look at that! Just look at what you've done!'

'*You* did it!' Paul argued. 'Besides, you can still read it.'

With a cavernous breath Nathaniel controlled his temper. 'Did I explain to you, Paul,' he said, 'just how important these figures are? I have here the entire financial autopsy for my silly little company for the current financial year. Are you with me so far?'

'Don't patronise me, Nat.'

'Please listen. There are no copies because Acquisitions decided, in its wisdom, to buy a tinkertoy model of copier, and we're are still waiting for the engineer to fix it. Again. Think about that, an engineer!'

Paul had decided once more to plead for reason. 'But you can still *read* everything,' he said, with an angular whine to his voice that Nathaniel could all but ignore these days.

'And this is an auditable document,' Nat said. 'An inspector *loves* this sort of incompetence. Inspectors love giving companies like mine a kick in the shins.'

Now that reason had been proven dysfunctional, Paul would resort to spiky self-defence. He said, 'You're just being *melo*.' This was his abbreviation for *melodramatic*. And once he had made this announcement he left the room.

Nathaniel cradled his head in his hands, his elbows on the table.

Pages rippled. By now the burning sensation that leaked across his abdomen when he was stressed was in full flow. *I am falling to pieces*, he thought. Numbers were bleeding in the whites of his eyes, like floaters.

Mid-evening. I still have a few hours, thought Nat. *I'll have a bath. Calm down.*

So deciding, he all but winched his bodyweight up the stairs on legs that had no strength. In the bathroom, Paul was admiring his new dental work in the mirror. They shuffled in the poky room without a word being exchanged. Nathaniel drew the bath. Firmly wedged in the heat and the plastic curtain a few minutes later, Nat was nodding off and was surprised to hear a knock at the door. Paul had brought him his drink as a peace offering. Paul leaned over and kissed Nat's bald spot.

Nat fell asleep dreaming of numbers that scuttled about the table downstairs like insects.

Gravity wanted his bones. Over the course of ten minutes, Nat slid down the soap-lacquered side of the bathtub, and the water licked at his chin. Water entered his ears with a pop and a suck, and Nat coasted an inch or two deeper. Unguented water lapped around his lips; they were a puddle. Nat opened his mouth, and swallowed.

He dreamed of a star. A star that would look in-place on top of a Christmas tree, but it was embedded into the cushion of the night, slightly wonky. It looked like a drunken king's crown. The star flapped its prongs like an undersea life form. It was encrusted and barnacled, and it sang to Nat.

Straining to hear the words made Nat twitch his head to one side. Water leaked against his tonsils. He coughed. I'm drowning, he thought, but the realisation brought no sense of panic. No sense of anything at all. Nat was drowning, but he couldn't drag himself away from the star. It sang the secrets of the universe; for Nat it was like someone was whispering through a gale. And he wanted to learn.

He came awake with the suddenness of a window blind snapping open.

Disappointment rang in his ears as he coughed up his

137

lungs.

Nat climbed into his car and hissed a prayer into the rear-view mirror. The car had been playing up for the last fortnight, and even now, as it started, it went into a series of curtsies. Finally the engine mumbled an acquiescence. Nat reversed out into the avenue. His head was full of two jealous sets of information, but the one he must concentrate on for now was that of the financial liberties being taken by certain members of staff.

Surprisingly, Katie Lenglert was waiting in his outer office. 'Good morning, Nathaniel,' she said, her accent like a tickle. Nat had always found her attractive. 'Would you have a moment?'

'I was going to call for you this morning,' Nat replied, non-committal. 'Could I just have a moment to get a coffee?'

'I'll get it,' Katie replied. 'Black, two sugars, yes?'

'Yes,' Nat replied. *She knows she's up the Suwannee*, he thought. *Your goose is cooked. Never mind a disciplinary; you're lucky if I don't call the police.* He hung his coat, played his voicemail and checked his diary. The coffee came, in the hands of a contrite Katie Lenglert. As she sat, Nat realised that she'd even chosen a short skirt for the occasion.

Beating about no bush whatsoever, Nat said, 'It's about your expenses.'

Katie paused. 'What is? What about them?'

Nat frowned. 'Isn't that why you wanted to see me?'

'No. Have I done something wrong?'

'Well, you haven't done much *right*, to tell you the truth,' he replied. 'But why did you want to see me?' If not to apologise and beg forgiveness.

'Well,' she said weirdly 'It's about your destiny.'

'Excuse me?' Was Destiny an account that the firm was working on?

'Are you sure you know what shape your destiny's taking? It's about the dream you had last night. It's time, Nathaniel.'

The dream from last night was a nice warm wash, and it flowed through him now: he had heard the heavens, jamming on an odd karaoke. Suddenly Nathaniel had the impression that he hadn't woken up. In an attempt to restore some order he went on, 'There are serious errors of judgement on your expenses forms.'

To which Katie's reply was unequivocal. 'Fuck my expenses form,' she said. 'You've got close, and you don't even know you've done it.'

'Done what? Close to what?'

'To the secrets. Jesus, Nat. Wake up.'

'Please. Go slowly.'

'We've been watching you for some time now.'

Rooted in Nat's breast, there was still a sense of curdled pride. Once more he attempted to redress the balance of superiority.

'I could say the same thing,' he mumbled.

Katie shook her head. 'You're close enough for us to be able to use you. We've waited a while.'

Nat said, 'Who's *we*?'

'Paul and I.'

'Paul who?'

'Your partner – Paul. The man who shares your bed with you every night?'

Jealousy rang its silly bell. 'And how do you know Paul?' Nat asked, blinking.

'Aren't you warm in here?' Katie enquired.

'Getting warmer by the second. Answer my question, if

you'd be so kind.'

'Okay. Here comes the difficult part.' Katie paused. 'I met Paul under the sea – the North Sea. It was bloody freezing, I can tell you. And then again I met him in a stream; this was a few years later…'

Nat interrupted. 'You know, I could call for security.'

'We drowned, Nat. Paul and I *drowned*.'

Nat's eyeballs swelled. He was cross, but he had got to the point where he had to know the answers.

'Explain your understanding of drowned,' he said.

'I mean, he and I took water into our lungs and we *died*. Is that clear enough?' Katie met Nat's gaze with full hostility. Then she softened. 'Sorry. As you might imagine, talking about the day one passed away is hardly a happy topic.'

'I can imagine.'

'People talk a lot of nonsense, Nat, about those moments,' said Katie. 'It's *not* a tunnel of light – or at least it wasn't for us, for Paul and I. It was very much like an acceptance. And do you know what I saw? I saw a constellation of stars, and I heard voices: they were trying to tell me something. But I couldn't get it. I couldn't get there – to the answers.'

'Where does Paul fit into this?' Nat asked.

'Well, at the time he didn't fit in anywhere: I was nine years old. Family holiday in Scotland – at the coast. Unbelievable, I still think, taking a family up there. For some reason I decided to go into the water, freezing though it was. Anyway, the rest writes itself, as you know. I did find the Chamber, although it was only years later that I heard it called that.'

'And what is it?'

'It's the room you go to when you're drowning, to put it simply. You go there, and only part of you comes back. My parents dragged a nine year-old's body from the waves, but part of me took up residence in the Chamber. Imprisonment might be closer to the truth, but not quite. You're in there until another poor bugger ends his life in the same place – the exact same place, which is not often, as you can imagine.'

'And this was Paul.'

'Right.'

'Well, I don't want to burst your bubble,' said Nat, 'but Paul's never even been to Scotland. We have a conversation like this every time I say how much I liked going up there as a student. He says he'd rather have his nipples chewed off than go to the frozen north. I don't feel I'm misquoting him with that either.'

Katie crossed her legs. 'The man you know as Paul might never have been to Scotland, but a *part* of him has, and that part died. His name was Jim, or James. He was an artist. He did the dumb artist thing, like: *some random woman doesn't want me – what the hell? I'll kill myself.*'

'So what was your name, before you were Katie?'

'Jean,' said Katie. 'Are you trying to trick me?'

'I'm waiting you out, Katie, and trying to see where you are going with this.'

'I already told you where it's going. It's going to your destiny.'

'Forgive me, I forgot.' There was no disguising the bitterness in Nat's tones. 'So he came to rescue you, did he?'

'That's right. He drowned in exactly the same place, just off the harbour there in Portree, so he was able to do that. The part of me that'd seen the skies and the part of him that had seen the skies were freed from the Chamber, and we joined the composite bodies that you know and love: Katie and Paul.'

'I don't love you,' said Nat.

'And you don't know Paul,' said Katie. 'But that's by the

bye. We're both of us made up of drowned souls, Nathaniel, and we're trying to get home – we're trying to find the way to the place you saw in your dreams.'

'How many souls? How many souls are inside you?'

'Thousands. Another one joins – a man for Paul and a woman for me, it always seems to be – every time one or the other rescues the other one. Do you follow me?'

'In Scotland?'

'No. There are millions and millions of Chambers in this country alone. Where there's water, there might be a drowning; and where's there's a drowning there's the possibility of a Chamber. And then the possibility of a subsequent rescue.'

There was no conversation for a good few seconds. Nat despised being spoken to by his staff in any tones other than respectful ebullience, but he couldn't stop himself listening to this woman – nor looking at her – nor posing the dangerous question.

'So what do you imagine this has to do with me?' he asked.

Katie's reply was immediate. 'You've been going there regularly since you were a child,' she said. 'You've forgotten it all. What we want to know is how the hell you've been doing it without a single drop of water entering your mouth.'

There was a pause. Then Nat tipped his head back on his neck and poured the hot coffee into his mouth, with the cup an inch from his lips. He had to drown; he had to go now. The coffee gurgled in the throat-well, and Nat spluttered.

'Come with me,' he said, standing up with coffee printed on his chin.

Katie stood. She smoothed her skirt. A worried expression was on her face.

There was something very restrictive about the *uni* in universe, and until now a secret had been kept about how private it was. Nat stepped forward and took Katie in his arms; her expression changed to a madwoman's rictus of rage. However, Nathaniel could hear no words; his ears were full of water, and blood, and singing.

Closing his eyes allowed him to escape to the Chamber, where he could write words, bathsful of words, which would fizz like his early morning nosebleeds, when he'd tried to swim under the waves for too long, until his head would ring with the pressure, all those years in his youth, when he and his family had lived by the coast, where the River Ness meets the Moray Firth.

And now, the pleasure: the ecstasy of the lightshows behind his eyes, finally learning all of the secrets.

Paul, Nathaniel knew, would have been so *proud*.

But Paul had died a long time earlier. 143

The Car-Eaters

'HOW LOST *ARE* YOU?' Dreadnought asked.

'On a scale of one to what, boss?'

'Okay. Stupid question. Tell me what you see.'

'Fields. Mud. Fuckload of sheep.'

'Right.'

'And we're gonna have to be a bit nifty here, boss. Gary hasn't had a wank for three hours and he's eyeing up the blonde one…'

Dreadnought heard a wash of laughter and a muted *Fuck off, Charlie!* – presumably from the aggrieved and accused Gary Brooker. The speaker wasn't clear because the mobile-to-mobile connection was not too shrewd. Displeased by the light-hearted approach to the failure of executing the simplest of instructions that his team seemed to have adopted, Dreadnought now said, 'Shut it.'

Something on Charlie's face – or a gesticulation of some kind – must have communicated the manager's displeasure. The mirth was snuffed out immediately.

Dreadnought paused. 'We can safely assume you're in the countryside.'

'Well, we're not in the petting zoo, boss! Of course we're in the countryside! *Nightmare* out there. Them cows are giving me the 'eebies.'

'You said sheep,' said Dreadnought.

'*Yeah.* And there's also some cows. What of it?' asked Charlie.

Dreadnought sucked air in through his teeth; it tasted of brandy and cigars. Standing up, he was made acutely aware of how woozy the two combined, over the previous seven hours, had made him feel. It was all he could do to make it over to the window.

'Boss?' It was Charlie's voice.

'Yeah, I'm here. Thinking.'

'You had a few?'

'Monoliday innaye. Listen.' He sniffed back an oil slick of mucus. 'Where do you *think* you might be?'

'In the village of Fuck-knows-where, mate.'

Dreadnought sighed. 'The wriggler gave us *directions*.'

'They were useless. "Barrel up the M14 and turn left when you see the windmill." There *was* no fucking windmill!'

'Are you sure you were on the right road?' the boss asked.

'Yeah! Billy guided us,' Charlie replied.

'Billy!

'Yeah!'

Again, Dreadnought paused. 'You gave,' he said slowly – wishing to clarify the situation. 'The *roadmap*. To *Billy.* You on crack or summing?'

'What?'

'Charlie. Billy couldn't find his own *cock* in a light drizzle. The fuck you're giving him the *roadmap* for, cunt?'

'He's from this part of the country!'

Irrefutable. Dreadnought decided to let the point go. 'Re-trace your steps. Get back on the M.'

'We did that! It took us to the village of Carnimagine Weirder.'

Fighting his own combative instincts (and the influences of booze), Dreadnought said, 'I'm losing patience, Charlie. What you want me to suggest?' Dreadnought demanded, slamming a palm down on the windowsill. The dolphin knickknack and the framed signed photo of Leonard Cohen from when he was

just a kid fresh from Montreal, jumped up like startled parakeets. 'I'm paying you two grand for two hours' work. I'm
hardly a slum landlord, mate.'

'I didn't say you was!' Charlie protested.

The call ended shortly afterwards. Feeling helpless, stupid and enraged, Dreadnought stepped into the lounge and
screamed at the television screen for a little while. The television was not on. But there was something richly satisfying
about venting spleen on a darkened version of your own reflection. Following that (feeling better) Dreadnought played the
Everly Brothers' album at a battlefield volume, and started to
get ready for his night out with Mazza.

Shower. Talc and aftershave (no shave needed). Pin-striped
whistle. Hello, *sailor*, Dreadnought thought, regarding his strut
in the full-length bedroom mirror. He examined his physique
from different angles. *Looking good…* The only sensible negative
conclusion that he could draw was this: *getting fat, mate.* How
does a fit bird like Mazza fancy a hobgoblin like you? Think
positive. Find that mobile.

It had to be in the house somewhere. Dreadnought had
been looking for it, on and off, for the last three hours. He had
tried calling his mobile number from the landline. No use. *The
phone you are calling has been switched off. Please try again later.* Well,
there wasn't much later to go. It was already five p.m. And
Dreadnought had been drinking since ten in the morn. The
day's holiday that he'd elected to take was to celebrate the occasion of Mazza's birthday. At dawn he'd given her a card and
bunged her two hundred pounds, instructing her to *have a good
day.*

What had she been up to? Dreadnought wondered, pouring
another drink. His last, he vowed. He filled the wine glass with
brandy. The gym was a cert, she would have done that: she

146

was addicted to the place. The Corner Sauna? Perhaps. Then a leisurely lunch with some of her mates – he didn't like to call them *girlfriends*, as she did: too erotic – and a feminine appraisal of many a waiter and passer-by, from both the rear and front.

Fair do's. Only human, weren't she? Dreadnought downed the brandy and had a little weep for a while.

I'm mashed, he realised. Dreadnought laughed into the bedroom mirror. The meal at Pekinese Pete's – the meal that was due to follow – seemed as heavy as an anchor to him now. And where the hell was Mazza anyway?

Dreadnought imagined her gone. He imagined a Mazza-shaped space beside him, on the couch. The shape had no colour, texture or aroma – but he knew that it had once been her. As he got to his feet (one final brandy, he believed) the shape moved slightly; it fidgeted for a more comfortable position.

The telephone rang: the *Bonanza* theme tune. Dreadnought thumbed the green key. 'Yo.'

'That the Dreadnought?' he was asked.

'Yeah. Who's this?'

'The night have a very short memory, man.' (An African accent. Dreadnought rifled through his mental filing cabinets.) 'It forget *you* long before *you* forget *it*.'

Dreadnought sniffed triumphantly. 'That you, Bovril?'

'No, man. You don't need me.'

'No, mate. Plenty more fish in the sea,' Dreadnought said. 'Just educate my grey matter for a minute, eh? Be a pal. Why do you need *me*?'

'I *don't* need you. But your wife does. Dinner for two, is it? With you charming missus. Do you want to hear her scream? She got a very pretty scream.'

It was Bovril on the other end of the line, Dreadnought

was certain. Bovril: named not because of the colour of his
skin (Dreadnought's first assumption, and a rare concession of
his to a racist slur) but because of his build: the cunt was beefy.
Bovril was famed for his April Fool jokes – the sort that went
on for 365 days of the year.

Nevertheless, Dreadnought said, 'No. I've heard her when
she's seen a spider climbing from the plughole. Why don't you
let me speak to her instead?'

'No dice.'

By this point Dreadnought had developed an increase in
heartbeat-volume, not to mention a light pancake of perspiration. 'So what do you actually *want* there, Chuckles?'

'What I *want* is to hurt her regardless. On general principle.
I have a superstition about letting a woman out of a locked
room unharmed. But what I'm gonna *get* is to get you to call
off the hounds.'

'What hounds?'

'Them sniffing up the M14,' said the caller. 'Call 'em off,
bro.'

Dreadnought waited. He examined his pulse, as though it
would Morse him the relevant information.

'I don't know what you're referring to,' said Dreadnought.

The caller laughed. 'Textbook, man. A *textbook* response…
Lionel? Give her a prod there. Give her a tickle.'

A bloodcurdling scream can remind you of those good
things in life: of the times when you didn't need to scream
against maltreatment. But the one that Dreadnought heard
now was different. It convinced him, albeit briefly, that his beloved Mazza was being nudged, shouldered, prodded into a
mincer. It didn't even *sound* like her.

'Enough!' he shouted.

'Lionel,' he heard. 'Pit stop, man.'

'Okay,' said Dreadnought. 'You're working for Des Lewis.'

'I don't remember providing that info.'

'You want me to call off the strike on his lockup. Have I got that right?'

'Right as rain showers.'

'Cool. It's done. Just let her go.'

'Man? She on the Tube in a lickety-split. No further damage guaranteed. Spit shake?'

'Spit shake,' Dreadnought agreed, mired in those two words: *further damage*. Dreadnought opened the window. London – at this hour, in this season – smelt of old fruit and zoos. A fly struggled in: for the warmth. Dreadnought almost wept again as he crushed the thing on his manual typewriter, using a yellowing copy of *The Sun*.

Coffee! he decided. He dropped the tabloid into the trash. He filled the kettle. Business. Dreadnought placed the phone to the left sideburn. It drilled its code into the early evening (outside, the air was turning mauve) and after a few rings Charlie said:

'We found the cunt.'

'Finally,' said Dreadnought. 'Now come home. All expenses covered.'

'But Dreadnought. We ain't done the ness.'

'I understand. Come home.'

Charlie sounded disappointed, like a child who had had his ice cream cone snatched away. 'Aw, Dreadnought,' he said. 'I was looking forward to that. Ain't scalded a place for yonks.'

'I'll give you another gig, Charlie.'

A key skittled in the front door lock. The door opened: the customary cat's mewing. Dreadnought froze.

'Mazza?' Dreadnought called.

'Yeah. Who else you expecting? Sorry I'm late. I was chatting to a drunken doctor in The Bloody Chamber. He was such a *lech*, Boo. You'd a lamped him. He couldn't keep his eyes off me chest. And Lorraine said – What's up?'

'You're okay,' said Dreadnought.

By now she was in the bedroom, unbuttoning her blouse. 'What *is* it?' she asked.

'I was worried about you, that's all.'

'So you went on the lash. Nice one. I feel so flattered. Come on.'

'Come on what?' Dreadnought asked.

'Get changed.'

'I *am* changed!'

Mazza snorted. 'I ain't going out with someone who stinks like an ashtray.'

Dreadnought could summon no suitable riposte. Instead he inquired after the whereabouts of his mobile phone – Mazza denied all knowledge – and unzipped his fly with a sigh of longsuffering perturbation.

Bewildered by what had happened, Dreadnought had re-suited himself and gelled back his hair. Though he disliked having been told what to do, he acknowledged the improvement.

At Pekinese Pete's they were shown to a corner table.

'Take it easy on the drink, Boo,' Mazza warned her man.

'I will. But it's your birthday. A bottle of bubbly, my son,' he instructed the waiter. Dreadnought was in very good spirits. 'And I don't need to read this,' he added. 'I know exactly what I want: a steak. With loads of chips.'

'Certainly, sir. And madam: would you like a few minutes to decide?'

'I'll have a steak too, please,' she said. 'Medium rare.'

'Of course. And how would you like *your* steak done, sir,' the waiter asked.

'Incinerate the cunt.'

'Dreadnought!'

'What?'

'Your manners!'

'*What?*'

'We're in a public place!'

'Sorry. Incinerate the cunt if you'd be so *kaned.*' Dreadnought leaned back and lit a cigarette. 'Please and sugar bollocks,' he continued.

The waiter (visibly shaken) now offered a court-jester bow, and withdrew.

'He'll spit on your food,' said Mazza.

'And he'll go home in three cabs. What's the matter, babe?' 151

Mazza was staring at the tablecloth. It took her a few seconds to compose her thoughts. 'I just wanted a nice night out. Is that so much to ask?'

Appearing wounded, Dreadnought said, 'But I *am* having a nice night out!'

'Lower your voice. Please,' said Mazza.

'Okay,' the man said in a reigned-in volume.

'You used the C-word to our waiter, Boo! For fuck's *sake…*'

Dreadnought's brow flexed and held. To give him due credit, he did seem to be on the verge of confusion. When he said, 'Do you mean *cunt?*' his wife was almost charmed.

'Yes, Dreadnought. I mean that word.'

'But I say cunt all the time!'

'I know. And will you *please* just lower your fucking voice?' said Mazza.

The hands were held up, palms facing. '*Mea culpa*, toots. Forgive me.'

Under no circumstances was he going to wake up tomorrow morning. The bottle of brandy at home had been chased by a magnum of champagne with the meal. And then of course there had been the mandatory palate-cleansing White Horse whiskies while Mazza had settled into her mango sorbet...

Questioning the non-appearance of any talent for walking, Dreadnought claimed Mazza in an amorous form of headlock. They performed a ragged three-legged race to the Bentley. No sooner had they arrived (and briefly bickered, as they had on the way here, through the subject of who would drive) than a voice arrested their attention.

'Yo,' it said. 'You the man.'

Dreadnought turned. Mazza turned.

The interlocutor was as wiry as a greyhound's penis, as Dreadnought would later review the altercation.

'You eating all your greens?'

Not alone either. The Wire was flanked by three average-sized but bored-looking Bengali lads. It was the expressions of inscrutable indifference that bothered Dreadnought the most: the welcoming committee had already formed the opinion that what was due to follow was going to be simple. Either they were tastier than they appeared or the myth of safety in numbers had yet to be disproved to them.

'So what's for dinner, Big D for Dreadnought?'

Dreadnought frowned. 'Horseshit soup,' he answered. 'With dumplings and fucking turnips. Now get *away* from me, lads. You don't want me.' And he remained fairly impressed with his turn of phrase.

'Young lion, you is!'

The wallflowers glanced wearily in Dreadnought's direction. So unimpressed did they seem that one – to the left as Dreadnought returned the attention – went as far as to begin cleaning out his thumbnails with what looked like a plectrum.

'He *sly*. Missus just get her Get Outta Jail card and he here with another!' Spoken in stately tones that smacked of genuine appreciation. 'Can't fail to be impressed with you *panache*.'

'Dreadnought?' Mazza's grip tightened. 'What's he talking about?'

'*This* is my missus,' said Dreadnought. 'Dunno who you *think* you had.'

'Her name Mazza.'

'That's right.'

The other man pointed. 'She too?' he asked with high-pitched incredulity, his teeth now bared as flawless as a baby dolphin's. 'Man! He even bang bitches the same *name*!'

'Style.' This was one of the other young men, speaking for the first time and apparently cleaning his own teeth with his tongue.

153

'What you want?'

'*Work* for you, D.'

'Excuse me?'

'Work, man. We show *nish*. A. Teef. You follow me?'

Dreadnought smiled: he couldn't help himself. 'Where you boys learn your patter? Or *you* patter, I should say. What you show me is *cliché*. What you *show* me's incompetence. You got that, bollocks? You trounce the wrong fucking bird and then expect me to roll over and fart show tunes for you. Get *back* on your donkeys and fuck off back to Tower Hamlets and Brick Lane. We're leaving. Nice offer, ladies.'

With which Mazza unlocked the driver's door.

'Carn, babe.'

'Dreadnought.'

Long-sufferingly, Dreadnought turned, a barnacled sneer *aglow* on his features. 'Don't tell me.'

'Dreadnought Xavier Flex.'

'Don't tell me. You're gonna steal me crayons. You're gonna report me to the Head.'

'We gonna hang the girl in the back of the van.'

For a second Dreadnought said nothing. Watching the manner in which his head sank into his shoulders (his jowls pooled outwards) was akin to watching a deckchair collapse. In fact, he was coping with a digestive matter. The result was a furious and fiery eructation – one of such severity that it made his lips flap. 'Let's see her then,' he instructed.

'Dreadnought, please…' said Mazza.

By flinging his right hand to the side and pulling it backwards quickly, the threatener managed to make his fingers snap together. 'You the man, baby. Round the corner, by the trash: the blue V Dub.'

Dreadnought looked at Mazza and put a finger to his lips. 'No backchat, sweetie, okay? Get in and lock the doors. I'm not back in ten minutes, call Charlie. If anyone gets in your way they're a bowling pin. Got it? And what do we do with bowling pins?'

Mazza hesitated. 'Knock 'em down?' she asked.

Dreadnought nodded. 'That's me girl.'

He kissed her forehead and watched her curl into the driver's seat.

'Gentlemen? Shall we?' Maintaining an air of collected displeasure, Dreadnought led the way to the aforementioned vehicle. He was delighted to hear a muttered: 'Nuts of marble, man…'

And don't you forget it, he thought. Not bothering to twist his neck, he raised his voice slightly and said: 'You boys got names you'd like to share?'

The one in charge answered first. 'Garveenathan.'

Dreadnought sniffed. 'Sri Lankan. Where do you get your African tones?'

'Mum's boyfriend.'

'Don't *tell* him, man!' said a voice that Dreadnought didn't know. He stopped walking a mere five metres from the Volkswagen.

Then he turned a one-eighty. Eyeing each of Garveenathan's accomplices in turn, Dreadnought asked: 'Which one of you posers said that? Eh?' He stepped towards the one closest to him. 'Was it you, ratboy?'

'Mighta been.'

Dreadnought's arm moved quickly: it was no more than a blur until, a fraction of a second later, his fingers had secured a puckered grip on the lad's testicles. 'What *is* it then, son?' said Dreadnought into the youngster's mangled howl. 'A case of practice makes perfect? Eh? Practise being a cunt long enough and you'll get there. *Eh?*'

'What?'

'"What, *sir?*" you piece of shit,' Dreadnought corrected. '"What, *sir.*"' His eyes were wide open, staring straight into his victim's lowered, crinkled lids; after another second his attention had rolled up the shutters. Nevertheless, Dreadnought now addressed the remainder of the group. 'Nobody − and I do mean *nobody* − fucking moves. Or imagine pigshit through a sieve: you've got the idea. Now you.' Dreadnought smiled. 'Where the *dickens*, dear boy, does a ponce like you get off, telling your leader what he should and shouldn't do? And *kindly*, for the love of Christ, get your hands off my fingers before I become aggrieved.'

'You ain't my leader, man.'

'*Name.*'

'What?'

Dreadnought squeezed harder.

'What, sir?' said the other man.

'It's roll call time. I asked your *name*.'

'Muzahid.'

'Good. Nicely remembered,' said Dreadnought. 'Well, Muzahid; listen up. When I said *leader* I weren't talking about myself. I was talking about Garveenathan there. Tell him you're sorry – for your disrespect.'

Having little choice in the matter, Muzahid apologised; no time at all later, Dreadnought had released the gonads and was rubbing his hands together, as if for warmth.

'You've earned some respect there, Garveenathan my son,' said Dreadnought, turning his back on the group and seeming to address the blue van. 'Someone else might've weighed in there like a Sumo. You kept your head, mate. Nice one.' Dreadnought started walking. 'Now. Didn't your mums tell you it's bad manners to keep a lady waiting. That's *their* job. Get the fucking doors open.'

Muzahid was endeavouring to regain some lost face. 'I coulda slice you up, man.'

'At the expense of your toolkit?' asked Dreadnought. 'Where'd you get him from, Garveenathan-son. He's embarrassing you. No sense of priorities. Send him to bed without his supper. And get *this door open*. I'm going grey fuck's sake.'

Threats made Dreadnought sharper: giving or receiving them – it didn't much matter. The groundwork had been done. He had singled out one of their pack. It was this one who would push Dreadnought into the back of the van: to re-assert himself in the eyes of his peers. Straight from the Ark, mate...

Naturally the van contained no whimpering lady; no one was trussed up or hogtied or bound. There was a grey fireman's blanket and a blue box of tools; a couple of dog-eared

156

computer game mags. A shovel. But there was no one being held prisoner.

The scream? The one he'd heard over the phone? It had come to Dreadnought during the meal: a BBC sound effects CD. Every music library had one. So, even as Dreadnought was shoved forwards onto the blanket (the brim of the van ledge bit his thighs and upper legs), he had a brief instant to re-acknowledge that the lads had at least done something original. Flattering, in its way: that they'd want to impress him so badly. Whatever the motive for the upcoming abduction ended up being, there might be some work for these boys after all.

Dreadnought went through the motions – the grunt of disapproval, the ragged cuss – as he waited for his team to pile out of the restaurant. To be sure, it would be Charlie who led. Charlie Peacock, Gary Brooker, then probably Old Bill, Wedg- es, Drama and Strawberry Jeff. You never knew: maybe even Pekinese Pete would join in, for the laugh.

As it happened, the restaurant-owner did not join in; but it was all over swiftly, regardless. Dreadnought stood straight- ening his tie and checking his cufflinks while he waited for the volume of moaning to die down. No hurry.

'Not bad, lads,' he finally said to the men, defeated, blood- ied, who now sat cross-legged (at Charlie's insistence: made it harder to stand up quickly) on the cold car park ground. 'Not bad at all. Now, who you working for?'

It took a while. It usually did, if the game was any good. Garveenathan was silently elected spokesman, and he breathed the three syllables of their employer's name – he breathed them into Dreadnought's knees.

'Well well well,' said Dreadnought, to whom the words *Des Lewis* had come as a surprise. Not that it didn't make sense, of course; it made perfect sense. Lewis gets wind that Dreadnought's boys are coming. He sets up a counter-attack. Logic. But Lewis was a salesman; where did he make the connections? A salesman with form, undoubtedly – twice imprisoned for selling inadequate and dangerous goods: a fire-friendly, holds-its-tongue fire alarm and some pseudo-elastic bungee rope – so maybe, while inside, Lewis had talked to someone who'd talked to someone…

Dreadnought reconsidered. He registered his opinion and the reason for it.

'It's bollocks, mate. Des Lewis ain't got the nous,' he said. 'Yeah. He owes me money but he didn't know my team was on their way. Or if he did then someone's squealed. And I'll address that issue in due course.' He smiled. 'No. You heard the words Des Lewis for the first time this afternoon, on the phone. So I'll repeat: *who are you working for?*'

'Boss?' This was Gary Brooker. 'Should we do this somewhere less public?' he said.

'We're nearly there, Gaz,' said Dreadnought. 'No point wasting precious petrol. All someone has to do is give me a name and a reason. Then we can all be on our way. I need a wee. I'm going back inside. In the meantime, fellas, I would urge you to rethink your code of loyalty. An honourable silence is one thing, but Charlie-Boy?'

'Boss?'

'What happened to the last cunt who wouldn't tell me summing?'

'We glued his lips together, boss.'

'We did indeed. Hold that thought while I go and point Percy,' said Dreadnought, exiting stage left. 'Charlie. You're in charge,' he called over his shoulder as an afterthought.

'Couldn't you just go against the bins, boss?' asked Charlie.

'We are not animals. Besides, I want to check on Mazza. It

is her *birthday*, after all.' And he wanted a little more thinking time, too. He'd established that someone had called Pekinese Pete's to check if a Mr Flex had dining reservations for that evening. Pete had confirmed to the caller that Mr Flex had, at eight o'clock. Pete had been adamant that the caller had spoken with a British accent: it had been the voice of whoever was paying the boys' salaries. But how would Des Lewis have known where Dreadnought and Mazza had intended to dine? How would anyone?

The Bentley was not in the place where he'd left it. Evidently Mazza had taken his instructions to the letter: she had left the premises (but Charlie's mobile hadn't rung).

A *doctor*... What had Mazza's words been this afternoon? She was sorry she was late; a drunken doctor had been eyeing her up... in The Bloody Chamber. Who was he, this 'doctor'? What had Mazza told him?

Call off the hounds, Garveenathan had demanded – again, on the phone. If Des Lewis hadn't been involved... who currently perceived Dreadnought to be a threat?

'Dreadnought?'

The man turned to face the entrance to the restaurant. It had been constructed, unconvincingly in Dreadnought's opinion, to resemble a dragon's open maw; there were lanterns on its upper lip, which looked like zits. Marzena, the Head Waitress, was waving Dreadnought over.

'You've got a call.'

'Ominous,' he tried to joke as he approached her long body. But it really was ominous. Not for the first time, he had the feeling that he was being watched.

Inside, the lights, the noise – the purple heat. The telephone on the front desk was mock old-fashioned: the finger on the dial and turn variety.

'You're speaking to Dreadnought,' the man declared.

'I feel like the Head of State for such a privilege.'

'Return the courtesy. Who's this?'

'Mr Smith or Mr Jones. You decide.'

'And you want what?' Dreadnought asked.

'You to rescue your damsel in distress.'

'Oh I see. Another Mazza-wannabe, yeah? Well lemme tell you a story. That record's so worn, mate. What's this all about?'

The next voice Dreadnought heard was his wife's.

'He's telling the truth, Boo,' she said.

'Boo?' Dreadnought heard at an equal volume.

'You on speaker phone?' he asked.

'*Boo?*' laughed Mr Smith. 'That's priceless.'

'Yeah yeah.' Dreadnought's mood was poised equidistant between rage and incredulity. 'I believe you've got Mazza. Now what do you want me to do about it?'

'There's a hundred thousand things you could do,' said Mr Smith.

'Right.'

'And they've all got the Queen's head on them.'

'Money?' asked Dreadnought. 'This timewasting charade has been about *money*? You sad, mindless amateur.' Dreadnought marshalled his questions. 'What were the Asian lads for?'

'Decoy.'

'Great,' said Dreadnought, self-disgustedly. 'How far away did you smell me? Where you at?'

'Boo? I'm in the village of Fuck-knows-where.'

Dreadnought waited. More than the faked Mazza scream had that afternoon; more than the appearances of Garveenathan and company had, a mere ten minutes earlier; more even than hearing the wife's tones on the blower – these words *chilled him.*

It was too much of a coincidence. *Fuck-knows-where:* what Charlie had said on the phone, earlier on. But *Charlie?* Charlie had been on the Dreadnought payroll for the better part of two decades.

I want to understand, thought Dreadnought. There's got to be a rational explanation.

Dreadnought cut quite a figure as he sprinted from the reception area of Pekinese Pete's to the car park around the corner. To his own consternation, he arrived in need of oxygen.

'Charlie-mate,' he said. 'The fuck you been speaking to?'

'Eh?'

'Coz if it's you, Charlie, you're pudding and pie. You got me?'

'Boss. What's tickled your ring?' asked Charlie Peacock.   161

'Been with me how long?' asked Dreadnought.

'Eighteen.'

'And I ever give you grief?'

'Nah.'

'So *why*, Charlie? Why fist me like this?'

Charlie was frowning. 'I don't know what you're on about,' he said.

Dreadnought paused. Then he pointed a finger at the ringleader of the opposition, saying: '*This* cunt? He's bread. Fetch some fat from the kitchens. Set fire to his shins and let's see how much he knows or don't know. Now.'

'Boss,' said Charlie, nonplussed. 'It's done. Ask and you'll receive.'

'I know that,' Dreadnought added. He sniffed. Then he said, 'The van. Charlie. Get in that van and find my mobile phone. Cunt's in there somewhere – or else we been bugged.'

Dreadnought's brain was saying: *No way, no way...* It

couldn't be happening. This couldn't be true.

She wouldn't...

Given the aggravated exaggeration of his facial features, Dreadnought's lips were nearly as wide as his visage. His lips were all but touching his earlobes. It was Mazza who had opined, early on, that when he took this mood upon himself, he resembled nothing more than a perturbed rabbit.

'And *these* comedians,' he went on, referring to the now battle-weary *bandidos* – shrunken, defeated and desperate. Salt-bespattered worms. 'They can get to work. I've had my dinner. Now it's their turn. Eat this fucking van,' he said, turning his attention to the rear doors of the same.

She was leaving him. Or she had left him.

What was worse?

162

Charlie had clambered aboard. But Dreadnought had fought his way through a certain fog and had reasoned, of course, that the mobile would have to be in the van in which Charlie had travelled that morning: not this one.

'Come on out, Charlie,' said Dreadnought.

Mazza was leaving him and she had hatched a plan to get money out of him, to boot. The latter hurt him more than the former. Deep down he had always known that keeping her by his side would be like cuddling ice cream. Sooner or later... The mist was red in Dreadnought's eyes.

'Why these cunts not eating?' he asked Gary Brooker.

Brooker held his hands up. 'Run out of knives and forks, boss,' he said.

Dreadnought punched him in the stomach.

'Cheeking *me*,' he wished to affirm. 'Cheeking *me*, you cheese?'

Doubled over, Brooker said, 'No, boss. Just a joke...'

'Well don't. Gandhi. Get munching on that fucking hubcap. Start this second. Go.' Dreadnought did the rabbit look again, aiming for inscrutable insouciance. 'Who's got a mobile?' he asked.

Strawberry Jeff volunteered.

The number was second nature. Eventually it was answered.

'Mazza.'

After a long pause, Dreadnought's wife said: 'Boo.'

'Why, babe?'

'…Why what?' said Mazza.

'You're unreal to me now, you know that don't you?'

'Is it time for threats, Boo?'

'For you it is. Why not *tell* me?' Dreadnought asked.

'Because…'

Dreadnought ended the call. Systematically he looked around. 'I don't see much *van* being eaten,' he remarked, wiping a tear from his eye.

Scrounge

SWANS GLIDED IN THE DISTANCE. They were too far away for Albert to throw bread at, although there'd been a time when they would have been within his range. He didn't like that. Sighing, he stood – to a symphony of creaks. He hated everything about being old. The rattling of his joints; the shortness of breath. Memory problems – and a frequently insistent bladder… He hated it all. Loathed this patient shuffle to which he'd been reduced for the last few years. He hated having to do everything in slow motion.

The daily walk to the park, come rain or shine, had long since lost its allure. Back at home Albert prepared a sandwich, even though he'd be collected in less than an hour and taken into the bosom of his son's family for Sunday dinner. They always ate too late – and they didn't give him enough to keep a gerbil going. Nor did the tightfistedness end there. Margaret, Albert's daughter-in-law, kept a stern and proprietorial eye on the drink as well. A schooner of sherry while they discussed the week's events, both international and within the family; a glass of medium white while the food was going down. Albert sighed the latest in a day-long chain of sighs, and he had a brandy to gee-up his thought processes.

In the car an air of preposterous gloom presided. Albert's grandson, Blake, was sulking on the back seat: an hour earlier his team had suffered a trouncing. When Albert spotted the boy's football shirt he made his usual inquiry: 'Did you win?'

'No. They gutted us, man.'

'Don't call your grandfather *man*.'

'Jesus.'

'And don't take the Saviour's name in vain.'

'We played crap,' Blake added.

Now that is just taking the Michael, thought Albert, ninety minutes later. 'Yum yum,' he said, instantly berating himself for his choice of words. Yum *yum*? Three Brussel sprouts: count 'em – three! A leaf of roast beef; four excellently crispy but tiny potatoes. A slick of gravy, dark as ichor.

He had learned not to eat at his usual speed – eating being one of the few things that Albert could still manage quickly – because he'd be all but licking the plate clean while the rest of his alien brood were chewing every slice of shaved carrot thirty-six times. Keeping that pace was not easy.

Blake perked up by the time the ice-cream was served. He asked his grandfather if he wanted to play computer games. Albert followed the boy upstairs.

Donning the headgear always reminded Albert, unpleasantly, of his potholing days, in his twenties and thirties – before his friend had drowned. There was something claustrophobic and final about the apparatus: the other image he sometimes received was that of the condemned man's cowl.

'What's the game?' Albert asked.

'You're a French assassin.'

'*Hee haw.*'

'Gramps. And you've gotta rescue the girl in the warehouse. She's been kidnapped by aliens and they're going to eat her brains.'

Probably more nutritious than what I've just sat through, thought Albert. 'Okay. Do I have any weapons?'

'Your gun fires acid.'

'Charming…'

'But you only have a few rounds left.'

'So the odds are against me, eh?' Albert winked. 'Go on then – let's start.' Why a *French* assassin? he thought as he moved towards a sugar cube-sized warehouse in the distance, across the car park. Why a *warehouse*? Why wait before snacking on a kidnapped girl's brain?

Helpfully, his alien ambushers announced their presence, with whoops and yells; now where did they come from? Albert wondered. They all squared up. His grandson had taught him the rudimentary principles of such games on many occasions: deal with the worst threat first. Well, this one – an Oriental skinny guy – was carrying a gun. Albert hoofed him in the gonads. The gun went off, but the bullet soared into the air.

Roundhouse kick; headbutt. Down they went, the buggers, two by two. Albert had started to mimic the clichéd cries. The fight was soon over. Albert resumed his stroll towards the waiting princess.

He had another fight to kill time, on the building's threshold, then he carried the young woman in a fireman's lift – back into the sunlight, to freedom. In his ear she whispered, 'Thank you.' She looked very similar to his daughter-in-law, with her raven bob and her pretty upturned nose.

The background music faded. The air smelled like barbecue coals, and Albert tugged the headgear from his features with a little more force than was necessary, but he was starting to feel trapped.

What he saw made him think – inappropriately – of his favourite brandy glass, which had been chipped and scuffed over the years, so that it scarcely resembled a glass at all.

That glass was what came to mind when Albert viewed his grandson, viewed Blake. 'Oh dear Christ,' Albert muttered.

The boy lay almost at a right angle to himself. But the bend was not at the waist. On a blood-skanked carpet, Blake was bent at the right hip – his left hip bone had split through the skin and shirt both and was protruding like an elephant's tusk. A horrified expression was on the boy's face – and this alone, if Albert had seen nothing else, would have been enough to seize and squeeze his heart.

Was it instinct or inevitability that lead Albert to inspect his own hands?

And was it the sight or the inference that told his stomach to roll over and beg?

His hands were covered in blood.

The air seemed to sizzle.

Something snapped – and Albert was aware of the noise of feet on the staircase.

The pain in his heart slipped away – fired out as if from a slingshot. What is happening to me? he had to wonder – before his fingers began to tingle. He reached for the holster, inexplicably athwart his waist and hips.

Dear God no… he screamed inside his head.

Inside his head…

Where another voice was waiting, although it spoke not a single word right now. Albert could feel it – feel *him*.

Don't do it, Albert shouted as he watched his own arm being held out horizontal, stiff – and ready.

He tried very hard to shout out loud.

Shut up! he was told, and the accent was markedly French.

The bedroom door swung open.

Albert's son – Blake's father – formed an expression of terror with his whole body. There was no time for words. A capsule of concentrated acid crossed the distance between the French assassin's gun and the man of the house's mouth in a hundredth of a second. The bolt sheared his lower lip clean off; it impacted with Blake's wallpaper and slid down the prints of footballers like a slug.

Albert's daughter-in-law squealed. Uselessly she made a break for the stairs and was halfway down the flight when the French assassin's second shot drilled a hole in her pinched-to-gether shoulder blades. The impact set her sailing into the air like a hang-glider.

Crack.

She landed on the boot-rack, on the phone stand, on her face.

'*Hee haw,*' said the French assassin.

'Dear Lord,' said Albert sickly.

Faster than had seemed possible in more than a decade, Albert walked to the park. Not that he was aware of much of the journey. He had passed out. When he woke, his arms were swinging like a sergeant-major's, and in one of his hands, the left, was the acid-gun.

He was trying to blot out the memories.

'Why are you doing this?' he asked as he passed a queue of people at a cashpoint. Some turned.

It's what you wanted, said the Frenchman inside Albert's head.

'What is?'

'Liberty. Equality... Egalitarianism.' Out loud.

Despite the velocity of their dash, Albert did not feel out of breath. He felt cramped from head to feet; and an alarm bell rang between his ears, just above the assassin's timbre.

The park.

Sprout-green grass spread for a mile in every direction, but Albert and the assassin weren't here to admire nature. At a trot they reached the pond, at which point the assassin raised Albert's left arm.

'Don't do it,' Albert pleaded.

A few shrieks were heard at the sight of the old man spraying the water with bolts of acid. One of the swan detonated; its neck was detached and formed a question mark briefly before it landed back down in the dappled tide.

I'm helping you to fight back… said the assassin.

I don't want to fight back, Albert replied.

Yes, you do.

The gun was out of ammunition. The air hissed with settling water; there were whimpers; there was bird flight – heavy wings stretching.

And it's what I do, Albert: I rescue people.

'I don't need rescuing…' Albert reached for rationality. The extra energy that he now commanded; the weapon in his grip… However weird it seemed, he was still inside the game.

With his free hand he flapped at his head, trying to remove headgear that wasn't there. The Frenchman, perplexed, had to ask him what he thought he was doing. 'I'm not here,' Albert concluded. 'This isn't happening.'

The Family Massacre that didn't happen?

I have to get out of the game, thought Albert.

What game?

Be quiet… Albert turned the gun up to his own face.

No! shouted the Frenchman.

The acid opened his face up, like a magazine on a lawn, being pawed at by a breeze. A jolt – like an electric shock – and Albert was back in Blake's bedroom. Sweating and swearing as he pulled off the headgear.

Blake looked worried. 'You okay, Gramps?' he asked.

'Yes, I'm fine,' Albert lied, now acutely aware of a pain on the underside of his upper right arm. When he lifted up the limb he could see that his shirt was ripped and there was blood confusing an open wound.

The pain became worse.

'What the hell happened?' he asked, as stars moved in front of his vision.

There was the smell of something foul about the room, but what the boy said next made Albert forget about passing out.

He said, 'I was hungry. I took a bite. You don't mind, do you?'

'You did what?' Albert squinted.

'I'm sorry, I couldn't wait!' said Blake, with the fear in his eyes of one who hopes that a parent won't be informed of a misdemeanour.

'Blake! Dad!' came a voice calling up from downstairs. 'Dinner's ready!'

'But we've had dinner,' said Albert.

The boy looked at him blankly. After a second or two he said, 'Are you sure you're okay?' in the kind of voice that doesn't yearn for an answer. It was a way of backing out of the door.

Albert was certainly hungry. There were many things that he could deny about today, but that fact was not one of them. He stood. The room needed air – and possibly so did he.

Down the stairs. And still nothing made sense. His arm pounded with pain. There was rage in his eyes; he felt exhausted.

He followed Blake into the kitchen. Gasped loudly enough for his son and his daughter-in-law to look up from their meals.

It wasn't the latter's uncanny resemblance to the woman in the game that had provoked this response, however. Nor, particularly, was it the sight of the two parents, naked, standing beside the kitchen table; nor even the daubs of blood down their chests and in their pubic wigs...

170

'Take your clothes off, Dad. You don't want to ruin your nice suit.'

No. It was the vision of the man from the game, the gun wielder, lying flat out, snapped sideways, on the table. He was raw with bruising, but had he still lived that would have been the least of his problems. Albert's younger generation had already begun to devour him. As Albert watched, his daughter-in-law scooped a handful of innards through a well in the victim's torso. She raised them to her mouth as Blake said:

'Cool. What flavour?'

Albert's son swallowed, 'French,' he said.

171

Window Shopping

VERY SOON THE MAN WHO has been carrying the tools will knock on the glass and want to know what I am doing here. He will be polite but firm; he will insist on knowing my business while making it clear that he would not be discharging his duties if he kept silent on my being there. Then, in the course of leaning down to speak through the window he will see the laptop on the passenger seat and the puppy in the back, asleep on a nest of towels and blankets.

My observer is one of the school's grounds-men. He has circled the car four times now, not getting any closer on each occasion, but completing his circumference at a faster rate on each pass. Every time he orbits, he carries a different tool – most recently a shovel – and I try to imagine what he must think. The car I am in park abuts the school's playgrounds, after all, and I have parked in a space near the link-fence that separates the two functional areas. Every time a bell rings from within the school building a different year group is released, and seventy or eighty children engage in a twenty-minute play session a matter of metres from the passenger door window.

He might think I am window shopping, but I am not. I am waiting for my stepfather to emerge from the building, his meeting soon completed. When I see him, I will make a show of hurrying over to the entrance. I might even stand beside him, hip to hip, and ease an arm around his waist to support his weight. I aim to claim his briefcase, and to help him back to my mother's car, moving as slowly as he needs to in the aftermath of the operation on his feet that has required me to drive him to this school in the first place. As we leave the property, I hope to see the grounds-man. And I will offer him a wink.

But Mark surprises me. I have returned to the essay I must write and submit this holiday, with the warm laptop now spread-eagled on my knees, when the car boot opens behind me. In the sudden wash of cold air from outside, Doris the dog wakes and protests with a single yelp. Mark has exited the school by a different door and has circled around to me unnoticed. I haven't so much heard the tapping of his walking stick and being crept up on like this makes me feel unaccountably ashamed.

'You were quick,' I tell him. 'How did it go?'

'That's the mortgage sorted out for the next six months,' he replies. 'Home, James!' – and I start the engine. 'Did you get any work done?' he asks, clicking the seatbelt buckle into place.

'A bit,' I lie. 'And Doris has been asleep all the time you were in there.' The puppy wears a harness that is locked into one of the back seat's safety slots. All the same, now that Mark has returned, Doris strains against the belt in an effort to reach her pack leader. The way that Mark ignores the bitch makes her want him more: she italicises her body on the back seat.

Universities had lured my friends away from our pleasant town. At the end of our exams we had scattered in different directions, to institutions of learning across the land. My maths result having been no worse than the other two, I had chosen a Widening Participation university as far east as a train line would take me, to study a subject that I learn in the same mechanical manner with which I had mastered 'Frère Jacques' on the recorder at Lower School.

Now I am back early for the long summer break, with a weekend job in a bakery to fund the occasional evening's entertainment, and a chauffeuring role that I had not anticipated, my mum being too busy with her own work to drive her husband around between appointments.

'I can't complain,' I tell Andy Brett, over a pint. 'They're putting me up, room and board, for twelve weeks. All they're asking is I drive Mark around in a car I enjoy driving anyway. And take the puppy to the park for her socialisation twice a day. It's okay.'

The venue where we find ourselves talking is a pub called The Doghouse, next door to a plumbing supplies store called Dirty Hose (unbelievably enough), which was called something else the last time I was in this part of town. But then again, so was The Doghouse. The last time I was here it was known as Slide, and it was gay.

I am only surprised to see Andy Brett here in the way that I am surprised to see anyone I know. (I would have been amazed to see him in Slide!) Separated by ability streams at school, we had never been good friends but smoking on the school premises had bonded us. He used to do motor mechanics when I had a free period on a Wednesday. We would often meet in an alcove by the outdoors cupboard where they kept boxes of tennis balls and shot putts and javelins.

'Do you live this way then?' Andy asks.

'No. I was looking for Slide.'

Andy nods. 'Went bust. So you're a benny on the loose then? Don't stun me much, mate, I must admit. Thought as much.'

'Really. It must be the tattoo on my forehead.'

He doesn't acknowledge my sarcasm. 'There's another one, though,' he comments. 'Do you fancy another pint?'

For the first time I realise that Andy must have been drinking – and with a degree of dedication – before I met him by accident tonight. Now that I focus on them, his eyes are wanderers, loose in their puffy orbits.

'No thanks, I have to drive. Another what?'

'Trade bar,' Andy answers. He concludes his pint with a wipe of his chops and an air-ripping belch. 'Go there myself, time to time. I'm not a poof, like. Just watch the girls chatting themselves up. Gimme the *right* fuckin' 'orn.'

I hope the set of my lips and my tone suggests emotional coolness bordering on fragility. 'Fancy that,' I say to him calmly.

'Do you wanna go?'

'*I'd* do it. *I'd* pretend to be a Muslim. Get myself involved – get close to the boss. Then *bomp*. Lets his hair down, I'm *in* there, mate. Put a spanner down his throat. I'll give *him* twelve virgins in Heaven, mate. Won't have a working cock time I'm finished with him.'

175

It's nearly nine o'clock in a bar I don't know – and it's actually *called* Trade. The trade is threadbare – easy on the eye but nothing more – and because I have the car, a Coke or a Becks Blue is all I dare order. By very stark contrast, Andy Brett is totally abandoned by logic – he is wasted. We're not long in Trade before I start to regret agreeing to accompanying him here. I have to collect Mark from the bowling alley at ten; it's not worth driving home if I have to leave again as soon as I get there. Instead I am obliged to listen to Andy's smeared diction and vociferous views.

'So where's your boyfriend?' he asks me at one point. 'Is he here or in Norfolk?'

'Neither. I haven't got one.' It's not so much that I think I owe Andy an explanation; it's more that I'm bored and that talking will kill a few minutes. 'We had to part. He couldn't keep his pencil in his pocket.'

Andy takes a moment to digest this. When he eventually

laughs, a smoke-coloured bubble appears at his left nostril.

'Gotcha. We're all the same.'

'*I'm* not,' I protest. 'I was faithful to him. I even gave him a third chance – *two* indiscretions – but he doubted I'd end it. And there's nothing worse than being thought of as predictable. So I changed the locks, metaphorically speaking.'

'So who do you fancy tonight?'

'…in what way?'

'In the shagging way, of course. The revenge shag.'

'No one. I have to pick up my stepfather at nine-thirty. I volunteered.' I lie about the pick-up time in order to plant the seed that I'll be leaving shortly.

'Where from?'

I explain about the bowling alley. 'He's in a league – they play every week. Just a practice tonight so he'll have a few beers with his friends.'

'Well, that's only a few minutes in the car. You could still get your end away.'

I laugh. 'As easy as that, eh? You're an expert all of a sudden.'

'Well, they have glory holes in the gents. They can't make it *much* easier for a quick one!'

'No, they don't!'

'Go and look if you don't believe me! I think it's between stalls three and four, but it might be two and three. Pop your piece in the hole and see who tickles your fancy. Anonymous.'

'Yes, I know how a glory hole works, thanks very much. I just can't believe they'd have one in a town pub – it must be against the law.'

Andy shrugs. 'Maybe it is, I don't know. But they had 'em last time I was here.'

By standing up I bring a smile to Andy's face. 'I need a

pee,' I tell him.

'But I bet you check it out while you're there.' He also stands – for a second I think he is going to accompany me to the gents. 'I'll get another drink while you're away. Do you want another soft one ... in a manner of speaking?'

Although I've already taken in more liquid than is comfortable, I decide 'One more Coke, please – just a small one,' and then I leave the table.

As I cross the bar I see the grounds-man – the man who carried the tools – the man who works at the Lower School where my stepfather had his meeting this morning. The man who looked at me strangely while I waited in the car with a laptop and a puppy...

The grounds-man is playing a machine that is wider and taller than he is. He inserts a two-pound coin and a jingle sounds – the theme tune of a quiz show popular with some of my friends at university.

177

An urge to explain everything to him is overwhelming. I stop in my tracks, not close enough to him to be a pest, but close enough for him to notice me in his peripheral vision. Once he has slapped a large button marked C, a tone sounds that makes it clear he has selected the wrong option.

'Can I help you?' he asks with a Spanish accent. He turns to me slowly in a manner that is both sultry and rather excitingly menacing.

'I wanted to tell you what I was doing this morning, in the playground.'

'...I beg your pardon?'

'Well, not *in* the playground – *near* the playground. I was parked and you were working.'

'I don't work,' the grounds-man interrupts.

'At the school.'

He shakes his head briskly. 'I don't work at a school. I gamble.'

'But I saw you, mate!' I protest.

He takes a step towards me. 'You didn't see me this morning. You've never seen me before this moment.' His breath is sweet with what I take to be wine consumption. 'And after this moment you will never see me again, I would think. Now. Was there anything else? I intend to play this machine until I win what I've put into it. So if you'll excuse me…'

And he turns his back on me once more. Bewildered and obscurely hurt by his rejection, I head to the toilets. It is not as if I had expected the beginnings of a lifelong friendship with the grounds-man but his behaviour has bothered me. If he doesn't work at the school, what was he doing there? Stealing tools? *Pretending* to work there in order to get closer to the children?

I enter the toilet cubicle that is third in line. I lock myself in. Sure enough, as Andy had said, there is a hole in the partition at waist-height. In fact, there are two – one on either side of the space. Theoretically, someone in the third stall could indulge in anonymous fun with someone in stalls two and four – simultaneously, even.

Suddenly the idea is intoxicating … but I am here to urinate, so that's what I do.

Except…

Except I hear the door to the main bar open – there is a wash of bass and a storm of cymbals and synths – and I know that someone has entered the gents. I know who it is as well. I can picture the grounds-man; he is looking for me. Although I don't understand his technique of seduction, he has made a virtue of confusion. He knows that his aloofness has made me want him.

I'm almost breathless. He enters Stall Two, on my left as I stand facing the cistern (although I have finished emptying my bladder). A few seconds pass. There is nervousness but it's the good kind of nervousness. It stretches the front of my trousers.

Do I dare?

'Are you shopping?' his whispered voice asks me. I can only just hear him.

'Yes.'

He slides two fingers through the glory hole and makes them wiggle.

'Follow me,' he whispers – and he withdraws his digits. But he has invited me over and it would be rude to turn down such an invitation.

The hole is a little low for me. By widening the space be-   179
tween my ankles, I am able to aim my erection through the gap. If you want to consider *vulnerable moments*, I might suggest that this is about as vulnerable as life throws at you.

The grounds-man starts licking the end of it. Within a few seconds I have relaxed; I've stopped worrying that we will be caught – the management must be aware of what goes on in here, after all. When he takes it into his mouth, I know that there is nothing else to think about.

It does not take long – I have never been able to hang on. The grounds-man spits into the toilet bowl and whispers, 'I must be going.' When he whispers, I note, his Spanish accent is lost. Perhaps it had not been a true accent in the first place.

He unlocks his door. 'I have to go the bowling alley,' he explains in his normal voice. 'My stepson is picking me up at ten. It's been exciting. See you!'

I wait for the old man with the hip surgery to leave the gents. I wait a long time.

Mr Konstantin's Visitors

(with M.F. Korn)

A PEARL OF PERSPIRATION exploded on the watch face.

It was nine a.m. – which meant that there were only three hours to go until the Tuesday delivery. Konstantin coughed, sponging his brow with his shirtsleeve, as he gulped down the latest in a long series of panic attacks.

He dreaded Tuesdays. Though he was never a good sleeper, his slumber patterns took a drastic dive every Monday night. It was terrible. He was up every hour, or for couple of hours. A whizz, a sandpaper yodel into the toilet's throat, a slurp of cranberry juice: it didn't matter. His mind could conjure up any number of reasons for him to drag his sackcloth body from the earthy damp of the years-unchanged sheets.

Every Tuesday, Konstantin felt like death warmed up.

Tuesday was the day that pretty Sushi from Noddy's All-Dayer brought the supplies: the food, the brandy, the cigars, the light bulbs, the detergent. And Konstantin hated visitors of any kind, even if he was so low on food he hadn't eaten properly for a couple of days. As was currently the case. All he had left in the fridge was a hunk of stiff bread, a withered carrot, a few cloves of garlic, and a plastic bottle of mayonnaise, dry and cracking, that he hadn't been able to finish for months.

Visitors meant germs. Sushi passed the parcel to Mrs Apesbury, Konstantin's neighbour, and from there the complicated negotiation was undertaken. Complicated, and by all accounts painful. Even a visit from the neighbour meant the outside world… and Konstantin wished to live in his snailshell, for now and forever more. The house was fortress enough for him. The outside world was dangerous. It had killed Benny B., and Benny T., and Konstantin's own brother, Maho. A traffic accident, a drive-by, and a fire, respectively: Konstantin preferred to live with the cobwebs of his dreams where he did not go out.

There was nothing safe about going out.

But, on the other hand, he had noticed the continuous barking of a dog that someone had abandoned on a back seat of a car, directly across the road from Konstantin's blush-red brickwork. In a scruffy-looking Buick.

Whose dog was it?

Whose car was it?

The dog's cascade of noise leaked into Konstantin's every moment, every prayer, The four televisions being always on, and tuned to the 24 hour news channels. Occasionally he thumbed the remote, but only to find new angles on same world events that everyone else was panicking about. He watched everything simultaneously. It beat the hell out of answering the phone (especially during thunderstorms, since he had been told that he could get electrocuted) and Caller ID was his saviour. Every day he had telemarketers trying to penetrate his missile shield of protection, but the privacy detector kept most of them out. If it showed that the calls were blocked, he didn't pick up. Even if a name showed up on his caller ID, then he would let it ring until the answering machine picked up.

Konstantin had a friend who had helped him set up this command central 'War Room,' as he called it, in his tilted, crockety apartment. More like a last-stand-bunker, the windows so covered with shades that only occasionally peeked out from under the blankets and draperies, all full of dust. He was never much of a housekeeper. He hadn't dared to allow anyone to come in and clean up. He had his neighbour, Mrs Apesbury, put his newspaper through his door slot, one of the

181

Achilles heels in his armour.

Apart from the feelings that he now had for that *dog.*

Whose dog was this? He had tried to phone Mrs Apesbury about it, but there'd been no answer. Confronting his fear of the outside world, he had then called ASPCA, and then the county animal control centre. For an animal to qualify as being in danger, he was told, there had to be evidence of actual abuse, physical or mental. 'Well, what the hell do you call being stuck in a hot car?' Konstantin protested. 'A laugh a minute? The poor mutt's killing himself in there!'

'It's a private matter, sir,' Konstantin was informed. 'It's between the car owner and the dog.'

Konstantin had a flash of inspiration. 'I've never seen that car before,' he said. 'Say it's stolen. Send your people.'

'Have you made enquiries locally to that effect?'

Enquiries to that effect? Konstantin closed his eyes. Did they *train* these co-eds to speak like this? 'No. No I haven't made 'enquiries locally to that effect.' And to be honest with you, I didn't expect this call to give you such a hard time. The simple facts are, there's an animal suffering and you're refusing to do anything about it. It's disgraceful.'

But the call was, if nothing else, a helpful reminder of why Konstantin had chosen the indoor life—this whole shut-in business. True, he wanted to live out his lifespan without an atrocity happening: his own accidental death, by stovetop fire, or toilet drowning, for example. After all, the world was a monstrous aberration of living chaos, while every other known planet in the universe had only blissful solitude. This why in his home he felt safe, most of the time. No one could stab him at a grocery quick mart; which seemed to happen every day somewhere according to the news channels. No one could attack him if he didn't think about taking a walk. Nor would there

182

be any head-on collisions; why, the interstate were all like NA-SCAR tracks now, the cars going 90 miles an hour. Sports utility vehicles flipping over and over with five kids inside. Madmen everywhere. Outside, the world was filled with madmen!

And with officious office staff like this girl.

Konstantin opened his eyes again. The silence between him and his interlocutor had stretched on too long, and he was just about to demand to speak to a manager (for which he had a different kind of phobia) when it suddenly became clear a simple insult to the girl's integrity was all that had been needed from the start.

'There's really no need to take that tone of voice with me, sir,' she told him. 'I'm only doing my job. But I'll say in my report that you are certain the car's been stolen. Expect our visit in the next four hours, if that's convenient.'

She did not stay on the line long enough to hear him say that it wasn't. *Oh dear Lord*, thought Konstantin. *Expect our visit.* The words made him need to sit down. He hadn't thought this through; and certainly hadn't anticipated any further involvement. 'Oh Lord,' he said, feeling sick and beginning to tremble. *Mrs Apesbury!* he thought. *I'll call her and she can talk to the coming do-gooders!*

But still Mrs Apesbury was not answering the phone again. And so wrapped up in his own distress as he was, that Konstantin did not even spare a thought for her own possible predicament as to why *she* was away from her phone. Maybe she'd tripped and fallen on a throw-rug; maybe she'd broken her neck, he would later think, when further calls were not responded to. Or maybe she sliced her hand off in the garbage disposal and was bleeding to death on the kitchen floor, her eyelids fluttering as she wonders who keeps calling her, and if she has the strength to crawl to the phone in time. Konstantin had a morbid mind sometimes, and this new game was fun, as the often were.

For now, however, it was a case of panic stations for him. When the knock did come at his door he cowered. He actually did exactly that – he hid behind his sofa. There he found a constellation of dropped coins, many quarters, and an old magazine about male health and fitness. He found a sock to put his coins into.

The doorbell rang again: it was the opening chords of Eric Clapton's 'Layla', and Konstantin had long since considered changing it when the batteries ran out.

Again, the summons. And again.

Konstantin, protected by the sofa but feeling vulnerable, started to cry.

184

When his tears had dried to slug-trails on his cheeks, he stood up, attempting to convince himself of his own worth. He even did a couple of stretches, lunging himself down to his left and right side. Life wasn't so bad, was the message that he was trying to convey to his invisible audience. Then he tiptoed to the bay window.

The visitor, or visitors, had left, but the dog in the car outside had not. When Konstantin peeled back the curtain for just a tiny peek, the vision that met his eyes actually broke his heart. The dog was still in the car, but its nose was pressed to the side window. Not barking, not howling: just watching Konstantin's house and window and using its brown eyes to plead for further action.

'Christ.'

Konstantin rushed to the fridge for a glass of juice. But there was no juice left. Old bread, a few sad vegetables and cracked mayonnaise, but no juice. Instead he had a glass of water. Then he had another, wondering what to do next. He wished and wished that Mrs Apesbury would answer her phone – or even better, that she would collect for him a packet or two more of cigars per visit. He was all out. And he desperately fancied a smoke right about now.

The pain he felt was crucifying him. Not the pain of nicotine withdrawal, but the discomfort of guilt. What the presence of human beings had failed to do, the simple presence of a mutt in a hassle had achieved. Deep down – below the heart – Konstantin knew that he would have to get dressed and go out and check on the animal…

Are you sure?

Konstantin felt scared. He turned his attention on the War Room televisions echoing doom. 'Twenty killed by crazed gunman at a Shoe Factory,' '206 people killed in a jet crash over the Atlantic.' The CBS anchorman, he was sure, was talking directly to him: 'Is milk really healthy, or is it harming your children?' 'New science reveals that pesticides in your home can kill your children.' The woman on ABC was similarly choosy about who she spoke to. Into Konstantin's ears, and Konstantin's ears alone, she said: 'More poisoned grapes found in California,' 'E-Coli in 20,000 pounds of ground beef causes recall,' and 'New study reveals that cell phones may cause brain cancer…'

At the same time, the NBC newsreader cooed in: 'Court finds Firestone Radials caused thousands of crashes. Executives covered this information up.' 'Radon in your cellar, a deadly silent killer.' 'The Riverside Serial Killer left a cryptic note, telling where the thirty bodies were, but the police are baffled over his whereabouts…'

Konstantin heard very little of it. In lieu of paying attention, he sweated, and he cursed. The dog, he realized, was in a similar predicament to his own. Trapped. And dying: quite possibly dying, like he was. *I have to go out there*, Konstantin realized – but the notion pumped hot squirts of fear throughout his body. What would happen as soon as he left the house? *Anything* could be waiting out there! Gang bangers, biding their time in the bushes for him to step out, with brass knuckles and loaded pistols. Kids' bicycles to trip over and break his neck. Angry neighbours, outraged by his side yard covered waist deep in filth, to engage in fistfights. Youths, smelling his fear, to knife him.

There was something else wrong, too. Konstantin's stomach somersaulted. Ah yes, thought the man: what about some *food?* Konstantin realized that he hadn't eaten anything substantial in more than 24 hours. It was time to fill his belly. The problem was though it was Tuesday, Mrs Apesbury had yet to bring the supplies – and there was very little worth 'writing home about,' as they say, in the refrigerator…. In part as a way of avoiding any new thought-conversation with the dog, Konstantin moved into the kitchen to distance himself from the window, and by extension the car, in case that helped. There his stomach squirmed.

Lord love us, he thought, *we have to eat.* And he plucked from the racks the dead carrot, the dense, dry bread, the garlic, the bottle of mayo. And he shaved his root vegetable; he hacked off two slices from the loaf; he diced the garlic.

Are you coming to free me or what? asked the dog, Unexpectedly.

Much to his dismay, Konstantin found himself answering – aloud. 'I'm coming as soon as I've had my lunch, okay.'

Well, no hurry, obviously, the hound replied, sarcastically. *Don't worry about the heat or anything, I'm just dying here…*

Konstantin sprayed thick mayonnaise on the concoction, its edges yellowed, to kill the flavours. And he started to eat what he'd created, thinking: It's one of life's pleasures – to destroy what you've just made. Five bites in, and Konstantin was beginning to feel fortified: beginning to feel that he could do it – he could leave the house, he could dash to the dog on the back seat. He could do a good deed.

In the bathroom near the front door, he took a leak and felt his stomach *drowning* in his nervousness. He wished he hadn't drunk all of his week's supply of brandy. Instead Konstantin fancied a drink, a smoke, a lie-down – not to mention a hearty regurgitation. The recent repast was not settling comfortably into his body: surely not after so many hours of nutritional abstinence. Still, with what strength that remained, through a fog of thought, Konstantin opened the door.

'Is this what I really want?' he asked aloud.

The dog started barking. *Don't be so selfish,* Konstantin heard. *This isn't about what you want or don't want. This is about helping out another of God's creatures….me!*

Konstantin steeled. He was as ready as he'd ever be. The thought of taking a step outside curdled his innards, but he knew that he couldn't allow the poor animal to die, not now that the ASPCA, and the county animal control services had failed – categorically failed – against their mission statement.

Burping up nervous gas, Konstantin opened the door. The outside air smelt of bright sun, citrus fruit and gasoline. The sky was as blue as a premature puppy. Konstantin endeavoured to file away his terrors: it was only fifteen metres to the car, he calculated, if that; he could do it – and he could do it because he *had* to do it.

He slammed the door instead. *I can't do it,* he told himself. But there were no more excuses, nothing else left to eat and there was nothing left to drink. So Konstantin poured and drank a few glasses of water. *That's the least I could give the dog,* he thought: *a bowl of water.*

So deciding, Konstantin sniffed away as much pressure as he could, opened his front door again – and stepped down into the tiled area that separated his lawn from his front door. His legs felt weak. He spilled some of the water with which he'd filled a cereal bowl. In exactly the same way, his eyes were leaking. There was something, he knew – there was something that was snapping inside him: something emotional. *I have to do this*, he told himself – again and again, like a mantra. And for the first time in over a year, Konstantin tasted the clean, dry sunshine, although he concentrated on keeping all of the water in the bowl.

When he reached the parked car, Konstantin could feel the heat off its metal from five steps away. There it occurred to him that he might have to bust a window: if the animal welfare organization had failed to complete its mission, then there was no reason to suspect that he, Konstantin, would be able to gain access to the distressed hound. Instead the passenger side door opened easily, to Konstantin's surprise…

I love you, boy, thought Konstantin as he placed the bowl of water on the sidewalk. The dog dived out and there was a throaty splash as he lunged for the bowl.

And Konstantin, with a hissed wince, clutched at his left breast: a reaction to the sudden manifestation of pain. He put his fingerprints on the car, its heat radiating through them – to keep himself balanced. The agony wildfired though his body. He swore aloud. And then– *Oh my Lord*, he thought as the heart attack (*what else could it be?*) settled down like a bad mood over a family dining room. The dog did not cease drinking. It didn't notice Konstantin's distress. But what else did he expect?

Leaning against the car, a greasy spot where his head rested, Konstantin waved to the person in the distance, who had just appeared. If Mrs Apesbury was still alive – and here Kon-

stantin entertained himself with a moment of morbid specula-
tion – that had to be her: that pear-shaped woman, approaching. Because that was how it worked. She would arrive in time
to save him…

'Mrs Apes…' Konstantin began, and he felt a wealth of
shadows as they deepened on his face. His chest had caught
fire; but there was also pain in his gut, his trachea, and – it
seemed – on every rung of the ladder down his spine.

Is she really there? Konstantin wondered – because she
was not getting any closer, despite the fact that she appeared
to be walking, counterbalanced by grocery bags in both hands.
Like a kid down a water-chute, Konstantin slid down along
the car's flank, and ended up in a heap on his side, gasping for
breath.

There the dog licked his face – respectfully, lovingly. Trust-
ingly.

'Get an ambulance,' he said, appealing to the hound's
augmented intelligence. But the animal simply cocked its face
away, and breathed something meaty into Konstantin's pores.
It wagged its tail, like a moron shaking his head. Konstantin
experienced the rough blush of fear. He didn't know what was
going on. The dog didn't love him anymore: it didn't wish to
communicate. Nor did Mrs Apesbury long to visit.

It broke his heart when the dog ran away, fear in its eyes.

It broke his soul when the paramedics arrived, sirens blaring, but failed to notice him, slumped by the vehicle. Konstantin couldn't shout. Could only watch as two large black men in
their whites slipped into his home, their boots crashing through
the door. Could only sigh. Lying there he did notice a dog-
sized raven on his roof. He licked his lips, in search of moisture
– there was none. And he stared through the walls, to where
the medics were working, checking each of his rooms. In the

189

kitchen they picked up the plate on which he'd prepared his final sandwich. They sniffed the bottle of mayo. They frowned.

'What killed him?' Konstantin heard a courtroom judge enquire. 'Simple loneliness?'

'No.' This was the first paramedic, but his opinion was enforced by the nodding head of Mrs A. 'It was bad mayonnaise, your honour. Terribly, bad mayonnaise.'

Brainwreck Mealtimes

I. Cocktails

It was late when Solomon arrived home. Armed with a packed and heavy briefcase, he dragged his key from the lock, and entered the building where he smelt the evidence of a burnt meal from Flat Nine. He was tired. After he had eased the door closed, he shuffled through the remaining unclaimed mail in the basket (nothing for him) and took himself up the stairs. It was time for his bed.

The cleanliness of the air within was what alerted Solomon to the fact that change had occurred in his flat. He deposited his briefcase. The air should have smelt of old cigarette smoke. Instead, it was cold and moving. *Christ*, thought Solomon, moving quickly into the lounge, *I must've left the balcony doors open all day…*

Or…

For less than a second Solomon imagined that it was his brother that had somehow gained entrance to the flat. Another black man was standing by Solomon's low coffee table.

But it wasn't Zach. Zach was taller, with more meat on his bones and less hair on his head. This man Solomon had never seen before. His fear arrived in the form of anger.

'What the hell are you doing in my flat?' asked Solomon.

'Easy, tiger,' said the man standing by the low table. The hands he held up were empty, plump, their palms as pink as ham – in distinct contradiction to the cappuccino colouring of his sausage-like fingers. His hands were a breakfast apiece. 'It's nothing much.'

'You're in my flat! Get out!'

191

'Sure thing. I'm leaving, man, I'm leaving.'

An exit would require close contact between the two of them in the hallway. *He could attack me*, thought Solomon, going on to wonder how he would reach the telephone. His heart burned; his mouth dried up.

'Got nothing worth stealing anyway,' said the visitor. 'You live like a monk, man.'

Solomon frowned. 'Thanks for the social commentary. How did you get in?'

'Balcony doors, mate. Weren't too canny if you wanna know the truth of it. You'll have a proper burglar one day…'

'What are *you* then?' asked Solomon, regaining a semblance of confidence.

'Desperate, mate. Money-desperate. I'm a painter-decorator.'

'…This is getting surreal…'

'You're telling me. What's the most expensive thing you own?' asked the man who was yet to be a burglar.

'My computer. And you're not having it.'

'And what's with all these *books*?'

Solomon shrugged. 'I like to read. You should try it.'

'Hark at *you*, guy. Sarcasm an' all.'

Then the intruder did something that Solomon had not expected, and what was more he did it quickly. It was almost as though a film had been unprofessionally spliced. One second he was standing up, a picture of petulant self-defeat; the next, he had plumped himself down on Solomon's buxom couch, and was *crying*, leaning forward, his shrubbery head imprisoned in his hands, sniffing and whimpering like a pup.

Solomon wanted to move in close to put his arms around the man.

'It's okay, it's okay,' said Solomon, remaining neither deaf nor blind to the fact that this might be a scam – a sympathy-inducing, weakness-inducing crocodile tears.

'It's Clement. Name's Clement.'

'Oh. Well I'm sorry…' That was wrong. 'I'm *Solomon*,' the other man forced out. 'Welcome to my home.'

Slowly Clement raised his face. The eyes burned palely – silhouetted islands in twin pink lakes – and the lips had lives and directions of their own. 'Oh *guy*,' said Clement, 'I'm so sorry. I'm just… God. I'm just *so sorry*.'

Fearing another outbreak of emotion, Solomon said, 'It's okay. It's okay, friend.'

'I just need so much *money*,' Clement explained.

'Me too,' Solomon replied.

'I know, I know: I'm a cunt. I should leave.'

There was a second or two of emptiness, and then Solomon said something that surprised them both.

'Would you like a drink?' he asked.

193

II. Entrée

'A drink?' repeated Clement as if the word was a trap. 'Are you having one?'

I'm tireder than I thought, Solomon told himself. He stared into the bleachlit guts of the refrigerator. The wine bottle was hiding itself in the back like a sniper.

Solomon blinked. There! It had been there all along, and now he retrieved it with an archaeologist's glee: the touch to his fingertips as cold and gluey as mud.

'No. I don't drink,' he said. 'But I have some wine.' He exhibited the crock of gold. 'My brother left it here the other night. He stayed over.'

'Sure. Glass a wine could be good. How come you don't drink?' asked Clement.

'Recovering.'

'Cool. Bad luck.'

Solomon poured and then replaced the stone-cold bottle. He filled the kettle and flicked the switch; the kettle made sounds of waking, of toil.

Clement chose his moment (he waited another three seconds) before asking: 'How long?'

'Three years…'

'Good for you, man. I sometimes think…'

'Seven months…'

Clement raised his fluffy brows. 'And?'

'Nine days.'

Clement nodded. 'My sister was the same, yeah? Like a *sump*. And you know how I find out? I'm on a train, right – I'm working on a paint job, in me overalls? – and he's *sitting* there, man: two seats away. The boss: her manager. Don't even know me, right? – but I was at their Christmas bash, as a guest, and I knew *him*. He gets a call. And he's like, "Shit day, actually. Really rough one – *Charles*. I had to let Beverley go." Well, I almost lamped the cunt. And then he's like, "She came in drunk again." It was that word did it. *Again*. So he sends one of the girls in the office into the toilets to follow her in, right? She's not even subtle about it: doing a line of Charles Dance on the sink.'

'Cocaine?' Solomon wished to clarify.

'And this girl's like, "Sorry, Bev." And *Beverley's* like, "Sokay. Just do it. Just make it happen: the next thing. Make it *happen*."'

'…Jesus. So what did you do?' asked Solomon.

'Went round there. Give her a squeeze,' said Clement.

Solomon had just enough time to wonder whether squeeze was a euphemism for slap, punch, kick – before Clement added:

'The least I could do. Bit a comfort, yeah? Time for help, I said. She just cried and said *yeah*: help's good.'

Clement sighed. He plucked at his left eyebrow and inflated his lips to a comic cubic-capacity. In truth, Solomon now feared a recurrence of the weeping; but it didn't transpire. Understanding, growth and wealth – spiritual wealth – fled his features.

With a voice as stiff as a starched collar Clement continued. 'And then there's the girlfriend. She wants to get her tits done. I say, Dee? Get 'em done on the National Health. She says no. "National Health's rubbish. Come out with two different sizes, whatever they got in stock." Jesus.' He laughed. 'What a carry on, eh? What a *carve up*.'

'I'd like to help,' said Solomon quietly, 'I really would, but you see…'

'No, mate – you're all right,' said Clement with an air of low appreciation. 'Books ain't gonna do it, are they?'

'I doubt it.'

'No. Stupid idea.'

At which point a scratching noise could be heard, a slithering and a skittering; it was the sound of a key in the lock on Solomon's door. Both Solomon and Clement remained still.

The door opened. Preceded by giggling and by mock-urgent insistences for quiet, a man and a woman in their thirties fell into the flat. Clearly, they'd been drinking: if the behaviour hadn't given this away, the fumes they were producing would have taken on the challenge. Equally clearly, there was a sexual agenda that the two of them intended to adhere to. With a smile on her face, the woman leaned back against the wall and pulled her partner closer by tugging on his tie. As he slipped his hands onto her derriere, she licked the underside of his chin and worked on his belt buckle…

Solomon got to his feet. 'Excuse me,' he said as he breached the threshold into the hallway. How perfectly *British*, he thought. His mind raced. A few months earlier, his mother had called to ask if Solomon would give his brother, Zach, a key to the flat; his mother (Solomon suspected) had at least grown tired of picking up the tab for Zach's taxis. Zach would sometimes work in Solomon's town on IT support contracts. On such occasions, Zach would round off his days with explosively alcoholic sessions in The Dirty Rat, where he would attempt to seduce a particular co-worker into bed. When that failed (or when her boyfriend turned up) Zach would realise that he was too late to make the train connections home. He'd take a taxi to the next town along – to Mum's place – and she would be forced to pay.

Solomon had said no to the key idea. He didn't want his flat to be used as a hotel. If Zach called on an evening when Solomon was still awake, then of course he could crash for the night, but otherwise... So. Mum had given her own key, had she? Well, Solomon was not best pleased about *that*; but how on earth had these two strangers got hold of it?

The man and the woman kissed in the hallway. She kneaded his protruding penis through his pleated pants.

'Get out of my flat,' said Solomon, experiencing a rush of déjà vu. But so engrossed in their moment were they that they failed to hear his demand. Indeed, the woman's apparent efforts to yank the man's erection from his body, groping through the unzipped fly, now intensified.

Solomon was less than a metre from them. 'For Christ's sake – *stop*,' he pleaded. Or at least, he thought – at least *acknowledge* me. But other matters burned in Solomon's mind. Why, for instance, had the couple shown no surprise at the lights being on?

'Wait,' breathed the man, looking past her.

Solomon's face burned with acceptance and relief, but only briefly.

'I need the loo,' the man went on. 'You get into bed...'

'I want to watch,' she replied.

'*Listen* to me,' said Solomon. He didn't know it yet but his hands had started shaking.

'Hey, lovebirds!' said Clement from a point very close to Solomon's back. (He hadn't heard him approach.) 'The flat's booked for the night, all right? Be on your way.'

The irony of the utterance was not lost on Solomon, but it was buried under a rising pile of panic. His ears were awash with blood-noise. Disconnecting himself from his lover's clutches, the man walked directly at Solomon, a twinkling smile on his face and a single word – 'Cheeky!' – on his lips.　　197

'Be quick!' said the woman, ducking left into Solomon's bedroom.

'Jesus,' said Clement.

The male lover closed the gap between his partner and Solomon in two small steps. Solomon raised his hands...

The pain that he had expected – the jolt of brisk contact – did not arrive. What came was infinitely worse: a discordant recognition of his own pulse, but raised to rock-stadium decibelage. A scream of his own blood; a weakening of limbs and a cracking of joints... The only sensation that Solomon had in his banks was a memory of slotting a light bulb into a socket in a low-rent Egyptian hotel. The shock he'd received for his troubles had thrown him from the bed.

'*Nooooo*...' screamed Solomon... as the untethered lover moved quickly through a body that seemed to have lost all substance.

Solomon tingled and spasmed. He fell down on the carpet.

Effortlessly the man plucked his way out of Solomon's spine and cranium; Solomon's drink spilled against the door to the storage cupboard. The glass cracked neatly: bowl and stem. And Solomon looked up. What he saw was as bad as what he'd experienced:

Clement, stunned (his mouth open, the circumference of his eyes unenlargeable), swiping at the shoulders of a man who could walk through walls...

Said man now torched the bathroom light; he stood before the sink, fully clothed but with his large manhood maintaining its salute. He eschewed the lavatory itself, and began to go into the basin. Solomon even sympathised: waking on many an occasion in a similar state, he'd been obliged to stand two metres from the toilet and put his faith in the Hands of God, moving closer only as the urgency dwindled.

'He's pissing in your sink, guy!' said Clement, but the remark held little vigour. It sounded as though Clement had just been trepanned and asked to comment on an aspect of higher physics. 'He went *right through you*, man...'

Solomon's body felt far from normal and far from resilient. Though able to pick himself off the floor, Solomon was unable to train his mind to travel in one direction at a time; unable to identify a source for the problem's solution.

They can't hear us, he thought. *They can't see us. We're not here.*

'He went right through you,' Clement repeated.

'Or *they're* not here,' continued Solomon.

III. Pudding and Pie

During the first ten minutes of the intruders' lovemaking, Solomon and Clement learned their names, or at least their monikers. Responding to something he did correctly with his tongue or nose or chin (it was hard to tell) the woman gasped and said, '*Yes*, Bob…' All they learned from the man, however, was 'Babes'. It seemed to work.

'We shouldn't be watching this,' said Clement, failing to remove his eyes from the spectacle.

'They're in my bed!' Solomon protested.

Babes slid down and took her place on Bob's hips, looking at the mirror on the wall. Bob regarded her back and with calmly lingering fingertips he traced both the carnation tattoo on her spine and the dimples in her buttocks.

Solomon wondered how the world would appear when he awoke from this dream. Would the sky be thrashing and molten? Would there still be life on earth?

Solomon worked for a brick and tile company; his work was telephones and his working life was ordered. At twelve-thirty he had a lunch break. Around three he loosened his tie, sensing the finishing line of another day. *This couldn't be happening.*

Clement had shown no indication of wanting to leave. In single file he and Solomon had followed Bob into the bedroom, where Babes, naked, had already established her place in the king-sized bed. Astonished, the two black men had watched the scene unravel.

'Do you see her reflection?' Solomon asked. He stood by the door. On the other hand, Clement had moved some laundry from the reading chair and had deposited the clothes and towels on top of the television.

'Yeah, man,' said Clement. 'She got *nice* tits. I wouldn't mind…'

'Her tits don't enter into it,' Solomon snapped. 'You see her, right?'

'Yeah.'

'And do you see yourself? In the mirror.'

'What?'

Solomon's tone softened. 'Please, Clement. One party in this room is alive and one party in this room is dead.' He gulped. The fajitas he'd eaten at the petrol station came back to haunt him with a savage burp. It hadn't been as difficult to say it as he'd imagined it would be. 'I think the first thing we should be doing is making sure which is which.'

Clement rose.

'Christ,' said Clement an hour later, 'ain't they got homes to go to?'

'That's not funny,' said Solomon.

'Sorry. But look at 'em, man! I'd be snoozing by now. You can't fault his stamina. Guy's an animal,' said Clement, not without awe.

'The chair,' said Babes.

All eyes now on the chair, but only one pair focusing on the man who was lounging on its cushions. Briefly but potently, Solomon imagined that Clement had been *seen*. But no: the words were a suggestion, a request – an order.

The lovers started to relocate.

'Oh man,' said Clement.

'Get up!' said Solomon. '*Get up!*'

Clement stayed put. An irascible but childish grin swept the years from his features. 'Wanna feel, man,' he said quietly. 'Never been in a threeway.'

Bob – sweating Bob, with his wide hips and his nova of back-hair – sat down on the reading chair and slid through Clement without displacing him any more than a few centimetres to either side. Clement's dark face lapped inside and outside of Bob's, like an undertow. The noise? The noise was shock and late evening trainwreck; the noise was rhumba and thunder and tidal. Clement shrieked. His eyeballs rolled out of their sockets, then snapped back home with the sound of a fish being reeled in.

Babes joined the two gentlemen, her knees on the armrests, her breasts against both Bob's and Clement's lips. Like a proud mother hen she settled down and wriggled for comfort.

Clement's head lurched backwards. 'Weird mango, man,' said Clement. 'This is some *damn* weird mango…' With which he reached through the lovers to unbutton his own fly.

Babes laid her hands on the windowsill. Only Solomon noticed this, and assumed at first that it was for the purpose of supporting herself – an anchor. But she was reaching under the curtains for something. Solomon watched her find it… withdraw it. Its edges caught the only light available, which was coming from the hallway – shining through Solomon.

'No,' Solomon had time to mouth. Intending to knock the knife from Babes' hand, he strode forward, his fists bunched, his blood malarial. But his strike connected with nothing. Unlike Babes' strike. Confidently, powerfully, she drove the blade into the back of Bob's head. There blood came running…

Bob screamed. Bob had the voice of a pig, mid-slaughter. Not that it was enough to deter his attacker's ministrations: as though she were trying to unblock a drain she now ensured that the knife wriggled ably in his lower skull. She was numb: or so it seemed. Dead-fish cold was her face. Her eyes were painted marbles.

'Oh I love you,' said Babes.

Bob attempted to rise from his seat. But it was too late. Blood was flowing down his and Clement's shoulders. (Clement wasn't shrieking. What had *he* felt?) And Babes leaned backwards…

Again, Solomon attempted to deflect the strike. It was ineffectual: the blade clipped into Bob's throat and a fresh geyser erupted. Bob's vocal protests now gurgled moistly; waves of blood ran down his chin and onto his tie.

Clement and Solomon could do nothing but watch. It was not over quickly. Seemingly without a care in the world, Babes pulled herself off her impaler and stood by as Bob slid to the right and half-fell over the armrest. For the first time in minutes, his face and Clement's became fully detached. And for all its liquidity, Clement's appeared frozen.

'Don't call me Babes,' said Babes. 'My name is Georgie,' said Georgie. 'As in Georgie Porgy, pudding and pie.' She smiled. 'Kissed the boys and made them cry.'

Said Solomon: 'Jesus.'

Said Georgie: 'Christ. Do you have to make so much *mess*?'

Georgie dipped down onto her haunches and set about removing Bob's fingers.

IV. Main Course

'I'm leaving,' said Clement.

'No you're not. Nor am I.'

'We can't stop her, man!'

'We don't know that,' said Solomon.

'She goes right through us! Or the other way round… I can't watch this.'

Georgie was now slicing fillets from the dead man's podgy jawbone. She was whistling an Elvis Presley tune – 'Heartbreak Hotel' – and mumbling the odd word or phrase.

Clement and Solomon adjourned to the lounge.

'It's down at the end of Lonely Street,' they heard.

'We haven't tried merging ourselves,' said Solomon.

'I ain't merging with no one, mate!' said Clement. 'But I agree. Do you know something? We have a *job* to do, don't we?

There's a *reason* why we're here.'

'I think so.'

'Good. What is it?' Clement asked.

'I don't know. What do ghosts usually do? Haunt people.'

'Are we *ghosts*?' The notion shocked Clement.

'I don't know what else we can be. What's the name of your girlfriend, Clement?'

'Dee,' said Clement defiantly.

'Short for?'

Clement paused. 'I don't remember.'

Solomon nodded. 'As I thought,' he said, well aware of the arrogance of the statement. 'Listen. I don't remember where I was tonight. I know I was at *work*, but what do I do? It was midnight when I got in. I'm in a suit, Clement; I'm not fighting fires or dealing with Uzi drive-bys all night, so what do I do that gets me home in the early hours? I don't even think this is my flat. I can't find my keys.'

'Where's the electricity meter?' Clement asked.

'No idea. See?'

'She killed us,' said Clement with slow discovery. 'Like she did that dude in there.'

'I think you're right. I think we fucked her and then she did us with a knife.'

'Well I fucked her *first*, you came later.'

'Whatever. If we're dead, Clement, we're dead. Question is, what we gonna do about it?'

Clement's brow stiffened. 'Wait,' he said.

'For what?'

'For Bob to join us.'

Solomon nodded. 'Stand up,' he said.

They touched. The boom of blood and the whine of gristle did not materialize; instead a soothing purr and a distant

203

sea-like gossip reached their ears.

'Closer,' said Solomon.

Like waves, like breezes, they moved into one another, eyes closed and emitting babyish sighs of chuckling contentment. The pains of which they had been unaware – the heartburn, the knee-twitch and the sleep-deprived eyes – melted away. All was calm. Vision was sharpened. Clement peeked into Solomon's lungs; and Solomon strolled around the rooms of both Clement's head and his apartment. He saw Dee. She was young; she was white; she was dreaming of a man who had a mop-head for a face and dusters for hands. She was crying in her sleep.

'And now… the end is near,' sang Georgie, having moved onto another notch in her repertoire.

United but overlapping as a result of their different walking styles, Solomon and Clement made it back into the bedroom. It was like, Solomon mused briefly, a three-legged race at school. A sense of farce prevailed. Until the two men saw the abattoir, at least.

Georgie had all but removed Bob's head. She had wrapped his severed nose, lips and ears in a pouch made from the tie that she'd wrenched from her victim's throat.

'Jesus,' said Clement.

'I did it… *my. Way,*' sang Georgie.

'Are we strong enough, do you think?' asked Solomon.

'Where's Bob?'

'I don't know.'

'Bob?' said Solomon.

Although Georgie failed to notice it, so engrossed was she in the excavation of Bob's shining eyes, the air shifted. The temperature dipped; the walls smelt of oranges and Brie. A dog howled plaintively in the distance. Pelicans squawked and muttered, flying past the window in formation.

'Can you hear me, Bob?' asked Solomon.

'Come on, man.'

'… and through it all…' sang Georgie.

'Bob, we need you…'

The reading chair twitched in a sudden heat haze. Transparent but fully-formed in front of it, Bob sat up and left his solid shell. His face spoke of pain, of betrayal.

'Where am I?' he asked with a voice too close to falsetto. '*Fuck*,' he continued, his eyes on the dentistry that Georgie was now executing with vim. Ineffectually, Bob swiped at Georgie's paws and weapon.

'What can I do?' Bob shrieked.

'It's too late, man,' said Clement. 'Join us. Teach her a lesson.'

205

Bob rose. He was clothed, rippling, and in perfect proportion. Unlike his carpet-bound counterpart, he still owned his features and even his tie. But he was scared. He tucked his rig in and zipped himself up. He coughed.

Contact. The three men merged cell and sinew; as one they regarded the mirror and recoiled from the image, despite the sense of peace that prevailed. It was something about the atrocious consanguinity of the features; the shock of all-at-once hairstyles; the cornflake-yellow teeth and anchored-open mouth.

Nor were the three men the only ones to notice the transformation. Transfixed and agog, Georgie now looked up from her surgery. Her eyes were heavy with the unknowable.

'No…' said Solomon, Clement and Bob; but the word did not sound like their voice. It was nobody's choice of word either. It had come from somewhere else, using the three spirits as its trumpet. It was loud.

Decked out from head to foot in Bob's blood, Georgie stood. A whimpering flow of urine coursed its way down her left thigh. She covered her breasts and her eyes were open to the size of tablespoons.

'*No more*,' roared the men. '*No more*.'

What are we saying? thought Solomon – while he was still capable of independent decision-making and opinion.

'*You'll get caught*,' Georgie was told.

She bowed her head and gently cupped her pubic hair.

I want to scare her, thought Solomon.

I want to leave, thought Clement.

I want her to die, thought Bob.

Worth

RIGHT ON TIME, AS the first of the razors sliced the first of his bristles, Belswain experienced his sympathy pains.

First the hip—the left hip—with the pain nipping neatly through the bone and into his backside.

Sometimes this agony alone was enough to floor him. On more than one occasion he'd awoken to the drip-drip-drip of soapy water falling onto his face, having collapsed unconscious with the faucets still running.

Then came the apparent laceration to his sternum. Whether standing or lying down, Belswain would buckle in two; quite possibly whimper—quite possibly beg for a cessation to this monthly torture.

His pleas were never answered. Yet always, when Belswain was dripping invisibly from non-existent wounds, his memory could call her back; she was there, behind his eyes somewhere, and she could hear him, she could react to his moans—but she couldn't do anything to delay her revenge, not even by one tiny instant.

Belswain was digging too hard with the razor. He'd drawn blood. He felt sick. As his strength guttered out and his stomach spasmed, he was suddenly aware of who was in the room with him.

And his understanding of the pains was complete.

It wasn't often that Belswain felt obliged to explain his plans, or the reason for them, but when he did it was usually around the first of the month. Come what may, the first of the month was Shave Day. He would enter a gas station restroom,

207

a hotel, a supermarket, a gym, or even—once—a bordello, and he would make himself as presentable as possible. Take some new clothes from the trunk of the car and try, for a week or so, to re-enter the human race.

Today was the 29th of June, and Belswain looked a shambles. Not that there was anyone to witness the condition, however: this was Utah, and Belswain was driving through the salt flats. If ever there was a place where the surroundings matched his appearance, he thought, it was Maggotville, here: Maggotville, Utah. Population: minus numbers. But the bleakness was oddly cheering. Belswain laughed and hoisted a cheek to break wind. As the power windows dipped, air as hot as animal breath caved in through the gap. Furthermore, the air smelt of onions but Belswain was unwilling to rely any longer on the rattling aircon.

With joyful buoyancy of heart he flicked on the radio, expecting little. Static belched free, but then the waves cleared and some cross-eyed honkytonk—with nothing quite gelling—spattered out.

Belswain shrank into his seat—because of the noise. Not the noise of the off-key pianist, but a sudden shredding roar that had capitalized his attention. He didn't speak but his face screamed volumes.

The din swelled—expanded—bled more noise—and was just as suddenly receding. To Belswain's right, away from the road, and above the sand and twig-like bones, a vapour trail was pushing before it a saucer-shaped object.

'Holy Jesus,' said Belswain. The Nova swerved like cloud-curves.

An apostrophe of smoke curled up in the distance. Belswain revisited his curse; he slowed the vehicle. Leaning the left-side of his face against the wheel he kept his eyes peeled for signs of movement.

The crash had taken place too far away; nothing could be done from here. Belswain entertained the thought of moving closer. As he opened his car door the afternoon heat made a claim for his calf; it tugged. Sighing, Belswain complied and exited the vehicle. He was wearing dark colours, as ever, and the temperature's ferocity impressed him immediately. As an afterthought he reached for his bottle of water, on the back seat. The plastic was as warm as a baked potato, and having taken a breath or two, he ventured away from the beaten path; his ankles sinking deep into the sand.

Belswain gripped the bottle of warm water harder. Its presence was comforting. Looking over his shoulder at the car provided a similar reassurance but a doubt presented itself immediately. Say the vehicle wouldn't start when he returned to it. What then? Apart from what had flown across his bows—whatever that would turn out to be—Belswain had seen no traffic for the last two hours. Surely someone used this road though, he attempted to convince himself. Maybe I should've left the engine running. Who would steal it?

But Belswain had no idea how long the rescue operation would take: nor indeed if any rescue would be necessary. Allowing the gas in the tank to waste away would have been a bad idea, he decided. He wished he owned a cell phone. Maybe the radio will be working in the cockpit, he thought. For despite the evidence—the saucer shape, the peculiar drone of the engine—Belswain was telling himself that what he'd seen was a helicopter. A military chopper, most likely, he thought as his eyes took in the wreckage: from a distance it resembled an ant-mound. No blades, his mind replied; no landing... *doobries*.

His vision blurred. He blinked until he got matters back under control. His head felt hot. Such hair as remained on his crown grew in tatty circles, with aisles of burnable flesh in between. He had a hat to prevent any exposure to the sun— an Australian bushman's hat, minus the dangling wine corks. Wouldn't that be ironic, thought Belswain: the poisoner poisoned, the biter bitten—the rescuer, poleaxed by heatstroke, requiring the assistance of the next Good Samaritan to venture along Ghost Road.

His left hip twinged. 'Mother of Jesus,' said Belswain aloud; his voice sucked dry air into the back of his throat. The plastic bottle squeaked a protest, and Belswain realized that he was squeezing it too hard. But it was no wonder that he was…

'A flying saucer,' he said.

A now-landbound broken flying saucer, true, but a saucer nonetheless. 'A flying saucer,' Belswain repeated, by no means certain of what to do with the information. No instinct to run was enforced, but neither did Belswain feel compelled to put a foot forward. He was waiting for something to happen.

Seconds dwindled away. The sun on Belswain's head, finally, was the impetus needed. He could feel his scalp turning red, and he stepped forward, his shirt melting into his skin and the water in the bottle now as hot as coffee.

The air around the wounded saucer was shimmering. The saucer was radiating heat—as if it had recently slipped through the earth's prophylactic diaphragm of gases. It hadn't burned up on entry; it had suffered a worse indignity.

This could make me famous, thought Belswain. Maybe that was the use to which his life could be put. He wondered how he could copyright the moment, and then he wished he had a camera in addition to the phone. Perhaps recognition was what he'd been chasing all along—respect in the eyes of others.

He circled the mangled cutlery of the saucer, looking for

the way in. It was small: not much bigger than twice the size of Belswain's car. And it was grey. However, on closer inspection it did not exhibit what Belswain had come to think of as typical flying saucer attributes. For one thing the metal—and it was undoubtedly metal—was not smooth and seamless. If anything, the welding looked like something of a botched job. Belswain frowned. The central dome was of darkened glass, scarcely otherworldly, no more glamorous than the windows of a rock star's limousine. Bizarre, he concluded.

Belswain jumped: a hatch thudded open. The water fell to the dust—and Belswain's breath clogged up his lungs. He whimpered.

But the figure struggling free was entirely human.

A weather-worn, penny-red face—about sixty—with shoots of snow-white hair. This pilot was slim and trim; he was wearing the dark green coveralls of a gas station mechanic or a neurosurgeon.

Spying Belswain was evidently a moment loaded with surrealism—and Belswain could see his point. Why would anyone be out here on the skin of the desert? Half in and half out of the hatch, the pilot paused and surprising Belswain said loudly:

'Are you him?'

'Am I who?'

'My Angel of Death.'

Belswain had been called many things in his forty-two years, but never an Angel of Death. He said, 'No.'

'In that case,' said the pilot, 'would you mind giving me a friggin' hand?'

When Belswain launched himself onto the saucer, the hot metal shifted under his feet like a rickety bridge. That this old boy had built the contraption was suddenly in no doubt; but the question of why needed a bit of explanation.

It was a hermit's cell: it was the sort of place that Belswain had read about over the years—the sort of place that was inhabited by millionaire recluses and mad scientists. Or someone with a foot in either camp, perhaps.

Belswain was impressed. As Reeves led him deeper into the ground, through interconnected honeycombs, Belswain said, 'This is beautiful. It must've taken you years.'

'Decades, actually. Two of 'em,' Reeves replied. 'Take a seat.' They had arrived at the small barroom. Reeves slipped behind the bar and Belswain perched himself on a heavy stool. 'I suppose you think I'm obsessive.' Reeves cackled. 'What do you drink?'

'I don't. Can I have a Coke?'

'No. I'm not letting the man who helped me out of a jam go away with just a soda.'

The truth was painful but it needed to be said. 'I'm a recovering alcoholic,' Belswain told his host, 'and a Coke on a hot day like this is a perfect thank-you.'

Reeves considered this. 'Coke it is,' he decided. 'You don't mind if I do, though, do you?'

'I don't mind.'

'You won't get the heebie-jeebies.'

'No.'

'Good.' Reeves poured himself a tumbler full of whiskey, to the brim. He took a good long swallow and then topped it up. He poured Belswain a Coca-Cola from the fridge, with the latter not caring about the sand that he saw had found its way into the bottom of the glass. They clinked. 'Chin chin,' said Reeves.

'Down the hatch.'

They drank.

'So what were you doing out there anyway?' Reeves asked. The two of them had shared very little conversation in the car from the site of the crash to Reeves' home. Introductions had been made ('Jim Reeves—like the singer?' Belswain had nodded. 'My dad had some of his records,' he'd said) but a stunned silence had prevailed.

'Everyone's gotta be somewhere,' said Belswain.

'True.'

'Anyway, I could ask you the same question.'

Reeves nodded. 'You want to know about the saucer,' he said. 'Understandable. You're not a reporter by any chance, are you?'

'No.'

'Or a Federal agent?'

'No. Why do you ask?'

213

Reeves shrugged. 'It's entirely possible you were sent out to find me. Still wondering what you were doing out there...'

'Couldn't I've just been going from one place to the next?' asked Belswain, a little amused.

'Suppose so.' Reeves drank.

'You sound disappointed.'

Again, Reeves shrugged. 'Wouldn't hurt to be taken seriously once in a while,' he said. 'Shown a bit of respect.' He brightened. 'So what is your trade, if you don't mind me asking?'

'I don't work anymore,' said Belswain, 'but I used to work in a furniture warehouse. Nothing exciting.'

'Depends on your point of view. And now you drive across the desert. I'm intrigued.'

'Across the country, actually. What I do is trace state boundaries, more or less. Knocking 'em down one by one.'

Reeves replied, 'You're sewing the country together. Big

patchwork quilt.'

'I guess so.' But the image was far from wholesome. Pain twanged in his left hip.

'Looking for what?'

'A way that I can be useful, maybe.'

'And how long a you been doing that?'

'Two years plus.'

Reeves smiled. 'And I was worried you'd think me obsessive. So what did you do that was so awful?' he wanted to know. He took the top off the whiskey bottle again, in order that Belswain might be spared the accusatory stare.'

'Excuse me?'

Reeves faced Belswain once more. 'What you're just described, my friend, is a penance for a sin you committed,' he explained before smiling again. 'Unless you happen to be going through the worst friggin' mid-life crisis I ever heard about.'

Sighing, Belswain said heavily, 'Maybe both. It's true: I'm paying a price,' he admitted.

'Me too.' Reeves nodded.

'Oh yeah? What did you do?' That came out rather aggressively, rather insolently, Belswain was aware; he would have to make an effort to moderate his voice. The problem was, the subject of his misdemeanour could still get to him, could still retrace the wound and flick it hard, stop it healing: the hip, the ripe fruit of the sternum. Yet he needed to tell; it was compulsive—to tell anyone who showed any interest whatever. Almost as though he longed to be punished by another's derision or disapproval.

'No. You show me yours and then I'll show you mine,' said Reeves. 'What did you do?'

'Are you ready? I killed a child. Driving.'

'Drunk?'

'Oh yes.'

A second or two passed, and then Belswain said, 'And you?'

'I found a UFO,' Reeves answered.

'Well I'm not sure that qualifies as a sin,' said Belswain.

It was Reeves' turn to sound disgruntled, and it would take Belswain mere seconds to understand that people liked having made their mistakes; that they were personal, these errors, not matter how frequently they were shared; and that no one had any right to try to diminish them or make the perpetrator of the sin feel better. Feeling bad is what makes me feel good, Belswain would realise.

'Why, what's your definition of a sin?' Reeves demanded.

Belswain was ready. 'Something you do that makes your life suffer ever after,' he said.

Having drained his glass Reeves smacked his lips. 'Then my friend, I've committed a sin—because since I found the friggin' thing my life ain't been worth what a gecko shits.'

Two years down the road, and Belswain could still feel the violence of the impact. Could still feel the thud—hear the scream... his own scream. And he could still see the wipers smear the blood across the windshield, like a rich preservative on a thin slice of bread.

Sometimes the memory woke him up; usually, however, it didn't—it was easier for Belswain to punish himself if he remained asleep. The guilt when he opened his eyes was that bit more intense.

'Do you mind me asking?' said Reeves—'but how do you fund this? You worked in a furniture place and you haven't worked for two years.'

'My father had money. He left it to me when he died,' Belswain answered. He was on his third Coke, feeling gassy, desiring a whiskey. 'I mean, that's parental love for you. Not only does he stand by you, he also leaves you everything he has—and he takes the rap for you.'

'He took the rap?'

Belswain nodded. 'He was in the car at the time. We told the police he was driving. No one saw it to contradict us.'

'Did he get into trouble?'

'No...' Belswain was recalling the girl's body in her summer frock: she'd been knocked out of her shoes, her left hip mashed. 'She ran out in front of the car.'

'Jesus.'

'And this'll be where you ask me to leave,' said Belswain.

Reeves shook his head. 'You don't have to leave,' he said. 'In fact I was about to ask if you wanted to stay the night. As you can see, I have plenty of space—spare towels and razors. What would you say?'

'I'd say thank you.'

Reeves nodded. 'You made a terrible mistake, and you're sorry. That's good enough for me. Sometimes I feel that making mistakes is what we were put on this good earth to do.'

Belswain grinned. 'I feel a UFO segue coming on,' he said.

'A UFO Segue is what they'll call the bio-pic of my life,' said Reeves. 'UFOs've been with me since the age of nine.' He was starting to slur his words. 'We lived in Wyoming—me, my sisters, Mom and Dad. And a UFO lands one night. Does nothing. Just lands... Are you sure I can't tempt you to something stronger than soda?' he asked for the second time. 'I feel awful guilty getting messed up in front of you.'

'Then don't.'

'Don't feel guilty, I hope you mean—unless you're presuming to tell me what to do in my own home.'

216

Never: never try to rationalize with a drunk, Belswain informed himself. Didn't he know that well enough?

'No offence intended, my friend.'

Reeves nodded. 'None taken,' he said—almost grudgingly. 'None taken, I'm sure.'

He was driving too fast.

He and his father were gridlocked on a difference of opinion.

He was not paying attention to the road.

Nails. The subject of the disagreement was nails, of all things. He was chauffeuring Dad over to the 'Hammer Time!' hardware store to buy nails. Belswain had volunteered to help his father fix the back yard fence, but they had different ways of going about the task. They always did. So Belswain made it a point of getting tight on a few fists of rum before he drove across town...

He hit her.

'You have to wonder, when it happens—why me? Why this ten metre squared pile of rocks and lizardshit? Why not ten miles down the road, in Maggotville, where others can see it-'

Belswain interrupted. 'What did you say the next town along's called?' he said.

'Maggotville. Well, Margaretville really, but if you stop there long enough you'll understand.'

'And how long's long enough?'

'About ten minutes.' Reeves scattered a seriously whiskey-sodden laugh in Belswain's direction.

'It's the strangest coincidence,' said the other man. 'I called it that in my head but I was just joking.'

'But why not there, is my point? Why not slap-bang in the

217

middle of the city? Why the desert?'

'It reminds them of home?' Belswain ventured. 'They're claustrophobic? They're bad drivers?'

'No. It's because, when you climb Mount Everest you don't want—or expect—to find a party on the plateau, do you know what I mean? They're lonesome travellers—but sometimes they can't resist making friends, just like we do.'

'They come in peace.'

Reeves nodded. 'They come in peace. Or else, why the fuck come alone?'

'So what happened?'

'I was out back…'

Reeves was having his mid-morning drink, playing horse-shoes in the yard—life being tough for a retired software engineer—when to a fan of baking air, the saucer hit the ground like a tossed discus. It careened and dug a hole in the earth.

Having run back to fetch his handgun, Reeves set about chasing the whale. The saucer had stopped rotating fifteen metres from Reeves' house: he regarded it, now, as his property. Finders keepers.

A ramp was lowered—an electric sigh. Reeves had his feet apart, the handgun at shoulder height, 'ready to blow the friggin' alien bastard to kingdom come'.

The legs were spindly and scaly; there were terrible claws on each foot. Apart from the head the alien was small—no taller than four feet high—with the reptilian appearance continuing up to the crest on its head. The belly was distended. The colour was winter-leaf green, out of place in itself in the bathroom pastels of the desert. Its head was long, the mouth as wide (Reeves assumed) as a shark's.

Reeves' right forefinger squeezed the trigger…

'And you killed him?' said Belswain, biting into the pause.

'No. He snapped a mind-thing on me. I couldn't complete; I was frozen. It was like I was holding my breath,' said Reeves. 'Then the son of a bitch unfolded these drabby grey wings and flapped his way free of the saucer. My friend—I wasn't even scared.' Reeves was shaking his head. 'I couldn't feel a thing...'

Belswain winced: the old phantom wounds: the hip, the sternum.

'You okay?'

'Yeah. Just sympathy pains, I guess.'

'You know what's good for that, don't you? A good glass of whiskey.'

Belswain had been sober for two years, or so he endeavoured to convince himself; but slips had occurred. A beer here, a chaser there... What the hell? He thought in response to ancient juices now starting to boil in his body again. One can't hurt.

'Sure, okay. Thanks.'

It sailed through Belswain on a perfect thermal; the wake it left behind sluiced through his brain. The signals were easily remembered: Belswain's stomach lining ignited with pleasure.

The pains, however, did not disperse.

Suddenly Belswain thought of his father. He tried not to do so too often, but drink was the expressway back into the past. He dipped himself into long-gone arguments, with his father enmisted by the vapour from a singing kettle; he recalled the sting of having to ask for readmission to the family home, aged twenty-seven, on the breakdown of his first and only marriage. But another memory was more insistent than either.

Dad's face, constipated with a pain that he couldn't pass through his system. And Belswain could remember frowning, unable to make head nor tail of the man's suffering. Not even certain that he was required to help.

219

'Ask yourself this,' his father had said on another occasion altogether. 'What is your worth to the world around you? What use are you? Because if you can't be of use then I'll personally buy you another bottle and I'll personally stand here until you've drunk yourself into a coma—or into your deathbed.'

One of Dad's many anti-booze spiels, recalled here and now by Belswain... Was it shame that tinkered with Belswain's feelings at this moment?—shame at seeing the wagon from which he'd fallen, rolling on? It felt like disappointment and confusion.

'Listen.' This was Reeves, disturbing the reverie, 'you want to see it, right? The UFO. You've waited long enough—I'm impressed by your patience.'

'You learn a lot of that, on the road,' Belswain answered, needing to know more, much more...

'I can imagine. Finish your drink.'

'I don't want to get smashed,' said Belswain.

'You're already smashed. You were smashed before you took a sip,' said Reeves, weirdly, as he got to his feet. He collected his handgun from behind the bar.

Belswain felt drunk on Reeves' behalf. Ignoring the query of why Reeves wished to take a weapon, Belswain asked, 'Would you mind if I took another one of those with me?'

'Help yourself.'

Belswain poured as Reeves used the bar as a walking stick. What an odd expression that is, thought Belswain: help yourself. But it's true, because no other swine'll help you... This had been the core message from Belswain's father, almost up until his dying breath. Help yourself, but be useful to humanity in some way. The old man had carried on in this fashion until the day that he had set Belswain free to embark on this mission—by dying.

The whiskey formed a meniscus just above the lip of the glass. Caring little for the disapproval of his host, Belswain leaned over and sucked away a few millimetres. Then he picked up the glass, feeling woozy, feeling sweatier than when he'd come in. He staggered out.

Ponytailed and jodhpurred, she had ridden her bicycle a few blocks closer to the main stem in order to collect a CD for her father's birthday present. She was crossing the road on foot to buy his card when—

When he hit her.

Belswain hit her.

Belswain scooped her slight body up as surely as a field-er takes a low ball into his mitt. But it wasn't the girl who screamed. Nor was it Belswain's father. The girl was clipped on her left hip and thrown into the windshield before acrobatting her way in a noisy beer-keg roll over the roof.

The car was brought to a halt.

'Ohmigod ohmigod…' said Belswain, fiddling with con- trols. Accidentally he engaged the wipers: the rubber strips scratched wearily across the dry and cobwebbed glass. They smeared the child's blood as if they were trying to see the back of it.

'Ohmigod ohmigod…'

'Change positions,' said Belswain's father. 'I was driving, okay? Okay?'

You're kidding, thought Belswain. A cattle barn? He keeps a flying saucer in the cattle barn?

The air was pure toaster-emission. An effusion of sweat coursed from Belswain's skin, as if it had been waiting. The drink had already swallowed his powers of rational thinking, but even so, the inappropriateness of the storage space seemed comical. Not that Belswain could think of a better place…

'So from that day on,' Reeves was saying, 'I've been studying the friggin' saucer, tryin' to copy the design. Trying to learn about the electrics, the hydraulics-'

'Trying to fly,' said Belswain.

'Well, exactly.' They had reached the barn doors and Reeves was choosing his keys with the fussy patience of an artist mixing his colours.

Belswain hated the wait. The sun was cracking open his bald spots, he was certain; in truth, the mixture of whiskey gulped too quickly and the merciless sun, was giving him double vision. Belswain watched two separate Reeveses poke two separate keys into two separate padlocks.

A graceless whine accompanied Reeves' opening the door; a workshop odour puffed out. 'I couldn't begin to tell you how many drafts and changes I had to make,' said Reeves, 'but I was a man possessed. I wanted a flying saucer of my own and that was all there was to it.'

Believing that Reeves was fishing for a compliment, Belswain said, 'You've done extremely well. I thought it was the real thing—that's why I followed you in the first place.'

'But I can't fly more than about a mile; I always crash.'

'Well that's a disadvantage, certainly.'

They stepped inside, and the change in light-quality messed with Belswain's head. Purple bruises appeared in the air—the air being dense and heavy—and Belswain saw in one of these bruises the little girl's face: the little girl that he had knocked into oblivion. She was smiling. Belswain was perplexed. He could sense her pain—the pain in her left hip, in her sternum—but this was not a recollection of the accident. Indeed, the scene was different altogether: in this new version the girl stepped backward, up onto the kerb, and avoided Belswain's inebriated swervings. Her smile had faded, but the little girl was still alive.

'Holy cow.'

Reeves had flicked on the lights; what was revealed was an obsessive's view of the world. Less a workshop than a shrine to the otherworldly, it was full of fledgling saucers, abandoned sketches and cannibalised and aborted engines. Tools were lying around everywhere: tables and tables of tools and junk and fuses and scrap.

The vista wobbled; what Belswain could see all melted together, but it was simple enough to make out the original flying saucer—the prototype—which was just as small as Reeves' copy. Belswain's side and stomach—and now face—were throbbing like buggery, in one of his father's immortal expressions. His face had never been part of the problem before; was he sunburnt? *Christ, I feel awful*, thought Belswain as he raised the glass he'd brought with him to his lips. He set the glass on a bench, beside a hammer.

'And the authorities won't take you seriously?' Belswain asked. 'I'd say the evidence was…'

He thought of his father. Dad was asking that question again—the one about Belswain's usefulness. But he was asking it at a very strange time: as he was bouncing over the roof of Belswain's car. Belswain's scalp was shrinking, or so it felt—pulling his memories together and getting them all muddled up.

'I never told the authorities,' said Reeves, and moving quickly on he added, 'Do you want to see the alien?'

'He's here?' Belswain turned to face the Reeves Triplets; he struggled to decode the other man's expression.

'Sure. They wouldn't give him a job at the bank,' Reeves

223

replied. Evidently he imagined this to be highly amusing.

'Where is he?'

They walked along a cluttered aisle to a door at the back of the barn. As they did so Belswain thought of the day of the accident, but by now his head was so scrambled that he couldn't even remember who it was that his car had struck.

Belswain was in agony. I can hardly walk, he said to himself—but he had to see what was on offer. Nervous and distracted by pain, he ran a hand through his month-old beard...

And everything dipped and faded.

A sink was before him, and he was gripping its soap-slimy sides. He was sweating and sick; but it was entirely plausible that he was also dying, judging by the discomfort that was burning in his hip, his butt, his sternum.

'Sympathy pains,' he hissed.

Looking up into the mirror, Belswain also looked through the windscreen and the little girl's face collided with the glass. He heard her as she rumbled and rolled across his roof.

He screamed. She did not have the time for such a luxury.

The mirror was cracked with the impact.

Belswain stared into the web, and his face was in pieces—as badly so as his beard was: the beard that he had only just started to shear away. Painlessly, the disposable razor that he'd dropped had landed on his right big toe, but Belswain was not thinking about the razor. Not the razor, not the sink of greyed water, and not the haphazard approach he had to shaving.

Was it Shave Day? Was it really the first of the month?

Belswain shrieked.

The girl's face was in the mirror, in slices.

And everything brightened, but Belswain still felt sick—

and confused.

He was still leafing through the folds of his beard. Shave Day hadn't arrived, so what was he thinking of? Belswain burped. It tasted of sick.

I haven't shaved, he thought.

A burning arrow poked through his sternum.

He hissed. With stupidly bad timing he looked forward to ridding himself of his beard. He frowned. So drunk was he (on so little drink!) that he had the strangest sense of déjà vu—that he'd already removed his bristles.

Reeves unbolted and opened the door.

Belswain could see clearly, although the picture was in triplicate: surprise, indignation and shock had sharpened his focus.

The alien was in a cage. And the creature was exactly as Reeves had described it: short, reptilian, and scaly, with a comb on its head. The colours were dark, and the eyes did not look friendly. Spittle was drooling from its wide, shark-like maw.

225

'I don't know what to say,' Belswain admitted.

'How about 'Hello'?'

Belswain was amazed. 'Can it understand me?'

'No, not really,' said Reeves, 'but it understands a peaceful intention.'

'So why's it in a cage?'

Declining to answer the question, Reeves said instead, 'He let his guard down for a second when he had me in a mindlock. And I shot him. Since then he's been my friggin' puppy, ain't you boy? Go closer if you want to.'

'I'm scared.'

'My friend, he's a rat in a box, nothing more.'

'What if he puts a mind-thing on me?'

'Then I'll remind him of the damage this baby can do.' Reeves replied, patting the gun.

Despite everything—the pains, the wooziness—Belswain was curious. He stepped into the room and his eyeline connected with the creature's. It was the closest he'd come to a religious experience...

Blackness temporarily covered Belswain's eyes: a response to the shock of having the door close behind him. The metal sang in its frame, and Belswain panicked. What made matters worse, of course, was hearing the bolts banging shut.

Reeves was on the other side.

'Reeves!' Belswain cried. 'Lemme out!' He banged his fists against the door face. 'Lemme out, you bastard!'

No reply. Belswain heard a screech. Turning quickly he sucked air that felt solid in his chest.

The alien had opened the door to its cage. The creature had never been trapped.

Belswain started to swear.

The alien started to approach.

'Ohmigod... ohmigod...'

It reached him in only a few steps, and its strength was astonishing. But at its first strike—a claw to Belswain's left hip—the victim understood.

There were no mind tricks that this lifeform could perform; this animal's means of communication was violence. Jim Reeves had ensnared an alien being—an animal which now dug its fist into Belswain's sternum. Belswain screamed.

Flashback: the first Coca-Cola that Reeves had poured into the glass—the grains of sand that were saturated. Only they weren't grains of sand, Belswain now knew. 'What the fuck did you give me?' he demanded—or maybe he didn't. The flesh of his lower torso was shredded away.

Would he wake up with soap-drenched water in his face?

Was he worth any damned thing?

226

Belswain saw her ponytail and her milk-tea-coloured jodh-purs, and he rejected the present, even as the alien was brushing some of the flesh from his back. Whatever drug he'd been given, it had thoroughly squirreled his way of thinking and had turned him into something else. He had no idea of how much had been true, and how much a fabrication. Had he really followed a flying saucer? Had he really met a man named Reeves?

On the other hand, his use to the world was simple and unequivocal; and his father would have been so proud—whoever his father had been.

Belswain was food.

And there was no such thing as a sympathy pain.

A Wound

KEEP ME WARM, she said, and I leaned towards her and placed my left arm around her shoulders, our leather jackets croaking like bullfrogs. Her hair smelt of good shampoo, and of marijuana smoke – a memento of the gig. We were happy, I think. She wore the same shade of lipstick as the lead singer had, but mine was darker still.

The bus crowned the hill and a businessman in a weary old suit climbed down, his briefcase at his outer thigh like an obedient dog.

Apart from the driver we were alone.

We weren't saying much. The long pauses were not uncomfortable. My ears rang, and it was difficult to hear anything above the whine of the engine. Before long we were heading into the outer estates. The shops had been closed and boarded blind for the night.

I thought of the holiday in Dakar; of the tent we had shared, and of the way that the sea had gossiped gently in the distance.

Keep me warm, she had said, for even then the nights had chilled us. I had lain on top of her with her coat pulled open, and the grungy work smock had felt rough. She had pushed her tongue between my strips of teeth, as if that too had suffered from the night air. I had grown into her belly. Without a sound she had placed her hands low down my back, and then slipped the tips of her fingers beneath the rope-tied waist of my baggy, thick trousers. Her fingerprints, Brailling me, cool – cool as ice.

She was always cold. She had a problem with her circulation, and there was no fat to warm her on her hips. But I gathered that there was more than this to her request for my embrace. Not once in our time together had she been through the outer estates without needing a cuddle; she was terrified of where we lived.

The driver appeared none too confident either. Despite the low temperature, a sweat-stain the shape of South America had leaked through his regulation shirt – at the top of his arm. I'm sorry about the busted heating, he called back, and I told him we were fine.

Again, my thoughts ambled back to Dakar. We were centimetres, now, from the hot perimeter ashes of the fire I had crafted. A red and orange chiaroscuro on her breasts, and the hurried juggling with the rope at my waist. Her nose on my scrotum; the sticky dabs of her tongue on the crenellations. 229 Then her legs, arched and strong, dipping down onto my feelings.

Contiguity.

The sound, the light, the impression: all visited at one and the same time. I understood. Hearing the bang was the worst; even worse than the blood that squirted up onto my chin. The bolt broke through the window and squared her on the temple. She had no time to scream. Her head deliquesced – shards of glass and fists of blood moving sideways across the bus. A mural on the window across the aisle. A headless woman, or nearly, by my side, now slumped.

The driver shrieked.

What did you call me? I had asked. We were fused. It had taken a lot of strength for her to push herself off the cliff: to jump. Reaching for her discarded clothing, she pouted, already guilty, and said – Nothing.

I thought of the time that Brodie had given me the sack

from *Slipped Discs*. And God, how I'd loved that job. But his betrayal was no different. All betrayal is a test, and I have to respond accordingly.

With surprising calm – You called me Robert, I told her. I propped myself up on an elbow. Who's Robert?

No one.

But the donning of her clothes had told a different tale altogether.

I had held his hand tight in the till – that's what I did. Until he'd agreed to my severance pay. A regular, monthly bonus; he'd heard of the company I kept.

What was that? the driver wailed. I'd been fossilised in glass, blood and bone. Leaves of brain, reeking, had coagulated on my cheek, my chin.

230   Panicked, all I could say was – A wound.

Are you testing me? I had asked Brodie.

No.

And are you testing me? I had asked her.

No.

Be careful, I had said.

Mary Mother, the driver bellowed. I heard his heavy foot as it stamped down on the pedal… and I heard my own eyelids click shut. The engine gunned. Forwards, we raced; but that would only take us deeper into the undergrowth, I realised. My heart was beating something fierce. Opening my eyes, I turned my head to see the damage – but not to her: to the bus's other window. Red and grey tumours were sliding down the screen.

Seeking solace in the majestic, I had strolled to the sea. Calmly I had asked it for answers. Mauve waves, arriving as tubes. Bits of shell beneath my feet. I had known of her approach before she arrived: she was small, lithe – but graceless, plodding in her movements. She kicked up stones.

Just a friend, she told me.

Then why? I asked. Why now?

She'd been seeing him for two months before the plane had taken us to that place. If at all she could be believed, she had attempted to finish it more than once. – But you brought him with you instead, I replied. In your head.

I'm sorry.

You will be. You're not as strong as you think, I told her.

I'm not strong at all. Neither are you. You need help.

Another bolt – another pot-shot. Once more, the sounds and sights joined hands. The driver's window was reduced to confetti, and his head cracked open like a dropped egg. He was thrust up and over his gate, like a mare escaping a stable. Sludge and slime all around.

The vehicle moved on. Momentum.

It swerved, it righted; through a child's play area it careened. When it finally drew to a halt, I whimpered. A swing oscillated on its chunky chains – slipping in through the windshield of the bus on groaning links.

Tears. A meniscus of tears in my eyes, slow to shed. The stench of death was pungent. I had no idea of what to do next. I waited.

You're not as strong as you think, she told me again, in my mind.

Silence.

I'm sorry, she repeated – over breakfast, over joints, and as we queued for surfboards and for seafood. I'm sorry. As we bussed to the airport, as we sank rum doubles and played the video games, killing Martians – So sorry.

Please forgive me.

I forgive you. If you tell me it's over, I forgive you. Just make a choice.

I want *you*, she said, clutching my forearm – a resolute grip. The relief was salty. While fingering her earrings I kissed her eyebrows. – Hush now.

As though myopic, quaint and feeble, the attackers circled the bus; the rings got smaller. Having spent very little at the gig on t-shirts or mug-trees, I had a hundred pounds burning in my pocket. This I would lose.

The man who eventually forced the door was Oriental, with a tattooed neck; a length of chain-link fence was his jewellery. He said –

What's your name?

I said – Mark.

Stepping over the driver's corpse – You got the money? he asked with a nod. Servile, apologetic. Respectful.

From the tight grenade of tenners I unfolded five notes, saying – What about your footprints, in the blood?

Forget about it. I was never here. None of us were.

I don't forgive you, I had told her as we landed. I had bought her a brooch in the market the following Saturday, and repeated – I don't.

She had nodded. You said that, she had told me.

Where's my money? I had asked Brodie the next month. On being told that I would receive nothing more, I used a disc. It was a band called Minus Child. I used the disc, blunt and awkward, as I might a circular saw.

His neck was only scratched, but he said – Enough. The till...

In the evening she had made spaghetti, and I'd said it again.

The question is, she had replied, do you want me to stay with you? Do you want us to stay together, for now? Until we find a way forward?

I guess. I'd been shovelling pasta and pesto into my mouth.

She had kissed me. – Then we move away from this area. Deal?

No. I like it here, I'd replied. Here, where my reputation was secure; where I had earned a scintilla of fearful respect.

More than me? she'd asked.

More than you, I hadn't answered. Instead I had punched her groin. She doubled over and screamed in scissors at me. But the groin was the only place to attack: it was how she had wounded me first.

Out of interest, said the Oriental man – what did she do?

My reply was immediate but non-committal. Damaged me.

How?

That's none of your business. You've got your money.

He shrugged. Just trying to make conversation, he said. – Did you love her?

Once. Not now.

What was there left to love?

Smiling softly, he said – Are you sure?

Yes!

Then why are you crying? he wanted to know.

I couldn't answer. The sea was a long way away.

233

Culchie

(with Lawrence Dyer)

THE CULCHIE DREAMED of running a race but falling forward before he reached the twitching white ribbon, held horizontal above the finish line by two of his old enemies from school, their faces leering as he fell, the grit biting his cheek. He awoke to face a familiar window, no curtains to border it, the glass tickled from outside by a prolonged fall of snow that seemed heavy for this time of year – the snowstorm had started hours before he had collapsed into sleep – but which he found refreshing and reassuring. As a boy he'd always liked snow. He watched it for five minutes. Snow reminded him of back home.

His hair as tangled as a string of Christmas lights in a box, the culchie moved into the bathroom and razored his jaw line with a diamond-cutter's precision. He flossed and gargled, then chose from a collection of wigs, the hairpieces pegged on a line in the boiler cupboard like so many bats in a belfry. Blond today, he decided, straight and neat. He settled the hairpiece's warmth over his own lush locks, and preened with comb and gel until he was satisfied.

Eschewing the option of an adhesive – but very realistic — moustache, the culchie opened a drawer in the bedroom and selected a pair of spectacles. The lenses were non-prescription, clear glass; the arms concealed a sequencer no-wired to his laptop, so that the right arm throbbed when he had incoming mail. Sometimes these specs could be a distraction and he would choose a different pair for a job, to escape mail; other times he wore none at all. Today he was expecting a mail or

234

two: it was his birthday.

September the fifteenth was the day, culchie's birthday, and this morning he was going out to celebrate. He was going to kill a total stranger.

Once had he been asked to kill someone he knew. He had resented this intrusion of the familiar into the anonymous; he had taken out his resentment on the man who offered the con-tract (there would be no more contracts from *that* source).

Reaching for the opened envelope, he looked once more at the face of the woman he was to erase. Zoe Jane Stedway was the name. There was something in that strong face that set her apart, an Egyptian definition, a hint of the ancient, the unassailable. At the same time, something familiar.

At least he didn't read *victim* into the features, which was good. The culchie liked a challenge, and he disliked preying on the weak, even if, as it was, the money was good.

With a shrug he directed his attention back to his reflection in the mirror. The ivory-white sphere that had replaced his left eyeball had grown larger in the night. Now it was distorting his eye-socket, and a sore, red crack had spread up his forehead. The culchie knew it could not be long before this growing thing split open his brain.

It had been inserted originally by his masters, a replace-ment for the eye – his non-targeting eye — and it contained a camera, so that they could watch, vicariously sharing the moment of death with him and the victim. But something was going wrong: the implant was expanding. He adjusted his glasses, staring with his good eye at the reflection of the pale grey sphere behind the left lens, its surface slightly moist, blank and unseeing — watching him, no doubt. It was fortunate that people he met could not see the sphere – he had tested it on the night-waiter who brought his room-service breakfast of kippers and toast at three in the morning.

'Do you see anything in my eye?' he had asked the stooping pudgy man as he set down the tray, 'I seem to have something in it.'

At first the waiter would not look – out of deference, it seemed. But when he did, when he looked closely, he had replied humbly, 'I'm sorry sir, I can't see anything.'

'My eye looks normal to you?'

'Yes sir. Will there be anything else?' he had asked, as if reluctant to believe that the sole desire of a man at three in the morning was salty fish.

The waiter now long gone and having caught up on some rest, the culchie inspected the grey sphere closely, wondering if anyone was watching his reflection in the mirror at that moment.

On the other side of the eye, on the other side of the camera, perusing these bathroom preparations with disdain, blown up as they were on a wall-sized display, the culchie watched himself.

In the old days, until Uncle Shane passed away (or was knocked away, as some of the local jokes ran), they would play Dare and Chicken on the road back home down the hill from The Slow Mile. There was often a practical reason for this. The road from the pub was one lane: there was not always a matter of choice in a drunken walker's participation in daredevil japes. If a car was sliding down this one-track corkscrew en route to the village (the vehicle often captained, it had to be said, by someone else who'd been a patron of The Slow Mile that evening) then dodging it was both fun and fairground.

Good times, they had been. That was how it was back then, back there; but one night, after a few, Uncle Shane was not so lucky, not so fleet of foot. 'Ah, when it's your time it's your time,' he used to say, tankard gripped; and sure enough, when that night arrived, no amount of smoky ale-breath was enough of a deterrent to shield himself from the tractor that bore down on him. So... so Uncle Shane passed away... or was knocked away, as some of the local jokes ran. Jokes that the culchie drew to mind as he stood outside The Slow Mile in the gloaming. Waiting to go in; listening to the alehouse Babel – the raucous punchlines, the roars of approval, a radio commentary – on a boxing match, was it? Hard to tell, and it didn't matter.

The culchie hadn't been back since the funeral, and he felt peculiar. For one thing, he wasn't a culchie here. This place was home – real home – where a sky, even a sky gloomed by a hint of storm, was something to see: vast and powerful. City skies could only impress a country bumpkin when the snow fell as thick as soot swept from a chimney; and that was rare enough. As far as people here were concerned, he had left them to make his way in the city – never mind it was a small city – and with that he lived as an urbanite now.

For a second thing, it was he who had driven the tractor.

He opened the door. Cosy warmth and booze bouquet: firm but loving sensations: the wide and kind embrace: the closest thing to a parent he'd ever known: The Slow Mile. The culchie smiled as Uncle Sean shouted:

'Flynn! .Sam! Boys! See who's come back to visit!'

The old man stood up and held up his arms.

'Come and give your uncle a hug, you city quare.'

On the other side of the camera the culchie watched; he saw himself embracing Uncle Sean, then shaking hands with Sam and Dara. Young Michael, still only seventeen, held out his fist, and the culchie pressed his own against the lad's.

'What brings you back to our little henhouse, Flynn?' Dara asked with a wry grin. From the other side of the screen the whole thing looked fragile, as if the characters were not real, but made of a brittle substance. Movie-prop glass, perhaps. He had only to flick Uncle Sean with his finger and thumb and the man would dissolve into a shower of sugared shards. With a sweep of his arm he could cut a swathe through them all: there would be a moment in which they all looked down in surprise at the route of his hand through their bodies.

Beside the spacious booth in which the culchie sat – wall-screen with the pub scene in front of him, darkness behind – he could see a woman looking at her own piece of animated wall. She was tall, over-weight – 'big-boned', Dara would have described her — in her late twenties. The culchie hadn't seen her before today, and was surprised that they had put someone new into the booth next to him, where Old Gringer normally sat. Perhaps Gringer had popped his clogs.

The culchie watched the woman for a moment, watching her own screen – some domestic scene with a child screaming – then she seemed to become aware of him and turned his way. Caught in the moment, he muttered, 'What you in for?' She twitched her cheeks and inclined her head in an expression that said: *What? I can't hear you.*

'What you in for?' he repeated in a loud voice, wishing he hadn't caught her attention.

'Killed my husband,' her muffled voice came back from behind the plexiglass. She took a long drag on a cigarette.

'Abusive?'

'No.' With a shrug she added, 'Just got bored.'

The culchie felt mildly alarmed. He always did when he found out what the others were in for: he was alarmed that their masters considered *him* as bad as *them*. And his profession older than the hills of Donegal!

Back on the screen the culchie was laughing – laughing fit to kill himself at some dirty joke Dara had told – while on the other side of the little round table young Michael looked uncomfortable. The culchie in the plexiglass booth watched without amusement. Behind him he could feel the presence of his masters, with their own camera watching him watching himself. Away off to the left and behind he could just make out the commentary of the live TV feed: the unseen audience must be enjoying watching him watch himself. If he concentrated he could hear the words of the commentary (at least he *thought* he could):

'Will Flynn decide to accept the offer or not? It's his moment of decision coming up any moment now.'

If the voice was real, it was his own, though he couldn't account for it. The snatch of commentary faded from his hearing but he knew what it had said was right. Another decision had to be made.

Zoe Jane Stedway wanted letters before and after her name, and those letters read *Dr.* and *PhD*. Every morning, while fighting with either the dissolving scraps of dreams, her duvet or her disappointment, she would remind herself that the letters were why she rose at this godforsaken hour; why she stood in the drizzle of an underachieving shower; and why her breakfast consisted of what she had left in the saucepan the previous evening. *Those letters.* She had a long way to go before she earned them, and this was something that she had no choice but to accept every morning when she opened up the pet shop to the general public. It would be worth it, she had promised herself, in the long run; propitious times awaited her, a few years down the road.

This morning she was late. Snow as thick as TV static had fallen through the early hours, which had elevated Zoe's hopes for a day off work… Very quickly, however, she had seen the schoolgirl error in the plan. A day off work? Dream on, Zo! Even if Armageddon had swept a fiery forearm across the city, the animals still had to be fed and watered. Jobs needed to be done. So it was that Zoe ventured into the dregs of the blizzard, in fawn-coloured dawn light, beneath a weak and mostly-hidden sun the unhealthy colour of aged meat, simply knowing that there'd be no buses; simply knowing that the shop would have no customers. Simply knowing that there must be better ways of funding a doctorate.

She was bushed by the time she arrived at the shop front. Not used either to the length of the walk or the effort of striding through snow, her legs burned at thigh and shin. She was ready for a cuppa.

'Good morning,' Zoe said to the man sitting on one of the stone benches along the parade – the one nearest to Yvette's Pets – the man so wrapped up and hunched in heavy clothing that he made Zoe think of a penguin sheltering from a blizzard of its own. Was he waiting for her to start the day's trading? Zoe removed a bunch of keys from her handbag, her ungloved fingers tingling. The visitor returned Zoe's hello and stood up. Evidently yes, he had been waiting for her. Who'd have thought it? Today, of all days. Urgent dog food requirements, perhaps; from what Zoe had seen of his face, he looked like a dog guy. You got wise to shoppers' habits after three years of studying faces.

'Sorry I'm late,' Zoe added.

'Not at all. Sorry *I'm* late. I won't keep you long.'

The alarm system harped impatiently. Having rubbed her boots quickly on a plush pelt-like mat, Zoe dashed in a skate towards the counter halfway along the length of the shop, on the right. Slips notwithstanding she had thirty seconds to disable the alarm before it started to bleat into the open air with fresh vigour. She moved past a bank of fish tanks, each containing a different species, and past a pen of bath sponge-sized copper-coloured rabbits. Elsewhere a guinea pig wheeked for food; the aviary of budgerigars, love birds and parakeets exploded into noisy flapping life.

Behind her, the customer approached the counter.

Zoe turned and fixed the man with the full beam of her best professional smile. 'What can I do for you this morning?' she asked.

'It's my birthday today.'

Okay… 'And you uh… you want to treat yourself to something?'

'In a manner of speaking, yes. That's a nice way of putting it.'

Distant warmth of a faint Irish accent; Zoe imagined herself listening to the sea from a few streets away from the beach. It reminded her of something – childhood, probably, some scene. What was this? Prompted by her punter's silence Zoe added, 'What kind of thing were you thinking about?'

The shop door clicked shut; it had taken its time to close, the progress slowed by a heavy hydraulic hinge at the top.

Was it the fact that this customer had caught her on the back foot that was making her nervous? At the closing of the door the quality of sound around her hadn't altered – the birds still squawked and chirruped, and there was no noise coming in from the snowy street anyway – but the air felt denser and harder to breathe, Zoe thought.

The customer opened his greatcoat.

'Oh my God…' Zoe whispered on seeing what had been

concealed. Her fingers rose to her lips; blood quickly leached from her features.

'This can fire two hundred and fifty rounds a minute. Does that sound impressive?' the man asked with what sounded like genuine curiosity in his voice. He seemed content to wait for an answer.

Zoe couldn't move; she could scarcely breathe. Inside the lagging of her coat her limbs felt heavy – and the weapon was still strapped across the man's chest. He hadn't even pointed it at her yet.

Maybe he wouldn't…

It took a few seconds before Zoe could find her tongue. 'It sounds,' she croaked, 'completely unnecessary. It's just a pet shop. The till's emptied every evening; there's nothing for you…'

'Do I look like I need chump change, my dear? I asked you a question.'

'N-No, that's a nice coat…'

'Not that question. I asked you if that sounds impressive.'

'.I don't know anything about guns.'

'Take a guess. I'm not actually a paragon of patience by the way.'

A heavy bowl of gas had lodged in Zoe's chest; it was still hard for her to breathe. Meeting her attacker's eyes with her own line of vision, Zoe nodded, hoping that a gesticulation would suffice.

'I can see why you'd think so,' the man continued, 'but it's largely a meaningless term, rounds per minute. Bolt-action rifles or artillery pieces are faster by a mile, but as I say, it's a meaningless term. Why? Because not many firearms'll sustain a whole minute's worth of fire, did you know that? And do you know why?'

'Run out of bullets?' Zoe managed.

'And the heat. Heat's lethal – leads to weapon failure. Even now! We've got better with water-cooled systems, but it's not an ideal science, not by a long chalk, Zoe, and most of the water-cooled weapons are heavy. This one's light as a feather, so it is. If the situation were different I'd give you a go, believe me I would, so you could see what I mean.'

'…You know my name.'

'I do indeed, Ms Stedway, 29B Margin Mews.'

'I haven't done anything. W-what do you want of me?'

'What do you think I want?'

Zoe's voice was low and laboured. 'I sell millet for budgerigars and spare perches. I sell little castles for kids to put in their fish tanks. Why would you know anything about –'

The Irishman interrupted her.

243

'What it is you're studying there, Zoe?'

'…Studying? It's a PhD. What's-'

'But what's the subject, Dr Stedway-to-be?'

'Risk Management.'

The Irishman laughed. 'Well you'd better get typing, darling! You've got a whole lot of risk to manage right now! You've been slow off the old boat, haven't you just.'

The counter separated them. How fast could he possibly be? Zoe wondered. True, she had yet to unlock the door to the back rooms – the little kitchenette area, the toilet and sink in an area no larger than a goal mouth. Could she unlock the door, put it between them, then lock it again – all before the Irishman made it round to her side of the counter?

Perhaps…

It must be the fifteenth or sixteenth time the culchie had watched this scene: Zoe making a dash for the back rooms, he chasing after her; she fumbling her keys, dropping them, backing up against the locked door as he raised the gun to point at her. Why did they keep showing it to him? It had become mundane. And each time he knew that the TV audience would see the camera angle switch between his motionless face and the heart monitor that was supposed to reveal something of his true feelings by showing his heart rate increase. But it wouldn't increase. So what was the point?

On the screen the final scene was almost over. If things followed true-to-type it would soon start up again, beginning with the morning of his last contract. He'd be looking at himself in the mirror again, about to shave. He would see the swollen eye-implant and guess that he had not long before it killed him.

Now he reached up to his eye socket and felt the edges of the hole where once had been his eye, and after that the implant. The implant hadn't killed him, just left a flappy hole – not so bad once you got used to it. There was room for a glass eye, but he had never had the opportunity to get one made. He had ended up here, instead, playing out this pointless game, day after day.

Perhaps they would make him watch it over and over again, week after week, year after year, until he died? And why the commentary, what was the point of that? It seemed to repeat too. Surely he couldn't be that interesting to a TV audience?

Unless he *was* the TV audience.

'Just tell me why,' Zoe demanded, a last desperate attempt to bring reason into this nightmare. At her back she could feel the cold wood of the back room door. But it might as well be the wall of an outlandish prison, the man before her a firing squad. By her right foot she could see her keys, splayed out on the floor. Now they meant nothing: they might be the last thing

244

she ever saw.

'I don't have to tell you anything,' the Irishman said evenly. 'I don't have to account for my actions.'

'*Please.*'

'.Your name was selected randomly.'

'By you?'

'Oh, good Lord no. I'm just the executioner.'

'Then by who?'

The question seemed to fox the visitor. 'By the audience, of course. So are you ready to put on a show?'

'No.'

'Good. That means you'll fight harder. That's good for the audience.'

'*What* audience?'

The man laughed. 'Oh I see,' he whispered. 'You're al- 245 ready in character.'

'I work in a *pet shop*,' Zoe tried to reiterate. 'I don't know anything about an audience or anything else.'

The culchie raised the weapon to her eyeline.

'Are you certain you don't want to play along?' he asked.

She stared at him in disbelief: she had no answer. The man was mad, he was going to kill her. But perhaps she could delay it, could actually play along, play for time. Her voice came out as a dry rasp, and she tried to swallow the dust that seemed to clog her throat. 'I want to play along,' she managed.

The culchie nodded.

'But I don't know how. I need your help.'

She had tried to keep her voice even, but there was a squeak of desperation at the end. The culchie lifted his gaze, then reassumed his firing stance, peering down the gun barrel at her again.

'For God's sake!' Zoe screamed. 'Tell me what you want

me to do!'

'*You have to find a way to fight back*,' the assassin whispered.

Inside the booth the culchie felt the iron wrist restraints cut in suddenly. Squinting, he forced his attention back to the screen. Something unexpected was happening! On the screen Zoe had stooped to retrieve the keys. The culchie saw himself fire — and miss — then Zoe rose up and heaved a pile of freebie local papers and advertising rags into his face – they had been on the counter. The assassin flapped his arms and then saw the door into the backroom closing. *Too quickly for reality.* The assassin fired again, punching a hole in the centre of the door, the silencer on the gun making the sound little more than a thud.

It made no sense, he had watched this scene hundreds of times: her crumpled face as she slid down the locked door to the floor, the way she clutched at her chest, the trickle of blood from the corner of her mouth as she lay on the floor arms akimbo, her lifeless eyes staring mindlessly at the ceiling. How could it be different this time?

Seeking an answer he twisted from side to side, peering through the plexiglass, looking for the truth. But the booths on either side were empty, and the dim figures in booths further away seemed to be concentrating on their own nightmares. But he had killed her! Never mind the video footage of it that they made him watch, he *knew* he had killed her. He *remembered* killing her! How could she have got away this time?

He dipped his head and closed his eyes. If his wrists had been free he would have put his head into his hands.

He was disturbed from this moment of mental escape by a click to his right. He jerked his head up to see someone opening the door to the booth. Was it time already for him to go back to the cold dark room they kept him in at night?

246

Then he saw who was opening the door.

It was Zoe.

'What brings you back to our little henhouse, Flynn?' Dara asked with a wry grin.

'Some unfinished business, Dar.'

'Oh sure,' said Uncle Shane (although he was dead, *knocked away* as the jokes ran), and he sucked on his pipe like a shilling-a-minute hooer. Cumuli of smoke enveloped his well-shaven features. 'And we all know what your business's name is, don't we, boys?'

As if it had been rehearsed the lads cried, '*MARIE!*'

Mirth had a lasso, and it rounded up everyone in The Slow Mile, even those who hadn't been privy to the conversation. Within a second or two everyone was laughing.

The only one who didn't get the joke was the culchie.

'What?' he kept asking. 'What is it?'

'How long have you been gone, boy?' asked Uncle Sean. 'Two years?' He snorted with an 'Aye! Aye, you've got the terrible *twos'* worth of business to settle!'

Another eruption of laughter.

'The fockcha mean, Sean?'

'The *screaming* terrible twos' worth, no less!'

'Yeejit,' said the culchie. 'The fock's the eejit spouting now?'

'She weren't *alone*, boy,' Sam elucidated, 'when you went away.' He sipped on the end of a cigar. 'Your little'un's two years old, and a bonny one an all.'

The culchie snorted. 'Chat shite so you do. Don't *know* no Marie!'

'Your *missus*, son! Your *missus*! Don't tell me the *grandeurs* of the Big Smoke are *amnesiac* quality now or I'll know you'll be chatten the bollocks.'

The culchie paused. 'I have a daughter?'

'God help him, he's got a brain too,' said dead Uncle Shane.

'O'fock,' he seemed to say.

'Oh-fock indeed. And she's on her way over, son, it's only fair to focken mention. You might want to scarper if the city's life's not quared your survival instincts. She's not likely to be showing you much of a sense of humour.'

'But how did she know I was here?'

'Jungle drums, how do you think? Y'daft bastard: she was coming here *anyway*, it's nothing to do with you. She works the bar when Mairead clocks off.'

The culchie closed his eyes.

'What's her name?' he asked, experiencing a weird sense of premonition. He was certain of what was about to be said, and he was right.

Uncle Shane answered, 'Zoe. Lovely little child, so she is. Apple of your eye.'

'She will be.'

Shane raised his drink to his lips.

'Apple of the *nation's* eye,' the culchie continued.

'You say what now?'

'She'll be a star.' The culchie smiled. 'I'll see to that.'

'Flynn, look at me, *look at me!*'

Zoe cupped his face in both hands, looking imploringly into his eyes. 'It's going to be fine. Just try to concentrate. Focus on what I'm saying.'

With an effort he tried to do what she told him, but there was something constricting about her hands, her gaze, too much like the walls of the booth, the iron manacles cutting into his wrists. Images teased him; scenes from his life fought for his attention. He wrenched himself away from her, tripped over the rim of the booth at the bottom of the door opening and fell headlong onto the stark white floor.

The fall winded him, but as he sucked in air some kind of clarity came and he dragged himself up to his knees. He stared at Zoe. Her cheeks were grey, hollowed. She was dressed in the same drab overalls he wore himself: she too was one of the accused, then? One of those forced to watch their crimes over and over again.

'But you're dead,' he said matter-of-factly. 'I shot you.'

'No, you didn't. It's what they made you believe. It isn't true.'

'In the pet shop,' the culchie continued. 'I had your name and address. It was my birthday. I shot you.'

'No, you didn't. It's me – *Zoe*. Your *daughter*.'

Flynn could hardly take it all in. 'Then who did I shoot?'

'You didn't shoot anyone – the audience changed their minds. They felt sorry for me. So now we've got a chance but we'll have to be swift.'

Although Flynn was convinced of the young woman's urgency, and although he would cooperate, it felt as though he'd awoken from something more enfolding and malleable than sleep. A promise to cooperate notwithstanding, however, he had a question that couldn't wait.

'What *audience*?'

'Not *now*. Come on!'

Zoe used code embedded in a thumbnail to open the manacles on his wrists; they sighed as they yawned and let him free.

Beyond the booth the corridor was long and brightly-lit. Zoe skipped out of the booth and took a few steps before she understood that Flynn had not joined her. She turned around.

'Flynn,' she slightly panted. 'At best we've got minutes. Possibly seconds. Before they realise I'm helping you.'

The culchie shook his head. 'I can't, Zoe.'

'You *can't*? Do you know where you *are*?'

'No. Maybe that's the point,' Flynn admitted.

'We're breaking you all free, Dad. It's taken months to get this far, and I'm not going to let you spoil it for —'

Flynn interrupted. 'You work here?'

'Of course! I'm undercover.'

'I don't believe you, girl; sorry.'

Zoe's eyes cleaned themselves of an appearance of guilty sadness: now she was furious and met Flynn's gaze with a more resolute expression. 'It doesn't matter now. I have to get you out while the power's down. They don't know how I did it — but you can bet they'll be working it out soon. It's now or never, Flynn.'

250

'It's never. I belong here.'

At this moment the woman who had killed her husband ran by, closely followed by two more people he recognised: Uncle Shane and Uncle Sean, presumably escaping from other booths. Looking past Zoe, Flynn could see that up and down the intersecting corridor yet more people were breaking out of their booths, and running. More and more with every second; the hubbub rising.

It's now or never, Flynn.

Limping slightly, Flynn followed Zoe to the double doors at the end of the corridor. It seemed that they were among the last people left in the place now.

The doors swung open towards Zoe, Flynn and a few other escapees in the corridor. Stepping into view and framed in the open doorway, barring their way, stood three men dressed primarily in white. Flynn struggled to stop his forward momentum, his weak legs working to keep him upright.

The three men had a rifle each hardwired into the length

of their right arms.

'Dear, *dear* Mr Flynn, *do* be careful,' the central figure, a tall immaculately groomed man, said with a click of his tongue. Then he turned to Zoe. 'I'm ashamed of you. I thought you were better than this.'

Flynn gaped. Zoe clutched his arm painfully.

With a nod to the men accompanying him the tall man said, 'Take them to Final Processing.'

Flynn said, 'No, I've got a better idea.'

And Zoe said, 'Flynn.?'

'A *better idea?*' the tall man queried, the corners of his mouth tweaked into a cat's cradle of laughter lines.

'Better for audience figures,' Flynn bluffed. 'They don't want to watch the same crud over and over, I appreciate that. So they sent you three. And my so-called daughter. To spice up their lives.'

Zoe had taken hold of Flynn's right sleeve. In a whisper she asked, 'What are you talking about?'

'This is part of the drama. They're watching.'

'Watching *what?*'

'Yes,' said the tall man. 'That's a question that intrigues us too. Watching what, if you'd be so kind, Mr Flynn?'

'Watching me watching myself,' Flynn explained. 'Taking the pieces of my past – my *real* past – and twisting them into dramas for you. Including this: right now. Including you in a pet shop. Including me in Ireland. It's all fake. There's another level; there *has* to be – because *this* can't be it all.'

None of Flynn's interlocutors knew how best to respond.

Flynn closed his eyes. His fists clenched at his sides, he tried to corral all of his memories: it was like hugging fog but he told himself not to give up. He saw a view from a tractor window; heard the foul thud of impact as he ploughed down

Uncle Shane on the road from The Slow Mile. He saw the self-application of a disguise; he heard a waiter's confirmation that he did not look in any way peculiar. (He tasted kippers at the back of this throat.) He saw Zoe.

Zoe.

Flynn opened his eyes, half expecting to see her smiling at him in triumph; but her expression was one of worry.

'This isn't my story anyway,' he told her. 'I think it's yours.'

The corridor clicked into darkness.

Flynn felt for Zoe's hand; the two of them gripped together. When he woke up next, he was certain, it would be to a scene that neither of them understood.

Entelecheia

IN THE TREES, the angels.

They swarm every path of light, shimmering in the sunshine. Millions of angels.

Sartrus was the Garden and the Garden was vast, and somewhere a Choir sang. In a clearing near the Choir, an angel named Aurasistacia painted. He had a talent for art, and used it for both pleasure and critical acclaim. Even by the standards of the Celestial, he was vain.

It was Sartrus that Aurasistacia was committing to canvas, his brush strokes steady and sure. He had painted the scene more than a thousand times and he was bored.

No angel had a status higher than Hypsistacia. He ruled the Garden and was without age.

Before him, Aurasistacia, the Painter, cowered. *I would like,* Aurasistacia said, not daring to utter the superior's name, *to enter the Orchard for an afternoon.*

Hypsistacia shone blue with confusion; the air around him increasing in temperature. His energy scalded Aurasistacia's faces.

It is not your time to enter Orchard. You know the laws, Aurasistacia; you must wait. I shall tell you when it is your time. You must be patient.

The Creator had spoken.

What Aurasistacia was planning had been forbidden for eons – since well before Hypsistacia had obtained Entelecheia and Theandric Power.

Aurasistacia wanted to pick fruit. He paled to a rubicelle hue.

Through the yellow air came the sound of singing: a four- or six-piece Choir, *a capella.*

As Aurasistacia flew through the trees, he heard the sounds of the Choir ampliate. He headed towards the Garden wall that separated Sartrus from the Orchard. As he did, he shimmered red with excitement and fear.

Aurasistacia, a voice called.

The angel pretended not to hear.

Aurasistacia, the voice said again, with more authority this time.

The Painter slowed to a halt in mid-air, and turned. He hoped his red colour was replaced by his customary grey. But in the roasting heat, his red gave away his strong emotions of excitement and petrification. Happiness provoked a pale purple. It was for this particular colour that Aurasistacia now struggled to achieve. He wanted to give the angel who had called his name the impression that he was pleased to see her. The colour was slow in coming.

Sestiquito saw that Aurasistacia was frightened: his deep red colour was unmistakeable. Although her own colour for fear was a buttercup yellow, she had known Aurasistacia for thousands of years, and she knew what colours he displayed.

Why are you not painting? she asked.

I am tired of painting, Aurasistacia told her honestly.

Sestiquito's grey was replaced momentarily by a very pale yellow. *You must not say that. Hypsistacia will hear you and you will be punished.* She floated to Aurasistacia's level. *Where are you going?* she asked, while being pushed to one side by a warm breeze from below.

Nowhere in particular, Aurasistacia answered. *I simply need a rest from painting.*

Sestiquito sounded incredulous. *You are the Painter. You cannot be tired of painting.*

I have come to see my painting as a waste of my time. I want to pursue other interests, Aurasistacia told her. *A more worthwhile type of creation.*

Hypsistacia will never let you.

Hypsistacia may never know.

The warm breeze floated through the trees. They could not remember their lives on Earth: no angel could. This information was forbidden by the Entelecheia Scriptures. The only angel with access to this knowledge was Hypsistacia, the Creator.

Aurasistacia explained his plan to Sestiquito. Her colours changed as he did so.

Hypsistacia will punish you, Sestiquito replied. *You will be gone to the Moon. Is the risk worth it? Soon enough you will be called to Sing and you will enter the Orchard naturally.*

Still Aurasistacia flew away.

Sestiquito was left turning to the deep dark green of her weighty sadness. If she had been human she would have cried. Seconds passed. She decided to follow the angel she loved. She opened herself like an unfurling flag and let the breath of Sartrus take her in the direction that Aurasistacia had flown. She put her mind into the chase; she must try to stop him.

Hypsistacia had preached of what happened to those who tried to get into the Orchard before their time. For at least eight thousand years, his admonitions had been sufficient to strangle any ambition of premature access to what lay beyond the wall.

Now, Aurasistacia halted his flight at the Garden/Orchard boundary. Blood-red with terror, he trod air and regarded its smooth red brick; it was chilly to the touch. Thousands of years

255

in the brilliant heat of Sartrus had conditioned Aurasistacia into believing that the cold of the wall did not exist.

Painter!

Aurasistacia's official title was shouted from somewhere behind. Aurasistacia turned, predicting who would have called him. He was correct: it was Ferbasilicia and Gelatiquito, the Guards, the male and female respectively.

Aurasistacia could not deepen his red colour: he was as scared as he would ever become. He knew that no Choir sang for him and the silence weighed ominous.

Did he dare risk the wall?

The Guards moved towards him.

Every angel in Sartrus knew the Entelecheia Scriptures word perfectly. Every angel obeyed them for fear of the punishment for not doing so. The Scriptures decreed that Sartus was the only home that angels could claim. Aurasistacia knew this, and yet he had striven to find another, a way in to the Orchard. At least, to Hypsistacia, roaring black with anger, it appeared this way. Hypsistacia did not know that the Painter had intended to pick fruit.

I have no meaningful function, Aurasistacia told him.

The Creator lost some of his black colour to display the blue of his confusion. *You have,* he told Aurasistacia, *a very important function.*

I paint trees. After five thousand years of doing so, I find this most unsatisfactory.

Do you desire a new occupation? Hypsistacia asked.

Aurasistacia was silent. Should he tell the Creator of his idea?

I desire, he said, *a new type of creation. I told you of my wish to enter the Orchard just for an afternoon, but I did not tell you why.*

Hypsistacia crackled: the heat gushing from him made Aurasistacia itch and feel uncomfortable. He would have liked to move further from the Creator, but Hypsistacia had told him where to float; if he moved from his place, his punishment would certainly be severe.

And will you tell me now? Hypsistacia asked.

The names of male angels ended in *–cia;* the names of female angels ended in *–quito.* The Scriptures said that this was to be so: it was so. Each angel had a title and an identity.

Sartrus housed more angels than it was possible to count in a handful of human lifetimes. Each knew what his or her function was and would be from then. Because of this awareness, there was widespread incredulity when the word became known of how Aurasistacia had attempted to enter the Orchard early.

257

Angels are required to perform their given tasks until they are called to be part of a Choir. The Choir might be two-, three-, four-five, or six-piece. No angel knew what until he or she was called. When the Choir was assembled, it practised its song until it was perfect; and when the song was perfect, only then was the Choir allowed to entered the Orchard.

Inside the Orchard there were billions of trees, in perfect rows, bearing fruit that did not ripen at the same time. It was the songs of the Choir that sang the fruit to ripeness.

Then when a fruit falls from the tree, a baby is born on Earth. As it is written in the Scriptures, that on Earth no child shall be born perfect; and the fruit must be bruised by the fall from the tree to the ground.

What happens to the Choir after the Fruit has fallen is not written, and by this no angle knows.

What Hypsistacia had expected to hear from Aurasistacia was the Painter had intended to sing a fruit to harvest by himself. The Creator had imagined that the Painter had wanted to create his own little being on Earth, rather than wait for his chance to sing as part of a Choir.

This would have been sinistrous. However, what Aurasistacia had *actually* planned to do once inside the Orchard – when the Painter had admitted all – was *pick* a single fruit.

Hypsistacia had been horrified by the confession. And if Sestiquito had not reported Aurasistacia's notion, the Painter might have got away with the crime.

Aurasistacia was sent away in a ball of lightning, and like Sestiquito had foretold him, sentenced to the Black Moon. Upon casting his angle away, Hypsistacia sat, burning pink, in his cave; he trembled in a way that he had not for millennia, his authority had been challenged; and he wondered how Aurasistacia had imagined that he would be able to get away with what he'd planned. Hypsistacia considered the possibility that he no longer ruled the other angels with a hard enough fist made of iron.

Entelecheia is the reward: it must be earned by an angel who lives his or her life cycle more than once, like Hypsistacia. For most all angels, that life consists of thousands of years in Sartrus, executing on an appointed task. Then one day the angel is called to be part of a Choir; the Choir rehearses, and then, in the Orchard, while singing to the trees, the songs cause the temperature rises. The heat helps the fruit to fall; where the angels, locked beneath the soaring brick walls, roast among the trees, burning like hot straw. Their energies ignite as the Choir's song soars and reaches for completion. Colours flash – emotion on emotion – and the angels cry weep sing, scalding in orgasm and they burn themselves out of existence.

After which each angel finds itself on the surface of a far-away place – a beach that stretches deep into the sky. The place has sand of many different colours. There are no trees and the place is nameless. It is a junction, from which two clear paths lead.

One path leads to a Black Moon; *one* to a White.

Aurasistacia's first attempts at escape were feeble. He flew through the night for miles, day, weeks, searching for some-thing that might help, but found nothing. He flew *vertically*, up into the sea of black above, for what seemed like miles, ages, but when he looked down he would only be a thousand feet from the dark rocks that he was sentenced to, at the very most. He would then return to the black surface where hordes of humans would flock around – often new arrivals, experiencing through him their first taste of Divinity.

259

With this, Aurasistacia soon became annoyed and impa-tient with the humans and his prison. Some of them hurled themselves at his feet much to his initial delight; but after the first hundred years of his incarceration, the attention ceased to amuse the angel. In fact, he was quickly sickened by the fawn-ing, two-legged souls.

Only after three hundred years of his sentence did Aur-asistacia breathe a first breath of hope. Then he glowed dimly in a freezing cavern, in a darkness that seemed to *thump*. Some human souls – modifying themselves in an effort to attain the perfect shape and physiognomy for a chance in the presence of angels – had left slippery, squirming scraps of themselves on the floor. And while he stared at a few of these dimming wisps of human material, Aurasistacia heard the hum of air being moved, and he knew something had changed.

He saw in the darkness a fuzzy sort of grey appear; and in the grey was something like a path, or a river. Aurasistacia flew towards the brightening light – and *flew through it* – wondering if someone on Earth was experiencing a vision of him. If so, could he not send his mind down the path to connect with such a visionary?

Aurasistacia focused his mind and imagination into one flashing green burst of energy, and with a scream of outrage, he flicked it in the direction of the grey path. Then he screamed again, this time with pain, when the bolt of thought and energy hit the path; but it was a pain that felt like escape: his mind leaving the surface of the Black Moon!

When he could see, he saw that he stood in front of a pretty girl, about four years of age, who quivered at what she saw. She clutched a teddy bear to her thin chest, her face displaying a rare purity of terror that Aurasistacia would never enjoy provoking.

The grey path dissolved to darkness.

Fewer than ten years later, Aurasistacia noticed something that immediately started him burning pink with confusion: a luminous bright blue airborne river, which disappeared into the distance, again in his cave.

Concentrating as hard as he could, he pushed his mind along the blue river. It was far from being a simple journey, and the merest progress took seventeen weeks of agonising effort. And then, one day, he found himself *in* the river – in the freezing water, tossed from bank to bank – with the understanding that the destination could not be far away.

Family Whorls

'IF YOU DON'T SAY IT,' the therapist threatened, 'I'm walking out and I shan't return.'

I wanted to tell him to see if I cared, but I couldn't speak. As soon as my brain recognised the confrontation in the words to be uttered by my tongue, the message went to my mouth. *Don't let him speak.* The words made it no further than my throat. They died there, crushed against one another. My mouth opened; I managed a gurgling grunt and a long tear of saliva which fell onto my shirt.

'So be it,' my therapist said after a minute had passed. He closed his briefcase and left my father's study, closing the door gently behind him. Not even a goodbye.

'Goodbye,' I said perfectly, and wiped my nose.

I heard muffled voices. I went to a bookshelf and took down my father's copy of the *Complete Shakespeare*. Opening the book arbitrarily I started reading halfway through *Coriolanus*. I knew the play well; it didn't matter where I started.

A raised voice broke my concentration. Then another. Then a curt goodbye (I think) and the front door was shut.

The study door opened. Father stood in the doorway, his face red, his brow crenellated. I could almost see smoke coming out of his ears, like it does with Yosemite Sam on the Bugs Bunny cartoons. Sharking in, Mother appeared in the background. She would stay—or at least pretend to be—neutral; take neither side in the oncoming argument. My father would shout about how he'd paid for the best speech therapist; and he would accuse me of not *wanting* to learn to talk again.

After a while his ranting fell on deaf ears. That's a joke, by the way. I'd *pretend* to be listening; my eyes would follow his lips as carefully as they always did. But instead I'd be listening to my fingertips.

I was twelve when I discovered them. They talk to me at night in whispers, as if they're scared they'll wake my father and mother up, but I know no one else can hear them. Sometimes they talk to me when I'm in town as well; a few times I've made the mistake of answering and passers-by have thought I was talking to *them*.

I'm fifteen now, and bright for my age, or so I've been told. But who can you trust?

My ears ring sometimes and I don't like it at all; they whistle, and that's even worse. I'll get a second or two of slurred babble through a door in my mind that suddenly opens, and I'll think my hearing has returned. It's a trick my brain likes to play. I try not to get excited when sounds invade, just to teach my brain a lesson. Because there's no point trying to fool myself: my hearing's never coming back. I'm stuck with this low, maddening hum.

All I'll ever hear are my fingertips.

Twelve. The age of twelve was when I had the accident. The doctors still think I'll never recover, but I'll show those cunts. Maybe I'll never a dance a tango, but one day I'll learn to place one foot in front of the other and walk. They'll see.

I used to be funny. Jokes on the spur of the moment; to have my classmates in stitches. Now my brain's too slow. Amusing apothegms arrive, but they are quickly carted away; arriving stillborn. Mother smiles and so does Father, but laugh nervous laughs.

'Why don't you go out and play? Play on your bike.'

262

My legs are match sticks; my pelvis was crushed and my ribs were broken; my heart was knocked out of place. And I think about the rest of my life – in this wheelchair.

'Dr Smithson is upset with you,' my father had said, standing in the doorway. His tone was angry: his lips were hardly moving. 'He says you're not trying your hardest.'

I *am* trying, I said, aware of the double meaning in the word.

'Ar-ham tr-hyig,' was how it came out.

'He says you're not. He says you're perfectly capable of saying the things he asks. He wants to know why you don't want to do it.'

Because I'm nearly dead, I thought; *by the time I've learned, they'll be putting your clever little boy in the ground. I'm dribbling down my chin and you haven't even noticed, and I don't know if my brain will know to wipe my face and interpret what you're saying, both at the same time. Is that answer enough?*

'Do,' I said simply. I put the *Complete Shakespeare* on the desk.

'I'm not going to argue with you,' my father said. 'Your mother and I...' and there was mother, right behind God. '... are at our wits' end.'

I opened my mouth and more dribble rained. Words collided in my throat. I was going to choke if one didn't come through and let some air in. *Was I turning blue?* If I'd had a voice I could have said, with sharpened sarcasm: '*You're* both at your wits' end! Look at me!'

'Car-room.'

And I could breathe.

'What?'

I'm not saying it again.

'Cartoons,' my mother told him. 'He wants to watch cartoons, don't you dear?'

As my father turned to debate the issue, I stopped listening, unsure of why I'd said 'cartoon'. This is another joke my brain likes to play: surprising me with unexpected words. Truth was, I didn't want to watch a cartoon. I wanted to listen to my fingertips.

I was riding my bicycle. A bright, sunny day. I was with my best friend, but he's not my best friend anymore. He doesn't want to know me. He's scared of me. Most people are.

We were twelve and riding our bikes in the countryside. We both saw the lorry. We rode abreast, my friend in the middle of the road. A small lorry and a narrow road. The lorry came from the opposite direction. I looked over my shoulder, just to see where he was, and I swerved away from the edge of the road. The lorry was much too close. I could feel the air underneath it, dragging me under, sucking my hair. It was a vacuum cleaner.

I don't remember anything else.

When I woke, I was in a different world. My eyes offered me indistinct images; my nose was at a funny angle. When I touched my face I felt plasters; when I touched my chest I felt pain; when I touched my groin I felt nothing. People spoke in a droning monotone; I understood nothing, and that made me cry. When I cried, I coughed up blood; when I saw blood, I panicked; when I panicked, my head hurt.

Before long my fingers began a discourse.

They didn't open little mouths, of course; if not for the fact that my fingertips *tingled* when I heard the voices, I don't think I'd ever have known who was speaking.

Hello, they said.

I was puzzled. I thought it was a doctor, or someone come

to visit me, although I could see no one.

'Urrah.'

What I said I couldn't actually hear, so my failure with 'hello' didn't scare me. *That* fear was still to come. I was to learn I'd lost the ability to speak when my eyesight improved, about seven weeks after the accident. Only then did I notice that when I spoke, baffled expressions arrived on my listeners' faces. I'd speak again. It dawned on me that they didn't understand. I hadn't realised I was just a mind. My visitors struggled with what I tried to say and I was too blind to notice. They wrote me messages for replies, which I held an inch from my face, trying to recall how each letter sounded. All I could hear when I spoke was that hum.

How are you feeling?

The tingling sensation in my fingers was nice. They were talking to me. My fingers! Not one voice, but ten, in unison. And *I could hear them*! No more scribbled notes, no straining my eyes. The joy was overwhelming, overbalancing.

265

Time passed, and eventually I left the hospital. Twelve years old and being pushed along like an old man. My legs were fucked. The doctors hadn't needed to tell me I'd never walk again: it was perfectly obvious those twigs would never be able to support my weight.

I'd been told to rest but I grew hungry for a pursuit. I started reading Shakespeare. I started with my father's *King Lear*— and the passion fizzled out. Not only did I fail to *understand* Shakespeare, I threw the book across the study in frustration.

My second pursuit was learning to lip-read, and I persevered with the play. I looked up words from the play in the dictionary. I wrote the story down in numbered points. By the time I'd read *King Lear* four times, I understood it. I began *All's*

Well That Ends Well. My lip-reading got better.

My elocution lessons began, and I hated my therapist immediately. Nevertheless, I tried to do as she said.

'After me: The dog chased the cat.'

'Thar-dur-aaay-aht.'

'Chased the cat.'

'Aaay-aht.'

'Once more. The dog chased…'

I stopped listening. My fingers were more interesting; they'd begun dancing, just for me, and they were singing as they jigged:

> *The doctor is a cow, the doctor is a cow;*
> *Eee-aye-eddy-oh, the doctor is a cow.*

A nursery rhyme tune. I started to chuckle.

After a while my first therapist left, with the declaration that I would never learn to speak until I *wanted* to learn. A refrain that they have all offered since.

And they were right, I *didn't* want to learn.

They don't always speak in unison. Sometimes they argue and I don't like that. My thumbs have the loudest voices. I think my thumbs are fathers. I don't know which fingers are mothers. My thumbs are better fathers than my father. I like my thumbs a lot when they're not arguing with my fingers; and maybe if I didn't like my real mother, one of my fingers would emerge as my new mother.

'I've managed to persuade Dr Smithson,' my father said, 'to return to teach you.'

Bring out the flags, I thought; *let's hear those trumpets.*

'Ankoo,' I said.

My father seemed surprised. 'You're welcome,' he replied.

I wanted him to go. I'd have done anything to calm him down.

'You're getting to be a man now,' he said. Mother smiled. I tried to smile back, though how she was ever supposed to take pleasure from seeing my split lips and broken teeth I had no idea. A man indeed! What a consolation! *You're the world's tallest dwarf, son; how do you feel?* Soon I'd be able to drink, smoke and have sex. I was fifteen years old when my father spoke these silent words; but I'd never do the things a normal fifteen-year-old did, let alone any of the above.

I picked up the Shakespeare. My ears were ringing so I didn't want to talk anymore. I wanted to carry on with *Coriolanus*. I'd come to love Shakespeare's plays, the verticality of the language; and how the characters in them spoke beautifully. *Their* words never nearly killed them. Even barking-mad King Lear managed to string together great bursts and gusts of dialogue.

267

My fingers were talking among themselves; idle gossip. My pelvis ached, but I didn't ask for a pill. I wanted to be alone. As the study door closed behind my parents, I coughed up some blood and spat it as far as I could. It landed on the globe, then slid down through the fist of Africa.

Are you feeling okay? my fingers ask, in unison.

Fine, my brain says.

It's night and I'm in bed with the families. Now I have three families to myself: two hand-families and one human family. My older parents are asleep; my new parents tingle messages to me. I feel part of a unit with my fingers; not so much the outsider intruding. I think I'm too much for my original parents. My new parents think so too.

You could kill yourself, they suggest; but it's only a joke, and I quickly pooh-pooh the idea. They say, *Good. Why not try walking, in that case? And we'll help you.*

I have no answer. It's what I've wanted for three years: to walk; to be partly normal again. I try. My arms support my weight as I lower myself off the bed and onto the floor. A dizzying feeling, just to be supported upright again, after so long. What happens if I let go of the bed? I don't want to ride in that wheelchair for the rest of my life.

Go on, my fingertips urge. *You're on your own now.*

On my own. Like lonely Lear, who couldn't see truth and justice. But with my families' support. My arms are large; my muscles have been developed after three years of pushing my wheels; they can hold my weight easily.

268

Try! my fingers beg.

I let go. Agony shoots from the soles off my feet to my knobbly knees. Knees buckle. Pain burns through my thighs and ignites my groin. It hurts worse than when I need the toilet. Up the ladder of my verterbrae, strumming my heart *en route*, and into my skull. Mouth opens, screaming I think. *Nose bleeds.*

No, say fingers, *it's only snot. You're doing well. Another step!*

I fall. Something is knocked to the floor—the shadows shift: it's my nightlamp that's been upended—and I think I hear a thud. No; the sound was the air migrating through my body like ugly birds, to be released in a *whooooosh!* My bedroom door opens and the light is switched on. Father's face is red and old. He runs to me. Mother's not in the background.

Raise us, say my fingers.

I extend my arms. Father sees me as a baby wanting to be picked up and carried to bed. He wraps his arms around me and tries to lift. But he's too old; I'm too heavy.

'What were you doing?' he asks breathlessly.

My fingers circle his throat. My new fathers shout and dig themselves into the old man's Adam's apple. It's like preparing a chicken, and I read his scream. His eyes show befuddlement. So, I expect, do mine.

In the doorway Mother appears. Her hands go to her mouth. Is she whispering to her fingers? *No need*, I want to say; *they can read your mind*. She's crying.

'Doan cry,' I say, tightening my grip.

The man struggles, but my arms are strong, my grip is unbreakable. His eyes bulge; his tongue protrudes.

The body falls limp. Blood's filled his eye sockets and my mother's fainted, shocked into unconsciousness. And what do I feel? I feel touched. Emotional. My fingers have killed my burdensome old geezer for *me*, no one else. My little pinky fingers speak to me on their own and I move to my mother's prone body. My little fingers are my *new* mothers; I've discovered the truth at last! I place my hands on her neck.

My old folks didn't want me. My new ones wanted me to be part of them so much they were willing to fight for me. They were *jealous*. They hated the old man, this revolting old woman. She smells of talcum powder and Father's tobacco. Why hadn't I seen it before?

Now, they tingle, *you are our little boy*.

I frown at my mother because the light has changed again. Shadows have splintered and scattered like something spilt over the walls.

Father has picked up the nightlamp. And his lips are not moving now.

269

Blame

'I'M PREGNANT,' said Liz. 'It's yours, Mike.'

'Are you sure?' Mike asked.

'I'm sure. So's my doctor.'

'That it's mine, I mean.'

'Yes. And don't worry about offending me with comments like that, by the way. Who the hell else's would it be?'

'You've been married for thirteen years, Liz,' said Mike, trying to be equable.

'Well exactly. Who the hell else's would it be?'

'If that's the case, the choice is yours.'

'The choice is *ours*,' Liz replied with both strength and speed. She imagined Mike, two hundred miles away, in Sunderland, with his face creasing into asymmetrical segments.

'Tina's going to be home any second; I have to go.'

'So's Greg. We have a week or so,' said Liz, 'to decide.' She laughed. 'You can tell me what you think at your mum and dad's do, if you like.'

'That's not funny.'

'Isn't it?' Liz asked. 'I think it's *hilarious*.'

Greg was late but Liz didn't mind. She had a glass of wine and the cracked opened book that she was reviewing for a poetry website. It was good; it was by a Welsh writer named Carl ap Tegwyn. While savouring a particularly nutritious twelve-liner called 'Imbalance' she heard the key in the lock. Greg called hi and Liz heard him shake out his umbrella and remove his coat.

'Your dinner's ready,' she said. 'Just pop it in the microwave.'

'Thanks. How was your day?'

'Fine,' said Liz as Greg entered the room. 'I finished editing that guy's science fiction novel.'

'Any good?' Greg asked.

Feeling sorry for him (or was it for herself?), Liz shrugged. Even after thirteen years he could still make an enquiry about her day sound like he was creditably interested. She couldn't do that anymore. And Greg was aware of this inability: he had long since stopped calling her from the road to inform her of his updates.

'I woke up this morning, in the hotel,' he said, 'and I discovered that I really missed you.'

Liz smiled. 'That's sweet. I missed you too.'

'I had just woken from this funny dream,' he went on, and Liz knew that he'd been waiting all day to share this knowledge; he'd driven back from Wales, reciting it to perfection through the curtains of rain, to the rhythm of the wipers. 'I'd forgotten to invite Tom Waits to my mum and dad's anniversary. There was a big auditorium and everyone was waiting for him. And it was all my fault.'

'You're worried. Why? It's gonna be fine,' she said. 'It's only a speech. You've done hundreds of presentations.'

'Not to my mum and dad I haven't,' said Greg. 'Not on their thirty-fifth.'

'It'll be fine. I said I'd help if you need me.'

'Thanks. I'll just warm up my dinner.'

Liz did not want to share with her husband the two dreams of her own that she could recall. In the first, an actress from the soap opera that she favoured had worked as a waitress. She had taken Liz's order while strumming her own clitoris. *What do you suggest?* Liz had asked. *I suggest right now,* the actress/waitress had responded.

In the second, Liz had given birth to a tiger cub. It had woken her with a jolt.

'Can I put the telly on?' asked Greg, now encumbered with a loaded tray – the plate, the glass.

'Sure,' said Liz. 'I'm over here having a bath.'

Mike had fathered a child before. In the third year of university, at the age of twenty-one: her name was Paula. Both of their names were Paula – mother and daughter – and nobody in Mike's family knew anything of the incident. Paula, the senior, at the age of nineteen, had demanded from Mike no display of responsibility. No attention, no money – no guilt. It was, as she'd put it, just one of them things. And he'd graduated, and he'd left it be.

272   That was four years ago. Now this. Lighting another cigarette, Mike wondered what sort of mother his brother's wife would turn out to be: a quiet or a noisy one? Such thoughts entertained Mike's fibrillating heart, until Tina arrived home. 'Kiss kiss,' she said, and landed him one on the plump left earlobe. 'I wish you wouldn't smoke in here,' she added.

They did not talk about the day that had just passed, for the days were always the same here. Mike took the bus to the office and created models for marketing cold callers, based on the client's specifications (age, wage bracket); and Tina typed for a legal firm that had been in the news when an M.D. had overdosed in a small hotel room in Clacton.

Instead, they talked about the future. 'I'm nervous,' said Tina, using the remote to find a next track on the CD. She never liked songs with saxophones farting all over the place; she thought of them as undignified as mud wrestling. 'It's tonight. I'm not ready.'

'Yes you are. You're ready.' Mike knew that she was referring to her brown belt judo exam: that was all. Tina had been talking about little else for the last month. Mike was sick of hearing about it. *You think you've got worries!* he muttered inside his head. 'Why are you worrying, Teen? You can kick the bejesus out of anyone in your group, love.'

'It's not *about* that, Mike…'

'I know. I was joking.'

'Oh, sorry. Did you feed the cats?'

'No. I thought I'd let them starve today.'

'Touchy.'

'Well, as if. Of course I fed the bloody things. Muddy scratched me,' said Mike, exhibiting a negligible wound to his right thumb. 'I shouted at him.'

'You didn't!' Tina protested. 'My poor baby.'

'Me or him?' asked Mike.

273

'*You* can fend for yourself. *He* can't.'

'We could try, though, couldn't we? Kick him out and have a progress report in what? Five years?'

'You're mean,' Tina told him. 'I'd better get ready. Are you going to meet me afterwards for a drink?'

'Just you?'

'No, Mike, the judo crowd. As usual.'

'No thanks, then. As usual. Especially if your so-called instructor's going to be there.'

Tina left the room with her small hands collected into nuggety fists. 'Not tonight, Mike,' was all she had to offer. She did not slam the door; there was more weariness than anger to her egress. More sadness than anything else.

Submerged in a cherry-scented bath a few nights later, Liz reminded herself of her fallopial vital statistics. One abortion (at twenty) and one miscarriage (at twenty-one), both of them pre-Greg. She had met him when she was twenty-seven and he was eighteen; they had married a year later. She had been working for a publisher then, in a boxroom office in a mews of Kensington High Street; now she was freelance. So she had given up one set of chains for another. And it had worked.

To the surprise of Ruth and Dennis. These were the parents of Greg, who was now thirty-one, and Mike, the baby of the trio. Inbetween them, little Isabel had arrived, but she hadn't stayed long. By the time she hit fourteen she was all but engaged to a fisherman in Greece. She bred tropical birds and baked her own bread; and there were rumours she'd make it back for the anniversary, but rumours like this, in the past, had mostly piddled away down the drain.

Ruth and Dennis had disapproved of their eldest son and his older woman. It wouldn't last. *Well*, thought Liz, sliding soap along her calves, *they were right*. But they had been wrong for a long, long time.

The rot had set in a year earlier. The chemical, if not alchemic, process that solidifies boredom into a form of disgust – this had long since occurred. There was nothing now. There was no glue to hold them together; no centrifugal force on the decreasing spin of their roundabout. Merely the infrequent Indian Summer – a show of kindness, of life, of love – sun and breeze.

It's over, thought Liz. *It's got to be, hasn't it? I'm carrying another man's child. I shouldn't pretend it's Greg's.*

Over half an hour of bathtime had led to these few scant certainties; the rest of the time had passed in a melange of panic – a noisy ablution of words and thoughts through her mind. Thirty minutes of intrusive and scary blood-heatrise.

But I don't want to be with Mike either, thought Liz, who had scored a bullseye, right to the heart of her fear (she could see the blood), a second or two earlier, with a six-word sentence of dull simplicity – but one which had carried its own slowly-acting poison.

This could be my last chance.

She was still recovering from them when Greg knocked at the door.

'Are you going to be much longer?' he asked. 'I need to brush my teeth.'

'Come in,' said Liz, sliding deeper into the waves that she created.

At the basin he was behind her. And although she couldn't see her husband, she knew what he was doing: it was a matter of routine: he was counting the white hairs in his goatee and examining his fringe-line to see if he was receding any worse than before. Than yesterday. He was terrified of growing old, and showing it. 275

Join the club, thought Liz.

'Are you ready?' said Mike. 'If this is the way you want to go, you understand? Only *if*. It's gonna cost five hundred pounds. Private.'

Liz waited a few seconds for the nausea to subside. 'You flatter me, Mike,' she said. 'Private, eh?'

'Please Liz.'

'No, I'm grateful,' she continued in the same tone of voice.

'I'll pay, for Christ's sake!'

'It's not about the money, Mike. It's the assumption.'

'I said *if*. I said *IF*.'

Liz frowned. 'Okay, calm down. Thank you. But it's all academic: I'm keeping it.'

There was silence.

'And what?' said Mike. 'Pretend it's his.'

'No. Or yours.' This took courage. Liz reached for her Campari and soda. She sipped while Mike questioned her ear, not realizing that she was not ignoring him. She said: 'Wait a second. Just wait. This is what I'm gonna do.' The breath she took weighed her breasts in its capable hands and then let them go.

'I'm saying I met someone else,' she said. 'Someone from work.'

'You work at home, Liz,' said Mike.

'But not in a vacuum! I do meet people, you know!'

'All right. But he's going to want a name. Trust me. It's a guy thing.'

'Then I'll give him one. I'll make one up.'

Mike sighed. He was assessing probabilities, Liz guessed. He said, 'Risky, but…'

'You're in favour.'

'I suppose. If you're sure.'

'No I'm not sure. But it's the best I can do,' Liz replied. 'And at least you're off the hook.' Toasting the decision, she raised her glass to her lips. It was a calamitous moment: it was when she realized that this had better be the last drop of alcohol she had for the next eight months. She mourned its passing with a lowering of her eyelids.

'God…' said Mike.

'What?'

He paused. 'Is it wrong to want you as much as I do right now?' he asked.

'Yes.'

'Why? The damage has been done, Liz.'

'*Damage?*'

'You know what I mean…'

'It's a *child*. Not an injury.'

The phone call ended shortly afterwards. Liz poured the remains of her drink into the sink; two hundred miles away Mike filled a mug with water and put on a tie for work. *Another day.*

Liz wasn't thinking about him. She was thinking about a man named... Joseph? Tom, Lucas, Billy... Elvis? For a second – with a giggle – she embraced the continental and christened the father of her child Raoul. *Or what about Pedro?* Skating over the surface of the planet, she toyed with Yang, with Murat, with Budion; but with reluctance she understood that something closer to home would be required. If only to authenticate the appearance of the eventual child.

Nick, then. Nick was good.

She turned on her computer. Then she went back to the bedroom to fasten in her best earrings, the better to woo a stranger on a first date.

Bruising on Tina's left hip: this was Mike's current obsession; but it wouldn't be with him long, he knew. She was always bumping into things, and dropping spoons, and spilling her food, and pranging the car; she was clumsy. As he was kissing along the dotted line of her shaved pubic triangle that evening, Mike touched Tina's bruises and felt her tense. She had recently earned her brown belt in judo; where she was sure to have sustained a badge of skin colouring. This, however, did not prevent Mike's thoughts and suspicions from moving about like a spinning-top. And all he could think about was Tina's judo instructor: Terry.

'Did I hurt you?' Mike asked.

'It's just a bit sensitive,' Tina replied. 'Don't stop.'

Mike resumed his ministrations. Minutes later, when she arched her back a little – when she took on a slightly different flavour and consistency and started to grind against his nose – he guided her through until she began to breathe normally again. He rejoined her at the pillow and passed her taste and scent to her lips and tongue.

As she was climbing down his body, Mike asked, 'Where did the bruises come from?'

'My exam,' Tina told him. 'Bad landing on the mats.'

'I thought you were throwing *them*!'

'I was. But you can't win 'em all.'

'But you passed.'

'I passed. Do you want this or not?'

Clearly, given his size and shape, the answer was yes. Mike apologised. Seconds later she began, and Mike was able to conduct a constructive comparison with the work of his sister-in-law.

His mind was ablaze. One baby had already eluded him, and presumably the two Paulas existed perfectly well, even happily, in Scotland: without him. Mike was confused. Although it was bedtime and he hadn't had a drink, he felt hungover – clogged, disparaged. When the revelation arrived, Mike greeted it with some relief – as indeed he might greet the two Paulas one day – who could tell? – the two Paulas, who from time to time took turns in his thoughts in a sprightly dos-a-dos. It was this: he wanted to be this new child's father. On this occasion, he did not wish to give up his rights and that part of his body that seemed reserved – suddenly – for the task of rearing young. *So this is what it feels like*, Mike thought. *This is what it feels like to be broody… She can have her mystery man, her lover. But I'm going to be the father*, he decided, aware only distantly that walls could fall as the result of such determination.

'What's the matter?' Mike heard from his lower torso. 'Are you tired?'

No strength, he realized; no yield… She was querying his lack of ardour.

'Yes. Tired.'

Tina moved into his arms instead. 'I'll do it in the morning,' she said – and he felt her gratitude, her simplicity, as she quickly made the sounds that signalled she'd been lassoed, with efficiency, by sleep. He let her go. In the darkness Mike blinked on, his mouth watering. He imagined Tina and Terry. He wouldn't have been surprised: Tina, the student, bending her back for her brown belt – and Terry, the instructor, the other man… his squat face, the big metallic wristwatch. His fingers kneading, with no subtlety, a woman's hips…

Fog arrived on the day before the anniversary celebrations; for and rain. It was April. Psychotically cautious of driving in anything but perfect conditions (and never at night), Ruth was put on red alert by the waves of grey air that were tumbling past her window. So much so that she reached for the cordless.

Calling Mike at work proved problematic (a time-wasting tour of the toilet and the snacks machine), but she got him in the end. 'I'm serious,' she told her son. 'If it continues like this, you're not to travel down. I mean it.'

'Mum,' Mike protested. 'The restaurant's booked: your favourite. We'll be fine.'

'No, Mike. Not if it's like this.'

'Okay, Mum. We'll see tomorrow, shall we?'

'Okay. Bye, dear. Bye.'

Getting Greg on the other hand proved impossible. 'He's not answering the mobile,' Ruth explained to Liz, as if she needed a reason to call her daughter-in-law. 'I think it's switched off. All I'm calling for is to say, if it continues, don't come tomorrow.'

Liz was struck cold. Behind Ruth's words she could hear the phrases of jazz piano, but she found it the opposite of soothing. If *what* continued? The deception, the pregnancy? With effort, Liz managed to expunge from her head the notion that Mike had confessed. After all, why would he do so?

The *marriage*? Liz wondered.

'The fog, I mean. Treacherous, love.'

Unwilling, as ever, to give Ruth what she wanted – also stung by the concatenation of her mother-in-law's last two words, as if they'd been intended as a verdict, a report: *treacherous love* was just about on the money – Liz said, 'I'll have a word with Greg when he gets in.'

'Fine. But we won't be offended, okay, if you can't come.'

'Oh, you're only up the road,' said Liz, knowing that a token display of disappointment and protestation was the order of the day. 'We'll make it.'

'Not if it's bitter, love. We can reschedule.'

Till when? thought Liz. *August? Doomsday? Actually, that's not bad, as a title. 'Anniversary on Doomsday.'* Liz resolved to use that at some point in the future.

It was only after the call that Liz considered the following: the fact that Ruth didn't *want* them there. Didn't *want* the celebrations.

Perhaps – it was a linked thought – she didn't even want the marriage or anything that reminded her of it. Liz drank deeply on the knowledge that thirty-five years was only six fewer than she had personally been alive. *Good grief,* she thought: *that length of time, that duration – it somehow didn't seem fair.*

With the geographical constraints upon them, it was not a customary affair for the whole family to come together; but this occasion was special, and this time it had worked. Greg had collected Isabel from the airport – Isabel, travelling light, carrying nothing but a small plastic bag of underwear and socks. She'd lost weight; her cheekbones looked like cartoon hearts beneath her skin. Her husband, Theo, had remained at home.

Isabel always felt her brothers' bottoms when she kissed them hello. 'You need to exercise more,' she told Greg. 'You're getting flabby.'

'You're not.'

She laughed. 'I will be soon.'

'How do you mean?'

'Well. I'm not ill, Greg, so…'

'You're pregnant.'

'Congratulations to me.' She smiled.

'Congratulations. I'm stunned.'

'Thanks.'

'Is Theo happy?'

'Theo doesn't know. It's not his,' said Isabel. 'But don't tell anyone that yet.'

'Excuse me?'

'Come on, Greg, keep up. I've been seeing someone else. The baby was my decision. I thought *someone* should get the ball rolling.'

'Christ. We haven't even reached the *car* yet. What else are you going to tell me?' asked Greg.

'Well I've nearly kicked the heroin,' Isabel said lightly.

'*What?*'

'Joke. God, your face!' Again, Isabel laughed.

'Don't do that to me!'

'Sorry. You know, you're as adorable as ever when you're panic-stricken,' said Isabel.

'I'll take that as a compliment.'

281

On the open road, Greg turned down Queen and asked, 'So what about this new guy?'

'What about him?'

'Well, his name would be a start.'

'Kurt. He's American. Do you mind if I smoke? Don't tell Mum and Dad.'

'About the smoking?'

'About anything. I'll do it.'

'Sure. It's none of my business.'

Isabel sparked one up. The breath she exhaled, for a second, painted the windscreen silver and blue. 'He works at the language school down the road. Bought some of my bread in the market one time, and we got chatting. He's twenty-two.'

'He's your toy boy, like me.'

'You're not my toy boy,' said Isabel. 'Anyway. What about you and Mike?'

'We're fine. Mike's doing well.'

'I meant grandchildren for the aged P's. Any news?'

'Not from me,' said Greg. 'You've got more of an accent than last time, did you know that? I just noticed.'

'Greek or American?' asked Isabel.

The fog warning was ignored. The restaurant twinkled in its capes like rhinestones, both alluring and repulsive. *The Albino* was Mum's favourite place to eat, which said plenty about her taste for refined décor (she erred toward the glitzy) but nothing about her taste for good food. As it happened, what it served was fantastic, and it served it well.

They all met in the bar. It was more a late lunch than a dinner, and Mike, Tina and Greg had needed to book time off work. The median quality of the hour, however, was no hindrance to the place's trade; the bar was packed. Suits were eating sandwiches next to a no-man's-land of unused pool tables; a fruit machine conversed energetically with a young man in overalls who was touch-typing its oversized keys. Elsewhere, the tables were full to brimming with staff from the car dealership and the book remainder warehouse down the road.

Isabel grasped Mike's bottom and kissed him hell. 'You're tense,' she told him.

'Family things always make me tense.'

'Me too. We care more about our parents the further we are from them. Have you noticed that?'

Mike smiled. 'Yes. You told me that at Christmas,' he said.

'Well then. You can't accuse me of being unfaithful to my themes at least.'

'I wasn't going to accuse you of being unfaithful to anything. Or anyone.'

Isabel copied his smile – and it really was a copy. Although three years separated the brother and sister, as children they had often been confused for one another, particularly during Isabel's brief tomboy phase and Mike's experiment, aged four, with shoulder-length androgyny. 'You Colombo you,' she said. 'You're the first to know. Don't tell Mum and Dad, will you?'

'Of course not. But what's going on?' Mike asked.

'I've met someone else. I'm leaving Theo.'

'Jesus. Does he have any idea?'

Isabel shrugged. 'I doubt it,' she answered. 'He loves his fish more than me. Says they have more warmth. He may be right.'

'Well. I'm sure you know what you're doing.'

'I'm not. But thanks.'

Noting Isabel's excavation of a packet of cigarettes, Mike said, 'Can I have one of those, please?'

'Sure. Does Mum know you smoke yet?'

283

'No. But she will soon.'

'Does Tina?'

'Yes. But I'm not allowed to in the house.'

Isabel raised her eyebrows.

'The cats,' said Mike in explanation. Quick to move the conversation away from his own relationship he added: 'So this new guy…'

'Hank.'

'You're what? – going to move in with him or something?'

'Or move to the States. He's American.'

'Why not here?'

'Too expensive – for a family.' Isabel waited, then she nodded. 'Six weeks.' She smiled. 'I thought I should get the ball rolling,' she said. 'I always did want to be the first at everything, didn't I?'

Mike was too slow to stop himself. Alcohol could not be blamed as he'd only completed one pint of beer and was working on a second. His words floated out on a carpet of smoke, and he regretted them instantly.

'I don't know that you'll be the *first*,' he said. Isabel's face seemed to choke, and then settle. Her eyes glistened briefly with moisture.

Only a fraught hour later, in a chance encounter outside the lavatories, did Mike have a chance to request of his sister a deadweight favour that was along the same lines as that one she'd asked of him.

'It's a secret,' he said.

'It's cool, Mike. I won't tell.'

'No, it's not what you think.'

'It's *fine*. She's beautiful.'

'What?' asked Mike, wrongfooted.

'She's *radiant*. But I won't say a word,' Isabel promised. 'Swear. Okay? But Mike, off the record, okay? She's got the loveliest pregnant hair I've ever seen. Very pregnant hair. Very.'

'*Liz?*'

'No, Tina. What do you mean *Liz*?'

'I meant Tina.'

Isabel's face was a picture of clownish disapproval. 'You said Liz, Mike.'

'I meant Tina. What has *Tina* said to you?'

'No. What has Liz said to *you*?'

'Nothing.'

Isabel was still frowning. 'I'm all in a muddle now, Mike,' she said. 'Tina just told me she was pregnant. Is Liz as well?'

'I have no idea. Tina's *pregnant*?'

'Oh God. I didn't say anything, agreed? I had no idea…'

'*Tina?*' said Mike. 'She didn't say…'

'Don't blame me!'

Shrugging off Isabel's fingertipped attempts at distraction, Mike set off back for the table, his face a hornets' nest, a storm. He sat down.

'Cheer up, love,' said his mother.

The smile he stretched was akin to lifting weights, or to killing cockroaches: there seemed to be a better, easier alternative. Let the weights drop, and let the greedy little buggers breed, breed and breed…

Dennis was drunk. In itself, this was nothing new; but his desire to tell a long rally of weak jokes was most certainly a novelty. Now he was embarking on one that involved a leprechaun and a nun.

Mike leaned towards Tina, behind the back of Greg, who sat between them. 'A word,' he said. 'Outside.'

'Oi.' This was Dennis. 'It's customary to wait for the

285

punchline,' he said.

But I've already heard it, thought Mike, not referring to the gag.

Winter was in the air. Allowed free expression, it was dancing its chill from one car rooftop to the next; it was circulating the scents of dinner, of ale, of smoke…

'It was an accident,' said Tina, before Mike had a chance to recriminate.

'What was?'

'It just slipped out. I was happy. I'm sorry; I know I should have told you first. Obviously. But I was *happy*.'

Frustration tautened a knot in Mike's stomach. A motorbike's growl from the main road made him madder.

'*Who*, Tina?' he asked. 'Who?'

'Who what?'

'Is it? I'll count to ten.'

'*What?*'

'Whose baby are you carrying?' Mike demanded.

'What? How dare you… I mean *what?*'

'Terry's? Is it Terry? I want to know.'

'I can't believe you.'

'And I can't believe *you*.'

'It's *yours*, Mike.' Her eyes were wide open and red. '*Terry?* What the hell has *he* got to do with anything?'

'He wants you.'

'So what? You think I can't make my own mind up? Mike…'

'What's this all about?' asked Ruth, still at the table. Her eyes found Isabel.

'Great,' said the daughter. 'Blame me.'

'For what?' said Liz. Immediately she had spoken out of turn. This was family business, and there was a protocol to be followed.

286

'She *told* me!' Isabel protested.

'About what?' asked Dennis.

'I can't tell you!'

Ruth said, 'Yes you can. What difference is it going to make now?'

Oh Christ, thought Liz. *She knows.*

She meant Tina. What else could account for the goings-on? Tina knew that Mike had played an away-game or two, and just possibly she had yet to discover with whom. How else could it be accounted for that Liz had not been summoned into the cold?

Liz stared down at her glass of orange crush. It damned her, she knew: although she had offered to drive – even insisted – her husband of thirteen years, growing greyer, had put up a suitable resistance and taken the reins himself. Thus it was with suspicion that her initial request for a non-alcoholic drink had been met.

A glass of non-booze had damned her.

'Is this still our anniversary?' slurred Dennis, not sarcastically. 'Here's one. A guy goes into a doctor's and says 'I keep thinking I'm Tom Jones. Is this normal?' The doctor says – '

'It's over, Tina.'

'*Why?*' Tears were threatening, looming.

'Because I've been careful.'

'Since when? You're as careful as a lemming.'

No more fuel was needed. He had never done it before and he would never do it again, but Mike's right fist now curled and he lashed out, in a roundabout way, at his girlfriend's left temple. Blood was singing between his eyes.

Tina stepped backwards. She caught Mike's arm. She twisted it.

The Drive-By Heart

(with Paul Meloy)

I WAS ABOUT TO MARRY this American girl. Lorna. I met her on a trip when I was twenty and years later she turns up on business and gives me a call.

I don't think I was in love. But there was a resonation. I can see her eyes now, deep blue irises, dilated pupils, and whites like a Mediterranean beach.

But I moved on; travelled down the Pacific seaboard in a hired Mustang. Felt like God.

Noise of the ocean all the way down my right side like a tearaway gravity. You know the ocean is just another atmosphere? Like the stratosphere, the ionosphere. It's called the hydrosphere. It's just that it's beneath your feet. If you stand on a beach some time and turn your back to the sea, do this: put your head down between your legs and look out across the water. It's now above your head. Imagine a planet with a coat of blue water surrounding it and all else beneath. Very disorientating.

Anyway, those were good times.

Now I'm back in England. Years have passed and I'm not doing so well. I have a failed relationship behind me, a job uptown that's killing me and I'm living with my mother.

Then I get this call. It's Lorna.

We have a drink and a meal in London. She's got her own business and is *loaded*. She's got a failed relationship behind her, a job that's making a killing and she's just stopped living with the bastard. He used to find creative reasons to beat her up, like: you're in the house when I get home, that kind of intolerable provocation.

She cries and I hold her. She's small and slim and her short blonde hair smells of a summer we were once in charge of, long ago. I hear the broken endless smash of a tremendous glass atmosphere, and tilt her chin up and kiss her.

Six months later, I've given up my job, all my stuff's in a crate on board ship and is halfway across the Atlantic and I'm over there living in her apartment. She's out all day at the office leaving me to pad around this damned great place. It's like a palace and I think I'm God again. Seems like being in the States has a deifying effect on me. She's gorgeous and rich. She hasn't got on at me about getting a job. She wants it three times a night. And I'm getting doubts. I don't really like her so much now.

She's told me all this stuff she used to let the other stroker do to her and it just starts to turn me off. And stuff about her dad which has made me go cold.

This is one of the times I do a truly bad thing. I let her down and walk away. She hadn't begged me to go out there. She hadn't begged me to propose, swept away as I was with a heady longing for fucks gone by. She hadn't intended for me to become disgusted with her when she disclosed her secrets to me.

I leave her at the airport, shaking her off me like wet cement.

The phone calls start almost immediately.

I'm staying with a friend called Gary but he's out at work. I've told Gary that I'd be in search of employment of my own today – the guy doesn't want me sleeping on his sofa-bed for too long, if I know him at all – but in fact I'm enjoying a long soak. I'm thinking about the sea, about drowning, about all sorts of shit.

The phone rings: the mobile, about the size of a hockey puck as it slips around the steam-moistened toilet seat. 'Hello!' I eventually say.

'It's me.'

I can't think of anything sensible to give back so I say, 'It's me too.'

'It's us then. Let's see what else we can establish.'

The bathwater's hot enough to brew tea in, but I'm suddenly feeling cold. I have the stupidest thought that I'm about to be electrocuted in the suds by the phone-waves.

'Lorna,' I lie, 'I'm really sorry.'

'Don't use the S word,' she tells me automatically.

I feel like I've been given a slapped wrist: she had told me often enough to say it. Saying sorry to some guys is like an invitation, I had learned. Off comes the belt Lorna's still talking. 'I would've given you anything, Mick. Do you know that?' she asks. Her voice is like one of those sculptures that people make out of spun sugar. But a nauseating sense of self-disgust enfolds me at the image. I'm about to destroy her life even more than I already have and the best I can manage is a comparison with a glorified form of candyfloss.

'I know that,' I tell her. 'But maybe I can't just take from others for the rest of my life.' I'm intending to win through with some timely self-deprecation, but I've misunderstood the way she's feeling.

'I'm not 'others', Mick!' she screams. 'And don't you *dare* try to use your philosophy on me. Am I *ten*?' She's speaking quickly; I can hear her spittle fizz in my ear. 'You're what? Gonna convince me that I'm better off without you? Forget about it, baby. You think *you're* the baddest around? Grow up, what else can I say? You forgotten what I told you I been through, Mick? You're a *joke* in comparison.'

Scarcely able to forgive her malapropism on 'philosophy' when she meant 'psychology' I ask, robustly, 'So why do you wanna be with me, eh?'

'Don't flatter yourself. Why would I wanna be with a scumbag like you?'

I'm confused and affronted. 'So why you calling?' I ask, and I can hear my voice climbing again.

'To warn you about the payback.'

This offends me; this ruffles my feathers. I'd have more respect for her if she broke down into tears. Only scepticism rides my words when I say, 'Oh come on, Lorna, what are you trying to say? You wanna be a gangster or summing? What payback?' I feel bad about attacking her like this, and also silly that I am still sitting in the rapidly cooling water. 'You trying to tell me now you've got an iron streak? Give me a break. What's changed?' Oh, I'm getting into my stride now. 'Gimme one good reason,' I demand, 'One good reason why I should fear you, even though you've spent a decade telling me how fucked around and beaten up you used to get.'

Lorna doesn't hesitate. 'Now I'm rich,' she replies, 'things are different,' and hangs up.

'How goes the job hunt?' Gary asks later. As always he looks nearly drowned in his oversized suit and clown-cloppy shoes. Someone needs to tell him that the 80's are over. But it won't be me: I need this guy's hospitality and safety.

'A few sniffs,' I lie, unable to tell him that after the bath I hadn't even gone out. The call has me scared.

'They're looking for staff at the off-licence,' he tells me.

My response is sarcastic. 'The principle being, I suppose,

291

what doesn't kill me makes me stronger.' I throw a peanut at his chin but he ducks. 'Fuck off out of it, mate. How do I think I'd feel? Stuff almost destroyed me!'

'That was then and this is now,' he says, stupidly.

The truth is, I've spent the afternoon wondering if a woman with a bank balance that multiplies faster than bacteria could really find me and do me damage. *Imagine this*, I told myself: a lifetime of being the underdog and now you have cash. Wouldn't *you* want to give your tormentors a tickle or two?

My mobile rings. This is another thing that's been scaring me all afternoon—and I really am endeavouring to tell myself that Lorna, even as pissed off as she undoubtedly is, has no control over the simple laws of machinery and physics. You turn a phone off and the thing stays turned off until you or someone else turns it on again.

And yet my phone's been ringing all day.

I go for the off-licence job and get it anyway. It gets Gary off my back and puts four pounds seventy five an hour in my pocket.

I stand behind the counter and look out over the central aisle of stacked cans there in the stalls, and the shelves of wines on either side, like wealthier punters crammed into theatre boxes, and feel onstage. They're hushed, my public, awaiting either some homecoming performance or a benediction.

'Fuck off,' I say.

There's an electronic *ree-roo* and the door opens. A tall, skinny Asian comes in. He's wearing a knee-length overcoat, ripped jeans and sixteen-hole Doc Martin's.

The shop is suddenly very empty, but for us. He backs the door shut and stands looking at me with eyes communicating clearly the rash decisions made in his head much earlier in the day.

Something about the last twenty four hours lends a curious slackness to my responses and so I'm unable to do much more than hang my jaw open and steady myself against the counter top as he pulls a hammer and a handful of three inch nails out of his breast pocket.

Not having the luxury of a twelve gauge, or even the comforting heft of a baseball bat, the staple recourse of our Seven-Eleven cousins overseas, all I can do is watch, dry-mouthed and incredulous, as the fellow turns and begins hammering the nails, workmanlike, into the doorframe.

It takes a few seconds more to realise that the stroker is hammering us *in*. And I pause to wonder why, if this is a robbery, he hasn't just demanded I lock the door. So it isn't a robbery, I decide. Which leaves what?

'What you doing?' I ask. Better late than never.

He turns, and gives me that look that a dog might give you – just before it sinks its teeth. 'It's none of your effing business,' he tells me, and I decide not to point out the fatal flaw in his argument. A reach for the phone seems dangerous. But then again, so does the wait while he goes about his psychotic DIY.

At length he turns and says, 'We're ready.'

'For what?' I ask him.

Not knowing exactly why, unless a sense of self-preservation has suddenly gone haywire, I say: 'I can't open the till. I have to key something in. Stops people stealing.'

'Well, it ain't gonna stop *me* stealing, mate.'

'I meant staff.'

And he finds this amusing. 'So I'm safe and sound then. Open up.'

I experience a squirt of inspiration. 'You're on camera right now,' I tell my tormentor.

Unexpectedly, and worryingly, he appears amused. 'And that fact makes you feel better, does it? Come on, mate – use your noggin. Let's be having you.'

I reach for a bottle of the expensive spirits on a shelf above my head.

The man's voice is raspy. 'What you doing?' he asks, as if expecting me to then take a pot-shot at his head with the missile.

'I have to swipe something. Like I said, the till doesn't open by magic.'

He nods.

'And there's nothing much in it now anyway,' I warn him.

'Well *that's* not gonna do you any favours, mate.'

Lorna.

Lorna's face fills the screen at the back of my head. And I say to myself: Oh Christ.

Did she send this villain? Is the robbery just a front. From the elaboration of the misdemeanour so far I have to think – yes. Because it's not every day that a maniac nails your entrance door shut.

I take a gamble. 'Is this about the American girl? Lorna?'

'I don't know anyone called Lorna,' comes the reply, but I don't know whether to trust it or not. I thumb the key for a cash payment, and with an oily sound the tray springs open and taps my stomach. What I see inside is depressing, in more ways than one. Intending to soften the blow I say, 'Most people pay with cards these days.'

'What you got?'

'About fifty. Sixty, at a push.'

'Hand it over.'

I do so. And then he says, 'Do you want a smack in the mouth or something?'

'I swear to you, that's all…'

'No, mate. Do you *want* a smack in the mouth? For the sake of the camera, like. Make it look like you put up some token resistance. Otherwise, how's this gonna look to your boss?'

'I haven't got a boss,' I answer. 'I've just quit.'

'Well it's up to you. It was an honest offer.' He shrugs. 'So where's the fire escape?'

'Follow me.'

'Do you want me to wave the hammer at you threateningly?' the man wants to know.

I tell him that I can live without the mimes, and I lead him through to the back.

On the way we pass an opened crate of whisky. Surprising me completely, as if that's even possible, the thief says politely, 'Do you mind if I take one of those?'

'Be my guest,' I reply, holding open the door. A fluttery sense of panic – a frightened bird loose in a chimney – spasticates its way around my ribcage. I think of the job, which is not a great job: but it's the only job I've got. I say:

'About that fist in the face, mate.'

'Yeah.'

I sigh and tell him, 'Go for it.'

My phone rings at dawn, but I'm awake. I still haven't managed to turn the damned thing off, but to be fair to it (why should I be?) it hasn't actually chirruped for a little while. I expect to get bawled out by the off licence manager, but no

'Lorna.'

'I heard about your incident,' she tells me, with a voice like she's consumed a doughnut. 'Tough break,' she finishes.

'Bullshit. You set him up. What do you *want* from me?'

She is laughing. 'Me set him up? You gotta be joking. A

damned *burglary* and a smack in the kisser? If you believe nothing else, baby, you should believe that you're worth a shitload more trouble than that. We haven't even got *started*.'

'So how did you find out about what happened?'

She pauses, as though unsure as to whether it's too early to pass on the information. I know for a fact now that hell exists – because hell is waiting in frustration for an answer that is just beyond your eardrums. When she says 'I just felt the ripples along the line, babe' I know that I am in worse trouble than I've been contemplating.

'Explain yourself,' I demand.

Again, Lorna chuckles. 'Aren't we the tough guy all of a sudden?' she says.

'Come on, Lorna. What is it you want?'

'To watch the show,' she tells me. 'It's a good one so far '

'What *show*? What *is* this?'

Instead of answering, Lorna poses a question of her own. 'Tell me something,' she goes on. 'Has it ever occurred to you that luck can be influenced? Has it ever occurred to you that you never had it so good as when you were with me. Now look at you. Virtually destitute, and with a broken nose. And pop quiz, sweetheart. How long do you think you're gonna keep your keep your shitty job when the next thug comes in for a freebie?'

'You *did* set it up,' I interrupt with conviction.

'No, not me. You did that by yourself. I just cancelled your privileges.'

'And what were they?'

'Good luck. Money. Health '

Getting angry again, I call her on her last cited point. 'My health? What are you talking about? A broken nose'll heal in two shakes of a lamb's tail.'

'Sure. You'll just end up looking like a pub sax player. Cool for you.'

I'm frightened. And even more so when Lorna asks, 'Tell me, lover. Have you seen a doctor recently?'

I haven't seen a doctor in about three years. 'No.'

'Well it might be a good idea,' says Lorna. 'We wouldn't want you catching your death, now would we?'

And the phone goes dead.

I help myself to a couple of drinks for my breakfast. In Gary's filing cabinet I locate a dice of cannabis resin. I roll that dice, and by ten a.m. I have smoked and drunk myself into a state of clinical paranoia. I keep thinking of the similarities between wild mushrooms and city umbrellas. I am both scared and exhilarated and terrified by the thought of venturing outside.

I can't but think that an articulated lorry, or given the way things are now, a damned Pantechnicon, is going to flatten me into a pizza base. But at the moment the hypochondria is taking its toll.

Suddenly I don't feel right. I need to get to a hospital, fast.

Lorna can see into the bad things that are going on in my life. Even when she wasn't there, she was always my lucky charm, even just in looking back at my time with her, but then I crossed her and what I would normally attract into my orbit has arrived. It just took a time for them to arrive.

The pre-eminent thought as I go out to taste the wind is this:

Somehow and someway, I have to make it up to Lorna. Saying sorry is not enough.

She needs a good reason to strengthen my protection again.

'Which is what?' my brain wants to know. When I tell it

that I don't damned know, the cab driver twists round with his eyebrows pinched into one long fuzzy caterpillar. Evidently I have spoken aloud, and I sheepishly cough and say sorry until he decides that it will be safer to get me to my destination than risk a scene by kicking me out.

My phone rings. These days a phone is as important as a wallet. Even the driver was taking a call as I hailed him down. Seeing that no breach of protocol will be achieved, I take my call too, already knowing who'll be on the other end.

I'm wrong.

'Hello, mate,' says Gary, 'You at home?'

'*Niet*,' I say. 'Job-hunting. Why?'

'You didn't leave anything on, did you?'

I can hear a slow rinse of distant traffic through the phone line. He's travelling somewhere, and I'm guessing, back to his house.

'Just had the weirdest damned phone call, mate,' he explains. 'A woman's just told me my house is on fire. I'm on my way there right now.'

'I didn't leave anything on,' I reply... but did I get rid of the evidence of my smoking session? 'And I can tell you who made the call.'

'Where are you?'

I'm aware that he might be thinking I'm running away. Could Lorna have arranged for someone to burn down Gary's house? Has there been enough time?

My skull is being circled by unwanted thoughts.

The traffic is like undergrowth, but we're both hacking our way through.

The Ion Offices are on the seventh floor of an old building that makes me think of a pensioner in his overcoat. Getting through the front door is easy, but that's as far as my ribbon of luck will stretch. It snaps.

'Who are you here to see?' the desk-jockey asks.

'Lorna Landbridge,' I reply. And I realise that I haven't used the surname in a good few years. In my current state it's a little bit like a rainmaker remembering the spell to make it drizzle. I felt that I should be doing a rain dance any second now.

'And you are?'

I can sense his salty disapproval, and I can see his puffed-up feathers. It can't be often, in a place like this, that he can get to feel superior to someone.

'Mick Keren,' I tell him. When was the last time I used my *own* surname?

That's the sort of thing you do when you're feeling anon- 299 ymous or if you want to impress someone. *Christ*, I think. *I've been wide open for anyone to see for a long time.*

'Just a jiff.'

It's one of those moments. What else can I say? For once, the dope has failed to catapult me into a zombie-breathed state of inertia, full of slow-forward and bubble- encasement. For once, I've been fucked up the back, and it's as if I have a jet-pack roaring out of the back of my spine.

I make a break for the lifts when one opens.

The stroker yelps, but I don't stop. It is one of those mo-ments – like dashing for a departing train, or clearing a clut-tered desk-top with your elbow – that is about as far as a sad, diminished brain will lean towards true heroism.

Lorna in the flesh doesn't scare me, I realise.

Or at least, the thought of it – of her – doesn't scare me.

Seventh floor. A Klee print on the wall, and a fat-leafed plant bidding welcome with open arms. I know where I'm going, although I've never been here. The offices have been set out exactly how those in America were. It's a likeness that makes me sick. I feel like I'm being buried alive; like a croco-dile with a javelin between its scales.

I realise that I am still catastrophically stoned.

She's waiting for me outside her secretary's vestibule. Sur-prisingly she is wearing a long, deep smile on her face, and I brace up the courage to ask:

'Is it money or power? What have you got?'

And she says to me, 'What makes you think I can't have both?'

So I wipe the sweat from my forehead. 'You don't want to hear me say the S word,'

I tell her, 'So how about this? You change me. You *change* me, Lorna. Make it all go away. Make me a better person, and let's see if it don't have a backwards result. Let's see if we can't re-juggle the past. Can you do that?'

Lorna says nothing.

'Can you *do* that?' I repeat.

'You sad sack of spunk,' she tells me. 'What makes you think I'm not already doing it? What makes you think that this *act* of yours'll do anything whatever? Grow up.'

She turns away from me.

'Don't leave me like this!' I whinny.

'Grow up,' she repeats as she walks away.

I'm ushered out: flapped out like a fart from under a duvet. Rain gives me something to think about. I consider how wet I'm going to get as I walk away.

The taxi driver hasn't waited. I don't blame him.

Gary is waiting at what used to be his home.

It's like a pig circus. Activity. Noise. So much *noise*.

He doesn't say a word. He strolls towards me with a stern but flat expression on his face. The only sound he makes is when his fist strikes my left temple.

I hobble backwards. My windpipe is convulsing, although that's nowhere near where he hit me. I'm finding it difficult to breathe.

Maybe it's the shock of seeing the black box that used to be a home.

It has been burnt so profoundly that not a colour remains, other than black. It looks so precarious and precious; one touch, I think, one fingertip prod and the whole thing will climb down in floating leaves of ash.

'You stupid little prick,' says Gary, and turns his back on me.

'I didn't do it,' I protest. 'It was the American girl.'   301

'Sure.'

'She *paid* someone to do it, mate, I swear to you.'

Gary turns. I have his attention, if not his unconditional belief.

'I'm all ears, Mick,' he says, a touch of irony in his words.

A battle-cruiser is designed to sail without fuss, without non-sense or incident, in all weathers and in all storms: impenetra-ble, sleek, slightly sexy in its fastidious infallibility. When some-thing punctures its hull, there have to be a few questions asked. There has to be a spirit of disbelief and slow resignation.

That's how I'd been feeling about my life.

Everything tickety-boo.

Now this.

I've been invaded by bad luck. Colonised. Deported to for-eign sands.

And I don't know what the hell to do about it.

It occurs to me (and I shudder to think) that if Lorna was out of the way, then the bad luck trail would be derailed. But that's the stuff of gangster fiction.

Wipe her. Get her out of the way.

But it's not how the real world works.

I have dreams in which we look down on the kitchen work surface and the breadcrumbs spell PAY NOW. I owe big time.

Overdraft. An overdraft of fortune to be paid back.

'What's your name?' I say to the next call I receive on the mobile.

'Jeanette.'

'And why do you want me to buy your windows?' I ask.

The question foxes her. '*Why?*'

'Why?' I repeat. 'Do you believe in your product?'

'Yes.'

'Really?'

'Yes.'

'Then I'll buy some,' I say, knowing full well that this won't be the case. It occurs to me that the simplest solution would be to draw a razor across my neck, my wrist. See it all crumble— the edifice of sand and muscle. See the luck rot to nothing.

I pick up the phone.

'Anything you want,' I say, when I eventually get through to Lorna. 'I'll do anything you want if you let me off.'

For her part, Lorna is unrepentant. 'Why should I?' she asks.

'Because we used to care for each other.'

"Used to' is a long time ago,' she tells me—just before she replaces the receiver. But she's right. There are only tomorrows in 'used to'.

This is why I've doused my body, from head to foot, in cold water. As some of it dries, it's like floating, or falling, from the sea into the clouds. The impression is calming. The motor is running: the motor of Gary's car.

His blood is on the forecourt. A tyre-tooled crack in his skull.

The jump-leads: clamped painfully to my left nipple and to the goosefleshed undertug of my scrotum Yes. I'm ready.

I'm going to test fate if it's the last thing I do.

Will it work? Will it?

'Lorna,' I say into the phone. 'Listen to this.'

303

Rapscallion

TINA OPENED THE WINDOW. 'I can't believe you can't smell it,' she said.

'I'm sorry – I've got a cold.'

'You couldn't smell it before. There's something *in* here, I tell you.'

Mick was eager to re-establish peace.

'Maybe a rat's died behind the cupboard,' she suggested.

'I doubt it. Why would I only smell it every now and then?'

'I don't know. But come on – we'll be late.'

They always had a squash court booked early on Tuesdays.

'Maybe it's me,' Tina announced. 'Maybe there's something wrong with my nose.'

'You have a beautiful nose.'

'I'm serious, Mick. Should I see a doctor?'

'Because you smell things better than I do?' Mick was incredulous. 'It's the other way around. Book *me* an appointment.'

Tina seethed. 'I hate it when you win,' she said. 'You get so flippant.'

'I always win.'

'Well, exactly.'

They moved furniture. Halfway through the process of rocking the tall-boy across the wooden floor, Mick was struck by an image that she immediately wanted to write down: it was like dancing with an ogre. They were still shifting furniture as midnight neared.

'There's nothing here, Teen,' said Mick.

'I know. Can you smell it *now?*'

'No. Do you want a cup of tea?'

Tina was not quite sulking – more baffled, her ego bruised. 'It's *here*. No, thank you.'

'Bed?'

'No, thank you.'

Mick frowned and said, 'Well, *I'm* having a cup of tea and then going to bed. I'll help you move this stuff back in the morning.'

Tina dreamt of a car-sized rat. It was wedged in the spare room, gnawing on the tall-boy with its long yellow teeth. Its gums dripped blood and its nose tasted the air.

'My name is Rapscallion,' it said with a gross contortion of its maw. 'I rape ghosts.'

After using the lavatory, Tina stepped into the spare room. The light was poor – the curtains kept the morning at bay – but there was definitely something on the floorboards.

Small and vaguely triangular.

'What *is* that?' she asked the tall-boy.

Her flippy rode up to the top of her thighs as she bent at the waist for a better view. Stomach and heart made the identification simultaneously. Tina recoiled from the object as if it had moved – she felt that she'd been punched in the heart.

'Mick!' Her voice was thin and reedy. 'Michaela!' she managed at a higher volume.

Deep sleeper did little to describe Mick's nightly comas, but she and Tina had been together for nearly a year and had tuned themselves to the other's various frequencies. Tina's words sang of panic – the address buried into Mick's unconscious and pricked at her sleep.

305

'What is it?'

The first policeman confirmed the identification.

'It's a nose,' he repeated, scratching his own. He used the blunt ends of two pens to pincer-raise the nose from the floor. Tina held open a small, clear polythene bag; but she could scarcely bear to keep it in her hands after the constable had dropped the nose in. It weighed, she thought, offensively little.

Taking the bag, the policeman raised it to his line of sight. He examined the smoothness of the nostrils, the speckly pores.

Mick had grown impatient. 'We were hoping you'd offer an explanation, actually.'

The policeman paused before responding. 'Do you have a cat?' he asked. 'Cats have been known to bring home all sorts of things.'

'Sorry. No, we don't have a cat.'

Tina had explained why the furniture in the room was in such disarray. Now she was eager to conclude the meeting amicably. 'At least we've solved the mystery of the bad smells,' she said.

'I'm afraid I can't smell a thing,' the constable told her.

The second policeman looked like nothing of the sort. A squat little man with a mop of oil-saturated hair, he was unshaven, pink-eyed and had a questionable attitude to personal hygiene. He showed Mick a laminated card with his photograph on it and the words DEPARTMENT OF ENQUIRIES.

'That's pretty vague,' Mick said.

'It is until you hear some of the enquiries.' He had an accent that made Mick think of Dracula. 'Then it all becomes very specific. May I come in?'

'Sure. Tina's gone to work, though. Not sure if I'll be of

use.'

Unbelievably, in Mick's opinion, the visitor's name was Rapscallion. On hearing this, Mick was even more desperate to know where the man might have come from. Although he'd never been in their house before, he led the way flawlessly to the spare room.

The floorboards creaked as he entered.

'You can smell it, can't you?' Mick said.

'The air is pungent.'

'Then why can't *I* smell it? Why couldn't the policeman?'

'You don't want to,' said Rapscallion, 'and my guess is, neither did he.'

'But neither does Tina!' Mick protested.

Rapscallion dipped down onto his haunches: a drum-solo of clicks and creaks was efficiently dispatched. 'Your friend has not been offered a choice in the matter. Besides, you'll smell it soon enough if we don't nip this in the bud.'

'Well, I'm not saying I *want* to smell it, but I do want to know what it is, and where that nose came from, and why.'

Rapscallion shrugged. 'It was probably a joke,' he replied. 'The dead have a fantastic sense of humour, you know.'

'The dead? So we *do* have a ghost?'

'Not yet,' Rapscallion told her. 'Is Tina's work local?'

'Not far.' Mick felt singed by proximity to white-hot information. 'She gets on the bus. She works in a travel agent's.'

'Could you ask her to come home, please?'

'She only went in to get away from all this,' Mick replied. 'I'm not sure she'll want to come back.'

Rapscallion turned his head. 'I thought I said this already – she doesn't have a choice.'

'Why not?'

'Because they've selected her. Because what she smells is

nothing to do with this room. She's smelling herself.'

Mick phoned the bucket shop, only to be told that Tina had already set off for home. 'She wasn't feeling very well.' Mick relayed the information.

'Drowsy? Nauseous?' Rapscallion asked.

'He didn't say.'

'I wouldn't be surprised. It takes a lot out of someone, being an engine.'

Mick paused. Then she said, 'Will you explain any of this?'

'I will. When she arrives.'

'You're Rapscallion, aren't you?' said Tina.

'At your service.'

Mick was surprised. 'You've met?'

Tina didn't know what to say. Rapscallion fielded the query. 'You've seen me where? In your dreams?'

A nod.

'You wouldn't be the first.'

'But you were a rat – you were huge.'

For the first time Rapscallion smiled. 'Well as you can see,' he said, 'I'm neither in my earthbound identity.'

'But why did she dream of you?'

'They know me, that's why.'

'The dead?' said Tina.

Rapscallion nodded. 'The dead,' he confirmed.

'So we *do* have a ghost problem,' Mick ventured.

'Not yet. A ghost-in-embryo problem, at best; so no real problem at all.' Rapscallion sluiced tea through his incisors. He had appalled his interlocutors by taking eight sugars in a single cup. 'What you have is an *energy* problem. There's a world of difference.'

'Explain,' said Tina.

They were not in the spare room; they were in the lounge, having tea to dilute the panic. 'There are ghosts and there are ghosts,' said Rapscallion. 'And I know the guys you've got here. I banished them in the first place.'

Rapscallion slurped down the rest of his drink. He even smacked his lips, like a connoisseur. He said to Tina, 'You're their choice. You're their engine. They think you're going to help them come back.'

'Nose-first,' said Mick.

Tina ignored the interjection. 'You *rape* ghosts,' she said, recalling her dream. 'What exactly does that mean?' The she doubted her own conviction. 'Am I right?' she wanted to know.

Rapscallion nodded his head.

309

'We have a counter-force,' he said. 'We go in with it – and blast them to pieces.' He shrugged. 'It's about that simple. I have to block up the passages and bung you up. They love a decent channel.'

'The dead?' said Tina.

'The dead.'

On the other hand, Mick was incredulous. 'What exactly are you talking about? Forgive me for being the bolshy one, but I don't have a clue.'

Rapscallion faced her.

'What I'm talking about is this,' he said. 'I'm suggesting that if you've got cotton buds you use them: you block up your partner's ears and nostrils. If you've got tampons, you use them: front and rear. Then stuff one in your mouth.'

'I'll avert my eyes,' said Rapscallion; but Tina told him not to be so ridiculous.

'You've seen a lot more than my *body*,' she explained.

In the spare room, the furniture had been shoved to the sides of the room. Perspiring, Tina lay on her front on the bare floorboards. Rapscallion stood astride her, with his eyes screwed tightly shut and his gaze lifted up to the ceiling. In each fist he squeezed a tampon.

There was a commotion – something distant – the sound of ice sliding down a roof.

Mick was frightened. She watched as Tina tensed.

'Tina?'

'Mokay-Mick,' said Tina, through the sanitary towel in her mouth.

From outside the room, a series of thuds landed on the front door.

310

Mick whimpered and said, 'Rapscallion, please…'

Another series of blows on the front door. Mick felt cold. The dead had come to claim her and Tina, and she knew that this man was nowhere near strong enough to defend them all.

'Arms-er laddoor,' said Tina.

'No, don't,' said the Master of Ceremonies.

The atmosphere was thick – squid-like and rubbery – and Mick was now looking for any excuse to get out of the spare room before another nose appeared. True enough, there was more flesh appearing – on the floorboards.

Straight – like a neck. The shallow curve of a new set of shoulders.

Mick broke.

At the front door – and only there – she acknowledged the shouts that had followed her. To the best of ability, she rebuffed them. She opened the door, to reveal the very first policeman – whose name, if she'd ever known it, had since swum away from her memory.

'They're coming,' said Mick, inviting the policeman over the threshold.

'Who?'

'The ones that Rapscallion wanted to defeat.'

The officer led the way. 'Who the hell is Rapscallion?' Mick heard him say, before remembering the great sense of humour that the dead were supposed to possess.

Back in the spare room, Tina started to scream.

The house was suddenly filled with rain that exploded from clouds that scuttered across the ceilings. A disgraceful smell of phosphorous and ignited rubber swept through the rooms.

Worse than anything, however, was the laughter.

Perhaps the dead had discovered the best joke of all.

'I'm so sorry,' said Mick, as she knelt down to take Tina – crying Tina – into her arms.

Scared stiff, the policeman swung his truncheon, while Rapscallion melted into the floorboards. Belly laughs, gutsy and huge, bid him a fond farewell.

Parts to Play

RELYING ON THE FACT that she'd be missed, the actress Diana Pearce swallowed half a bottle of pain-relief capsules.

When she woke, she assumed the overdose to have been a failure. But there was no headache or nausea. Why was she invisible to mirrors and unable to pick anything up or switch anything on? Nor did Diana have an appetite, a sense of time, or bodily functions.

It took great mental energy but she was free to float, and into the big wide world she ventured, using her mind as an engine.

The funeral came and went. Diana managed to stay concentrated enough on being present: a slip of the mind and she would have been whipped back to the flat. The eulogy made her tired; she could feel the fake emotion. She was disappointed at how few people turned up, and in one case at who turned up with whom. Diana's agent arrived with Diana's ex-husband, but the actress had long suspected that one. What hurt was that neither of them had felt comfortable telling her. Then again, Diana's temper on set had been legendary.

Diana was aware that she was no happier than she'd been in the flesh. Watching the sadness in her city depressed her further. She got on well with the young man who moved into her flat and took up her old space. Diana watched him get dressed in the morning: into a black suit and a pink shirt and tie. Some mornings she was certain that she could smell his hair gel, and even hear the scrape of his toothbrush bristles across his overbite.

Four times Diana tried to introduce herself to the new tenant. As one might tackle an opposing rugby player or deal with a burglar, Diana charged headlong at his wiry body. And slipped through, sliding embarrassingly up the bathroom wall, or over the kitchen lino. Each time the man swatted the air, trying to scare off a non-existent insect.

Nonetheless, Diana discovered a means to contentment: learning to write. Very quickly she convinced herself that this was what her life had lacked.

She had a woman named Claire for assistance.

It was late one night when Claire received Diana's first message. Claire would say later that the pointer on the board had moved so quickly it'd been hard to make sense of the words.

Diana herself had been equally as surprised; it was the first thing she could control—this way station between the corporeal world and the spiritual. Lacking patience but appreciative of the need for clarity, Diana sent the introductory message again. She sensed Claire's shock and befuddlement.

My name is Diana Pearce. Do you know me?

'No.'

As Claire had been attempting to contact a fellow named Brendan, Diana knew she shouldn't be too upset.

To begin with, Diana gave little away: she needed those secrets after all. Instead she tried writing poetry and prose, but her efforts were unsuccessful—although Claire loved them. Claire would coo her breathless glee. Diana would just get angry, and cancel transmission.

A year after first contact, Diana completed a short story with which she was satisfied. She instructed Claire to send it to a magazine, and six months later it was published under a pseudonym: *Claire Peters*. Ecstatically Diana followed up on her victory with a piece that was promptly rejected by the same periodical.

Downhearted and lost, she told Claire to send all the work she'd transcribed in the last twelve months to the magazine. Thinking that Diana meant to send it all at once, Claire bundled the monsters into a huge padded envelope and mailed it, using the one received paycheck to cover the postage.

The following week Claire got a letter from the mag: *Present your work properly or don't waste our time.*

Unsure of what she'd done wrong, Claire blinked at the acidic scrawl for some time and decided not to tell Diana about it.

When the time came to begin the autobiography, Diana had lived with Claire for two years. She dished the dirt. She had no choice, and besides, every actress has revenge brewing somewhere. What better time to vent that spleen than when you are already dead? Existence was interesting again.

She'd let the man with the pink ties have the flat, once and for all.

TV called. And although the cameras, the hosts and the money were enticing at first, Claire soon lost the thrill of being chased. Several times Diana had to order her to show up. Demonstrations were expected, and were given. Laughter trickled down from sceptical audiences. One time Claire burst into tears at the ridicule a particular host dragged her through.

Diana still loved the exposure, though getting out of the house tired her more than ever. At night she told Claire that the book would make her rich.

They were halfway through *Playing Parts: The Sin, Sex and Scandal of Diana Pearce*, and Claire had received her seventh lawsuit. This one had come from a disgruntled actor who'd been frightened that Claire could know a specific secret.

Twelve weeks on the bestseller list, and Diana started to feel another slump approaching. Claire had more friends and Diana was jealous. Claire told her not to be silly, but for Diana the circus was over and all that remained was the churned-up field of her life. She regretted telling so many intimate secrets.

She started to accuse Claire of crimes that she knew were not true.

Diana had never had a child, and as an actress she had never played the mother. But now, she decided, was a good time to have a baby.

315

To Diana's astonishment, Claire agreed, and having joked about asking Mr Pink Ties for a contribution, steps were taken to adopt a girl.

Claire-Anna grew up under two foster mothers. The girl was happy. She was loved inescapably. When she was old enough not to know better, Claire-Anna felt trapped by the new twenty-room place, and moved to a flat in a nearby city. If she'd known (despite the protests and proclamations) of how heartbreaking her exit would be, she might have stayed. She married twice.

I married twice.

Twenty-five years after Diana moved in with Claire…

Claire died in a car crash. She'd given the chauffeur the day off and if she'd been in the back seat she might have been safe.

Diana fell silent. She never spoke to another living being, despite inexpert efforts when the board was finally found.

She didn't want to play the role of the dead woman blabbing.

So there's no happy ending to this story; but given time you eventually get over the death of a loved one. I'm twenty-five now; I've come to terms with her passing away, but sometimes I feel they're with me, in the room.

If I smoke I feel a sense of disapproval.

At the age of eighteen I could have discovered the identity of my biological mother. To be honest, one more seemed greedy.

316

I've played Ophelia—in a town hall, to an audience of thirty-three.

I've been in several soaps, pouring pints or jogging past the camera.

I look like Diana.

The man in Diana's old apartment—Mr Pink Ties?

Drunk one afternoon, I went round to see him, to ask a few questions and see if he remembered anything. He looked at me as though I were insane, but that didn't stop him asking me out for dinner. And I accepted. You only live once.

I'm happy. If I could think of anything else to ask for, I would.

This morning I stabbed Mr Pink Ties dead with a dull bread knife.

Eden Across the Water

A MIDDLE-AGED EX-CON named Jack Charrott has unusual dreams that a youth called Rick Shawdon shares. They do not know each other, although Rick delivers a newspaper to Jack's flat every morning. When Jack is visited and attacked in his sleep, by a wraith-like creature, Rick sees this attack too, and decides to investigate.

Meanwhile, a murder has been discovered by the police, and investigations are underway. Two constables, bored with their worthless assignments, leave their posts and by chance meet the man who has committed the murder. Blade (as he calls himself) has blood on his face from a *second* murder, and becomes agitated when the constables ask routine questions. There is a fight, during which P.C. Bob Dooley disappears into thin air. He is taken away to the place – Gangullus – from which Jack's wraith-visitor emerged. On his escape, Blade vows that he will go there as well. Blade later kills Rick Shawdon's mother.

A family man named Duncan Scrivener is unhappy with his second family, his failing antiques business, and his life in general. He visits his childhood home, only to find it replaced by tower blocks, wherein he has an encounter with two punks. What he does not know is that Redman Terrace casts a spell on any of its few visitors and all of its inhabitants. A man named Michael – who, years earlier, was humiliatingly expelled from Gangullus by his enemy, the Wizard Bees – has set up residence on this dreary estate. He turns everyone there into one of his ever-growing army, which he expects to use one day against

317

Bees. Though he doesn't know it, Duncan will have no choice but to return to Redman Terrace and become one of the warriors. In the meantime, his family begin to notice changes in his behaviour.

In Gangullus, the Wizard Bees (who is not really a wizard at all) consults a heavy-lipped prophet called Kookoo about the sense of doom that he feels. It is Bees who sent the wraith to Jack Charrott. Not able to visit the outside world himself, Bees has sent a messenger that will gestate inside Jack. The messenger is a bee/human child crossbreed, and in its sting is the message's information: to fight against Michael's legions.

Are you with me so far?

318

Rick Shawdon, in mourning with his father, is visited by the second police officer who was present at the fight with Blade. P.C. Clive Ferniss tells Rick that he knows who murdered his mother. They ally. Rick visits Jack and finds him radically changed for the worse. The bee-child gestating inside him is endangering his health. But it serves a purpose when it enables Rick to travel – first mentally, then physically – to Gangullus.

Ferniss visits Blade, having learned where the killer lives. After a struggle, Blade *also* disappears to Gangullus, leaving Ferniss doubting his sanity.

Wounded, Rick awakes at a place halfway between Jack's flat and Gangullus. It is a forested area in which lives Gangullen, a man-beast who controls the numbers allowed between the everyday world and the hidden town which was named after him. What is strange, however, is that Rick has had no assistance from Gangullen to get there. This makes Gangullen afraid of him, and his fear turns quickly to violence.

Infected by Michael's spell, Duncan Scrivener is on the way to Redman Terrace when he has a car accident, which then results in a minor heart attack. He is taken to hospital.

Rick's friend Steve becomes involved when he visits Jack Charrott, worried about Rick. Jack tells him what has happened, and also the story of why he went to prison. This story is the key as to why the Wizard Bees has chosen Jack to be the host for the messenger. Steve is understandably concerned about Rick's (and his own) involvement with a one-time killer, but Rick's father is furious when he finds out.

In Gangullus, Blade is confused and bewildered, and demands answers to his questions from a young woman named Kelyeena. When she cannot help him, he is violent, but she manages to escape, and runs to enlist the help of the Libertines – a female gang who hate living in Gangullus and openly flaunt their derision to the nightly curfew. The women take Kelyeena to see the prophet Kookoo, who is also a colleague of theirs.

I am afraid to say that this is where things start to get complex.

Blade receives information from Wizard Bees, who is alarmed that someone has brought Blade in from the Outside. Bees has never been able to execute this trick himself, and he has no idea who his new enemy is. When it becomes clear that it is his friend Habe Caratatem, he is angry and upset. It reminds Bees of what happened with Michael, years earlier. Bees has been told by Kookoo that he will be threatened by an unknown person and sees Blade as this threat.

Rick is also in town. After advice, he goes to see Kookoo to get some help. He, Kookoo, Kelyeena (with whom Rick has fallen in love) and the Libertines become allied against their new common enemy – Blade. But there are several other matters to which they must attend.

Blade is let out of a trap that Bees set. Bees himself lets him out, but does so in such a way as to make Blade feel as though his own cunning has freed him. Bees also convinces Blade that he was acting on the orders of Habe Caratatem when he imprisoned him. As Bees wanted, Blade's anger turns to the other man. The Wizard Bees is adept at such mental trickery.

Meanwhile, on the Outside, suspended P.C. Clive Ferniss is following any clues that might help lead to some understanding. He ends up at the house of a widow Judith Hinton – a house in which Blade spent many days years earlier. Judith was a significant part of Blade's evolution into a cold-blooded killer, and now Ferniss discovers how and why. After some time, however, as a victim of Judith's subtle manipulation, he escapes, but despite his background, he has to burn down the house to do so, thereby killing his captor.

Duncan Scrivener is still in hospital. He is visited by the two punks who assaulted him at Redman Terrace. They have been sent by Michael to fetch him, but as they are leaving the hospital they encounter Duncan's stepdaughter, Samantha, who is coming to see him. There is a struggle, but the punks get away with Duncan. Some of Duncan's family go to Redman Terrace after learning from his youngest son that Duncan took him there one Sunday when he had custody. These members of Duncan's family do not find Duncan, but are all infected by the spell over Redman Terrace, and are forced to return later to be part of Michael's army.

While Steve and Rick's father are talking to Jack Charrott, Jack's parasite breaks free of his chest. At the same time, in Gangullus, Blade is destroying a once-man named Windows, through whom Bees was able to issue the wraith-creature into

Jack's flat. The man named Windows is the Wizard's only link to the Outside, and by destroying him, Blade is inadvertently destroying Jack's flat and the immediate environs. As the bee-child is born and begins attacking, the flats crumble.

The bee-child's task is to sting as many people as possible. Each sting contains a message from Bees: this is how the Wizard recruits his army.

In mourning for Jack, Rick is able to see through the eyes of the bee-child, as it has also been born of the Wizard. Rick witnesses several stings – which result in their victims achieving a zombie-like state, unseen to outsiders. He also sees the buildings of Redman Terrace as the bee hovers hover them, but does not know where the buildings are or what they signify. The bee also leads Steve and Rick's father there. Rick reads Kookoo's journals and learns the history of the town, including Michael's betrayal of Bees.

321

Intending to punish Habe Caratatem, Blade visits him, only to learn that he has been tricked – not only by Bees, but by his beloved cousin Cathleen, for whom Caratatem claims to have been working for years. Cathleen (Blade learning) has been manipulating him, albeit for his own good. It was Cathleen who got him the job working for Judith Hinton.

At Redman Terrace, Michael comes to understand that he has underestimated the Wizard when the latter's hypnotised army starts to congregate around the buildings. However, Michael does not release his own troops to combat the others. The police try to disperse the crowds, but many of them become a converted part of the throng while doing so.

In Gangullus, a friend of Blade's – Eternus – locates Bob Dooley, the policeman who vanished on the night of Blade's fight with the law. Dooley is persuaded to believe that Blade is not his enemy, although Bees *also* tries to convince Dooley of as much on learning that he is also in Gangullus.

But what has any of this have to do with water, you might well ask. The title said 'Eden Across the Water.'

So it did. Allow me to continue.

After learning that Cathleen has been associated for some time with Branx – the unseen god (or goddess as it may be) living far out to see on an island – Blade vows to sail out there to discover more of the truth. However, Rick also needs to go to the island, and he and the Prophet use the latter's fantastic wealth to purchase a small, sea-worthy, ship in which to do so. They take the remaining members of the Libertines, and Kelyeena. But the voyage is violent, and the perils they face claim lives of ones unknown.

At Redman Terrace, Michael has begun his spell which will bring Gangullus – the whole town – in to the Outside. His spell moves the island closer to Rick's ship, and it is only this which allows him to land on it. The crew of the ship, however, soon discover that there are no life forms on the island; it is one large power source, its radiation the so-called 'magic' that gets washed up on the shore. They ride the island as Michael's spell pulls the island closer to the mainland. Michael intends to create a tidal wave that will wash the town through to the Outside: through the exit he has prepared himself.

Certain people and animals sense the flood approaching. Bees escapes major injury by retreating to the far edge of town, and he is safely washed through the gateway between the buildings of Redman Terrace and spewed into the distance. Many of the town's inhabitants are not so fortunate, although Rick and his friends make it off the island (which has turned violent on them) and through without terrible injury. Kookoo

322

is the worst hurt, and does not regain enough strength to save his life for very long.

Michael's troops come to life and the long battle begins, with them attacking anyone to has made it alive through to the Outside. The spell can only be stopped when Bees himself has perished.

There are several reunions, including Blade's with Cathleen. Kelyeena confesses to Rick that she believes she is expecting his baby. They made love for the first time on the ship. Meanwhile, Blade discovers that Ferniss has killed Judith Hinton, and he vows revenge.

Using a newly discovered talent, Rick manages to pull through to the Outside the limbo forest in which Gangullen and his slaves live. He has scores to settle with the man-beast. However, Gangullen reacts violently, kicking out at Kelyeena, making her miscarry. Gangullen is frightened of Rick and flees away to safety.

After a fight at Redman Terrace between Blade and Dooley (and two of Michael's warriors), Blade leaves Dooley to fend for himself. Ferniss finds Dooley and there is another reunion, Ferniss bringing Dooley up to speed about who Blade is and what he has done.

Meanwhile, Rick has kidnapped Cathleen, the better to get at Blade. Rick has discovered where the Wizard Bees and Gangullen (now united), as well as some of their collective army, are hiding from Michael's roving warriors. Lying, deceiving, Rick takes control of the rabble and leads them to Redman Terrace in order to set Michael and Bees against one another, thereby bringing the struggle to an end. He has revenge to wreak upon several people to whom he has promised a fair leadership.

Duncan is also at Redman Terrace, with his own reasons

323

for getting even with Michael. He is one of the few on whom the spell has not worked properly, although he is charged with murderous instincts. He has suffered a long mental breakdown, and now genuinely believes himself to be Michael, and that the real Michael is a harmful impostor. The two men go into the buildings, although by this point the buildings are covered in a web of burning white light – Michael's way of protecting himself from Bees's hordes. Only a few can get through the heat.

Inside the perimeter of the buildings, Duncan kills Michael. Rick and Gangullen's slave Passionelle kill Gangullen as the spell starts to fall apart, the white light crumbling away from the web to litter the ground like snow. Blade and Bees fight, the former killing the latter; but Blade is desperate to find Cathleen. After a long search and struggle, Rick manages to send Blade back to the ruined drowned town of Gangullus. Blade is suspended in the water in a large bubble, the air inside which will eventually give out. For all the terrible things that Blade has done, Rick views a swift death as inappropriate.

The town is sealed shut for ever, like a tomb, as the buildings start to crumble. The fight is over. Rick and Steve recover in hospital. Duncan begins a slow return to mental health, although he will never reach fully physical health again. Jack's funeral is attended by all concerned (with many reporters hanging on) and Rick mentions that he relishes the idea of a long stint of boredom.

Though to be honest with you, I don't know if any of this is true.

324

Author's Note

Panic Soup is my third and final collection of shorter fiction, following *Paranoid Landscapes* in 2006 and *Sick Dice* in 2016. It contains some brand new stories and some brand new *old* stories. Allow me a moment to explain.

In the past I have told students that I do not regard a piece of writing as *truly finished* until it has been published. However, even after publication, I have found, some tales linger and flutter in the imagination, hoping for *one final draft*. While some of the stories in this collection appear for the first time, other stories had earlier incarnations of themselves published elsewhere. Although no story that was previously published appears here in its original form, I offer my thanks to the editors and colleagues who invited some of these stories into their comfortable paper houses or digital tenements.

'A Difficult Angle' was first published in my collection *Paranoid Landscapes*. The version here is shorter and punchier – and in my opinion it is a far more effective tale. These statements are also true of 'Parts to Play', 'Needles and Threes', 'Brainwreck Mealtimes', 'Nod Your Own Head', 'The Car-Eaters', 'Heart of the Seahorse' and 'Blame'.

'Worth' and 'The Drive-By Heart' first appeared in *Alternate Species*; 'A Wound' and 'Delivery Night' in *Dark Angel Rising*; 'Scrounge' in *Nemonymous*; 'Trite' and 'Things Break' in *SciFantastic*; 'Mr Konstantin's Visitors' in *Dream Zone* and *Die Earthman Die*; 'Family Whorls' in *Storyville*; 'The Pigeon' in *Masters of Terror*; 'Rivereyes' in *Infinity Plus*; 'Nod Your Own Head' in *Dusk*; and 'Don't Drown the Man Who Taught You to Swim' in *Redsine*.

'Window Shopping' was published in *Something Remains,* edited by Peter Coleborn and Pauline E. Dungate. It was an honour to be part of this book, and I mention it here for two reasons. The first is that every penny made from sales of *Something Remains* goes to Diabetes UK, a most worthy charity. The second is that *Something Remains* remembers our dear friend Joel Lane, who died unexpectedly in 2013.

Everything else is original to this collection.

326

About the author

David Mathew has a PhD in Education and Psychoanalysis and works as a Learning and Development Manager for the National Health Service (England).